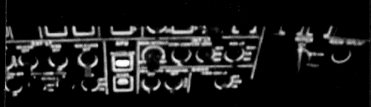

**WELCOME TO DREAMLAND
THIS IS ONLY A TEST.**

D1040276

DREAMLAND
DUTY ROSTER

Lt. Colonel Tecumseh "Dog" Bastian
Once one of the country's elite fighter jocks, now Dog is whipping Dreamland into shape the only way he knows how—with blood, sweat, and tears—and proving that his bite is just as bad as his bark. . . .

Captain Breanna Bastian Stockard
Like father, like daughter. Breanna is brash, quick-witted, and one of the best test pilots at Dreamland. But she wasn't prepared for the biggest test of her life: a crash that grounded her husband in more ways than one. . . .

Major Jeffrey "Zen" Stockard
A top fighter pilot until a crash at Dreamland left him paraplegic. Now, Zen is at the helm of the ambitious Flighthawk program, piloting the hypersonic remote-controlled aircraft from the seat of his wheelchair—and watching what's left of his marriage crash and burn. . . .

Major Mack "Knife" Smith
A top gun with an attitude to match. Knife had a MiG killed in the Gulf War—and won't let anyone forget it. Though resentful that his campaign to head Dreamland stalled, Knife's the guy you want on your wing when the bogies start biting. . . .

Major Nancy Cheshire
A woman in a man's world, Cheshire has more than proven herself as the Megafortress's senior project officer. But when Dog comes to town, Cheshire must stake out her territory once again—or watch the Megafortress project go down in flames. . . .

Captain Danny Freah
Freah made a name for himself by heading a daring rescue of a U-2 pilot in Iraq. Now, at the ripe old age of twenty-three, Freah's constantly under fire, as commander of the top-secret "Whiplash" rescue and support team—and Dog's right-hand man. . . .

continued . . .

SHADOWS OF STEEL

A surgical stealth campaign attempts to silence the enemy guns once and for all . . .

"A pulse-pounding novel of the near future that never ignores the human agony of combat."   —*San Francisco Chronicle*

"Brown is a master . . . bringing life to his characters with a few deft strokes. More than just a military thriller."
                                                                —*Publishers Weekly*

"State-of-the-art action in the air, on land, and at sea from a master of the future-shock game."   —*Kirkus Reviews*

STORMING HEAVEN

The New York Times *bestseller—Coast Guard Admiral Ian Hardcastle returns in a tale of covert warfare that will leave readers hanging on the edge of their seats . . .*

"Brown raises some provocative issues . . . His aeronautical knowledge is broad and accurate, and his flight scenes are first-rate."   —*Publishers Weekly*

"Fascinating . . . *Storming Heaven* will be an explosive success with fans of military technothrillers."   —*Booklist*

CHAINS OF COMMAND

The riveting story of Air Force involvement in a Russia-Ukraine border skirmish— that may result in all-out nuclear holocaust . . .

"*Chains of Command* is as convincing as nonfiction. Dale Brown is the best military writer in the country today and is a master at creating a sweeping epic and making it seem real."   —Clive Cussler

"Dale Brown takes a hard look at the future of America's Armed Forces . . . A great story of war in a modern unstable world. It's an exciting ride."   —Larry Bond

continued . . .

NIGHT OF THE HAWK

The exciting final flight of the "Old Dog"—
a shattering mission into Lithuania, where
the Soviets' past could launch a terrifying future . . .

"Dale Brown brings us the gripping conclusion of the saga that began so memorably with *Flight of the Old Dog*. A masterful mix of high technology and *human* courage."

—W.E.B. Griffin

SKY MASTERS

The incredible story of America's newest B-2 bomber,
engaged in a blistering battle of oil, honor,
and global power . . .

"*Sky Masters* is a knockout!" —Clive Cussler

"A gripping military thriller . . . Brown brings combat and technology together in an explosive tale as timely as this morning's news." —W.E.B. Griffin

HAMMERHEADS

The U.S. government creates an all-new drug-defense
agency, armed with the ultimate high-tech weaponry. The
war against drugs will never be the same . . .

"Classic . . . His most exciting techno-thriller."
—Publishers Weekly

"Whiz-bang technology and muscular, damn-the-torpedoes strategy." —Kirkus Reviews

DAY OF THE CHEETAH

*The shattering story of a Soviet hijacking
of America's most advanced fighter plane—
and the greatest high-tech chase of all time . . .*

"Quite a ride . . . Terrific. Authentic and gripping."
—*The New York Times*

"Breathtaking dogfights . . . Exhilarating high-tech adventure."
—*Library Journal*

SILVER TOWER

*A Soviet invasion of the Middle East sparks a
grueling counterattack from America's newest
laser defense system . . .*

"Riveting, action-packed . . . a fast-paced thriller that is
impossible to put down."
—UPI

"Intriguing political projections . . . Tense high-tech dogfights."
—*Publishers Weekly*

"High-tech, high-thrills . . . a slam-bang finale."
—*Kirkus Reviews*

FLIGHT OF THE OLD DOG

*Dale Brown's riveting debut novel. A battle-scarred
bomber is renovated with modern hardware to fight the
Soviets' devastating new technology . . .*

"A superbly crafted adventure . . . Exciting."
—W.E.B. Griffin

"Brown kept me glued to the chair . . . a shattering climax.
A terrific flying yarn."
—Stephen Coonts

DALE BROWN'S

DREAMLAND

nerve center

Written by
Dale Brown and Jim DeFelice

B
BERKLEY BOOKS, NEW YORK

This is a work of fiction. Names, characters, places, and incidents either are the product of the author's imagination or are used fictitiously, and any resemblance to actual persons, living or dead, business establishments, events, or locales is entirely coincidental.

DALE BROWN'S DREAMLAND: NERVE CENTER

A Berkley Book / published by arrangement with the author

PRINTING HISTORY
Berkley edition / July 2002

Visit our website at www.penguinputnam.com

ISBN: 0-425-18772-1

A BERKLEY BOOK®
Berkley Books are published by The Berkley Publishing Group, a division of Penguin Putnam Inc., 375 Hudson Street, New York, New York 10014.
BERKLEY and the "B" design are trademarks belonging to Penguin Putnam Inc.

PRINTED IN THE UNITED STATES OF AMERICA

10 9 8 7 6 5 4 3 2

I
Premonition

Allegro, Nevada
1 January 1997, 0410 (all times local)

USUALLY THE NIGHTMARES WERE ABOUT LOSING HIS legs.

Jeff "Zen" Stockard felt the jerk of the ejection seat as the planes collided, or saw the fireball that had seared into his brain. Sometimes the nightmares didn't replay anything that had really happened the day his spine was crushed; they were subtle in their horror, teasing his fear. He might sit in an empty room, watching while everyone else got up to leave, wondering why he couldn't move. Or he'd be in a bathtub, surrounded by an immense blue sea, bobbing as the swells turned to waves.

But tonight's nightmare had nothing to do with his legs. Tonight, the first night of the new year, a sun rose from the middle of his head, a sun of chromium red. Its glow burned holes in the void around him. A black core appeared in the middle of this sun, a whirlpool of force and gravity that grabbed back the rays, grabbed back his brain. Zen's body was pulled from the inside out toward the void, his bones and the muscles and the skin sucked into the vortex. And then his soul itself was consumed by magenta fire.

Zen shouted. His wife, Breanna, rolled next to him on the bed.

"Jeff, are you all right?"

He didn't hear her until she repeated the question a third time.

"I'm okay, Rap," he told her.

She mumbled something, shifting next to him in the bed. Jeff stared at the ceiling of their condominium bedroom, noticing as if for the first time the soft red glow from the alarm clock numerals. The red reminded him of the color of his flesh when it burned in the dream.

But as he stared, he realized the clock had nothing to do with the dream. The nightmare hadn't come from anything here, nor had it been seeded by his accident.

It had come from ANTARES, the computer-mind interface experiments that taught him to control a robot plane with his thoughts. The sun was part of the metaphor he used to go into Theta-alpha, the mental state where he could interface with the computer.

It had ended long ago. Anything from before the accident was long ago, but ANTARES seemed even further in the past, distant history for him and the rest of Dreamland, even though the program had only been officially shut down six months ago.

Breanna leaned over him. Stale perfume and smoke from the party they'd been to earlier wafted across his face; her breath carried the overly sweet scent of her last glass of Chardonnay.

"You okay?" she asked.

"Just a dream."

She ran her fingers across his forehead and down his cheek, obviously thinking he'd had a nightmare about his legs. With her touch she tried to console him for the inconsolable, sympathizing with him for something that couldn't be sympathized for. He took her hand gently, placing it back on her side.

"Go back to sleep, Bree," he said. "It was just a dumb dream. Old junk."

He closed his eyes and listened to the sound of her heart in the still room, the light, steady rhythm pulling him back to rest.

II
Night moves

Bunker B, Air Force High Technology Advanced Weapons Center (Dreamland), Nevada
9 January, 1405

THE HELICOPTERS KEPT GETTING IN THE WAY. ZEN barely kept his U/MF-3 from colliding with a Blackhawk, mashing his control stick left and flailing away at the last possible instant. He was so close to the helicopter's blades that the wash whipped his wings into a nearly uncontrollable spin, despite the computer's efforts to help him steady the plane.

Before he could fully recover, he found himself in the middle of a stream of lead, thrown by the two ZSU-23 antiaircraft guns he was assigned to hit. Fortunately, the guns were being sighted manually and the gunners couldn't keep up with Zen's hard zag back to the right. But the sharp maneuvers made it impossible for him to lock on his target. Zen pressed the trigger as the four-barreled mobile antiaircraft unit on the left slid through his targeting pipper, while he simultaneously tried to walk his Flighthawk back into the target by sticking his rudder with a quick jerk left. That might have worked—might have—in a plane like an A-10A Thunderbolt, built for low-speed, low-level target-thrashing. But the U/MF-3 Flighthawk was a different beast altogether, originally designed for high-altitude, high-Mach encounters.

Not that she couldn't fly down here in the mud. Just that

she didn't necessarily appreciate it. Zen found himself fighting for control as the small craft jerked herself right and left, shells bursting from beneath her belly as she tried to follow his commands. The spin had taken him too low, and his cannon fire had slowed him down. The unmanned aircraft was in serious danger of turning into a brick.

Stubbornly, Zen ignored the computerized voice that warned of an impending stall. He goosed off enough slugs to nail the flak-dealer, then tossed off a few prayers to get the Flighthawk's nose pointing skyward. The antiaircraft gun exploded with a brilliant crimson glow just as the assault leader announced that the helos were on the ground.

But before Zen could draw a breath to relax, the radar-warning receiver in the lead Flighthawk went berserk, screaming that an enemy fighter had somehow gotten close enough to launch AMRAAM air-to-air missiles at the helicopters Zen was supposed to be protecting.

MAJOR MACK "KNIFE" SMITH GRINNED AS HE POPPED his F-16 up over the mountains he'd been using to mask his approach. He'd snuck in behind the two fighters tasked to keep him at bay; the four helicopters carrying the enemy assault force floated naked in front of him. Four helicopters, four missiles, four turkeys ready to be gassed.

A quartet of AMRAAMS slid off his wings in quick succession. Preset for the encounter, the missiles turned on their active seekers, each homing in on their targets as their solid-fuel rockets burst them forward at speeds approaching Mach 4. It was overkill really—the helicopters were less than five miles away; the missiles barely lit their wicks before nailing their targets. The helos were history before their pilots even realized they were targeted.

Mack didn't have time to gloat. One of the helicopters' escorts flashed for his tail. Its pilot—Jeff Stockard—had been caught with his pants down, and now he wanted revenge.

Of course, the fact that he didn't have time to gloat did not actually mean that Knife wouldn't gloat. On the contrary— he flicked on his mike and gave a roar of laughter as he took his Viper into a nearly ninety-degree turn, pulling close to thirteen g's. The "stock" plane would quite possibly have rattled apart; Knife most certainly would have blacked out from the force of gravity pelting his body. But nothing at the Air Force High Technology Advanced Weapons Center—aka "Dreamland"—was stock. The F-16's forward canards and reshaped delta wings were fashioned from an experimental titanium-carbon combination that made them several times stronger than the ones the factory had first outfitted her with. Mack's flight suit was designed to keep blood flowing evenly throughout his body at fifteen g's, negative as well as positive.

It couldn't keep his heart from double-pumping as he took the turn and managed to get his pursuer in his sights. He got off a half-second slap shot as the enemy zigged downward. The odds against hitting the small, nimble U/MF fighter were at least a hundred to one, but he got close enough to force the SOB to break downward, keeping it an easy target for the F-16. Knife laughed so loud his helmet almost came off—he hadn't had this much fun in months.

ZEN WORKED HARD NOW. HIS BREATH GREW SHORT and the muscles in his shoulders hardened into cannonballs as he tried desperately to break his airplane out of the low-energy scissors he'd been tricked into.

Not tricked exactly. He'd blundered into it, failing to use his airplane properly. Failing to use his head—truth was, he'd been surprised twice in the space of ninety seconds. He was stuck now in a three-dimensional game of follow-the-leader where being the leader meant you had a fifty- or sixty-percent chance of landing in the other guy's gunsight.

The pursuer had to be careful not to be sucked into a turn or even a loop that would send his plane shooting ahead, effectively changing places. This was a real danger since the U/MF could turn tighter than even the high-maneuverability F-16 Knife was flying. Mack was no sucker, nor a fool, hanging back just far enough to stay with him, but still close enough to cut off any fancy stuff with gunfire.

Zen had three other Flighthawks hurrying to his rescue. Eventually, they'd force Mack to break off, turning the tables on the hunter. But eventually seemed to be taking forever.

The problem was, he couldn't control four of the robot planes at one time, not easily anyway. It was especially hard when they were tasked with different missions in different places. Changing mental gears wasn't bad enough—the U/MFs' control gear took forever to cycle into the right plane.

Forever being ten nanoseconds.

Three months ago, Jeff had saved Mack's sorry butt and oversized ego with a near-impossible foray into Libya. Shot down and captured while taking part in a covert operation, Smith had been headed to Iran to have his head chopped off when Dreamland's Spec Ops team, "Whiplash," intervened. Controlling the still-experimental U/MF-3 Flighthawks from a hastily modified weapons bay of an EB-52 Megafortress, Zen had found Smith and his captor in a small plane over the Mediterranean. When Smith was finally rescued, he was more grateful than a groom on his wedding night.

For about thirty seconds. Now they were back in their usual places, clawing each other at the nation's top center for weapons development. It didn't matter that this fight was being played out in a massive computer, projected on a series of screens in a high-tech hangar. Both men went at it like boxers competing for a ten-million-dollar winner-take-all purse.

At the end of the day, both men would go home with the knowledge that they'd helped test and perfect the next generation of front-line weapons for the country. More importantly—as far as they were concerned, at least—one would go home the winner, the other the loser.

Or, as Mack would put it if he won, "the peahead loser."

Tracers flared over Jeff's Flighthawk, arcing to his left. The burst of red ignited an idea in Zen's brain—he yanked hard on the stick, pointing his nose straight up, directly into Mack's path.

KEVIN MADRONE EDGED WHAT WAS LEFT OF HIS thumbnail against his tooth, watching the bird's-eye view of the dogfight on the large display screen. The Army captain could see that Mack had the advantage, but it wasn't quite enough to nail Zen. Their dogfight was incidental to the overall exercise, but he couldn't help watching. They were like old-fashioned gladiators, flailing at each other in the Colosseum, willing to go to any lengths to beat their opponents. There was something irresistible in their single-mindedness, something attractive in the danger they faced.

And frightening as well. Madrone whittled his nail, nervously razoring two sharp V's on the cartilage. Blood pricked from his finger as he finally broke away from the conflict to glance at the screen on his right, where one of the computers monitoring the encounter was kicking up data.

"Weapons test complete," declared the computer.

As the test supervisor, Madrone ought to end the encounter. But instead he turned back to it, drawn by the swirling energy and fascinated by his own fear.

The Flighthawk suddenly veered straight up. Mack's F-16 seemed to stutter in midair, less than two hundred feet from the smaller craft. The planes seemed to collide. Then it became obvious that the F-16 had veered off at the last possible instant, wings spinning violently. The Flighthawk somehow managed to flip its nose downward, lighting its cannon. Three or four slugs ripped through the F-16's wing, but Mack managed to zip off in the opposite direction, the craft in an invert.

The two pilots cursed at each other.

"You stinking cheater. You used a hole in the programming!" snapped Mack.

"Oh, like you didn't to nail the helos."

"Knock it off," said Kevin, snapping into his role as mission boss. "Exercise over."

Neither pilot acknowledged.

Aboard EB-52 BX-2 "Raven"
Range 2, Dreamland
9 January, 1415

"YOU HAVE TO KEEP YOUR SPEED UP OR YOU WON'T GET off the ground."

"I'm not stupid," snapped Lieutenant Colonel Tecumseh "Dog" Bastian, struggling to get the big EB-52 off Dreamland's Runway Number Two. The big plane was trimmed for takeoff, its four freshly tuned engines humming at maximum takeoff power. He even had a crisp takeoff kind of wind at eighteen and a half knots in his face.

And still he couldn't coax the plane into the sky. The mountains loomed ahead.

Worse—the computer-pilot-assist droned a stall warning in his ear.

"Daddy."

"I have it, Breanna," he snapped to the copilot, Captain Breanna "Rap" Stockard. Bree was not only acting as his mentor on his first flight in the big plane; she also happened to be his daughter. "I have it," he repeated.

But Colonel Bastian didn't have it. The Megafortress's nose stubbornly remained horizontal and its wheels on the pavement. He was nearly out of runway, and nothing he did— nothing—would get his forward speed over seventy-eight knots. Way too slow for anything but disaster.

Dog started to curse. In the next second, the plane magically lifted her chin, instantly gaining momentum. It wasn't until he went to clean his landing gear a few seconds later that Bastian realized what had happened—the computer had taken over.

His copilot, meanwhile, was having serious trouble stowing a smirk.

"What the hell, Bree?"

"You tried to take off with only one engine."

"What do you mean, one engine? They were all in the green." The colonel ignored a query from Dreamland Tower, which was monitoring the airplane's progress toward Range DL/2. "The controls—"

"You never punched it out of Sim-2," said Breanna. "You were looking at old numbers." She laughed uncontrollably.

They had used the plane's command computer's simulator module to run through a few mock takeoffs before starting down the field. The colonel realized now that he had failed to authorize the computer to switch back into real mode for takeoff. Obviously, Breanna had counted on the Megafortress's safety protocols to get them off the ground safely.

Which, of course, they had.

"That's dirty pool, Breanna," Dog told her. "You shut off the engines."

"No. I just dialed them down to ten percent. You weren't paying attention," she added. There was no trace of humor in her voice now—she was the veteran flight instructor verbally whacking a greenie pilot. "You didn't ask for a check, which you should have, because as you can see, my screen clearly indicates the proper output. Inattention is a killer. In any airplane except the Megafortress, you would have bought it."

"Any other plane and there's no way you could have done that," said Dog angrily. "You tricked me with a bogus reading."

"Your screen clearly says sim mode. You didn't go through the checks properly," she said. "This was a dramatic way to point that out. I'm sorry, Daddy," she added, her voice suddenly changing.

The change in tone killed him.

"No, you were absolutely one-hundred-percent right," said Bastian. He practically spat the words through his clenched teeth, then sighed. She *was* right, damn it—he hadn't dotted his stinking i's and it could have cost him his plane, his crew, and his life. "Can I get control back?"

Breanna reached to her panel. "On my mark, Daddy."

"*Don't* call me Daddy."

Bunker B, Dreamland
9 January, 1415

THE FLIGHTHAWK AND F-16 SWIRLED IN THE SKY, CAT and dog locked in a ferocious match. Neither could gain enough of an advantage over the other to end the battle. Then the big screen at the front of the room flashed white and a loud *pffffffff* cracked the speakers—Captain Madrone had cut the feed.

"I said, *knock it off.*" Madrone stood back from the console, folding his arms in front of his chest. At five eight and perhaps 140˙ in a winter uniform with boots, thermals, and two sweaters, Madrone hardly cut an imposing figure. Even for an engineer he was considered shy and quiet, and most people at Dreamland who knew him even casually could mention several nervous habits, beginning with his nail-biting. But somewhere in the recesses of his personality lurked a young lieutenant who had faced down a pair of tanks in Iraq. The same ferocious snap that had led his team to wipe out the tanks with nothing more than hand grenades now brought the joint-services team that had been fighting the mock battle on a new simulation system to rapid attention.

Except for the two men at the heart of the battle, that is.

"You fucking *cheated*," Zen told Mack, tossing off his Flighthawk control helmet. A control cable caught the custom-built device about a millimeter from the ground, just barely keeping it from turning into a bucket of ridiculously expensive but busted computer chips.

"I didn't cheat," said Smith, standing from his station on Madrone's left. "I just flew under the radar coverage. How is that cheating?"

"You flew beyond the parameters of the plane," said Zen. "You pulled over ten g's twice. And besides, no way no how could you have gotten past the F-15's at Mark Seven."

"The computer let me take the g's," said Mack. "As for the F-15's, where were they?"

"He got past us," admitted Captain Paul Owens, who'd been handling the F-15 combat air sweep from one of the back benches. "The damn simulator has a hole in the radar coverage big enough to fly a 747 through. You can't see anything under a thousand feet."

"Gentlemen, please." Dr. Ray Rubeo, one of the scientists overseeing the simulation, leaned over the railing at the back of the room. His voice had the world-weary tone a kindergarten teacher would use at the end of a long week. "I believe we have our data for today. I suggest everyone take the afternoon off to play with their Tinkertoys. Live-fire exercise in the morning. Tomorrow, please, keep the WWF routine on the ground."

Rubeo turned and walked from the room, shuddering slightly at the doorway, as if shaking a great chill from his body.

"Easier to walk away than fix the holes in the sim program," muttered Zen.

"I think he was right," said Madrone. "We all pretty much know what we have to do tomorrow."

He turned to Captain Rosenstein and Lieutenant Garuthers, who were to pilot the actual helicopters they would test tomorrow. The Army commanders were here to test new helicopter upgrades and combat communications in something approaching real conditions; they cared little for what they called the "Hair Force testosterone show," and were only too happy to knock off early.

Knife and Zen, meanwhile, traded snipes across the floor.

"You were lucky today," said Zen. "Tomorrow we're in real planes."

"Tomorrow I'm going to kick your ass all over town, you peahead loser," promised Knife. "I can do things in the MiG that would tear an F-16 apart, even with Dreamland's mods."

"I can nail a MiG with my eyes closed," said Zen.

"We'll see," said Mack. He popped the CD that had recorded his part of the exercise out of the console near him and left the room, practically whistling.

Zen wheeled toward his helmet, still shaking his head. He picked it up and handed it to Jennifer Gleason, one of the computer scientists on the Flighthawk project. Gleason smiled at him, pushing a strand of her long, brownish-blond hair back behind her ear. The computer screens bathed her face and neck an almost golden yellow; she looked like a nymph emerging from bed. A genius nymph—Dr. Gleason was among the world's leading authorities on AI circuitry and intelligence chips—but a nymph nonetheless.

Madrone stared at the curve of her two breasts in the slightly oversized black T-shirt she wore. Lowering his eyes to her hips, he watched them sway slightly while their owner went over some of the details of the encounter with Jeff. Madrone turned back to his station, pretending to sort through his papers, pretending not to be driven to sense-crushing distraction by an expert on gallium arsenic chips.

"We're seeing you tonight, right?"

"Uh, yeah," Madrone said, still distracted.

"You okay, Kevin?" Zen asked.

"I'm fine. Have to, uh, sort all this out, you know."

"Yeah. Listen, don't worry about the holes in the simulation program. Jennifer will work them out. Nail's bleeding," Zen added, smiling. "Bad habit."

Madrone nodded sheepishly. Stockard gripped the wheels of his chair and rolled himself back a foot or so. The others had left the control area, but Zen still made a show of looking around, a car thief checking if the coast were clear. "Listen, I have to give you a heads-up on tonight. Bree's playing matchmaker." Zen rolled his eyes and shrugged apologetically. "You know how it goes."

Madrone suddenly had a vision of Jennifer Gleason sitting

on the Stockards' couch in a short, wispy skirt, breasts loose beneath a silk white polo shirt.

"Abby Miller," added Jeff.

The vision evaporated.

"I'm sorry, Zen. What'd you say?" asked Madrone.

"Abby Miller. She's a civilian. She works over at Nellis in the public affairs office. I think she used to be a reporter or worked for a magazine or something. I'm not exactly sure how Bree first met her. You know Rap—she knows just about everybody. Uh, nice personality."

Madrone folded his thumb beneath his other fingers, holding his fist close to his side. "If Breanna likes her, she's okay," he said.

"That's the spirit." Zen gave him another sardonic grin, then began wheeling away. "Seven P.M. *sharp*. Bree'll have dinner timed out to the half second. Bring the wine."

Madrone suddenly felt real fear. "Wine? What kind?"

But Zen was halfway out the door and didn't respond.

Aboard Raven
9 January, 1415

NOWHERE IS IT WRITTEN THAT POINTY-NOSE FIGHTER jocks are better than all other pilots. No military regulation declares that just because a man—or woman—regularly subjects himself to eight or nine negative g's and hurtles his body through the air at several times the speed of sound is he—or she—better than those who proceed in a more considered fashion. Not one sheet in the mountains of official Air Force paperwork covering piloting and flying in general includes the words "Teen-jet jocks are superior to all others."

But every go-fast zippersuit who ever strapped a brain bucket on his head believes it is true. He—or she—did not get to fly the world's most advanced warbirds by being merely good. Personal preferences and luck aside, front-line fighter pilots in the U.S. Air Force are the best of the best. And most would have no problem telling you that.

Lieutenant Colonel Bastian was, more than anything else, a front-line fighter jock. It did not matter that his last mission in combat had been more than five years ago during the Gulf

War. Nor did it matter that that mission was actually in a bomber—the F-15E Strike Eagle, at the time one of the newest swords in the weapons trove. It did not even matter that his present post as a commander—a *ground* commander—was several hundred times more important than anything he had done during the war.

What mattered was that he *was* a fighter pilot. Dog thought like a fighter pilot. He talked like a fighter pilot. He walked—some might say swaggered—like a fighter pilot. One who had seen combat. One who had big hours in F-16's as well as F-15's. A fighter pilot who had flown F-4's, F-111's, and even an A-10A once or twice. A fighter pilot who had taken the stick of an F-117 and a turn in an F-22 demonstrator. In short, a zippersuit who could fly and had flown anything the Air Force had to offer, and had done it very well.

Except for today, when he was sitting at the helm of an antiquated, out-of-date, obsolete, lumbering, slow-as-a-cow-going-backward BUFF. A plane as old as he was, and twenty times as creaky.

Actually, if it *had* been simply a B-52, Dog might not have felt as bad. The Stratofortress's vintage controls took a hell of a lot of getting used to. Levers and knobs stuck out at all angles, the dash looked like the display case in a clock shop, and there was no way to get comfortable in the seat until a dozen hard landings form-fitted your butt. But the B-52 he was flying had been rebuilt from the fuel tanks outward as an *EB-52*. Rebuilt and reskinned, reengined and recontrolled, the Megafortress retained the soul of the old machine—the most capable and durable bomber of the Cold War era. But she flexed twenty-first-century muscles. It was like having the wisdom and experience of a sixty-five-year-old—and the muscles and reflexes of a twenty-one-year-old young buck.

As Breanna somewhat gushingly put it after they landed.

"I can do without the metaphors, thank you, Captain Stockard," snapped Dog, unhooking himself from the seat restraints.

Or rather, trying to unhook himself. Damn, he couldn't even undo a stinking belt buckle today.

"All I'm saying, Daddy, is that Raven takes a little getting used to. It's not your average F-16. I know that with a few more flights, you'll be right on top of it."

The restraint finally snapped clean. Dog unfolded himself from the seat, struggling to maintain what little was left of his dignity as he left the plane. The other crew members—he had foolishly agreed to fly with a navigator and a weapons officer—wisely made their way out the ventral hatch well ahead of him.

"Daddy—"

"And another thing, Captain." Bastian twisted at the back of the flight deck before starting downward. "Do not, under any circumstances, while we are on duty—at *work*—ever refer to me as Daddy, Dad, Pop, Poppy, Father, Papa, or anything in that vein. Got it?"

"Sir, yes, sir."

The Megafortress's stealthy carbon-resin skin was specially treated to withstand high temperatures. The runway apron, however, seemed to melt as Dog stalked from the plane, which was being refueled for a flight by another crew. He headed toward the ramp to the Megafortress's subterranean hangar, where a state-of-the-art simulator waited to replay his flying mistakes in bold colors.

A black Jimmy SUV with a row of flashing blue lights whipped off the access ramp to his right, speeding toward him. Dog stopped, thankful for the interruption, even if the flashing lights boded a problem. The Jimmy belonged to his head of base security, Captain Danny Freah. Danny was loath to use the blue lights—he claimed they made the truck look like it was leading a fire department parade—so something serious must be up.

But instead of Freah, Chief Master Sergeant Terence "Ax" Gibbs pulled down the driver's-side window as the truck rolled up.

"Colonel, you have visitors," said the sergeant.

"Visitors who?" snapped Dog.

"Secretary-to-be Keesh for one," said Ax. "A whole pack of muckety-mucks nipping at his heels."

An ex-Congressman, John Keesh was the new Administration's nominee for Defense Secretary. Bastian knew him vaguely from Washington, but hadn't seen or spoken to him for months. He was expected to be confirmed next week.

Last November's elections had completely rearranged the defense landscape, removing Bastian's chief patron and booster, National Security Director Deborah O'Day. Her likely replacement, Philip Freeman, was unknown to Bastian personally. The only ranking holdover from O'Day's staff was Jed Barclay, a young Harvard whiz kid who had more pimples than experience. His official title was Deputy NSC Assistant for Technology and Foreign Relations, though he had been more of a freelance troubleshooter for O'Day.

"Why the hell didn't somebody tell me Keesh was coming?" Bastian asked Ax.

"Advanced warning systems completely smoked," admitted the sergeant. "Captain Freah's already giving them the two-dollar tour."

Taken off guard, Dog settled for the passenger's seat as he contemplated what the surprise VIP tour might mean. That was a mistake, as Ax's screeching takeoff quickly confirmed. Bastian grabbed desperately for the door handle, trying to keep himself from shooting through the windshield as the sergeant threw the truck into reverse and whipped back toward the access road back to the main area of the base. Gibbs had no peer when it came to organizing an administrative staff and handling the paperwork of command. Driving was a different story.

"Flight go okay?" asked the sergeant. His voice sounded innocent, but Dog suspected it was anything but.

"It did not. Keep your eyes on the road."

"Yes, sir. Papers for you to sign," added the sergeant, thumbing toward the console between them where three thick folders were wedged tight.

"I'll read them if you'll slow down," said Dog as Gibbs took a turn on two wheels.

"Ah, I keep telling you, you don't have to read the stuff I give you. Requisitions for toilet paper and that kind of stuff." Gibbs jerked the Jimmy onto the road to Taj, Dreamland's command complex. "Anything important I forge."

"I hope you forged me a will," said Dog, gripping his hand-hold tighter.

" 'Xcuse me, Colonel?"

"Just watch the road." Dog finally managed to buckle his seat belt. "Now why the hell didn't you radio me when the Secretary's plane was inbound? And didn't someone on General Magnus's staff call to give us a heads-up?"

"Well, thing is, Colonel, number one, the Secretary didn't come by plane, he came via limo from Nellis. Second thing is, he just showed up there too, and made a beeline out to us without telling the base commander. Everybody is peed. General Magnus's staff didn't know anything about it. I think Captain Granson may lose a bar over it," added Ax. "Sergeant Fulton says it was his turn to keep track of the brass's brass."

Dog's stern frown cut Gibbs off in mid-chortle. Granson was an aide to Lieutenant General Magnus, Colonel Bastian's immediate superior in the streamlined chain of command established when Dreamland and its Whiplash Action Team became operational some months ago. Until the last election, Magnus had seemed on the short track to head the Air Force and maybe the Joint Chiefs. The fact that Keesh didn't give him a heads-up before inspecting one of his commands obviously meant he was off the track, at least for now.

"Last but not least," added Gibbs, "you left explicit orders not to be disturbed."

"Ax, if the President came, would you have radioed me?"

"Probably. Ought to be down in the Mudroom by now," added Gibbs, jerking the SUV to a stop so quickly it was a wonder the air bags didn't deploy. "Senator Densmore looks like he had a bumpy flight, Colonel. Might offer him a cocktail. Also, Congresswoman Timmons is wearing very expensive perfume, so she may have intentions. She's a widow, you know."

"Anything else, Ax?"

"Just my papers, sir."

Dog frowned at the folder. "I have to read them."

"Seriously, Colonel, they're just routine. You know, sir, if I can say something out of line—"

"You were born out of line, Sergeant."

"You're wasting your time on a lot of diddly-shit with the papers. I'll bring the stuff you really need to deal with to your attention. As for the rest—"

"Not my way, Ax." ·

"Yes, sir."

The Mudroom—only Gibbs called it that—was a secure command center on basement level three of the Taj. Dog found Danny regaling the visitors with tapes of Dreamland's successful Whiplash raid into Libya three months before.

Not too subtle.

Dog stood for a moment at the railing on the observer's deck at the rear of the room, watching the tape run on the composite screen. The entire twelve-by-twenty-one-foot surface was given over to a feed from one of the Flighthawks as it surveyed the bunker complex where American prisoners were being held. Keesh, five lawmakers from Congress, and an aide were standing about five feet from the screen, completely mesmerized by the action. A roof began moving on the left; puffs of smoke and small flames, carefully rendered by the equivalent of more than 250 laptop TFT displays, filled the big screen. The camera veered off, and Whiplash's assault team arrived in a combat-outfitted Osprey at the left corner of the screen.

"Just getting to the good part, I see," said Bastian from the railing.

Danny jerked his head around, surprised that Bastian had managed to come in so quietly. "Colonel," he said, pushing the remote control to freeze the video.

"It's okay, Danny. Don't stop now." Bastian rolled his arms together in front of his chest.

"We know how it ends," said Keesh, readjusting his thick, brown-framed glasses. They matched his brown suit. "But it is impressive."

"Thank you, Mr. Secretary," said Dog, not sure how to address him. "We did get some breaks."

"I was referring to the equipment," said Keesh, who obviously didn't mind the title.

"I think the colonel and his people deserve a compliment," said Congresswoman Timmons, the ranking member on the Defense Appropriations Committee.

"The colonel has already been complimented," said Keesh. "He's in charge of the most prestigious command in the Air Force."

Uh-oh, thought Dog, his crap detector snapping from search-and-scan to dogfight mode.

Nella McCormack stepped forward. Identifying herself as the Assistant Secretary for Technology "elect," she introduced the colonel to the rest of the delegation. "Colonel, we're on a tight schedule this afternoon," she said after Bastian pumped the hand of the Washington lawmaker. "We'd like to speak to you in confidence. Perhaps we could pick up the tour in your office?"

As he led the delegation back up to his office suite, Dog wondered if they had come to sack him. Prior to his arrival, Dreamland had been run by a three-star general. Bastian was almost certainly the lowest-ranking officer in command of a mainland base in the Air Force. Dreamland wasn't exactly a remote operating area either. HAWC had two main tasks: developing next-generation weapons for the Air Force and much of the rest of the military, and projecting that technology into trouble spots via Whiplash, its combined action squadron. Whiplash had a ground component headed by Danny Freah, and could draw on any of a number of high-tech planes, including the Megafortress and Flighthawks.

Ordinarily, the person heading such an operation would have a shoulder lit—some would say burdened—by at least two stars. So Bastian half expected that, once the new Administration got settled and figured out where everything was, he would be patted on the head and replaced. But Keesh wouldn't have brought an audience to can him, would he?

"Nice desk for a colonel," said Senator Densmore as they passed through Bastian's personal office to get to the conference room.

"It was actually the last commander's," said Bastian, placing his palms on the exquisite cherry of his desktop.

"Tecumseh, let me apologize for barging in on you unannounced," said Keesh as they all took seats around the two large tables in the conference room.

"We're here to give you some good news," said Congresswoman Timmons.

Dog felt a sudden pang. They couldn't be here to promote him, could they?

"We're going to greenlight an expansion of the U/MF program," said Densmore. "Both the Senate and the House will include it in their budgets, and of course the Administration is behind it."

"Well, that is good news," said Bastian. He meant it—the robot planes, in his opinion, were potentially the biggest development in aerial combat since AWACS. But he wasn't exactly sure why that news had to be delivered in person— nor why Magnus had been cut out of the loop. His confusion only grew as Keesh praised the Megafortress and JSF programs as well. Dog waited for the punch line, but none came.

"We have to be in our hotel at six," said Keesh finally. He rose. "Perhaps we could see the Flighthawks before we go? And the Megafortress?"

"Of course," said Bastian. He pulled the phone off the table and dialed Ax.

"Major Cheshire is waiting out here to give the nickel show," said Gibbs as soon as he clicked on the line. "Major Stockard seems to be tied up with another project today. I couldn't find him."

That had to be a lie, or at least a fudge; no one escaped the omnipotent intelligence of Chief Master Sergeant Terence Gibbs. On the other hand, Nancy Cheshire was the perfect tour guide. She headed the Megafortress project, but had worked with the Flighthawks enough to sing their praises. She'd also give the men in the delegation something to look at if they got bored. The fact that she had received the Air Force Cross for her role in the Libya action, as well as a Purple Heart, wouldn't hurt either.

Besides, while Nancy had a way with VIP types, Stockard tended to get impatient with people he thought were airheads. Which pretty much summed up his definition of anyone in Congress.

"Very good, Ax," said Dog. "We'll meet her at the elevator." As he put down the phone, he noticed Keesh nod to McCormack. So he wasn't surprised that McCormack touched Bastian's sleeve and signaled that she wanted to talk as the others filed out.

"My sergeant has some papers for me to sign," Dog told them. "I'll catch up with you at the hangar."

He closed the door.

"You're very smooth, Colonel," said McCormack.

"Actually, I think I was pretty obvious," said Bastian. "As were you."

"It's a game we play. Washington." She laughed. In her late thirties and not unattractive, she wore a light gray tweed pantsuit that made her look several pounds heavier than she probably was.

"So what's going on?"

"The Secretary is very impressed by your work here. He

wants to make sure that the base is properly funded. He sees very big things in your future."

If it hadn't been for his combat training, Dog would have responded with a terse "bullshit" and asked her to get to the point. As it was, he strained several muscles keeping his mouth shut. McCormack finally filled the silence.

"We're very impressed with the U/MFs. We'd like to see two dozen in the air by the end of the year."

"Two dozen by the end of the year? That's quite optimistic. At the moment, I only have four, and don't even have the funds to train more pilots."

"That can be taken care of."

"Okay," he said cautiously.

"We'd like them all in the air at the same time. The Secretary is very impressed with the Air Armada concept."

Dog suddenly sensed where she was going, but held his tongue.

"We believe ANTARES should be revived to control them," said McCormack.

"Oh," said Dog.

ANTARES stood for the Artificial Neural Transfer and Response System, and was a method for merging electronic data with a pilot's senses. It allowed a pilot to see—some suggested "feel" was more descriptive—radar data, engine-performance readouts, weapons status, and flight data in his brain. It also promised to allow him to control planes with just his mind. The multifaceted project had led to huge advances in computer-assisted flight controls, and in fact the Flighthawks' C^3 and the computer autopilots in the Megafortress were outgrowths of ANTARES. But after stupendous early success, ANTARES had been placed on permanent "hold" after being compromised by a Russian spy.

"Multiple-plane control was part of the original plan, under the Nerve Center option. It's quite all right, Colonel," McCormack added, obviously reacting to Bastian's hesitation. "I'm up to speed. I was part of the original team that came up with the concept several years ago."

"You knew Maraklov then."

"Captain James, yes." McCormack said the name so lightly she could have been talking about a friend from kindergarten—not one of the most devastating intelligence moles in history. "Colonel, let's put our cards on the table, shall we?"

"Please."

"Joining the Flighthawks to the Megafortress was a brilliant idea, a stroke of genius. Now we can move ahead and make the Flying Armada concept a reality. Nerve Center will give us a twenty- or even thirty-year lead on every other country in the world. Conflicts such as the Gulf War or Bosnia could be fought bloodlessly, at a fraction of the present costs."

"As long as we're being blunt," said Dog, "I think AN-TARES is a big, big mistake. Fifty years from now, maybe. But the computers we have, and maybe the human brain itself—maybe I'm just an old dog, but I don't trust it. There were a lot of problems with the program."

McCormack smiled smugly as he continued.

"If you're talking about putting major resources into the project, reviving flight testing and that sort of thing, I think our money could be better spent in a million ways," said Bastian. "The Flighthawk controls are heavily computerized as it is. Besides, there are only a dozen people or so with ANTARES experience left on the base, and all of them have other duties."

"Dr. Geraldo would be the logical person to revive AN-TARES," said McCormack. "She was involved in the early stages before returning to NASA, which gives her the necessary experience while avoiding the James taint. I understand she has already done some work on it since transferring here in November."

Martha Geraldo was a former NASA astrophysicist and psychologist with expertise in computer-human interaction. Her present assignment at Dreamland concerned development of the interfaces with flight computers. Dog had been aware of her ANTARES connection when she arrived, and in fact had asked her to prepare a study on what might be salvageable from the project. Now he realized that her transfer might have been part of a backdoor plot to revive the program all along.

"You've spoken to Dr. Geraldo about this?" he asked.

"No," said McCormack. She said it quickly, but with enough of a neutral tone that Dog couldn't tell if she was being honest. "That would be improper until I'm confirmed. But bluntly, Colonel—the new Secretary is very much in favor of ANTARES."

"What if I'm not?"

"Then someone who is will be found to fill this command."

Dreamland Shuttle Dock
9 January, 1745

MACK LEANED BACK AGAINST THE RAIL, SQUINTING AT the hills in the direction of Nellis Air Force Base, waiting for the Dolphin to arrive. Technically an Aerospatiale SA 366G Dauphin, the French helicopter had entered service as a Coast Guard recovery craft, and through a tortured series of events and horse trading, had come to serve here as part of the ferry service between Dreamland and Nellis. Known in military dress as a "Panther," the whirlybird was a smooth and steady performer that made quick work of the trip to the larger, "open" air base. But there was only one helicopter, and it did not always run according to schedule. Even a patient man could find himself cursing as he counted the rivets in the Plexiglas shed that served as the Dolphin's waiting area.

Major Smith was anything but patient. He paced, he turned, he muttered. He cursed. He kicked at the cracks. He stared at the mountain and the dry lake beds. He folded his arms and leaned against the side of the shelter, willing the stinking helicopter to appear.

It did not.

Two more passengers approached the platform from the hangar area. Mack glanced at them, saw they were civilians—and more importantly, male—and glanced away, uninterested. One of the two men stood in the shed for a second, lighting a cigarette, then nervously approached him. Mack turned and stared at him for a few seconds before realizing it was Kevin Madrone, in jeans and a baseball cap.

A Yankees cap. Figured.

"Hi, Major," said Madrone, taking a long pull on his cigarette.

"Hey, Twig."

Madrone winced at the nickname, which Mack had recently invented. It hadn't stuck yet, but it would.

Knife had worked with Madrone a lot during his earlier hitch at Dreamland. The Army wanted a secure weapons link with the Joint Strike Fighter, allowing it to provide target data to ground units and receive data from them. Madrone had come to the project as a weapons expert, but had proven adept at dealing with all sorts of complexities; he'd actually engineered part of the link himself when problems arose. But he seemed abnormally quiet, even for a geek.

"Major, you mad I killed the exercise?" Madrone asked Mack.

"Ah, shit, no," said Knife. "Don't worry about what Stockard says. He's so fucking competitive. He doesn't know when to turn it off, you know?"

Madrone shrugged.

Stockard probably chewed his ear, Mack thought. Just like the SOB. Zen was a good pilot—not great, but good, certainly. But like a lot of guys Mack knew, he had a serious ego problem. He just couldn't accept that anyone was better than him.

"Think we'll get off tomorrow? Weather's supposed to be bad," said Madrone. "Storms in the mountains. Worst winter in years, they say."

Talking about the weather. Poor guy was probably desperate to make conversation. Who could blame him, though? It sucked horse meat to stand out here waiting for the damn Dolphin.

"I'm thinking clear skies," said Mack.

"You're flying that Fulcrum?"

"Shit, yeah. I'll cook Stockard's ass. You watch."

"Problem is, he can't control four planes at once."

"I'd cook his butt one-on-one," said Mack. "I have plenty of times."

Madrone took off his baseball cap and looked at it, as if trying to decide whether to wear it or not. Finally he folded it up and slipped it into his jacket pocket.

Smart move, thought Mack. He considered saying something about how Jeff had screwed up so badly one time that it had cost him his legs, but he held off. He didn't like to hit a guy when he was down, even if it was true.

Besides, Stockard had helped save his butt in Africa. So maybe he owed him a little.

"The way they've reworked the MiG," he told Madrone, "it's a pretty nice piece of hardware now. I can outaccelerate an F-15. Stock F-15 anyway. Tough little customer. Anything less than an F-22, I think you'd have a tough time one-on-one. The simulated F-16 we were using? That's not even half as capable as the Fulcrum, not with Dreamland's alterations. Shit. We only used that model because they couldn't code the Fulcrum in—it was too far off the charts. Damn plane is beyond even the computer boys, it's so hot. Simulates what the Russkies will be flying in 2030—assuming they're not part of Iowa by then. Which they will be if they ever try and start something."

Madrone nodded. Almost down to the filter on his cigarette, he took one more pull, then tossed it to the ground.

"Of course, it all depends on the pilot," Mack went on. "Right pilot in an F-5E could take out the wrong pilot in a Raptor. All depends on using your plane. Knowing it. That's why I beat Stockard today. That's why I always beat Stockard."

"Yeah," said Madrone. He glanced in the direction the Dolphin ought to be coming from, as if trying to decide whether or not to have another cigarette.

"See, nothing against Zen personally," said Mack, "but he's a bit of an egomaniac. You know, figures he's the hottest stick on the patch, that kind of thing. Now with Libya—which, nothing against Zen, but hell, think about who we went against. Qaddafi? Come on. Guy wears dresses, for Christsake. So Jeff did well, or at least well enough, and that inflated his head. Shrink would probably tell you it's because he had a fragile ego to begin with. Penis envy or something like that."

Mack laughed, though he was only half kidding. Madrone seemed to smirk, then reached into the pocket of his shirt for another pack of cigarettes.

"Now his wife, Breanna? She's not that good a pilot at all. But she's lucky, and that's a lot more important. That, and she has one hellacious set of knockers."

Madrone lit his cigarette without saying anything. He didn't seem to be that bad a sort, just a little shy. And Army, but you could overlook that.

The Yankees thing, though. Well, he did come from New York, so maybe you could excuse that too.

"Say, I'm thinking of heading into Vegas tonight," said Mack. He unfolded his arms and shoved his hands into his pockets. "Check out MGM, maybe pick up some women. Been a while since I been to the City of Sin." He laughed—it had been a while for a lot of things. "Want to tag along?"

"Can't, sorry," said Madrone, lighting up.

"Heavy date?"

"Kinda," said the Army captain. He took a puff, then turned to his left—the Dolphin was just clearing the range. "Shit. I just lit this."

"Bad for you anyway," said Mack. "Who's the lucky girl?"

Madrone shrugged. "A friend of a friend."

"And?"

"It's Abby something or other. Rap is setting me up."

Mack suddenly got the picture. "Rap as in Bree Stockard?"

"Yeah. Zen and Breanna invited me to dinner."

The roar of the approaching helicopter helped drown out the sound of Mack grinding his teeth.

Allegro, Nevada
9 January, 1913

BREANNA SMOOTHED THE SHEET OF ALUMINUM AGAINST the top of the pan, her fingers sweeping the edges taut. The clock clicked over and now she had exactly sixty seconds to ignition. Plenty of time—she grabbed her freshly sharpened chef's knife and whipped through the scallions, stockpiling a supply of perfect two-mm-long ovals at the side of her chopping block. The timer binged and she hit the burner to finish steaming the carrots.

Of course, if Madrone didn't show up in ten seconds, she was going to have to put everything on hold. The carrots would survive, but the rice was iffy—it had only ten minutes to go.

Kevin was late. Not too late—she'd guessed that he'd be about fifteen minutes late, and had calculated dinner accordingly. But the outside parameter of her estimate was rapidly approaching.

Could it be that Jeff had warned him about Abby?

Not that Abby deserved a warning. On the contrary. But sometimes men were such geeks about meeting people of the opposite sex, especially when they were obviously perfect for each other.

If he didn't show in thirty seconds she was going to use the knife on him. And the ovals she cut wouldn't be pretty.

The doorbell rang. Breanna felt a surge of adrenaline and relief as she snapped into action. The four ruby-red pieces of fresh tuna were plucked from their marinade and deposited on the foiled broiling pan; fresh marinade was ladled on them, a dash of soy, a sprinkle of toasted sesame seeds, ginger shavings, the scallions. Oven open, broiler on, another dash of ginger and a pinch of sugar for the carrots, check the rice— bing-bang-boing. Breanna had it so well timed that she was ready at the kitchen door just as Madrone approached to greet her, holding a bottle of wine.

Cabernet Sauvignon. Just bottled too. Oh, well.

She took the bottle and hugged him. He was actually shaking a little from nervousness.

A good sign, she thought.

"Have you met Abby?" she said, putting the wine down on the counter and ushering him back into the living room.

"We just said hello," said Madrone.

"Abby used to work for CNN, didn't you?" she prompted, gently easing Kevin toward the couch.

Jeff frowned at her from his wheelchair. She smiled into his stare as Abby explained that she had worked for CNN Headline News Radio, and that she hadn't been anyone important, had actually been little more than an intern.

"But I'll bet it was exciting," suggested Bree.

"Sometimes," said Abby.

Breanna nudged the stereo a bit louder, hoping it would drown out her husband's snort. As much as she loved him, Jeff could be amazingly unsupportive at times.

"You just returned from a trip to Europe, didn't you, Kevin?" Bree prompted.

"Uh, couple of months ago. Business thing with, uh, NATO."

"NATO," said Bree, underlining its importance. "Get any sightseeing in?"

"Not really."

"Oh, come on, Kev. What about that laser-sighting system the Germans were trying to sell," said Jeff.

And the worst thing was, Breanna thought, he did it with such a straight face.

"Honey, why don't you open that excellent bottle of wine Kevin just brought," Breanna said, going to him and running her hand over his shoulder. Before he could object, she tucked her fingernail into his neck—an accepted signal that lives and possibly the sports channel rental were on the line if he refused.

"Good idea," he said, wheeling to the kitchen.

"You've been to Europe too, haven't you, Abby?"

"Rome," she said. "But it was years ago."

"Rome's a beautiful city," suggested Breanna. "Maybe not as romantic as Paris."

She glanced at Kevin. One of her timers buzzed and she quickly excused herself, having left him the perfect opening.

"Hey, your nail hurt," said Zen as she walked in. "You going to bite me next?"

"I may if you don't keep your voice down," Breanna hissed. "Don't be negative, Jeff," she added, going to the oven. "I think they're good together."

"Oh, a regular Bonnie and Clyde."

"Sshhh."

The tuna was perfect—she flipped the steaks over for a quick sear to finish them, then pulled the rice and the carrots from the stove, placing them in serving dishes.

"This is the good china," said Jeff.

"Well, you didn't think I'd use paper plates, did you? Get out there with that wine. No, wait—bring the sake too. We'll have a toast."

"Sake? A toast?"

"Every dinner has to have a toast."

"You trying to get them drunk?"

"If it'll help, yes."

Zen left shaking his head, but he did take the sake. Unfortunately, he was the only one drinking it when she came out with dinner.

"You sure this fish is cooked?" Jeff asked. "Looks raw."

"You'll have to excuse him," Bree told the others. "Jeff is a great pilot, but he doesn't know food. His idea of a meal comes in a box with a toy."

"I know raw, Bree."

"Actually, marriage is a wonderful thing," said Breanna. "We get along really well."

Even as a joke, it was a tactical mistake, quickly thickening the silence. Jeff had mentioned that Kevin had been married briefly before, though he was vague on the details. She took a heavy slug of the wine Zen had poured. It was acceptable, even if it was about two days old and clashed with the ginger and scallions.

AS HE FINISHED DESSERT, MADRONE'S HEAD STARTED to float. It wasn't the wine; he'd had only had a few sips. It was the food—he'd never had tuna like that before. And a chiffon chocolate soufflé for dessert. The Army captain wasn't exactly sure what that was, just that it was really, really good. Good-looking, a great cook, smart, funny, loving—Jeff had been out-of-his-mind lucky to find Breanna.

It was impossible to feel jealous of him. But seeing how perfect Breanna was, and what a great thing the two of them obviously had, did hurt.

It hurt because he'd had that himself.

Or thought he had.

But that was another lifetime now. Two lifetimes.

Abby wasn't beautiful, but she wasn't a dog either. She started talking about a movie she'd seen, a comedy—it seemed interesting, but Kevin couldn't think of any way to get into the conversation.

IT WAS NICE TO SEE BREE GO DOWN IN FLAMES EVERY so often. Zen sipped his beer, observing Kevin and Abby on the couch. It was obvious they weren't hitting it off. Abby talked about movies she'd seen and some plays she'd gone to when she was in London a year ago. Kevin had a dumb smile on his face, the kind you wore when you wanted to be anywhere but here.

Breanna kept trying to coax the conversation along. He could practically see the wisps of smoke coming from behind her ears.

Zen emptied the bottle and wheeled his chair around to the kitchen for another. Maneuvering through the tight hallway had come to seem almost natural, the movements so familiar that not even the effect of sake and a few beers slowed him down. He'd come a long way in the year and a half since the accident—and in just the last five months since returning to Dreamland.

Lying in the hospital, he didn't think he'd ever make it. He certainly didn't think he'd be here, back in his apartment, back with Bree. He hadn't thought it would be fair to her, living with a cripple.

He wasn't a cripple. Oh, he definitely was a cripple, but not a *cripple*. There was a difference. He'd come to realize that.

Thanks to Bree mostly. She didn't make it *okay* that he couldn't walk—but having her made a huge, huge difference.

Jeff opened the refrigerator and took out a Sierra Nevada. Bree, yes. The right woman made all the difference.

There was no reason Kevin and Abby shouldn't get along. Kevin was a bit shy and, admittedly, geeky, but Abby was shy too. Hell, they had plenty in common—starting with Bree and Jeff. It was just a question of getting down to it.

Zen popped the cap on the bottle and wheeled back into the living room, where a treacherous silence had descended. "Hey," he said, "let's talk baseball."

"Baseball?" said Bree. She gave him a look that, roughly translated, meant she would kill him when they were alone—if she could wait that long.

"Yeah," said Jeff, wheeling next to Abby. "Your father used to know Mickey Mantle, right, Ab?"

"Oh, sure," said Abby. "He worked for him. It's because of my dad that I'm a Yankees fan."

"Really?" said Kevin. He pushed forward on the couch. "So am I."

Dreamland
9 January, 2104

COLONEL BASTIAN WAS ABOUT THREE STEPS FROM THE door to the hangar when someone screamed a command behind him.

"On the ground, scumbag. Hands out! Now! Fucking now!"

Before Dog even realized the command was meant for him, the business end of an M-16-3A1 poked sharply into his neck.

"Down, fuckhead!"

"Son," Bastian said calmly, "I appreciate the fact that it's late and it's dark and you're doing your job. But that's *Colonel* Fuckhead to you."

"Yeah, right." The man grabbed Bastian by the arm and swirled him around. Someone behind the man turned on a flashlight, shining it in Bastian's eyes.

"Shit," said the sergeant who had accosted Bastian.

"Fuck. Ten-shun," snapped the flashlight bearer.

"Very funny," said the colonel.

"Um, no offense, sir," said the first man. He was Sergeant Perse Talcom, one of Danny Freah's Whiplash team.

"We, uh, we didn't know you were, uh, en route," said the other man, Sergeant Lee Liu, another Whiplasher.

"We just, you know. Shit, sir. No one's supposed to be out here after nineteen hundred hours. I mean, the geekers and all, the eggheads, but they usually call or get an escort. You didn't look like one of them."

"We're really, really sorry, sir," said Sergeant Liu.

"No problem," said Bastian. "Let me ask you something, Sergeant. Both of you. How come you're pulling guard duty?"

"SOP. Captain Freah's orders, sir," said Liu. "Normal rotation."

"Thinks we're fuckin' gettin' big heads," said Talcom. "Uh, excuse me, Colonel. Shit."

"I've heard the word before."

Bastian hid a smile as he returned their salutes, watching them slip back into the darkness. Then he slid his magnetic ID card through the security terminal next to the door. After he punched his access code, the panel above the card reader began to glow a faint green. He placed his thumb against it and the lock on the door clicked open.

The vestibule inside was bathed scarlet by the night-lights; a pair of surveillance cameras tracked Dog as he walked to the elevator. He had to rekey his ID code and give another thumb print for the doors to open. Once inside, he turned and waited. There were no buttons inside the elevator car; there was only one destination, the underground hangar-bunker that housed the Megafortress project offices and labs.

The bright hallway lights stung Dog's eyes as the doors snapped open. Activated by a computer when the elevator started downward, the fluorescent panels washed the scrubbed concrete with the equivalent of ten million candles, ensuring that the security cameras observing him had an excellent image. Lights flicked on in the distance as he started down the hallway. The surveillance, lighting, and environmental systems were run by a small computer optimized for economy as well as security; the brain could selectively shut down heating and even ventilating units depending on the time of day or other requirements. The vast bays on the left side of the hall, for example, were currently unheated; they held four B-52's undergoing conversion to EB-52 Megafortresses. One of the planes was being bathed by a strong flow of air—it had been painted earlier in the day, and the techies had arranged for perfect conditions to dry the coating of liquid Teflon properly.

Dog's destination was on the other side of the wide hallway, where a set of double doors led to a Z-shaped ramp upward. Black suitcases were piled along the side of the top of the ramp; wires snaked everywhere just beyond the railing. Tables crammed with electronics equipment—meters, oscilloscopes, computer displays—clustered just off the ramp. Bastian treaded his way to the large, cone-shaped mockup of the Megafortress cockpit in the middle of the room. He had just reached its slightly rickety-looking wooden stairs when a head popped out from a control station near the nose.

"Colonel, I was beginning to think you wouldn't make it," said Jennifer Gleason.

"Just kept getting waylaid," said Dog. The stairs were sturdier than they looked; they didn't even creak as he climbed up and slid into the pilot's seat. Intended more to help the developers play with the still-experimental plane's systems, the simulator did not fully duplicate flight conditions. But it did move on a flexible chassis, and Dog strapped himself in.

"You're all set," said Jennifer, coming up the stairs behind him. "Computer will follow your voice commands with the usual authorizations. You can run today's flight backwards and forwards as many times as you want."

"Thanks," he said.

As he reached for the control stick, the computer scientist placed her hand on his shoulder.

The world suddenly caught fire.

"You want me to hang around?" she asked.

He did, but not to monitor the practice session.

Dog told her no, and then began the arduous process of learning from his morning's mistakes.

Las Vegas
9 January, 2250

FOUR HUNDRED DOLLARS AHEAD ON TWENTY-FIVE-dollar chips playing blackjack—not bad, thought Mack, especially for fifteen minutes worth of work.

Four hundred bucks was a pile of money to anyone on a military salary, but to the other people around the table, especially the blonde on his right in her almost-see-through top, four hundred bucks was a tip for the doorman. Mack took his cards, noted the total—nineteen, a pat hand—and sipped his drink. The double shot of Jack Daniels stung his lips lightly as he took an infinitesimal sip.

"Hit me," said the blonde. Mack watched her chest heave as the dealer slid a card from the shoe.

Seven.

"Hit me," said the woman again.

A king materialized next to her chips. She curled her lip up but said nothing, silently turning over her cards as she submitted. She'd tried to hit sixteen.

Too dumb to make it with, Mack decided.

The dealer looked at him.

"I'm fine," he said.

The dealer revealed her cards—fourteen. By casino rules she had to hit. She made eighteen; everyone but Mack lost the round.

He kept playing, winning mostly, but his mind started wandering. He'd wandered into The Punch, one of the newest casinos in town. Its game rooms exuded sophistication—exotic wood trimmed the tables, waiters in dark suits prowled the aisles, the lighting was directed perfectly to make it easy to see your cards, yet it somehow seemed soft and incapable of producing a glare. But all the good-looking women here had rich sugar daddies on their arms. The pile of chips in front of him wasn't nearly as impressive as the Rolex on the old codger two seats away. Only his competitive juices kept Mack at the table.

That and the blonde's soft shoulder, which now leaned heavily against his arm.

"Nice music," he said. "I've never been in Punch before."

"It's all right," she said. Then she got up and walked away.

That did it. Mack took his cards, saw that he had a pair of red tens, and decided not only to split them but to put his whole wad on the bet. He busted on the first.

And hit blackjack on the second—good way to go out.

"Let me buy you a drink, Major," said the codger with the Rolex, appearing next to him as he swept up his chips.

"Do I know you?" Mack asked the old man.

"We've met several times," said the man. He had a vaguely Spanish accent, though Mack couldn't place it. "Fernando Valenz. Brazilian Air Attaché. I have an office in San Francisco, but I visit here often."

Portuguese, not Spanish. But that didn't help Mack. He was about to blow off the old guy when Valenz took his elbow. "A lot of pretty girls in the blue lounge, I'd wager."

The blue lounge was a private penthouse upstairs. Mack had heard stories that the waitresses there all were topless. He'd heard other stories as well.

What the hell, he thought, and he let Valenz lead him toward the elevator, which opened when Valenz placed a special key card in the lock slot. Inside the car, the Brazilian slicked back his white hair, flashing not just the Rolex but a black onyx ring whose jewel could have been used as a golf ball. Five-eight with a good-sized belly, he wore what had to be a hand-tailored suit and a silk turtleneck—a dandy, though forgivable given that the guy was probably sixty and a foreigner.

The geezer slipped a Franklin to the attendant who met them at the door to the lounge, then tented one for the waitress who approached with a gin and tonic.

She wore a top. So much for rumors.

Valenz told the woman to bring Mack a double Jack on the rocks, then steered him toward a pair of leather club chairs at the corner. The chairs sat in front of a large plate-glass with a good view of the city; Las Vegas in all its tacky glory spread out before him, neons wailing in the night.

"The Punch is a bit sophisticated for the city, wouldn't you say, Major?" asked Valenz.

"I guess," said Mack.

"Besides the Brazilian government, I work for Centurion Aeronautics," said Valenz. "We are consultants. We're always looking for new associates."

Mack smiled. He'd been expecting some sort of pitch. "I don't think I'd be a very good salesman," he said.

"Oh, not a salesman," said Valenz. He reached into his pocket and took out a leather case. "Smoke cigars, Major?"

"Not really," said Mack.

"Pity." Valenz opened the small case, which held three cigars. "Cubans."

"Thanks, I'll pass," said Mack. In the reflection of glass he saw several good-looking young women staring at them. Fully clothed—but interesting nonetheless.

"We need pilots who can talk to other pilots. My own country, for example—the Navy is thinking of buying MiG-29's from the Russians. Someone like yourself, with your experience, could help quite a bit."

Mack felt his heartbeat double. Did this SOB know he was working on the MiG-29 project? Or was that just a coincidence?

"What we do is all perfectly legal," said the Brazilian. "We have several Americans on our payroll. We obtain the necessary approvals. Some even remain with the Air Force."

Time to leave, thought Mack. He stood.

"You know what, I just remembered something I have to do."

"Take my card," insisted Valenz, standing. "A man like you appreciates the finer things in life. As I say, nothing illegal."

"Thanks," said Mack gruffly. But he did not remove the card from his pocket as he headed for the elevator.

Dreamland Perimeter
10 January, 0455

HIS LUNGS FROSTED WITH EACH BREATH, THE COLD morning air poking icy fingers inside his chest as he ran. Bastian struggled onward, flexing his shoulders and pushing his calf muscles deliberately, trying to flex his muscles to the max. It wasn't the cold so much as fatigue that dogged him as he ran the perimeter track; his body moved like a car tire breaking through a pile of icy sludge, each joint crackling and complaining. He'd gotten less than two hours sleep and his body wasn't about to let him forget it.

Dog was thinking about shutting his workout down at the three-mile mark—ordinarily he did five—when a lithe figure poked out of the shadows ahead. The runner trotted in place a second, still trying to get limber in the cold air.

"You're up early," said Jennifer Gleason, falling in alongside him as Dog drew up. He'd recognized her from her bright-red watch cap, which this morning was augmented by a set of blue ear muffs. Gleason was a serious runner, and wore a nylon shell workout suit over what seemed to be several layers of T's and sweats.

"So're you," grunted Bastian. He turned to follow the left fork of the path, even though that meant he'd be stretching his workout to six miles.

"Did you shut everything down when you left?" she asked.

"I did, Doc. I did."

Their running shoes slapped in unison against the macadam, a steady rap that paced their hearts. They ran in silence for nearly a mile. They crested a small hill overlooking the boneyard beyond Dreamland's above-ground hangars. The fuselages of ancient Cold War warriors and failed experiments lay exposed in the distance, sheltered only by the lingering shadows of the night.

Seeing the hulking outlines of the planes always spurred Dog on; he couldn't help but think of the inevitableness of time and decay. How many other commanders had run—or perhaps walked—across this very spot, their minds consumed by the problems of the day? The A-12 had done some testing here. Northrop's Flying Wing had pulled more than a few turns around the airspace. It wasn't Dreamland then; it wasn't even a base, just a long expanse of open land far from prying eyes.

Some of the Cheetah sleds, earlier variants of the hopped-up Eagle demonstrator, lay in the bone pile. At least one DreamStar mock-up sat beneath a wind-tattered tarp. It was a 707 whose nose had grown fangs, the early test bed for the forward airfoil of the plane destined to succeed the F-22. Or rather, the plane that had been intended to succeed the F-22. The fiasco that had brought Bastian to Dreamland had shelved DreamStar. And ANTARES, though obviously not for good.

"Let me ask you a question," said Dog, pulling up suddenly and putting his hand out in front of Jennifer.

His hand caught the soft looseness of her chest. In the dim light he saw surprise in her eyes.

"ANTARES," said Dog, dropping his hand awkwardly. "What do you—tell me what you think about it."

"What do you mean?" Her voice was thin and low, out of breath.

Dog leaned his body forward and fell back into an easy jog. "Your opinion on it."

"It was never my project per se," said Gleason, quickly catching up. "Bio-cyber connections aren't my thing."

"What about Nerve Center?"

"Some thing. It's part of ANTARES. It is ANTARES. No one here spoke of them separately."

"You say that like you don't like it."

"No. Not at all. I mean, eventually fluid organic interfaces will be part of the mix. It's inevitable. You've heard about the experiments that have brought sight to people with certain types of blindness."

"Sure."

She picked up the pace. Dog felt himself starting to strain now to keep up. Gleason's words came almost in staccato, pushed out with her breaths.

"That sort of thing—of course it's not as advanced as ANTARES. Well, ANTARES is a different model altogether technically."

Her voice either trailed off or her words were swallowed in a hard breath of air. Dog waited for her to continue or explain, but she didn't.

"Can ANTARES work?" They were really running now; Bastian had to struggle to get the words out.

"It did."

"For the Flighthawks?"

"Of course."

They took a turn to follow the fence. One of the security team's black SUVs approached slowly on its rounds. Dog waved, then realized he was falling behind. He tried lengthening his stride, pushing to catch up.

The fence tucked to the left up a very slight rise. Bastian's quarters were down a short road to the right. He goaded his legs to give him one last burst, but barely caught her as he reached the intersection. He slowed, walking, warming down; Jennifer circled back.

"It does work, Colonel. No question about it," she said, trotting backward in front of him as he walked, catching his breath. "Major Stockard already passed the first set of protocols and controlled one of the Phantoms using the Flighthawk protocols."

"You have—" His breath caught. He stopped and leaned down, hands on hips. "You have reservations."

"Not about the concept. I'm not an expert," she added.

"You've worked on the gateway translation computers and you know as much about AI and computers as anyone on the base, including Rubeo."

"ANTARES isn't a computer. That's the difference."

She trotted back and forth, a colt eager to get on with her workout. Her body swayed—even in thick warm-up gear, she was beautiful. If he hadn't been so exhausted from that sprint at the end, he might have grabbed her to him.

Thank God for exhaustion then. She was just a kid, the age of his daughter.

Ouch.

"I'm not an expert," she insisted. "The program was ready for the Flighthawks when it was shelved. Phase One testing with a Phantom was completed about a month before Major Stockard's accident. Nerve Center would have been the next step. We rewrote some of the hooks into the flight-control computers and tested them. We dropped some of the code in C^3 covering simultaneous flights for memory space, but with some of the changes we've made recently I doubt it would be a problem loading them back in."

"How long?"

"How long are they?"

"How long to load them back in?"

Jennifer shrugged. "Not long, if it's a priority."

"It may be."

"Your call."

Her whole manner toward him had changed. Damn his clumsiness for grabbing her chest. Damn—he could kick himself for being such a klutz.

"You don't like ANTARES, do you?" he said.

She started trotting away, resuming her workout. "Not my area of expertise."

"Thanks, Doc. I'm, uh, sorry."

"Sorry?" she called back.

"The way I, uh, bumped you before."

If she answered, her words were muffled by the wind as it suddenly picked up.

Dreamland
Aggressor Project Hangar
10 January, 0905

To Mack Smith, the plane looked like a black shark with slightly misplaced fins.

The MiG-29M/DE Dream Fulcrum, better known by its nickname "Sharkishki," had a boxer's stance. Her twin engines hung beneath a cobra cowl that melded seamlessly into her wings. Stock, the MiG-29 was a serious air-superiority fighter, not quite better than the F-16 or F/A-18, but close enough to cause a few beads of perspiration on an opponent's brow. But Sharkishki was anything but stock. Dreamland power-plant specialists had worked over her RD-33K turbofans to the point that she had a third more thrust at full military power than even the uprated engines she had come with. They now put out 35,000 pounds in afterburner mode, a good sight better than the Pratt & Whitneys on an F-15C. As the plane remained several thousand pounds lighter than the average Eagle, she could easily outaccelerate one. With the help of new leading- and trailing-edge control surfaces, her already impressive roll rate had been considerably improved, and variable-geometry nozzles helped cut down her turning radius. The notoriously bumpy MiG skin had been smoothed out by the Dreamland techies so that hardly a blemish remained.

But it was in the cockpit that the Sharkishki's improvements really shone. Her antiquated Russian avionics had been replaced with Dreamland's finest microchips. Her HUD was slaved to a trial version of the F-22 radar and target-tracking units; her own reasonably competent infrared search and tracking (IRST) system had been replaced with a longer-range passive-detection system capable of detecting warm toast at twenty nautical miles in the rain. While not without bugs, the all-weather infrared system allowed Sharkishki to detect and engage enemy fighters before they knew they were being detected; its small size and radar-defeating paint meant the plane could generally not be scanned by fighter-borne radars until they were about fifteen nautical miles away. Granted, detection by AWACS was a different story, and a pilot who knew he was going up against the Sharkishki could employ tactics to neutralize the improvements—but he had to know what he was up against.

Which was the point of the project. When she was finished, the MiG-29M/DE—DE stood for "Dreamland Enhanced"— would be turned over to an "aggressor" fighter squadron tasked with training exercises at nearby Nellis Air Base. Sharkishki would take the role of Russia's next-generation fighter, helping groom Air Force Top Guns for the future.

Kicking their butts was more the way Mack thought of it.

"Typical Russian piece of tin shit," groused Chief Master Sergeant "Greasy Hands" Parsons behind him on the runway, joining Mack and the crew chief on the preflight walk-around. Parsons had a large ceramic bowl of coffee in his twisted fingers, and a thick stub of a cigar in his mouth. "We ready to go, Alan?"

"Yes, Sergeant," said the chief, with considerably more snap and starch than he directed toward Mack. Parsons grunted. Then he spat some of his cigar juice out and took a swag of coffee. Shaking his head, he stepped close to the plane, frowning as he looked into the modified air intakes.

The original Russian grates, intended to keep out rocks and debris on poor runways, had been replaced with an interior baffle system that acted like a turbo-booster at high speed.

"Something wrong, Sergeant?" Mack asked.

"Piece of Commie tin-shit garbage. You sure you want to fly this crate, Major?"

"What's wrong with it?"

Parsons didn't answer, moving instead to the leading edge of the wing, where he pointed his cigar at the gap and demanded that the chief have it checked. A crewman ran up with a micrometer; the gap was shown to be within tolerances. That hardly suited Greasy Hands, who growled and continued around the aircraft. He soon had five men making last-second adjustments and checks, none of which were warranted, in Mack's opinion.

"This plane is more than ready," said Knife finally. "Ground crew did a hell of a job."

Parsons ducked out from under the fuselage, where he'd been inspecting the landing gear.

"You got a problem with me, Major?"

"Hell, no," said Mack. "Just lighten up. The ground crew kicked butt here."

"Excuse me?" asked Parsons.

"I said the ground crew kicked butt," Mack shouted.

"Well, thank you, Major," said the chief master sergeant, breaking into a wide grin. "Nice to hear an officer say that." He stepped so close to Mack that his breath nearly knocked the pilot over. "Now don't fuckin' break my plane."

Mack's mood didn't lift until he slid the throttle to takeoff power and kicked Sharkishki into the air nearly a half hour later. He cleaned the underside of the MiG, pulling in the landing gear, and yanked the stick back, taking the MiG in a steep climb that made him forget all about sergeants and their typical bullshit.

Knife hit his marks and leveled off, vectoring toward the range where the day's test was scheduled. He keyed into the shared frequency that would be used by all of the players in the exercise. Ringmaster—actually Army Captain Kevin Madrone, who was flying in an E-3 AWACS above, monitoring the test—acknowledged, then quickly reminded everyone of the ground rules: no hitting, no spitting, and no talking back.

The helicopters and the secure weapons links and com systems were the most important part of the exercise, but other systems were being tested as well: the MiG, an Army ground-point air-defense radar, and the Flighthawks. Zen was still learning to control four planes simultaneously, apparently a lot harder than it looked.

"Two minutes," said Ringmaster.

Mack hit his way-point at the edge of the range and prepared to attack.

Dreamland Security Office
10 January, 1015

DANNY FREAH FELT HIS EYELIDS TOUCH BOTTOM, AND only barely managed to keep from dropping the phone onto his desk as the conference call droned on. He'd gotten up at four this morning to talk to his wife on the phone. A college professor, she'd returned to New York a week ago for the new semester and he missed her badly. They'd burned three hours on the phone line, and even then he'd felt frustrated as soon as he'd hung up.

Not to mention dead tired, since he hadn't managed to get to sleep until a little after midnight. The day's schedule precluded any catnaps, and he'd already gone through the thermos of coffee he'd brought into the office to take the secure—and uninterruptible—conference call on security matters.

Fortunately, these briefings were held on the telephone; none of the three-dozen other participants in the conference call could see him prop his head up with his elbow.

Getting regular heads-up briefings from the special FBI unit on terrorism and espionage was a good idea. But like many good ideas, it had morphed into something bad. Originally intended to alert certain top security officials to possible activities directed against them, it now included a briefing from the State Department, and even reports on foreign diplomats traveling in "areas of interest," the definition of which seemed to have been gradually expanded to include all of North America.

"We have some diplomatic activity in San Francisco, where the Secretary of Defense is to address the Aerospace Convention today," said Pete Francois, the FBI's deputy director for EspTer, as they were calling the group. "I think we have a couple of sightings in Las Vegas as well. Debra, you want to handle that briefing?"

"Brazilian attaché in Vegas. Usual suspects in San Francisco. Nothing to report yet," said Debra Flanigan, the Special Agent in Charge who handled the area.

Danny wanted to kiss her.

"Just for the record," intoned Francois, "there are defense officials from fifty countries in San Francisco. Per regs, etc., unusual contacts to be reported."

"In triplicate," murmured Danny.

"Excuse me?" said Francois.

Freah nearly fell out of his chair. He hadn't meant to actually *say* that. He opened his mouth to apologize, then realized it was better to stay silent—and anonymous.

"I think someone said triplicate." Flanigan laughed. "Personally, I think two copies will do. But remember to blind-copy all the e-mails, please."

Dreamland Range 2
10 January, 1054

WITH THE COMPUTER TEMPORARILY CONTROLLING THE two Flighthawks that had already launched from the Megafortress, Jeff took his hands off the controls and set them on the rests of his seat. He pressed down to lift his butt up, shifting around to get more comfortable.

Once precarious, the airdrop of the robot planes from Raven was now routine, with the computer able to handle it completely. The EB-52's pilot nudged the Megafortress into a shallow dive as the computer counted down the sequence, initiating a zero-alpha maneuver.

"Five seconds," said the pilot—Breanna, sitting in for Major Cheshire, who was away at a defense conference in San Francisco.

Zen watched the instrument displays in his command helmet, power graphs at green, lift readings shifting from red diamonds—"no go"—to green upward arrows—"go."

The simple graphics of the lift readings belied the complexity of the forces acting on the small robot planes strapped to the EB-52's wings. The bomber's airframe threw wicked vortices against the small craft; upon launch the robot's complicated airfoil fought thirty-two different force vectors, all dependent on the mother ship's specific speed, altitude, and angle of attack. Air temperature also played a role in some regimes, though the engineers were still debating exactly how significant the effect was. In any event, the computer handled the drudge work of setting the leading-edge foils and micro-adjusting the rear maneuvering thrusters as Raven reached launch point.

"Away Three," said Zen, without touching the controls, and Flighthawk Three knifed downward, right wing angling upward to cut against the wind. "Away Four," he said, and Flighthawk Four launched, stumbling ever so slightly as the Megafortress momentarily bucked in her glide slope.

"Sorry about that," said Bree, but Zen wasn't listening—he was in full-blown pilot mode now, the main display in his helmet giving him a pilot's-eye view from the cockpit of Flighthawk One. The sitrep or God's-eye view at the upper right showed all of the positions of the Flighthawks. It also marked out the other planes in the exercise. Pilots' views from the other three robots were arrayed in a line next to it all the way across. A band at the bottom showed the instruments in the selected or "hot" Flighthawk. Though they had used it in combat, the interface remained a work in progress. Zen liked the helmet, since it came as close as possible to duplicating the in-the-cockpit experience. But the others on the team felt a dedicated console was preferable if more than one plane was to be controlled at a time, since the instrument readings for all of the planes could be displayed on different tubes, available at a glance. Today, Zen had the best of both worlds, flying with a scientist who monitored those displays at the next station. But the idea was for there to be eventually two different pilots, each with his own brood of robots.

A preset exercise like this allowed Stockard to work up a full set of routines for the robot planes' C^3 flight-control and strategy computer, augmenting the preset instructions and flight patterns with courses and default strategies to be implemented on voice command. Even so, a rapidly evolving situation could overwhelm both pilot and computer. Simply jumping from cockpit to cockpit—in other words, changing which Flighthawk he had manual control of—could be disorienting. It somehow taxed his muscles as much as his mind, as if he were physically levering himself up and out of his control seat into each plane. Controlling a four-ship of Flighthawks was like trying to ride four busting broncos simultaneously.

The testing program called for them to move up to eight in two months.

They'd work it out. Right now, Zen concentrated on nailing Mack. Yesterday's mock battle had convinced him he'd never take out Mack straight on—the MiG was more capable than the F-16, and Smith could be expected to push it to the limits.

Which would be Zen's advantage. He ducked the lead Flighthawk down to treetop level, or what would have been treetop level if there had been trees in the Nevada desert. Then he pushed down to anthill level and stepped on the gas.

Jeff's shoulders relaxed as the rushing terrain flew by in his helmet. His thumb nudged against the throttle slide on the right stick—the Flighthawk controls featured HOTAS (Hands-On Stick And Throttle) sticks combining most of the functions normally divided between throttle and control stick. As he notched full military power, the computer warned he was approaching a ridge. It gave him a countdown; he waited, then pulled the stick back hard with a half second to spare, shooting the Flighthawk straight up.

It was a bonehead move—the Flighthawk went from completely invisible to the fattest target in the world.

Exactly as planned.

MACK CHORTLED AS HIS LONG-RANGE IRST PICKED UP the Flighthawk climbing over the ridge eighteen miles away. He'd gotten by the F-15's so easily it was a joke, and now this. Zen had obviously miscalculated, not believing that the passive sensors in the MiG had been improved fourfold. He quickly selected one of his "Alamo" R-27 long-range air-to-air missiles. The fire-control system had been Westernized, making selection considerably quicker—one snap on the stick instead of a cross-body sequence of taps, and he had locked and launched.

Though mocked up so its performance would resemble the Russian Alamo air-to-air missile, the rocket was in fact an AMRAAM with a simulated warhead. In keeping with the theme of anticipating the Russians' next wave of technology, its guidance system smartly toggled its seeker from radar to infrared if it encountered ECMs once locked; that made the missile practically no-miss. In this case, the "Alamo" would fly toward the target until its proximity fuse recorded a hit. Then it would pop a parachute and descend to earth.

Mack knew from experience that the Flighthawks would hunt in two-ship elements. Mack guessed the second plane would be about a mile behind the first, and when he saw a flash on the IRST he quickly kicked off his second and last Alamo.

MACK'S SIMULATED ALAMO AIR-TO-AIR MISSILES ACTI-vated their radars the instant they launched, so even though he hadn't turned his own radar beacon on, Knife had effectively given away his position by firing.

Which was half the point of Zen's display with the Flight-hawk.

The other half had been achieved by dropping the delayed-fuse illumination flare, which Mack had hastily mistaken for the second Flighthawk.

A tiny cheat perhaps. But now Sharkishki was down to four missiles, all short-range Archers.

Not that the Vympel R-73 heat-seekers were to be taken lightly. On the contrary—the all-aspect, high-g missiles were more capable than even the most advanced Sidewinders. But they had to be fired from very close range, severely limiting Mack's choice of tactics.

Zen told the computer to take over Hawk One. As good as C³ was, its evasive maneuvers were unlikely to be enough to evade the missiles. But he'd already accepted its loss. Jeff jumped into the cockpit of Hawk Two, which was flying a preset course with Hawk Three at the eastern end of the range. He swung the nose to the north five degrees, heading for an intercept with Sharkishki. Three, flying three feet behind Two, tight to its left wing, followed the maneuver precisely.

The Army helicopters, meanwhile, reported that they were

five minutes from their landing zone. Zen jumped into the cockpit of Hawk Four, which was just starting the far leg of an orbit near the LZ. He poked up the nose of the plane, twisting toward the target area. As he climbed through two thousand feet, he shot out a double shot of radar-deflecting chaff. He ticked the wing up again, hit more chaff, and turned his nose toward the target, giving the Army Super Black-hawks a feed of their target area over the new system.

"Good, good, good," sang one of the Army observers.

Jeff turned Four back over to the computer and concentrated on Mack. The ZSU-23 antiaircraft guns protecting the target area wouldn't be a problem for at least three minutes.

MACK CURSED INTO HIS MASK. THE FLARE HAD BEEN A clever trick, forcing him to waste his last Alamo.

Zen would be counting on him to waste time looking for the other Flighthawk; more than likely it was lurking near the ridge where he'd found the first, undoubtedly hoping to get behind him for a tried-and-true rear-quarter attack.

That wasn't going to work, though, because he was going to ignore it. He goosed his throttle to dash ahead, eyes pasted on the passive IRST. Mack got two quick contacts out near the helo target area—the U/MFs, which were at twelve miles.

Damn, these Dreamland mods were good—his F-15 next-generation demonstrator couldn't find them with its passive gear until they were within five miles, pretty much dead-meat territory.

There wasn't much sense trying to lock them up at this point, since he had only the heat-seekers and was much too far to fire. Mack nudged his speed down. He wanted the package to come to him, and wouldn't commit to the attack until he knew where the helicopters were. Assuming he found them soon, he'd open the gates on the afterburners for a few seconds, shoot forward, and dust by the U/MFs. From there he'd take a wide turn and listen for the growl of his heat-seekers as they found the helicopters in the chilly morning air.

Most likely he'd pick them up as his nose passed the ridge.

Thirty seconds.

Forever.

No amount of Dreamland magic could uncramp the MiG's

cockpit. On the tall side for a fighter pilot, with broad shoulders and thick pecs, Mack had to poke his elbow practically through his side to get a comfortable angle on the throttle lever, whose slide seemed notched in the plane's external skin. The handle was directly over the emergency power settings and just ahead of the flaps—he glanced to make sure he had the proper grip, not wanting to screw something up. He settled his hand in place, looking back to the front in the poorly laid-out cockpit. The Russians knew a lot about mechanics, but they were light-years behind in ergonomics.

Now here was a mistake—a Flighthawk, coming at his nose, four miles away, without its wingman.

Dumb even for Jeff; he'd prematurely committed himself to an easily deflected attack, while leaving only one plane to guard the Super Blackhawks. Worse, the U/MF was an easy shot for an Alamo, whose all-aspect targeting gear made a front-quarter shot very tempting as they closed.

Too tempting to miss. He had four of the air-to-air missiles. Even if he used them all against the Flighthawks, he could take out the helicopters with his cannon.

The Alamo practically jumped up and down on his wing, begging to be launched. Poor Jeff. He was so anxious to nail him he'd gotten sloppy. Knife pressed the trigger on his stick, launching the Alamo.

As it left the rail, the Flighthawk split in two.

JEFF FURLED HIS EYES AT THE VISOR IMAGE. THIS WAS the tricky part—the MiG could outaccelerate the Flighthawks, and if Mack played it smart, he'd just get on his horse and shoot into the clear. That would leave only one Flighthawk to get between him and the essentially defenseless helicopters.

But Mack was Mack; he couldn't resist easy pickings. Sure enough, the U/MF's enhanced optics view caught a flare beneath Mack's wing; within two seconds C^3 had interpreted and calculated the threat. By then, Jeff had already pulled the two Flighthawks away from each other.

For about ten seconds, he controlled them simultaneously. He twisted and turned in opposite directions, pouring on the speed, flares kicking in every direction. The baffled Alamo thought its target had exploded.

Now Mack would be pissed that he'd been tricked for a second time, and go all out for the Flighthawks. But which one?

The closest. Sharkishki whipped onto Hawk Three, its superior acceleration quickly narrowing Jeff's brief lead. But the Flighthawk's thrust-vectoring tailpipe narrowed its IR signature, meaning that Knife had to get within three miles of the plane before he'd be able to launch. Zen verbally selected God's-eye view in his main screen, asked for distances—and then just as Mack entered firing range, he cut Hawk Two across the MiG's path.

MACK INTENSIFIED HIS STREAM OF CURSES AS HE closed on the target. The war-game dummies had been made from actual R-77 "Archer" all-aspect infrared missiles; while the Dreamland team had jettisoned the cumbersome helmet system the Russians used, they had retained (and improved) the targeting-handoff system, allowing Mack to simply designate the target and let the computer worry about firing. While that took a bit of initiative away from the pilot, it allowed him to concentrate entirely on his enemy—useful against the tricky little Flighthawks.

True, he knew when to fire better than any damn computer. But the automated system meant he'd be able to lock up both Hawks quickly. He'd launch, swerve, and find the other U/MF, which was climbing and looked to be angling for a turn behind him.

Bing-bang-boing. Dead Flighthawks all over the field.

Except it didn't work that way.

As Mack edged Sharkishki left, he designated Hawk Three, handing off to the computer. Within five seconds, the U/MF fell into the middle of his pipper. The missile growled, then barked; the AAM dropped from its rail. As Knife raised his eyes toward the sky where he thought the second bandit had flown, the system growled and fired another missile, and then a third.

Just as the computer had fired, the second Flighthawk had veered into his path, disgorging flares like a pyromaniac—prompting the automated system to lock on the extra targets. Stockard had taken advantage of a bug in the programming.

"Override, override," Mack screamed, trying to turn off the automatic firing feature.

As the computer acknowledged, a green flare lit the sky ahead. His first missile had simulated a splash.

Another flare ignited moments later in the vicinity of the second Flighthawk.

Served the damn cheater right—both his planes were splashed. The helos were dead ahead, defenseless.

Mack whipped his head backward, making sure the last Flighthawk hadn't caught up. It was nowhere in sight.

This turkey shoot was going to be very tasty, he thought, turning his gaze back toward the target area.

ZEN STRUGGLED TO HOLD HIS HEAD STRAIGHT UP, forcing as slow a breath as he could out of his lungs. His neck and shoulder muscles had gone spastic, knotting and cramping, pulling half of his spine out of whack, shooting pain all across his back. He felt disoriented, momentarily losing the connection between his body and his mind, as if he were truly in the cockpit of one of the Flighthawks, as if it truly had been shot down.

He'd caught Mack by surprise, but Smith had managed to hold on to his last missile, giving him a decided advantage as he zoomed toward the helicopters. Zen selected Hawk Four's cockpit view for his main screen, preparing to rise off the deck and confront the aggressor. The C³ flight-control and strategy computer had already taken over piloting the "downed" planes, flying them along a preplanned route back to one of Dreamland's runways to land. Their cockpit view screens sat at the top left-hand corner of his visor, shaded slightly in red.

As Zen quickly checked on them, he noticed something he hadn't counted on. Hawk One was still alive—C³ had managed to duck Mack's radar missile.

Cavalry.

"Attaboy!" said Zen out loud, his muscle cramps suddenly disappearing. He turned Hawk Four over to the computer, telling C³ to keep it on the preprogrammed course behind the helicopters as they came in, where it would be impossible for Sharkishki's radar to locate it. Then he pulled One out of the neutral orbit the computer had set, recording twelve g's as he rushed toward Knife's butt.

Twelve g's would have wiped out any normal pilot—and probably smashed most aircraft to bits. But the Flighthawk's stubby wings and thick fuselage were designed to withstand stresses approaching twenty g's. The plane stuttered in midair as its vectoring nozzle slammed it on course; inside five seconds Hawk One was galloping for Sharkishki's tail.

Slowed by the encounter with the other Flighthawks, the MiG was roughly six nautical miles ahead as Zen popped over the ridge—dead meat for a missile shot in a teen jet. But the Flighthawks' only weapons were cannons; while the guns had good range—roughly three nautical miles even in a maneuvering dogfight—he was still too far away. Zen had the throttle to the max, but couldn't gain on the MiG, which was now pouring on the kerosene as it closed on the Army target zone.

Ten miles. Mack would have the Blackhawks before the Flighthawk caught up.

"Helos hold," Zen ordered the Army pilots, hoping to keep them out of danger. As they acknowledged, he jumped into Hawk Four, swinging her up and over them, rising to meet Mack.

MACK'S HUD RADAR DISPLAY PAINTED A FLIGHTHAWK ahead, rushing to protect the helicopters.

Interesting. Zen had broken his usual pattern, letting two of the U/MFs operate alone. He was learning.

But the curve was steep. The Flighthawk would be dead meat as soon as Brother Archer growled on the wing tip.

Mack nudged his stick left, intending to take an angle into the target area that would let him swing toward the helicopters after he launched his Archer at the robot. As he did, his rear-looking radar found the small plane trailing him.

What the hell. Taking advantage of computer glitches was one thing, but bringing a plane back from the dead was total bullshit.

Should have expected nothing less from the stinking SOB. What a pathetic egotist, determined to win at all costs.

Knife would expose him to everyone, including his buddy

Twig Boy. And his wife, though God knows how she put up with what she did.

No way he was losing to a cheater. Mack reached for the afterburner. The Mikoyan flashed ahead with a sudden burst of speed, its pilot quickly revamping his attack plan.

ZEN SMILED AS THE MIG SHOT AHEAD.

"Helos go. Go!" he demanded.

"Hawk Flight—we have a bogey at two o'clock. Request—"

"Go! Go! Go!" screamed Zen. There wasn't time to explain. He jumped into Hawk Four, yanking straight up. Mack didn't fire, continuing to accelerate as he avoided the rear-quarter attack.

"Computer, Hawk One on air defense at LZ. Plan Two."

"Plan Two, acknowledged," said C³. It took control of the Flighthawk immediately, nosing it down to attack the two simulated ZSU antiaircraft guns on the ground.

Zen, meanwhile, concentrated on Sharkishki, banking in a wide turn in front of him. Zen pushed off left, then cut back, aiming to intercept from the side. Knife could have simply powered his way past and taken out the helicopters—but that wasn't Mack. Jeff knew he'd gun for the Flighthawk, concentrating totally on showing him up.

What Jeff didn't expect was Sharkishki's nose suddenly yanking in his direction and growing exponentially. Mack had him fat and slow; there was little Hawk One could do.

Except make Mack waste fuel. Sharkishki started with 3500 kg of jet fuel, killing nearly four hundred just to take off. The engagement rules called for Mack to reserve a thousand kg to get home, even though he needed far less with Dreamland's many runways nearby. Between his low-level flight and afterburner use, he ought to be nearing bingo, the point at which he had to give up and go home.

Knowing this was his enemy's Achilles' heel, Zen had had C³ keep track.

"Calculated time for enemy bingo is ninety-eight seconds at present flight characteristics," said the computer. *"Enemy craft has Archer-type missile loaded and prepared to fire."*

Jeff turned Hawk Four south and launched diversionary

flares. Mack followed, steadily closing the gap as Zen zigged and zagged. He needed to get closer to guarantee a hit.

Jeff ran out of flares as the MiG narrowed to four nautical miles from his tail. He pulled eleven g's trying to gun the Flighthawk back toward Sharkishki, but it was too late; the Archer ignited below the MiG's wing.

Jeff left the plane to the computer, returning to Hawk One. While he'd been leading Sharkishki away from the helicopters, C³ had been carrying out the attack on the ZSUs. It had been close—the computer had splashed both guns, but not before the lead Super Blackhawk took a simulated hit, causing minor damage but leaving the helo and its crew in the game.

"Bogey is at bingo," declared the computer.

"Helo Flight, you're cleared," said Zen, rushing over them in Hawk One. "You're bingo, Mack, bye-bye," said Zen. "Sorry to see you go."

"Fuck you I'm bingo," said Mack, winging toward the helicopters.

"Flight rules—" declared Madrone.

"Suck on your flight rules, Soldier Boy."

Dreamland Commander's Office
10 January, 1205

"RESPECTFULLY, I HAVE TO DISAGREE. DISAGREE." MARtha Geraldo shook her head and turned toward Colonel Bastian at the head of the conference table. "Ray is prejudiced against humans," she continued. "It colors everything he says. It is as bad as a mommie complex."

Steam seemed to shoot out of Dr. Rubeo's ears. Dog had learned day one that the scientist hated to be called "Ray." There was no way Geraldo didn't know that; she was obviously pushing his buttons.

Then again, she ought to be good at that sort of thing.

"I think calling it a complex is a pretty strong statement," said Bastian, even though it was fun to see Rubeo speechless.

They'd spent more than a half hour discussing the best way to proceed, or not proceed, if ANTARES was restarted as part of the Flighthawk project—a given, based on Dog's brief conversation with General Magnus this morning. Magnus was clearly angered by Keesh's end run. But while he sympathized with Dog's protest against ANTARES, he'd ordered Dog to proceed with the program "as expeditiously as possible." A contingency budget line—black, of course—had already been opened for the program. Magnus seemed to be playing his own brand of politics, trying to swim with the currents.

"I would prefer that we left psychological innuendo out of the discussion," said Rubeo, his voice so cold it was a wonder his breath didn't frost. "The interface is neither stable nor dependable. We don't even know precisely how ANTARES works."

"One of the biggest drawbacks with the present control system employed by the Flighthawks is the human element, as Dr. Rubeo has noted on several occasions," said Geraldo, ignoring Rubeo's last point—which was technically true, despite reams of data and elaborate theories. Her crisp tones matched her starched blue suit; military personnel aside, she was probably the most conservative dresser of any Dreamland worker, the scientists especially. With a rounded face and frosted hair, she looked like a slightly older, slightly more distinguished Bette Midler. She'd come from Cuba as a girl, though the only trace of an accent was a slight tendency to roll her r's when excited.

Like now.

"Those drawbacks, which Dr. Rubeo has himself outlined, can be overcome with ANTARES. I have kept abreast of the latest exercises, Colonel; four planes cannot be handled adequately with the present arrangement."

"Four can be. We should put our resources into the next generation of control computers," said Rubeo. Tall and rangy, in certain lights he looked like a young Abraham Lincoln.

This wasn't that kind of light. He looked and sounded a bit like an out-of-control animatronic character at Disney World.

"ANTARES made C^3 possible," said Geraldo.

"Piffle."

"You're suggesting that the computers would completely fly the planes," said Geraldo.

"They already do," said Rubeo.

"You cannot remove human beings from the equation." Geraldo held out her hands and looked at Bastian triumphantly, having played her trump card.

"I can't say I disagree with that," admitted Dog, "though I'm not sure I accept ANTARES as fully human."

"It's as human as language," said Geraldo. "That's all AN-TARES really is—a very special language. A way of talking to a computer, which happens to control an airplane. Or several."

"Piffle," repeated Rubeo. "It takes over three quarters of the subject's brain. Tell me that's human—tell me that's better than using computers as tools designed to do a specific job. Computers that we can document every function of, every byte of information and logic."

Bastian leaned over the table toward Geraldo. She reminded him a bit of the dean of students at his college, an almost matronly sort who could outdrink any sorority on campus.

"If we build on the previous program, what would be the next step?" he asked.

"First, we need a subject. My preference would be someone who is 'clean,' someone who not only hasn't worked with ANTARES before, but who doesn't know how to fly. If we work with a clean slate, we won't have barriers or bad habits to break. I believe from my review that the biggest hurdle to joining with the computer has been the learned patterns associated with flight. To use my language metaphor again—when you learn a new language, the old one gets in the way. And that goes for ANTARES as well. I would propose a whole host of changes from the old program, including some bio enhancements."

"Drugs," sputtered Rubeo.

"Yes, drugs," said Geraldo. "Supplements actually, designed to enhance neural and other brain functioning. The tests have already been conducted."

"Mmmm," said Dog noncommittally.

"On the other hand, using someone already familiar with the procedure would cut down on the start-up time." Geraldo nodded as if responding to an argument Dog hadn't made. "At present, there's only one person on base who has used ANTARES, and that is Major Jeff Stockard."

Geraldo opened the folder in her lap, consulting her notes.

"I'd prefer to have someone else," said Bastian. "Jeff is the only pilot presently assigned full-time to the Flighthawks."

He also didn't want to waste him on a project that, in his opinion, might—or should—end up being a dead end.

"But a non-pilot?" he added. "I don't know. What if something goes wrong? Who takes over the plane?"

"C^3," said Geraldo. "The computer defaults have been well tested. C^3 is very capable, Colonel; I actually agree with Dr. Rubeo that for all intents and purposes it could fly the planes. Just not as well."

She smiled at Rubeo, but he wasn't buying the bouquets.

"And unlike DreamStar, the ANTARES pilot will not actually be aboard the U/MFs," Geraldo added. "So there really is no necessity for the subject to be a pilot." She glanced at her folder notes. "I have also recorded a steep learning curve for pilots transitioning to the Flighthawk program. According to the records, there were three test pilots who washed out before Major Stockard. The last full-time pilot, Jim DiFalco, had a great deal of trouble right up until he transferred out of the program, and he had been a civilian test pilot. My suspicion is that the problem is very similar to the one with ANTARES—my language metaphor."

Dog nodded. DiFalco—a top engineer as well as a highly rated test pilot—had earned the nickname "Rock" while with the program.

"According to the simulation exercises," continued Geraldo, "with the exception of Major Stockard, the best raw scores in the Level 1 qualifying tests for the U/MFs were compiled by non-pilots."

"Exactly," said Rubeo. His face was no longer red, though he couldn't quite be called calm. "If a pilot has difficulty controlling the planes, then logically—"

"Logically we try someone other than a pilot," said Geraldo. "I've already worked up a likely profile. Thirty years old, male, single, technically oriented, in reasonable but not athletic shape, with a slightly beta-male outlook, someone willing to follow rather than lead. On the other hand, he would need to have survived conflict, so that he could draw on that experience for confidence. And of course, he will have to have volunteered, so he can use that as motivation."

"Witchcraft dressed up as psychobabble," muttered Rubeo.

"Let's give it a try," said Bastian, even though part of him agreed with Rubeo.

**Dreamland, Range 2
10 January, 1205**

MACK HAD NINE HUNDRED KG OF FUEL LEFT, OR JUST under two thousand pounds in American measurements. That was enough to fly the Fulcrum's goosed engines roughly a hundred miles, landing at his theoretical base.

But the way he looked at it, his base *wasn't* a hundred miles away. In fact, he could run the damn engines dry and glide down from here.

Almost. And almost was good enough at the moment, because he was going to nail that stubborn cheating SOB Stockard even if it meant getting out and pushing the MiG home.

Knife let his left wing roll down slightly, tucking into a circle behind the remaining Flighthawk, trying to get the bastard in his boresight. The small plane couldn't outrun him, but its tight turning radius made pursuing it tricky. Mack took a quick snap shot as the Flighthawk slashed right. But he was going too fast—he nosed down desperately as the smaller plane jerked to his right, trying to get a shot off before sailing beyond the Flighthawk. He lost his enemy, guessed where he'd be, goosed the throttle and shoved down, just ducking Hawk One's barrage.

Firing the cannon cost the robot considerable flight energy; it started to wallow as it angled to pursue Mack through a hard series of turns. Knife gained momentum, then flung the MiG back around, getting off a shot before the Flighthawk barreled away.

The helicopters were escaping south.

So be it; it was Zen he wanted.

As Knife banked to regroup, he found the tail end of the Flighthawk at the top of his HUD, just out of range. He squeezed the throttle for more power, nearly unsocketing his elbow as he jerked his arm.

He had the bastard now.

"TERMINATE," SAID MADRONE CALMLY OVER THE COM-mon frequency.

Zen flicked his stick, flashing the Hawk's nose upward before jerking into a steep dive, complying with Madrone's order.

Even if the engagement hadn't been terminated, he was confident he would have escaped—at best, the MiG could only get off four or five shots before sailing past the pesky Flighthawk.

Mack cursed in his ears as he swung his wings level.

"You're a fuckin' cheater, Stockard. Twig saved your ass."

"I'm a cheater? You're about six hundred kilos past bingo. You're walking home."

"At least I didn't resurrect a plane."

"You didn't hit it."

"Oh, yeah, right. The Alamo missed. Two Alamos—the other was in the same frickin' area and would have caught a whiff."

"Hey, ask the computer."

Mack's curse was cut off by another transmission from Madrone, calmly congratulating everyone for a successful "event."

That was one of the reasons Zen liked Madrone. Had someone else—anyone else—been running the gig, he would undoubtedly have scolded them.

Probably they deserved to be scolded, since they had pushed the envelope of the exercise, but that was how you learned, wasn't it?

The hopped-up MiG was a pretty hot plane, and Mack had flown it well. Still, by the parameters of the exercise, Zen had won, preserving the Super Blackhawks. He let the computer direct Hawk One back to base. He was exhausted, physically and mentally beat—more tired, in fact, than he had been during the actual fight in Tripoli.

"You okay, Jeff?" asked Jennifer Gleason over the interphone, the Megafortress's internal com system. She was sitting at the techie station a few feet away.

"Ready for a shower and a cold one," he told her.

"Shower, yes. I can smell you up here," put in Bree from the cockpit.

"That's probably Major Smith." Jennifer laughed. "I can't wait to see his face at the debrief."

"Maybe Bree will take pictures," said Jeff.

His wife didn't acknowledge. Maybe it was because they had, after all, lost three of their four planes.

Or maybe, he thought, she just didn't like Jennifer.

Dreamland Briefing Room 1
14 January, 1005

KEVIN MADRONE HAD CALCULATED THAT HE HAD JUST enough time to sneak a cup of coffee before heading to the meeting. But his math had been too optimistic—everyone's head turned as he came through the door. He quickly headed down the central aisle of the small amphitheater and slipped into a seat, staring down at Colonel Bastian, who was standing in front of the lectern. As he settled into his seat, Madrone saw that Jennifer Gleason had an empty seat a few rows further down and across from him. It was too late to change places, though.

"What we're looking at is expanding the Flighthawk program to include some of the project work that was originally sketched out under ANTARES," said Bastian. "Now I realize that that's going to seem controversial because of circumstances we're all too familiar with, which is one of the reasons I want to make sure we're all up to speed about what's going on. The promise of ANTARES itself isn't debatable. And we seem to be reaching a ceiling on the U/MFs."

"I disagree with that," said Jeff Stockard. He was sitting in his wheelchair at the lower right corner of the room. "We've gone from controlling two planes to four. We have plans in place to go to eight."

"Granted," said Bastian. "And there are other ways of tackling the problem. This will proceed in tandem."

Bastian continued to talk, but Madrone found his mind wandering as he looked up from Jeff and at Jennifer Gleason. The fluorescent lights of the briefing room made her strawberry-blond hair look almost pinkish; she twirled one side with her fingers, pushing it back behind her ear. As she did, she happened to glance back in his direction, caught him staring, then smiled.

Kevin smiled back, or at least he tried. His stomach was fluttering—he was back in junior high, listening to some endless history lecture, hopelessly in love with Shari Merced.

Kevin put his thumbnail to his lips, even though he'd sworn off the bad habit five times already today. He was so damn awkward with girls—with women. The other night he'd been tongue-tied with Abby. She'd seemed interested when he was talking about the time Don Mattingly had signed his score-card. But he'd felt so stinking nervous that when she dropped him off, he'd blown his chance for a kiss.

He could have kissed her, he should have kissed her, he might have kissed her. She wasn't his type, a little too giggly and talkative, he thought, but still—he could have, should have, would have kissed her.

But didn't.

What if he had the same chance with Jennifer? Would he take it?

Hell, yes. He hadn't always been this stinking nervous, this much of a wreck and a dweeb. Damn—she turned back in his direction and he quickly averted his eyes, pretended to be interested in something on the floor.

He'd never get into that situation with her. She didn't notice him. Why should she? It was like being back in junior high—the jocks, aka pilots, were the ones who got all the attention. He was just a nerd.

He had to find a way to get her to notice him.

"SO WE'LL SEEK VOLUNTEERS. THERE'LL BE PROFILE testing, physical, mental, that sort of thing."

Jennifer watched Colonel Bastian pace at the front of the room as he spoke, barely able to control his energy. He wasn't very tall, but his shoulders were wide, and swung back and forth with implicit urgency. His hands cut through the space around him as if they were the fighters he'd flown.

She leaned back in her chair, taking another sip of her Diet Coke. The cold metal of the can stung her lip. For some reason the AC was cranking in the room, and Jennifer felt a slight shiver run through her as she swallowed the soda.

She'd nearly melted the other morning when Colonel Bastian had touched her. She'd wanted him to sweep her up in his arms, smother her. A million volts had seemed to snap between them—but he'd done nothing. He saw her as just another scientist, a well-meaning geek probably.

He was damn smart, wise in ways you wouldn't expect. Like this—knowing people would worry about ANTARES, knowing there were reservations, he dealt with them head-on, got everyone aboard, made them part of the team.

He looked at her now and said something.

Volunteers, he was looking for volunteers for the ANTARES program.

"We won't be looking for pilots," said Bastian. "Dr. Geraldo can give us the whole brief, and we'll start in a few days. The profile is rather specific actually. At the moment, we believe we need males. Sorry, Jen."

Jennifer felt everyone look at her. Her face began to flush. Bastian smiled at her.

She wanted to say something. She wanted to say the program was a mistake.

She also wanted to say—what? That she was in love with him?

"I'd like to be in on it. Take a shot at being a subject," said Bill McKnight. McKnight was an aeronautical engineer who had worked on the DreamStar program.

"Me too," said Lee Ferguson. He was a communications expert and had designed the Flighthawk command system.

Bastian was still looking at her. Did he expect her to say something?

Shit, she thought. I have to. I couldn't get it out right the other morning.

How would she put it? What specifically were her objections? The fact that no one specifically knew what the subject's brain did while connected to the computer? The few odd, unaccountable glitches she had come across while adapting some of the early programming for C^3?

The fact that his broad shoulders and kind eyes looked so comforting, so warm?

Jennifer felt her hand starting to ascend against her will.

Someone behind her said he'd do it. Jennifer turned and saw Captain Kevin Madrone, the Army weapons specialist, staring right at her.

"I'd like to try," said Madrone, quickly looking away.

Someone else chimed in, and then someone else. This

wasn't the time to object, and she didn't trust herself besides. Jennifer realized she'd left her arm about halfway up on the small desk in front of her. As she lowered it, she felt so cold she began to shiver.

III
Head games

MADRONE SHIFTED UNCOMFORTABLY IN THE CHAIR, TRY-
ing to find a spot where the stiff plastic would feel comfortable against his back.

"It's kind of been a while since I thought about all of that,"
he told Geraldo. "My wife, I mean. Five years."

The psychiatrist put her hand to her mouth, pinching her
lower lip between her thumb and forefinger. She nodded, then
slowly reached for her coffee mug. She wanted him to talk
about Karen. It was almost as if she had a magnet in her
brain, trying to draw out the words, but Madrone resisted.

Not resisted exactly. He had nothing to say. He couldn't
even form a picture of Karen in his mind.

If he thought about it, if he analyzed it the way Dr. Geraldo
obviously wanted, he might have found the day that it had
happened, the moment he'd gotten over her. He'd been ob-
sessed with her for a long time after she'd left him, fantasizing
about getting her back, fantasizing about confronting her—
and yes, even fantasizing about killing her, though he would
never admit it.

Probably, that was what Geraldo wanted to hear. But he
wasn't going to tell her that.

Christina, his daughter, his poor dead daughter—she was
locked away in a place he'd allow no one to enter, not Geraldo, not even himself. He'd never mention her to anyone.

"You don't feel angry with her?" Geraldo asked.

"Well, a little. She left me. But . . ."

It really did feel like a magnet, pulling at him.

"After a while, it kind of went away. Slowly. I don't know. It seems almost trite."

"Time heals all wounds?" said the psychiatrist.

"Exactly." He glanced at his thumbnail, willing his hand still.

"And there's been no one else?"

"On that level. No."

"Afraid of commitment?"

"Not really. But being single does have some advantages."

Geraldo sat in her thick red chair, waiting to see if the magnet would pull anything else out. Finally, she seemed to decide it wouldn't.

"I have yet another test for you," she said apologetically. "It's another standardized test, but this one is a bit old-fashioned, no computer—pencil and paper. You have to fill in circles." She got up and went to a filing cabinet at the far end of the room. She returned with a manila folder and a pencil. "Would you like more coffee?"

"No, thanks."

As she started to hand the folder to him, the psychiatrist stopped. He looked up into her face; for the first time since the testing and interview sessions had begun, her face seemed like a real face, as if it belonged to someone he knew, an aunt maybe, not a scientist. The small wrinkles at the corners of her eyes and mouth furrowed deeper. Her body pitched down slightly, as if the tight iron bands that had held it loosened. Even her clothes—a dark navy-blue suit with a stiff white blouse—became less severe.

"Kevin, if you ever want to talk about your ex-wife, you can," she said. "Not as an official thing, of course. But if you feel the need."

He nodded slowly, then took the folder.

ZEN WHEELED HIS CHAIR BACK FROM THE MONITOR, watching as Geraldo left the room. Even though it was his job to help the psychiatrist make the final selection of an ANTARES subject, he felt like a voyeur spying on his friend.

He knew Madrone was divorced, even though Kevin said little about his ex-wife. Yet something about the way he talked about her surprised him. Over the past two years or so that they'd known each other, Kevin had seemed rather muted, not just shy, but not an emotional guy—as if being an engineer was deeply embedded in his personality. Even when he talked about things he liked, the Yankees and baseball, for example, he sounded as if he was reading down a column of numbers.

When he had talked about Karen, however, his eyes had changed. His motions had become, if not animated exactly, at least more fluid. Zen got the impression he was hiding something, struggling to keep something bottled away.

Anger? Did that make any difference for ANTARES?

Madrone had consistently scored the highest or second highest on all of the tests they'd given him, even the manual-dexterity and physical-endurance tests. His IQ, tested by computer no less than five times, had turned out to be an astounding 180. His only flaw was an inherent shyness and possibly a slight feeling of inferiority, or as Geraldo put it: "an image of self-worth that does not accurately reflect his abilities."

Zen wheeled toward the low table where he'd placed his coffee nearly an hour ago. Geraldo pushed through the door briskly.

"Very good, Major, don't you think?" she said, going immediately to the desk. She glanced at the monitor, then pulled a thick spiral notebook from the top drawer and made some notes.

"What do you think about his wife?" said Zen.

"Oh, the usual anger and resentment, some bewilderment," said Geraldo, still writing. "I think he honestly was blindsided. Perhaps it accounts for his reserve, no? The nail-biting under pressure, the cigarette-smoking—classic. Minor. To some extent the military has replaced his wife; he throws himself into work. Very common. Not an impediment. His emotions don't run all that deep. Not good for a marriage, but for ANTARES, it's a plus."

Zen didn't say anything. Geraldo pried into people's minds for a living. It had to be done, but sometimes the notion that a personality could be dissected and examined like a piece of code in a computer or the components of a jet engine bothered him. Zen had undergone a battery of tests and examinations as part of his rehab in the hospital. He'd gone through it because it was necessary, but he hadn't particularly liked it. Now he realized that people must have been watching him on hidden monitors just as he had watched Madrone. One more indignity; one more surrender.

Necessary, but still humiliating.

"I think he's the one," said Geraldo, putting down her pen finally. "But you're reluctant."

Her comment took him by surprise. "What do you mean?"

"You just seem reluctant. Should we bring Ross back in?"

"I'm not reluctant," said Zen.

Geraldo pushed back in her seat, swiveling gently. "You're his friend. You have doubts about the program, and you're worried about endangering him."

"I'm friends with a lot of people. He's the obvious choice, no doubt about it."

"You have reservations about ANTARES."

"Of course," said Zen. "We've gone over that."

"The spy did not compromise the project."

Spy. No one would even say the name Maraklov—or Captain James, as he had been known here. He had nearly ruined Dreamland, and all of them.

"It's not that," said Zen.

"Perhaps you should explain, Jeff. Are you feeling jealous?"

"Not in the least."

They'd been over it before, twice as a matter of fact, neither time very satisfactorily. Jeff believed in the concept of ANTARES; he was the only person left on the base who had gone through the program, and in fact still had the old-style chip implant in the side of his skull. He had always assumed he would be involved in the next stage of the project, always assumed it would eventually be green-lighted again after the Maraklov business died down.

But he had reservations, objections he couldn't quite put into words. His recent nightmare for one. The way he felt when he woke from it—as if a part of him he didn't completely trust or like had taken control of him.

There was no way to put those vague feelings into rational arguments. They sounded like reasons to continue studying ANTARES. They were, in fact.

"We've made numerous improvements," said Geraldo. She spoke as if she were making the case for the first time. "We're light-years ahead of where the project was when DreamStar was canceled. Fresh eyes—fresh minds—a new start. Kevin Madrone will be a perfect subject."

"I'm sure he will."

"So we have your approval?"

What was it that bugged him? Kevin or ANTARES?

Shit. The way Geraldo was looking at him, he could tell she thought it was jealousy—that he looked at Kevin as a potential rival on the Flighthawk program.

"I think Captain Madrone is the obvious choice," said Zen. "And I'll put that in writing."

"Very good," said Geraldo, standing. "We'll start this morning."

Aboard EB-52 BX-4 "Missouri"
Range 2, Dreamland
23 January, 0807

WAS IT THE FACT THAT HE WASN'T USED TO FLYING something so big? Or the fact that he wasn't used to flying with a copilot?

Or maybe he just felt odd flying a plane named after a Navy battleship.

Then again, it was better than Cheshire's suggestion— "Rosebud," ostensibly for the sled in *Citizen Kane.*

"Crosswind," prompted Major Cheshire from the copilot's station.

Colonel Bastian told the computer to make the crosswind correction, probably a half second before the computer would have taken over from him. He was near the edge of his localizer course, off center and coming in a bit too fast. He nudged the throttle glide slightly. The speed and engine readings flashed on the HUD, all green.

Was that temp on three nudging into yellow?

Just land.

Just land.

Dog blew a laboriously long breath from his lungs as he edged the stick ever so gently to move the big plane back into the sweet spot as it approached the landing. If he'd been flying an Eagle, he would have simply—

Irrelevant, he told himself.

"In the green," said Cheshire. "You're looking good. Temps are all normal."

The concrete seemed to expand as he approached. He could feel the heat wafting upward, gentle hands taking hold of him as he settled down.

Then all hell broke lose. The plane jerked suddenly to the side; a dozen warning buzzers went off. Cheshire shouted something at him.

He had no lateral control. The computer had begun to compensate. Stick dead.

No, he had stick. No rudder.

No tail?

He forced the plane down, felt a jolt as the wheels on the right undercarriage hit the ground. He could feel himself sliding to the right.

"Steer! You still have steering!" shouted Cheshire over the interphone.

"Okay," he managed. "Okay."

The plane straightened out. Their speed knocked down to twenty, then fifteen, then ten knots. Firmly in control now, Dog permitted his eyes to move to the left-hand multi-use display, which was slaved to the emergency status nodes.

Clean.

Clean?

"What the hell happened?" asked Bastian.

"You were doing such a good job I decided to complicate things," said Cheshire. "You just landed without a tail."

"Jesus."

"Well, he would have done a better job," said Cheshire, clearly enjoying herself. "Still, you did okay. I didn't take off the entire tail, just one of the stabilizers."

Actually, Cheshire had directed the plane's advanced flight computer to simulate the loss of one of the stabilizers. The flight profile was among several the major had preprogrammed into the flight computer as part of the advanced training Bastian had persuaded her to give him.

"You're worse than Rap," Dog told her.

"Thank you, Colonel."

"What would you have done if I crashed?"

"Oh, you wouldn't have crashed," she said. "We were always within specs. The computer has tested the profile on its own."

"You can't really fly without a tail," said Dog, who didn't trust the simulator modules in the flight computer, no matter how sophisticated they actually were. He turned back to the windshield. The SUV designated to shepherd them toward the maintenance area was just now approaching from his left, a little behind schedule.

"Sure, you can. If you're good. *You* could."

"Ha."

"You're better than you think, Colonel."

"I mean, the plane would auger in without a stabilizer."

"Over my desk there's a photograph of a B-52 that landed without a tail in Vietnam," said Cheshire. "And another that was shot nearly in half through the fuselage. Then there's the one with three quarters of its wing missing."

Dog grunted. He finally realized he'd been suckered into a sales job.

"Colonel, you might want to relax your grip on the yoke," said Cheshire. "You look like you're going to snap it off."

"Right." He trundled the plane to the edge of the runway, where three support vehicles had joined the SUV.

Missouri—better known as "Mo"—was testing a modified version of the PW4074 turbofan, and carried one apiece on the inside engine pylons. The PW4074 turbofans, highly efficient engines originally developed by Pratt & Whitney for Boeing's 777, were to be quickly checked by the ground crew. Assuming they were okay, the bomber would take off for a second tier of tests, then repeat the process for a third.

Dreamland's specialists had tweaked the systems to achieve somewhat more thrust; nowhere near as thirsty as the J57's that came stock on early B-52's, the jets were considerably more powerful. The Megafortress engineers were still diddling with the computer models and specs to determine what exactly their optimum arrangement might be. While the conventional wisdom was that one new engine could sit in place of two old ones on each pylon, the Dreamland whiz kids were fond of defying common wisdom. The vast airframe of the B-52 gave flight to all manner of fantasies. Computer models had been devised showing the plane with six and eight power plants. One odd design even called for two of the engines to be mounted at the rear, somewhat like a 727.

The goal was to improve low-level speed without decreasing overall unrefueled range. Stock, a B-52 could clock roughly 365 knots at sea level with the old power plants. The Megafortress, with its much cleaner airframe, notched roughly 425 nautical miles an hour. The engineers wanted 475, which was well beyond the venerable and trusty J57's.

Fifty knots didn't seem like much, but it would exponentially reduce the detection envelope for a Megafortress on a low-level attack mission. In practical terms, it would allow an EB-52 to evade all but the most sophisticated defense radars, and to get close enough to air-launch torpedoes against a surface ship, one of the design goals remaining to be achieved.

Do that and even the Navy might order up a few dozen. Missouri indeed.

Dog powered back, preparing to turn the plane around at the edge of the ramp. In some ways it was more difficult to guide the big plane on the ground than in the air, since the flight computer didn't help. Bastian found it nearly impossible to judge the clearance distance accurately, and twice twitched the control column, afraid he was about to clip one of the chase vehicles with his wings. But Bastian handled the turn expertly, stopping precisely parallel to the techies' yellow and black pickup.

"You have time for the second flight?" Cheshire asked.

"I wasn't planning on it," said Dog. Then he realized she had a funny expression on her face. "Did I do that bad?" he asked.

"No, I told you, you did fine," she said. "I was hoping to talk to you a minute."

"Fire away," Dog told her.

"I have to quick run over some of the numbers with Peter first, though," she said, referring to the engineer in charge of the engine testing. "A quick check and we're good to go."

"All right," said Dog. It wasn't like he wanted to go back to his office and the mounds of paperwork waiting for him.

Truth was, he would greatly prefer taking off again, even if it meant listening to Cheshire's pitch for more resources.

"Thanks, Colonel. I'll be right back. I appreciate it."

Dog undid his restraints and stretched his arms, watching out the cockpit windows as the ground crew gave the plane the once-over.

It wasn't just that he preferred flying to paperwork. He wanted to master the Megafortress, just as he had every other plane on the base.

Not every plane. He hadn't flown the two 767's or the 777 they were testing as tankers. But he had flown every combat plane. The F-22, the modified F-16, the Joint-Service Strike Fighter, even the SR-71D spy plane with its hypersonic hydrogen engines. Flown them all, and damn well.

But something about the Megafortress kept him at bay. He could fly it, but he wanted to *fly* it—to master it, twist it over and around and in and out of knots. He wanted to get out on the edge of the envelope with it. The flying battleship was the future of the Air Force.

He wanted to prove he was a great pilot. He wanted to prove . . .

That he was better than his daughter?

The idea shot into his head like the snap vector from an AWACS controller. Dog pushed up out of his seat, squeezing out of the Megafortress's cockpit. He didn't have to prove anything to anyone, especially himself, and definitely not Breanna. He had other things to do than fiddle around in the sky.

Cheshire met him on the ladder down to the lower deck.

"Colonel," she said. "You're leaving?"

"Sergeant Gibbs will be waiting. What did you want to say?"

Cheshire leaned against the bulkhead and began talking about the Megafortress project, saying that the engine tests were taking much longer than anticipated. The mechanical delays were only part of the problem. She needed more engineers—a common and justified complaint. The decision to develop the Megafortress as a mother ship for the Flighthawks was also stretching her people and the planes to the max.

"We only have the three planes," said Cheshire. "Raven,

Bear Two, and Mo. Galatica, the AWACS tester, won't be on board until at least next week."

Bastian nodded.

"We need at least two planes to complete the engine tests. Bear Two is needed for static tests, and Galatica still has to go through the usual flight trials. We won't have the others for at least three weeks. The tanker program is already on hold, and the backlog on the avionics tests is thicker than a phone book."

"The Flighthawks remain a priority," Dog told her, guessing what she was going to suggest. "Raven has to stay with them."

"I wasn't going to suggest we stop using the EB-52 as the Flighthawks' mother ship," she said. "Though I've heard the control gear won't fit in the Megafortress weapons bay once you reach eight U/MFs."

Obviously she'd been talking to Rubeo.

"That may be a problem," said Bastian. "That's why we're in business—to solve those sorts of things."

Damn Rubeo. He was throwing every possible objection in the way of ANTARES.

"We can't solve it if we don't have the resources," said Cheshire.

"Pete Rensling suggested using the 777 airframe as the AN-TARES mother ship," said Dog. "It has a huge bay, and the fuel tanks that would be needed for refueling were already part of the tanker testing."

"That's not a bad idea, if the wings could take it."

"Being studied right now. If it works, that will lessen some of the burden on you. In the meantime, I'll expedite more conversions as part of ANTARES."

"Thank you, Colonel," said Cheshire. She was smiling broadly. "Now how about more pilots?"

"I'm still working on that," said Bastian. There were presently only six qualified B-52 pilots on the base; since even with the new flight computers it typically took two to fly a Megafortress, there was only one crew per plane. Two of the pilots were due to be transferred next week.

"You better be careful, Colonel. If you get any good, we may slide you into the rotation."

"I'll help out anyway I can," said Bastian, smarting a bit from her tone.

"You sure you don't want to take this run? I still need another pilot."

"Maybe I will," he said. "As a matter of fact, let's go for it."

Dreamland Handheld Weapons Lab
23 January, 0807

"LATE, AS USUAL."

Danny grinned at the gray-haired woman in the white lab coat. Her frown turned into a smile, even as she shook her head and wagged her finger.

"Captain, you need a secretary to look after you," Annie Klondike told him. She turned and began walking briskly toward the back rooms of the handheld weapons lab.

"You want the job?" asked Freah, falling in alongside.

"You wouldn't last twenty-four hours."

Klondike shuffled toward the large room where the firing ranges were located.

"Annie, those new slippers?"

"Don't get fresh."

Klondike walked to a large gray box that sat in front of a series of drawer-shaped lockers. About eight feet wide and another six feet deep, the box came up to the diminutive weapons scientist's chest. It seemed to be made of a very hard plastic material. Klondike put her palms on the top and the box began to move. Fascinated, Danny watched as the box pulled itself apart, a shallow section remaining behind the top.

"Opens only with my palm print and could withstand a one-megaton explosion," said Klondike.

"This thing?" asked Danny. The shell material was no more than three inches thick.

"As long as it's not a direct hit. Of course, if it was one of *my* bombs—"

"You do nukes too, Annie?"

"In my youth, Captain. I'm retired from that."

"You shittin' me?"

Klondike lowered her face, but kept her eyes fixed on him, as if she were a Sunday school teacher peering over her glasses. She sighed, then again shook her head, shuffling over to the table.

"At the moment, the Combat Information Visor must be attached to the Smart Helmets," she said, turning her attention to the device Danny had come to inspect. "I have some hopes of miniaturizing it further, so that it can be used as goggles. I find the visor cumbersome, and I'm told some troops do not like the helmet."

"It's heavy," said Danny. The so-called Smart Helmet included a secure com link and a GPS system. It could withstand a direct hit by a fifty-caliber machine-gun bullet from fifty yards—though that produced a hell of a headache. Klondike's prototype visor added two additional functions: a long-range multi-made viewer, and an aiming screen for a specially adapted M-16.

The visor looked like a welder's shield. It shifted the helmet's center of gravity far forward when it was snapped on, promising severe neck strain.

"There are four native modes to the viewer," said Klondike, reaching to cinch the chin strap. "They select on the right, zoom and back out on the left. They toggle through in sequence. One is unenhanced. Two allows—wait, let's kill the lights."

Mode Two was infrared. Three was starlight-enhanced. Four actually did not work yet; they were perfecting a graphics Geiger counter, which would allow the unit to detect radioactive materials from twice the distance as the "sniffers" or portable Geiger counters Whiplash now packed on NBC missions. But the gear wasn't quite ready.

"I'd trade it for making it lighter," Danny said, fiddling with the helmet.

"Well, it won't make it heavier, because we hope to press the functions into a pair of chips. I'm sorry, Captain. The weight comes from the LED panes and the carbon-boron sliver-plates at the side," she added. "We've actually lightened it about a pound and a half since we began. Notice how the slide here is almost round?"

"Oh, yeah, first thing I noticed."

Klondike turned the lights on. "The helmet can accept inputs from external sensor systems, assuming they meet MAT/ 7 standards. You'll need an RCA plug, but once you plug in you're slaved to a Pave Low's infrared, assuming the helicopter's gear has been modified for an additional output. The host thinks it's the original screen. Adjustment's easy; we'll have it put on your C-17 the next time Quick-mover goes in for a lube."

While she was talking, Klondike had approached the gun drawers. These were locked with an old-fashioned key, which she kept on a string around her neck. She bent to one and opened it, then removed an M-16.

"I prefer my MP-5," Danny told her.

"Captain, please," said Klondike. "With all due respect to my friends at Heckler-Koch, submachine guns are meant to be sprayed, even theirs. A fine weapon under certain circumstances, but hardly a one-bullet, one-kill solution. Now come on or I'm going to miss my soap opera—or worse, *Jeopardy*."

The M-16A3's laser sight had been replaced with a small, stubby bar that had only a small pinhole at the barrel end. Nudging a slider on the top of the gun activated a VSRT or Very-Short-Range FM Transmitter, which allowed the gun to communicate with the targeting screen. A pair of cursors appeared on the view screen; as the gun was aimed horizontally, the cursors merged. A tear-shaped ring appeared around the cursor, showing the probable trajectory if the shot deteriorated because of the wind or distance.

"The cursor is absolutely right on to two hundred yards in all conditions," Annie told him after he'd put five bullets into the center of a target at three hundred feet. "But we haven't been able to reliably compensate for weather conditions beyond that. Additionally, you can't aim through water or glass as you can with the sniper rifle. But it's an improvement over the laser dot, both in distance and detectability. And it has the added bonus of persuading men to keep their helmets on," added Klondike, "no matter how heavy they may be."

"Ready for field testing?" asked Danny.

"Didn't you notice the helmet was formed for your head?" said Klondike.

"If I weren't married already, Annie . . ." said Danny.

Klondike's response was drowned out by the report of the rifle as he squeezed off the rest of the clip.

Dreamland, Aggressor Hangar
23 January, 0182

WHEN YOU WERE A GENERAL, YOU NEVER HAD A BAD day. Generals had drivers. Generals had staffs. Generals had people who made sure their stinking alarm clocks didn't malfunction so they didn't oversleep.

More importantly, when you were a general it didn't matter if you overslept.

Mack Smith wanted more than anything to be a general. He'd had a master plan from the day he entered the recruiting office, and until getting shot down over Somalia three months ago, he'd followed it perfectly: combat experience, an air kill (two), serious seat time in the country's most advanced planes. He had numerous connections inside and outside Washington, dozens of military godfathers—all of whom knew he had the right stuff and were willing to pull strings to make sure he got ahead.

His next step, command of a top-tier squadron, had seemed assured. For the last three months, though, everything seemed to be going wrong. The President—bit of a windbag, but still the commander in chief, don't forget that—had shaken his hand and thanked him—thanked him!—for doing such a "good job over there." Then he'd gone and lost the election. With him went the Defense Secretary, who had smiled and murmured something about a promotion to colonel.

Worse, Knife hadn't been able to snag an important assignment. The gig testing Sharkishki was the best he could manage, a bit of an end run that had brought him back to Dreamland against his wishes. He'd taken it in hopes that it would lead to an assignment at Nellis heading the Aggressor squadron, which was where the MiG and its brethren were headed next. Recently, though, there were rumors that the Aggressor squadron, which trained top-rung fighter pilots for combat, was overstaffed. It was possible he'd get there only on temporary duty, assigned to show the boys how to work the stick and rudder—a cushy job certainly, but not one calculated to take him to any great heights. It would also put him back where he had started, in search of a command billet.

Was he in the midst of a bad streak? Or were others out

to sabotage him? Everywhere there were minor annoyances trying to trip him up. Like his alarm clock. And this morning's Dolphin, whose pilot insisted on waiting at Nellis for nearly a half hour because he was the only passenger.

As if anyone else important might show up.

By the time Knife reached the hangar where he and the engineers were due to review the upgrades to the MiG's passive avionics, he was nearly forty-five minutes late.

Which didn't explain why his team wasn't here.

One look at the man who was, Major Franklin Thomas, and Mack knew his luck was going from bad to absolutely terrible. Thomas was a bean-counter who always came up three beans short. He also never delivered good news.

"You missed the meeting," said Thomas.

"What meeting?"

"0730. There was an e-mail on it last night."

"To me? Musta missed it."

"Major, I won't sugarcoat this," said Thomas. "The Advanced Aggressor program has been canceled."

"What?"

"Completely. The MiGs are going to be mothballed."

"You *have* to be shitting me." He gestured toward the three fuselages to the right, in various stages of renovation. "There's got to be ten million dollars of work tied up in those planes, and never mind what the airframes cost."

"The Aggressor program isn't going to make the cut," said Thomas. "The new Administration believes it's better to cut bait right now, rather than dragging it on. I can run through some of the numbers if you want."

"Oh, fuck that."

Thomas's lower lip quivered and his cheek jerked up nervously. "The Russians have canceled most of their developmental programs, so our efforts to anticipate them no longer make sense. We would be training against a nonexistent threat."

"Bullshit."

"E-ev-everyone's going to be reassigned to other Dreamland projects. Of course, we'll be securing the airframes that we have. Now you're not technically Dreamland personnel, so the colonel mentioned that he'd help find something for you if you need help."

"I don't need God's help," said Mack, practically spitting Dog's very unofficial and not exactly flattering nickname.

"Major, this isn't going to affect you adversely. It's just a little bump."

"Screw yourself, Thomas, okay? Just fucking screw yourself."

Aboard Mo
23 January, 0915

EVEN THE PEOPLE WHO FLEW B-52'S CALLED THEM BUFFs—Big Ugly Fat Fellas, or Fuckers, depending on whether there was a reverend around. The venerable Cold War bombers looked clean on the first sketch pads, but even by the late sixties wore a variety of blisters and stretch marks across their approximately 160-foot bodies. Each modification made the bomber a more potent weapon, but most also took a slight nick out of its aerodynamic qualities. Never fast to begin with, latter-day Stratofortresses positively labored in certain flight regimes, including low-level maneuvers.

Not the Megafortress. With a sleek needle nose, an ultra-clean fuselage, carbon-fiber reinforced wings, and a modified tailplane assembly, the EB-52 could accelerate through a forty-five-degree climb from one thousand feet, its speed touching 423.5 knots even though it carried a simulated weapons load of 28,000 pounds of iron bombs.

"We can go faster," Cheshire said as they climbed through seven thousand feet. She'd let him take the pilot's seat to continue his training.

"Engines at max," said Dog.

"Engines at maximum power," concurred the computer.

"We should have more thrust," complained Cheshire. "Eight thousand feet, going to ten thousand."

The outboard J57's rumbled noisily, as if Major Cheshire had annoyed them. Still, the airplane's indicated airspeed slipped back toward four hundred knots. Cheshire made some adjustments on her side of the control panel, but nothing seemed to have an effect. They reached ten thousand feet; Bastian began pushing the nose down, trimming the plane for level flight.

"Air speed 380 knots," reported the computer.

"How can that be?" said Dog.

"Problem with Test Engine Two," reported Cheshire, a moment before the computer flashed a warning on the status screen. The PW4074/DX engine's oil pressure shot down, then up off the scale. The temperature went red as well.

"Shutting down Two," reported Cheshire.

"Two, yes, shutting down Two," said Dog. His mind hesitated for a moment, his brain momentarily caught between a dozen different thoughts. The synapses were temporarily clogged by the memory of the only time in his life that he'd lost an engine in flight and couldn't get it relit.

Unfortunately, it was in an F-16 over the Atlantic. No amount of restarts, no amount of curses, could bring it back. He'd bailed out into a moonless night at ten thousand feet— and even with plenty of time to contemplate how cold the water would be, he'd underestimated the chill by half.

But he was in a Megafortress now.

"Trimming to compensate," Dog said calmly, remembering the routine Bree had taught him during the simulations.

"Good," said Cheshire. "Okay. Okay," she sang, running through the instruments on her side.

The Megafortress wobbled slightly. Mo's speed continued to drop steadily, but he was still in control.

"I'm going to bank around and try for Runway Two," Bastian told Cheshire.

"Two's no good," said Nancy. "The Flighthawks are using it for touch-and-go's. Three is our designated landing area."

"Three then." Bastian clicked his radio transmit button. "Dreamland Tower, this is Missouri. We have an emergency situation. One engine is out. Request permission to land on Runway Three."

"Tower. We acknowledge your emergency. Stand by."

Dog started to bank the plane. His hands were a little shaky and the artificial horizon showed he was tipping his wing a little too much.

"Temp in Engine Three going yellow, going—shit—climbing—red," reported Cheshire.

She said something else, but Dog couldn't process it. His stomach started fluttering to the side, as if it had somehow pulled loose inside his body.

Relax, he told himself. You can do this.

"Nine thousand feet, going to eight thousand," said Cheshire.

"Shut down Engine Three," said Dog.

"Through the turn first," prompted Cheshire. "I'm on the engine, Colonel," she explained.

Dog came out of the turn, leveling the wings while still in a gentle downward glide. Cheshire did a quick run through the indicators on the remaining engines, reporting that they were in the green. The tower came back, clearing them to land.

"Six thousand feet," said Cheshire. "One more orbit?"

"I think so," said Dog. But as he nudged into the bank, his left wing started to tip precipitously; the Megafortress began bucking and threatening to turn into a brick.

"Problem with the automatic trim control," reported Cheshire. "System failure in the automated flight-control computer, section three—the backup protocol for the engine tests introduced an error. All right, hang with it. This won't be fatal."

She then began running through some numbers, recording the section problems that the flight computer was giving her on the screen. Under other circumstances—like maybe sitting on the ground in his office—Dog would have appreciated the technical details and the prompt identification of the problem. Now, though, all he wanted was a solution.

"We're going to have to fly without the computer," said Cheshire finally. "I can't lock this out and it will be easier to just land and we can debug on the ground."

"I figured that out," said Dog, wrangling the big plane through the turn.

"If you want me to take it, just say the word."

He felt his anger boiling up, even though he knew she didn't mean it as an insult. "No, I'm okay," he said. "Tell me if I'm doing anything wrong."

"Wide turns," she said. "Very wide turns. We're more like an airliner than a fighter jet."

"Yup."

Part of him, a very, very small part of him, wanted to turn the plane over to Cheshire. A strong case could be made that it was the right thing to do—when all was said and done, he was a green pilot trying to deal with a very big problem. Even if he wasn't in over his head, it made sense to turn the stick over to Cheshire.

But Dog was way too stubborn for that. And besides, he wasn't in over his head—he came through another orbit much more smoothly, having worked the plane down to two thousand feet. They legged into final approach with a long, gentle glide.

"Come on, Mo," said Cheshire, talking to the plane. "You can do it, baby."

"Yeah, Mo," said Dog. "Go for it, sister."

Whether she heard them or not, the EB-52 stepped down daintily on the desert runway, her tires barely chirping.

She poked her nose up slightly, perhaps indignant to find a full escort of emergency vehicles roaring alongside her. But Bastian had no trouble controlling her, bringing her to a rest near the secondary access ramp at the middle of the field.

"Good work, Colonel," said Cheshire. "You handled that like a pro. Maybe we *will* use you as a pilot when Pistol and Billy leave."

ANTARES Bunker
27 January, 0755

KEVIN NODDED AT THE GUARD AS THE GATE SWUNG back from the road, the panel of chain links groaning and clicking as the metal wheels whirled. While the path was wide enough for a tractor-trailer, no vehicles were allowed past the checkpoint, not even the black SUVs used by Dreamland security.

Madrone proceeded past the gate and the three cement-reinforced metal pipes that stuck up from the roadway, walking toward the pillbox that served as the entrance to the ANTARES lab. Made of concrete, the building bore the scars from its use long ago as a target area for live-fire exercises, though it had been at least two decades since the last piece of lead had ricocheted off the thick gray exterior. The interior somehow managed to smell not only damp, but like fried chicken, perhaps because the main vents from the underground complex ran through an access shaft next to the stairway.

Madrone nearly lost his balance as he stepped down the tight spiral stairway. All of the qualifying tests for ANTARES had taken place over at Taj; coming to the lab yesterday had been a revelation—truthfully, he didn't even know it existed. The bunker facility had actually not been used during the program's first phase, except for some minor tests; it was only after ANTARES was officially shut down that the computers and other gear were consolidated here. Geraldo had been using it as an office and lab for a few months, but the scent of fresh paint managed to mingle with the heavier odors as Madrone stepped off the stairway and across the wide ramp. No human guards were posted beyond the gate, and like the rest of Dreamland, there were no signs to direct anyone; it was assumed that if you had business here, you knew where you were going.

The metal ramp led to a subterranean catacomb area with three large metal doors, none of which looked as if they had been opened in years. Madrone went to the door on the right, which was the only one that worked. It was also the only one with a magnetic card reader. He pushed his ID into the slot and the door slowly creaked upward. He took a breath, then ducked beneath it, passing into a long hallway whose raked cement walls and dull red overhead lights continued the early-bomb-shelter motif. At the end of the hallway he turned right, and was immediately blinded by light; before his eyes could adjust the door in front of him slid open, activated by a computer security system similar to the one that governed Taj's elevator.

Now the ambiance changed dramatically. He stepped onto a plush green carpet and walked down the hallway, barely glancing at the Impressionist paintings—elaborate canvas transfer prints complete with forged brush strokes like the real thing. As he neared Lab Room 1, the adagio of a Mozart Concerto—K.313, for flute and orchestra—filtered into the hallway, and he smelled the light perfume of Earl Grey tea.

"Good morning, Kevin, come in, come in," said Dr. Geraldo.

She was wearing a lab coat and her customary severe suit, but otherwise seemed more like a matron welcoming visitors to the family estate than a staid scientist. She ushered Kevin to a thick leather chair and went to get him some tea; somewhere along the way he'd mentioned that he preferred it to coffee.

"And a pineapple Danish," she said, appearing with a plate and cloth napkin. "Did you sleep well?" the psychiatrist asked him.

"As a matter of fact I did," he told her. "Best I've slept in weeks. Didn't have any dreams."

"We always have dreams," she said gently. "You mean that you don't remember them."

"True."

"How many cigarettes have you had this morning?"

Kevin laughed—not at her stern-grandmother scowl, but at the realization that he hadn't had any. He hadn't even thought of it.

"I think your pills are a cure for nicotine fits," he suggested.

"If so, you and I will share a fortune," she said kindly. Geraldo glanced toward his thumbs, which Kevin belatedly pulled into his fists; that was one habit he hadn't yet broken. "You've gained weight. Very good. You did your exercises?"

"Yes, ma'am. Full hour."

"Let me look at your spider," she said, standing on her tiptoes to examine the side of his skull above his ear. It was a bit of a joke—the integrated circuit placed there to facilitate the ANTARES connection looked like a flattened spider. "Itchy?"

"Not today," said Kevin.

"Yes, I think it's fine. I think it was only the irritation from the shaving bothering you."

He sipped his tea. Inside the next room, Geraldo's two assistants were making last-minute adjustments to the equipment. One of them made a joke that somehow involved the word "monkey," and the other laughed.

Monkey. That's what he was.

Madrone concentrated on the Danish as Geraldo reviewed the results of yesterday's session. She gave brain wave and serotonin levels, which he knew wouldn't be encouraging—they had failed to make a link.

The thing was, he didn't quite know what making a link really meant. Geraldo said it would be like shaking hands with the computer, except that it would seem imaginary. He'd feel it more than think it.

Neither description cleared up his confusion. Zen, who had gone through ANTARES before his crash, described it as a smack on the head with an anvil, followed by the warm buzz of a beer when you'd spent the day working outside in the sun.

That didn't help either. Not only had he never been hit by an anvil, Madrone rarely drank, and frankly didn't like the loss of control that came with being buzzed, let alone drunk.

Geraldo bent down in front of him, so close he could smell the tea on her breath. "You're worried this morning."

"A little nervous." He felt his thumb twitch.

"You'll be fine," she told him. "The link will come. It takes time. Everyone is different. There are different pathways. Trust me."

Shorn of its classified and complicated science, descriptions of the ANTARES system tended to sound either like Eastern religion or sci-fi fantasies. The bottom line was an age-old dream—ANTARES allowed a subject's brain to control mechanical devices. It was hardly magic, however. The subject could not simply think an item into existence, nor could he— for some reason not totally understood, no woman had ever been an effective ANTARES subject—move items by simply thinking of them. Thought impulses, which corresponded to minute chemical changes in synapses in different sections of the brain, controlled a series of sensitive ultralow-voltage electrical switches in the ANTARES interface unit, which in turn controlled the external object—in this case a gateway to a special version of C^3, the Flighthawk control computer.

But before Madrone could interface with C^3, he had to reach Theta-alpha, the scientists' shorthand for a mental state where he could produce and control the impulses of the hippocampus in his brain. The production of the waves were measured on an electroencephalograph. All humans, in fact all carnivorous animals, produced such waves. But few people could actually control them, let alone use them to project thoughts as instructions. Successful ANTARES subjects could do just that, using the brain waves as extensions of their thoughts, in effect talking to a computer without bothering to use their mouths.

In Theta-alpha, the brain began utilizing resources that it normally didn't tap. Or as an ANTARES researcher explained it on the introductory video: "Areas of the brain that normally go unused are suddenly put into service to control autonomous functions. The average person uses only thirty percent of his available brain capacity, but under Theta-alpha, the other seventy percent is suddenly put on line."

That seventy percent would be augmented by the computers it was interfaced with. When he mastered Theta and AN-TARES, Kevin would tap into their memories and, to some extent, computational abilities.

ANTARES had physical components. A special diet, drugs, and feedback manipulated serotonin and other chemical levels in the subject's brain. A chip implant in the skull supplied and regulated the vital connection to the ANTARES input and output system; this was physically taped to a receptor or, alternatively, overlain by a copper connection band in the AN-TARES control helmet. ANTARES subjects had to either sit in a special chair or wear a flight suit that contained a sensor that ran parallel to their spine, allowing the ANTARES monitoring units to record peripheral nervous-system impulses. But the most important component was the subject's mind, and his will to extend beyond himself. Kevin had to think himself beyond the interface into the object itself. As Geraldo was fond of saying, he had to discover a way to think in harmony with the machine. He needed to invent a new language with its own feelings, metaphors, and even thoughts.

"The important thing is not to push too hard," she told him now. "Let it come to you. It will. Are you ready?"

Madrone took a last bite of his pastry, then got up and followed her into the lab. He stripped off his shirt, holding his arms up while the techies carefully taped wire leads that would monitor his heartbeat and breathing. Shirt back on, he slipped into the subject chair, which looked like a slightly wider version of the one found in most dentist offices.

"Going to prick you, Captain," said Carrie, one of the assistants, as she picked up his hand. He nodded, trying not to stare at her breasts as she poked a small needle into his right thumb. She held the needle against his finger as she retrieved a roll of white adhesive tape from her lab coat pocket. A small tube ran from the needle to a device that measured gases in Madrone's bloodstream, analyzing his respiration rate during the experiment.

It was all but impossible not to imagine the outlines of her nipples rising as she attached the device.

In the meantime, the other assistant—Roger, whose long nose, wide stomach, and long legs made him look like a pregnant stork—got ready to put the ANTARES helmet on Kevin's head. The helmet was actually more a liner made of a flexible plastic with bumps and veins; a full flight helmet would go over it when they got to the point where he was actually working in a plane. Besides the thick metal band that connected with the chip, there were two classes of sensors strung in a thick net within the plastic. The first and most important picked up brain waves and fed them to the translating unit, backing up those that were fed through the chip and band interface. The other sensors helped the scientists track Madrone's physical state.

With the helmet on, Roger lowered a shieldlike set of visual sensors to track rapid eye movements over his eyes. These backed up the translating sensors, and gave the scientists another way of monitoring their progress. In the next stage of the experiments, the sensors would be part of the flight helmet and would be used by ANTARES to help it interpret his thought commands.

The physical feedback input from electrodes, which would be connected to the spider and grafted onto the nerves of the skin behind the eyes and ears, wouldn't be used until Madrone demonstrated he was capable of achieving and controlling Theta. The electrodes would allow the computer to send data to him, first by affecting his equilibrium, and then by interacting with his brain's Theta-alpha wave production.

A ponytail of wires connected the ANTARES helmet with a bank of workstations and two servers. These fed data to a set of supercomputers the next level down via a set of optical cables. The interface modules for the Flighthawk's C^3 units were still being worked on, but eventually would be hooked into a smaller, portable (and air-cooled) version of the ANTARES computer array.

Madrone sat stoically in the chair as the technicians prepared him. Geraldo had given him breathing exercises to do as a form of relaxation; he tried them now, imagining his lungs slowly squeezing the air from his chest. He pictured his upper body as a large balloon, gradually being emptied. He relaxed his arms and hands on the seat rests, easing himself into the chair. When the visor was placed on his face he accepted the darkness.

His lips and cheeks vibrated slightly, as if set off by some internal pitchfork tuned to their frequency. Someone placed headphones over his ears. The Mozart concerto played softly in the background.

The music called up memories of the past, times in junior and senior high school, learning the cello. Orchestra was his favorite class, though not his best—B's and B+'s compared to the A's and A+'s in math and science. The thickness of the notes matched the feel of the bow in his hand, the vibration shifting in his senses. Sounds morphed into movement through space, and space itself transformed, the high school halls a jungle of jagged shadows and sharp corners.

"Kevin, are you ready?"

Geraldo's voice intruded like a bully bursting from the shadows. Junior and senior high school were in the same building, seventh-graders mixing with towering twelfth-graders, always cowering in fear of being pummeled.

"Kevin?"

"Yes," said Madrone.

"Your hippocampus has grown two percent since our measurement twenty-four hours ago," said the scientist. "That is extremely good. Surprising even. Incredible."

"Off the chart," said Roger approvingly.

The hippocampus was one of the key areas of the brain involved in ANTARES, since it produced nearly all the Theta waves. Also responsible for memory control and other functions, it was actually a ridge at the bottom of each of the brain's lateral ventricles. Geraldo had explained that she wasn't sure the size of the ridge or the number of cells there mattered. Nonetheless, the ANTARES diet and drug regime included several hormones that were supposed to help stimulate the grown of brain cells.

"Our baseline frequencies this morning are 125 percent," continued Geraldo. "Kevin, I must say, we're doing very well. Very, very well. Can you feel the computer? If I try a simple tone, do you feel it? The feedback?"

He shook his head. Her praise was misplaced. He had no control over his thoughts, let alone the growth of his brain cells. He was worthless, a failure, useless. Karen had seen that and left.

His brain began to shift, ideas floating back and forth like pieces of paper caught in a breeze.

Something hot burned a hole on the side of his head.

Red grew there. His skull bones folded inward, became a flute.

Maria Mahon, the flute player in ninth-grade orchestra.

He had a crush on her. Thomas Lang, a senior, was her boyfriend.

Stuck-up rich kid bully slimebag.

Go out for the football team, his dad urged.

He broke his forearm and couldn't play the cello anymore.

Very red and hot.

The light notes moved down the scale. He was a horrible trumpet player. Try the bass, pound-pound-pounding.

Red knives poked him from the sides of the hall. Someone took a machine gun from the locker.

Respond with the York Gatling gun. He had one in his hands. His head was the radar he'd worked on.

Pounding red lava from the cortex of his brain.

Madrone heard words, hard words that shot across the pain, spun him in the displaced hallway of his distorted memories.

"Kevin, try to relax. Let your body sway with the music. You're fighting too hard."

Relax, relax, relax. Don't think about the bullies.

The tanks. He was in Iraq, alone with his men.

"Lieutenant?"

"Go left. I'm right. Just go!"

He screamed, running faster. He drew the Iraqis' fire and his men did their jobs, it was all so easy in his memory now, without the pain and the nervousness, knowing exactly how it would come out, the elation, the adrenaline at the end, the smell of the burning metal, the extra grenade still in his hand.

He could do it. He wanted to do it.

And then Karen. Christina being born in the hospital. Taking blood in the doctor's office when she was a week old because the TSH had been so elevated.

Normal, said the nurse, for a traumatic birth.

Except the birth hadn't been traumatic. Labor was only two hours and the kid nailed the Apgar charts.

Christina wailed as they pricked her heel. They couldn't get the blood to flow.

The second test, then the third. X-rays. Colonel Glavin, Theo P. Glavin, wouldn't give him the day off so he could be there.

"P" for Prick.

Oh, God, you bastards, why did you poison her?

Karen, don't you see—they killed her. They poisoned her and then me.

His wife looked at him from across the room, the empty white room at the back of the small church where they'd had the service for Christina, their poor, dead little girl. Karen's eyes stabbed at his chest, wounding him again, the memory so vivid it wasn't a memory but reality; he was in the church again, his daughter dead, his marriage crumbling, his life over. He'd been uncontrollable at the service, blurting out the truth, what he knew was the truth—they had poisoned her through him, killed her.

He'd get them, the bastards who'd exposed him to the radiation, exposed her—

"Kevin?"

"I can't do it, I'm sorry." Madrone snapped upright in the chair. He yanked off the helmet.

"Easy, easy," said Geraldo. Her fingers folded over his gently but firmly. "Let's break for lunch."

Her words or perhaps her touch pushed him back, somehow both surprising and calming him at the same time.

"Lunch?" he asked.

"Yes, it's lunchtime," she said. "Why don't you go over to the Red Room? Take a real break. We'll start from scratch at two o'clock."

"What time is it?" asked Madrone. He'd only just sat in the chair, perhaps five minutes ago.

"High noon," said Roger. "You've been attached for nearly two hours. Flirting with Theta-alpha the whole time. You're close." He put his thumb and forefinger a half centimeter apart. "You're damn close."

Dreamland All-Ranks Cafeteria
27 January, 1230

"HEY, MONKEY BRAIN," SAID MACK AS HE ENTERED THE food line in the mess hall and spotted Madrone in front of him. "How's it feel to have a microchip in your head?"

"Hi, Major." Madrone stood stiffly, eyes on the cook's helper who was cutting him some roast beef. Mack thought the Army captain looked even paler than normal. The ANTARES people must have started frying his brain already.

Gained a few pounds, though.

"Lot of food you got there," said Knife. "Bulking up for all that skull work, huh?"

"I'm hungry."

"That a boy. Go for the red meat. No more Twig, right? Got a new nickname—Microchip Brain. Monkey Boy."

The airman slicing the meat glanced in Mack's direction.

"No electrodes in your neck yet?" Mack asked Madrone, narrowing his eyes as if he were scanning for microscopic ANTARES implants. "Guess I can't ask you to toast my bread, huh?"

"Jeez, you're more obnoxious than usual today, Knife," said Zen, rolling in behind him.

"And why not, oh, exalted one," said Mack. He did a mock bow. "Your father-in-law just offered me a job as janitor here."

Actually, Bastian had tried to talk him into flying Megafortresses. Smith would take a job with a commuter airline, or even look up that Brazilian geezer who'd come on to him in Vegas, before stooping to flying BUFFs.

"I'm sure you'll get a good assignment soon," said Jeff.

The thing about Stockard that pissed Knife off was his ability to deliver a line like that without giving himself away. Anybody overhearing him undoubtedly thought he was being sincere.

Mack knew otherwise. But there was no real way to answer him, or at least Mack couldn't think of anything snappy. He compensated by making sure the airman cut him an extra slab of beef from the rare side of the roast, then helped himself to the rest of the spread. Known colloquially as the Red Room, this mess and the fancy food had once been reserved for special occasions. Bastian had thrown it open with his "all ranks, all the time" decree. Interestingly, most of the base personnel had responded by using the Red Room only for special occasions.

Mack decided he'd eat here until his next assignment was settled. Might as well. Odds were he'd end up getting shipped out to Alaska, or perhaps the Antarctic.

Bastian—whom he'd actually had to make an appointment to see—had pretended to be gracious after Mack turned down the Megafortress. He'd told him he could stay on as an "unassigned test pilot," whatever the hell that was supposed to mean. Obviously a career crusher. When Mack had said that was no good, Bastian had pointed out that the MiG project would live on for only a few weeks more. After filling out some odds and ends and collecting data for future simulations of next-generation Russian planes, the plane would head for deep storage. If Mack couldn't snag something before then, he might very well find himself assigned to something he didn't like, almost certainly not at Dreamland.

Things did look bleak. The only assignment Mack's preliminary trolling had turned up was as a maintenance officer for a squadron of A-10A Warthogs.

It was possible, maybe even likely, that the brass was trying to get him to glide into the sunset. The fact that he'd gotten waxed over Somalia probably embarrassed them. They just hadn't dared admitting it to his face at the time.

Bastards. Let them put their butts over a few dozen ZSUs and SA-9's. If he hadn't hung around there, an entire company of Marines and at least one helicopter would be Somalian tourist attractions right now.

Knife took his tray into the paneled eating area, his flight boots tromping on the thick red carpet that gave the room its name. Madrone sat by himself at a table for four in the corner. Mack walked over and put his tray down.

"Penny for your thoughts, Monkey Brain," said Mack. When Madrone didn't respond, Mack started humming the start of the John Lennon song "Mind Games."

Madrone shot him a glance, then put his head down, staring at his food.

"Silent treatment. I get it," said Knife.

Zen rolled across the room, tray in his lap. "Mind if I sit here, Kevin?" he asked.

"I'm kind of thinking," said Madrone softly.

Smith started to laugh. "What the hell are you thinking about?"

"Leave him alone, Smith."

"Come on, Zen, Kevvy can fight his own battles. Right, Kev?"

"I would like to be left alone," said Madrone, his voice a monotone so soft it was difficult to hear even in the quiet room.

"Hey, that's okay, Kevin," said Zen.

"Guess he doesn't like you today," said Mack.

Stockard said nothing, rolling backward and then across to the next table. Madrone stared down at his food.

Mack liked the guy, he really did. Maybe he shouldn't have busted his balls quite so hard.

"Hey, look, Kev, I didn't mean nothing, okay? Just bustin' your chops. If I was out of line, I'm sorry."

The Army captain raised his head slowly. His face had changed—his eyes were squeezed down in his forehead, under a long furrow.

"Go away, Major," he said.

Mack laughed. That's what he got for trying to be nice.

Madrone stared at his food for a few seconds more, then slowly pushed back his chair, stood, and walked from the room.

"See ya, Microchip Brain," said Mack, looking across at Jeff. "They got to him already." He shook his head. "They ought to bag ANTARES."

"For once I may have to agree with you," said Zen before turning back to his food.

ANTARES Bunker
27 January, 1555

THE CHAIR POKED INTO HIS BACK. HIS LEGS WERE LEAD. A thick snake had wrapped itself around his head.

"Relax now, Kevin," said Geraldo. "Do your breathing. You'll find Theta when the time is right."

What did it take to breathe? What muscles did he use?

Poor, poor Christina, lying so helpless in the hospital bed, smiling at him. She'd been born with anaplastic thyroid cancer, a rare, nearly inexplicable, and always fatal cancer. It could only have come from the radiation he'd been exposed to at Glass Mountain and Los Alamos. Poison.

No. He'd gone over all that, buried it a year after burying his daughter, after his wife left. Colonel Glavin helped him get a transfer. That was five long years ago.

He was the helpless one. Impotent.

That wasn't him, just a part of him. Once he'd been tough, once he'd been brave. The bullets splattering around him. He ran with the grenade in his hand.

Shit, the tape is gone. I pulled it, it's live.

Screw these bastards. Screw them all!

Knives, red and sharp, poking from every direction.

"Try to relax, Kevin," said Geraldo again.

"The music," he said. "Could you, could you change it?"

"The music's bothering you?"

He felt his heart pounding in his chest. "Yes. It's killing me."

"Carrie, the music."

"I'll get it, Doc," said Roger. There was some static in the background, then a loud click. "Oh, shit," said the techie.

A loud hush filled Kevin's ears, a kind of wind sound that must have come from some malfunction in the equipment, a crossed wire or something. There was a light popping noise in the background, a set of footsteps, and then a sound like thunder, two peals, three. The noise gave way to a storm, rain coursing down from enormous clouds, bursting overhead, then trickling slowly across and through a thick canopy of leaves. Light burst across his eyes, then darkness again, shapes receding.

He stood in a thick forest. Rain fell all around him. His pants were wet.

Alone in the middle of a vast tropical rain forest, alone and at peace.

"You're in," whispered Geraldo from far way. "You're in."

The forest felt beautiful and empty. Could he stay here?

A jaguar circled nearby. A snake slithered through the trees. It was more jungle than forest.

Rain. Storm.

"Kevin?"

Madrone felt something snap below his head, a sharp pain as if he'd overstretched a ligament. Someone pulled off the glasses.

Geraldo was standing in front of him, smiling. Her assistants were peering over her shoulders, expressions of awe on their faces.

"You were in Theta-alpha for twenty-eight minutes," said Geraldo. "And you responded to the computer."

"I was in Theta?"

What had the computer said to him? What had he seen? What had he felt?

He didn't remember anything except a vague, restful pleasure.

And danger at the edges, beyond the trees.

"Are you sure I was in Theta-alpha?" he asked again.

"Oh, yes. Oh, yes. You were in Theta and you responded to the computer. Just a pulse, but it was definitely there," said Geraldo. "I can't believe it. We've never, ever had results like this. Never. Not this early, not this long or fast."

"Let's do it again," Kevin said.

"So soon?" said Geraldo.

"Let's do it again," he insisted.

"Your pants," said Roger, pointing. He'd lost control of his bladder as he entered Theta.

It was immaterial. He had to get back there.

"Again," Kevin said sharply.

Dreamland Commander's Office
29 January, 1705

COLONEL BASTIAN PUSHED HIS LEGS UNDER HIS DESK, stretching out some of the knots that had twisted in his muscles. But there was no way to release the pressure of the one developing in his head.

"The way this works, Colonel," General Magnus continued over the secure phone, "reports come to my office."

"I understand the normal procedure, General," said Bastian, struggling to keep his voice level. "I was ordered—"

"You don't accept orders from anyone but me."

"The Assistant Secretary of Defense asked specifically for an eyes-only assessment of ANTARES. I delivered it. And I copied you ahead of time, despite her instructions not to."

"Chain of command. Chain of command."

Dog pushed the phone away, resisting the temptation to answer. He detested the political bullshit. Worse, he'd been maneuvered into a no-win situation. Magnus was his boss, but Washington wanted a direct say over what happened at Dreamland. Magnus hadn't minded that so much with the past Administration—he'd been tight with the NSC as well as the Joint Chiefs. But things were different now.

Nor did it help that Dog had told Washington what it didn't want to hear—go slow, if at all, on ANTARES.

"You still there, Bastian?"

"Yes, General, I am." Dog pulled the receiver back to his ear.

"You're a real piece of work, you know that?" Magnus said. "You're covering your ass fifty ways to Sunday on this."

"Actually, sir, I'm playing it straight. We're ramping up ANTARES, per your direct order. But at the same time, I don't think it should have priority."

Magnus snorted. "You sound like Brad Elliott more and more." He was referring to Dreamland's last commander.

"I'd take that as a great compliment, General."

"Just remember where the hell he is," snapped Magnus, breaking the connection abruptly.

As he hung up the phone, Dog realized the lieutenant general had never actually disagreed with the report on ANTARES. But it wasn't Magnus's opinion—or Bastian's—that counted. And the truth was, the program was galloping along.

The intercom buzzed.

"Next appointment, Senior Scientist Andrew Ichison," said Gibbs. "Mack Smith is also waiting, sir."

"Again?"

"Wants to check on the progress of his assignment, sir."

Dog could tell from Gibbs's tone that Smith was standing about three inches from him.

"Tell him there's nothing to report."

"I did that, sir."

"Slot him in."

"Your call, sir," said Ax, hanging up the phone.

Bastian pushed his chair back, waiting for Ichison to appear. The scientist had been part of the high-altitude spy glider project, which the Administration had cut. Dog had to tell him, along with twenty other civilians, there was no place for him at Dreamland, and probably anywhere else in the government.

ANTARES was hot. The advanced particle laser, the high-altitude spy glider, the HARM follow-ons, and the MiG Aggressor projects were not. Many of the senior military people who'd been working on them would be shunted into career dead ends. A good portion of the civilians would be left with nothing but a handshake and a reduced government pension for their years here.

Most accepted the news with grace. They thanked him for trying to hunt down jobs, and then giving them a personal heads-up on the prospects. And then there were people like Mack Smith—who barged into the office instead of Ichison.

"Major, you are to wait in line," Dog told him.

"Egghead told me to go first. Nice guy. So how are we doing, Colonel? Did you find something?"

"I offered you a job here."

"No offense, Dog, but you and I both know that's going nowhere. Unassigned test pilot—that's a man without a country."

"I meant the Megafortress project."

"Ah, I'm a jock. I'm not flying cows. Shit, Colonel, the EB-52 is a girl's plane, you know what I mean?"

"No, Major, I don't know what you're talking about."

"Hey, it's great for Cheshire and Rap, probably as much as they can handle. But guys like us—we're jocks, right? We belong in the best."

"You know, Mack, I've had a ball-buster of a day. In spite of that, and maybe in spite of my best judgment, I have actually made some inquiries on your behalf. But you know what? I have a tremendous headache. And when I get a headache, I sometimes forget to follow up on things. I don't answer important phone calls. Paperwork tends to get lost."

"Gotcha, Colonel." Mack jumped to his feet. "F-22 is going to need a commander, I hear."

Dog said nothing.

"How about a gig in Europe? Naples?"

"Good night, Major."

Mack took a few quick steps toward the door. "Hey, go easy on Ichison," he said, spinning around. "Not wrapped too tight. I told him there'd be plenty of people looking for an engineer with experience like him and he just about started crying."

"Thanks."

"Just doing my bit."

Allegro, Nevada
29 January, 2034

BREANNA TOOK HER BEER INSIDE INTO THE LIVING ROOM, curling up on the couch next to Jeff in his wheelchair. He had a folder with reports open on his lap, and seemed only vaguely interested in the basketball game on the TV; she reached for the TV controller.

"Don't change the station," he growled.

"Oh, come on, Jeff. You're not watching it."

"Yes, I am."

"What's the score?"

"Denver 45, Seattle 23."

"Blowout."

"Don't change the station."

"What a grouch," she said. She drew a curve on Jeff's skull behind his ear, sliding her finger down and back along his neck. "Come on. You don't want to watch TV. Let's watch a dirty movie."

"*Friends* is not a dirty movie. And that's what you're aiming at."

"After *Friends*."

Her hand shot toward the controller, but he was too fast, snatching it away.

But then, as she knew he would, he clicked it to her program.

"Whatcha doing anyway?" she asked him as the opening credits rolled.

"Classified."

"Excuse me?"

"It's just bullshit for Washington," said Jeff finally, closing the folder. "Flighthawks and ANTARES. Need-to-know bullshit."

"Don't let me stop you," said Breanna. "What are you getting me for Valentine's Day?"

"A six-pack of Anchor Steam."

"Very romantic."

Jeff tucked the folder away in his briefcase, locked it, then wheeled himself into the kitchen. By the time he returned with a beer, the program had started. As it happened, it was one of the two Breanna had already managed to see.

"Want to play Scrabble?" she asked.

Jeff agreed as long as she'd put the basketball game back on. Twenty minutes later, she was ahead by more than a hundred points.

"What's bothering you?" she asked her husband. "You didn't all of a sudden start rooting for the Sonics, did you?"

He shrugged.

Breanna put her fingers at the base of his neck, kneading gently. Finally he began to speak.

"I saw Kevin today. I think ANTARES is blowing his head to pieces."

"They only just started."

"He got into Theta-alpha already. I talked to Geraldo before I came home. She's excited as hell and pushed up the simulator tests. He'll be at Stage Five in a few days. Hell, maybe tomorrow."

"What's that mean?"

"Flying on the sim."

"Really?"

Jeff nodded his head but didn't say anything. ANTARES was one of the few things they didn't talk about before his accident, and not just because the program was highly classified. Something about the interface and the associated protocols, Breanna gathered, deeply bothered Zen. But when her husband didn't want to talk about something, he didn't; there was no sense pushing him.

Besides, there were better ways to spend the night.

Breanna slid her fingers under his shirt. "Loser has to draw the bath," she told him. "And gets the bottom."

"Bree—"

She leaned forward and kissed his temple, then rolled her tongue gently around his ear. "All right, you get the bottom whatever the score."

IV
Brainstorm

**Aboard Hawkmother
(Dreamland Boeing 777 Test Article 1)
Dreamland Range 23 West
18 February, 1007**

THE RAIN STARTED WITH A FEW SCATTERED DROPS, HIT-ting against the high leaves. Time extended; the sprinkle grew quicker, then slowed again, drops sliding and popping through a filter of gently spinning leaves. The wind began to pick up. A bird with long massive wings fluttered overhead as a snake unwound in the distance.

The dark night surrounding him grew even blacker. The rain fell more strongly, began to pound. A low peal of thunder heralded an intense outburst; more thunder, more, and then a fierce flash of lightning.

Kevin Madrone felt his brain fold open and his body catch fire; he exploded into the forest and the storm, becoming the rain, becoming the thunder, becoming the flame that flashed at the center of the universe.

I'm in.

Most of the other successful subjects described reaching Theta as something like a rusty nail slicing through their skull, followed by the rush of a roller coaster heading downhill. The sensation of pain had been a constant for all the subjects, nearly all of whom said it progressed incredibly as they moved beyond the Stage Two experiments, which involved simple manipulation of a sequence of lights. Stage Three involved manipulating a series of switches; Stage Four called for interpreting data from the interface unit. Most of the test subjects who managed to reach Theta washed out in those stages, never reaching Five, which called for controlling an aircraft simulator, much less Stage Six, which was actual flight.

But Madrone felt no pain on reaching Theta; it was all rush. He went from the Stage One tests to Stage Three on his second day. He was ready for the primitive simulator sequences the next afternoon; that afternoon, he told Geraldo he wanted to work with C³, the Flighthawk controller. When she told him the programming updates needed for the gateway link between ANTARES and C³ hadn't been completed, Madrone suggested he could help by working with the gear.

Overjoyed at their unprecedented progress, Geraldo called in the scientist working on the gateway software—Jennifer Gleason. The beautiful, ravishing Jennifer Gleason, who with his help completed it in two sessions.

Three days later, he was ready to fly for real. They moved to the Flighthawk command bunker, where with Zen as a backup, he got ready for a ground takeoff.

The plane nearly broke him in half.

He'd spent the night before chanting the procedure for takeoff and the flight plan, committing it all to memory—military thrust, brakes off, roll, speed to 130 indicated, back on the stick, maintain power, climb, clear gear, alpha to eight, 250 knots, indicator check, level flight at bearing 136, orbit twice. Walking into Bunker B that morning, he felt confident, as sure of himself as he had ever been. Someone asked him if he wanted a cigarette and he laughed. Someone else—Zen—remarked that he'd gained weight. Kevin nodded confidently, ready to nail this sucker down.

But in the control chair, full ANTARES flight helmet strapped on, sweat oozed upward from his spine to his neck. As he practiced changing the visor image from the forward video feed to the synthetic IR view, a fist grew inside his brain, knotting the inside of his head and then punching the top of his skull. Bile rose in his throat and he screamed—red and purple flares flew across his eyes, and then blackness as he lost the link.

They tried again. Nearly the same thing happened, this time even quicker. Kevin fought to hold the link. A spear of ice pounded into his ear, tearing a hole in his skull as he held on. He tried pushing the ice away, but couldn't reach it. Then he tried closing the hole. He went out of Theta and lost the link.

The rest of them wanted to take a break. Madrone said no. He'd already flown the plane on the simulator, and knew this was merely a kind of performance anxiety, the sort of thing that might happen to a star second baseman who thought too much about the throw to first. To get into Theta, he had to relax and let the process take over, walk blindly into the night.

And to fly the plane, he had to let the computer take over, let the data come to him—not as thoughts exactly, more as waves of feeling, the kind of thing you felt as you rode a bicycle into the wind on a mountain road. The computer knew how to fly—the key to ANTARES was to accept the knowledge the computer gave him, to learn to trust what seemed to his mind instincts. For when he was in Theta, the computer's knowledge became his instincts.

They began again. He warmed his head as soon as the jungle appeared, pulling the sun through the trees around him. The Flighthawk came to him gently, pulling itself over his consciousness like a warm mitten over a cold hand. He took his hand off the control stick and closed his eyes.

The image from the visor screen stayed in his brain, projected there by C^3, working through ANTARES. As he relaxed, he realized he could see much more in his head than with the visor—with the computer's help, he could see the video, IR, and radar-enhanced views simultaneously, three-dimensional overlays around his head. Seeing wasn't the right word—it was more like a new sense that had sprung into his mind.

To fly, he had only to release himself from the ground.

The U/MF lifted off the runway perfectly. For the next three hours, he learned to fly for real.

Zen coached him through the com connection, but Kevin knew he didn't need a teacher, not in the traditional sense. He had only to trust C^3, to understand the way it spoke to him, to make his brain and the computer's one. He learned that he was not to worry about the specific power setting or the compass heading or the rate of fuel burn. He could see those numbers if he wished; he could ask the computer to set them specifically if he wanted. But focusing on them made his head turn away from the front of his body, where it belonged; it was more natural to accept them, flowing within an ANTARES-tinged equilibrium.

He knew how to fly. He knew everything in the computer's extensive library. C^3 was part of him, his arms and legs. He became oblivious to the image in the control helmet; it was redundant. He didn't bother to use the complicated joystick controls—thought was so much faster.

They went from one plane to two planes on the third day. The day after that, they boarded Hawkmother—a specially modified 777 that housed ANTARES and C^3—and air-launched two U/MFs. The only thing that took some getting used to was the sensation of the plane he was sitting in. It felt unsettling to bank sharply while he was controlling the Flighthawks in level flight. Zen had laughed when he told him about that later—after months of flying the Flighthawks from the belly of an EB-52, Stockard told him, he still couldn't get used to that.

That made Kevin determined to beat it. By the third drop on the second day of trials, he had.

He amazed everyone with his progress. To Kevin, it seemed no more difficult than moving through the levels of a video game. He had merely to relax and feel the cues of the computer. And then he let his mind run, flying into the wide blueness. It made him hungry, it made him want to grow.

Geraldo had asked him yesterday if when he entered Theta he felt as if he'd become a Greek god. He'd laughed and said no. He couldn't describe exactly what it felt like—as if he walked onto the threshold of a different kind of existence. Thoughts felt different, more like the sensation that accompanied tasting exotic food for the first time. His appetite grew every moment; once in Theta, he needed to explore more, to see and feel as far beyond himself as possible. Flying the U/MFs, he felt, was merely a metaphor, a device he used to interpret the world. ANTARES demanded, and provoked, new metaphors—the rain forest, which had become the way he entered Theta; the world itself, a dark mass beyond his center core demanding to be explored.

It sounded like mumbo jumbo when he tried to explain it, even to Zen. So he didn't. Watching Jeff's eyes start to squint into a frown when he approached, he realized he'd already gone far beyond his friend; he'd gone far beyond everyone. He wouldn't discuss it; he couldn't. He'd just feel it.

Today, they would air-launch two Flighthawks and simulate a combat encounter with the MiG as an aggressor. It seemed laughably routine, even boring. Madrone knew he was ready for more—four, ten, twenty U/MFs. He could fly far beyond the petty, unambitious schedule they'd laid out. He could get beyond C^3's limitations. He hungered for something beyond the small scope of the robot planes' sensors.

It made him angry to be held back. He could see the emotion coming sometimes—the edge of his brain tinged with red. He thought about Glass Mountain and Los Alamos, about the bastards who had killed his daughter, Glavin especially, who was foolish enough to still think he had him fooled, pretending to be his friend by sending Christmas cards. He remembered the bastard doctors at Livermore, and how he'd been tricked into taking Christina to see them. They'd masqueraded as doctors with a radical new treatment for her cancer, but all they'd wanted to do was kill her more quickly, steal her last moments from him.

Sometimes he got so mad he almost lost Theta. He felt himself being pushed back to the edge of the forest. The jaguar roared, snapping at him from behind the trees.

Madrone fought against it, struggling to relax, concentrating on his breathing. He'd always been good at controlling his anger, keeping secrets; it was just a matter of focusing on what he wanted.

"Two minutes to launch sequence," said a thick voice from the side. Zen, the mission boss, monitoring the flight from Raven. "Yo—you ready, Kevin?"

It seemed like such a chore to answer. Once he was in Theta, leaving the realm of his thoughts to do anything physical, even just to talk, felt like an imposition.

"Of course," said Madrone.

"We're ready," concurred Geraldo, who was sitting nearby in the 777's control bay.

"Hawkmother?" said Zen, talking to the Boeing's pilot.

"In the green, Gameboy. Let's do it."

The others on the circuit agreed. Hawkmother began to nose downward, preparing for the roller-coaster maneuver that helped separate the robot planes from her wings. Kevin felt the weightlessness and the rushing wind currents as the plane approached Alpha and the release point.

Go, he thought, go.

Hawk One plunked off the wing, followed a half second later by Hawk Two. They stuttered slightly, shuddering off the turbulent vortexes from the 777's wings. The engines ramped quickly to full power. Madrone trimmed his control surfaces, felt his indicated airspeed move above three hundred knots, pass through 350. He shot upward, altitude-above-ground-level leaping to 5,232 feet for Hawk One, 5,145 feet for Two. He pushed harder and climbed through his first marker, notching eight thousand feet.

A leisurely stroll. He'd done this before. He wanted something new, something more challenging.

Aggressor Flight checked in.

Come for me, baby.

Madrone wanted more planes, more challenges. How far could his mind really go? What if it turned inward, examined the nooks and crannies of the interface and the ANTARES computer? What rooms were there?

A video camera had been rigged in the nose of Hawkmother to record the mission. The video was recorded onto a hard drive and could be accessed through the C^3 controls, where the techies had made use of a physical bus and a series of unused interrupts to get easy control of the device. That let them run a log coordinating all of the flight records—Hawkmother's as well as the Flighthawks' and ANTARES—off the same time scale.

It was also a connection he could squeeze down, providing the gateway let him. His brain could slither in, like a kid slinking through a subway turnstile. Once inside, he'd have control.

C^3 gave him an error message, a slight buzz of confusion poking against his temple. His wandering thoughts had confused it.

But he could see the video. It was part of him.

Pain. Great pain.

Stay in your head. Maintain discipline.

He could partition his brain. That was the trick to AN-TARES. Lock off different parts. Just as he'd locked off Christina.

The interface tried to suck everything out of you.

Kevin moved the Flighthawks into a combat spread 3,500 feet apart. He nudged Two upward slightly, offset three hundred feet higher than One's twelve thousand AGL.

A brown-red blanket of desert lay at his feet; clear blue surrounded his head. Instruments were green.

The MiG would appear dead ahead. He would close with Two, flushing his enemy, who could only choose to dive or run past. Either way, Mack Smith and his Sharkishki would be nailed.

The tactics were basic and simple. Change the distances, which were really just a function of the engines, and the formation and procedures for engaging the enemy would be familiar to Baron von Richtofen.

Too simple a task to waste his thoughts on.

Madrone was invincible with these planes. Why had it taken so long for him to arrive at this point? He'd wasted every moment of his life until now.

"Keep your separation," warned Zen.

"Hawk Leader," he snapped, acknowledging the petty and tedious reminder.

Aboard Raven
8 February, 1123

ZEN FROWNED AS HE STARED AT THE MAIN MONITOR DIS-play at his station. The sitrep or God's-eye-view projected the exercise in sharp, color-coded lines, depicting actual positions in solid against the briefed courses in dash. Everything matched, even the reds showing Mack in Sharkishki, which had just taken off en route to Area Two over the mountains.

So what the hell was bugging him?

The U/MFs had come off the wings a second too soon. Kevin had taken them from him, even though Zen had assigned himself the launch.

Maybe. Kevin had definitely come in before the planned handoff, which was supposed to be ten seconds after the launch, when the Flighthawks were well beyond the vortices. Whether he'd had control on the wing and actually initiated the release was difficult to tell, because in either case C^3 handled the actual sequence.

The flight computer did nearly everything under AN-TARES, or could. That was the way the designers wanted it— the computer was more efficient.

Jeff resented that, even though C^3 made it possible for him to fly as well. But he was angry about something else, even though he couldn't precisely define it. Something about Kevin—his attitude seemed more dismissive.

Jeff realized he might be hypersensitive. Maybe Geraldo was right; maybe he was just jealous. Madrone was flying his planes, after all.

There was one other thing. The 777 had been nicknamed "Hawkmother." It was natural, a prosaic if utilitarian name for the plane. But it also happened to be the call sign Zen had used the day of the accident that cost him his legs.

He'd thought of suggesting something different, but decided it would seem trivial or worse—superstitious.

"Dream Tower is requesting we change the scenario a bit," said Bree, punching the interphone circuit that restricted the communications to inside the plane.

Zen acknowledged, then flipped into the control circuit to find out what was going on. A live-fire exercise was taking longer than expected, the controller explained, and they wanted to maintain a suitable margin of error. The new area for the Aggressor drill was well to the southwest, over another stretch of empty desert at the edge of the mountains.

"Yeah, okay, we can do that. Gameboy acknowledges," said Zen. He went back on the shared line to tell Madrone and the others about the change.

"Already have the course plotted," said Kevin before he could say anything.

Zen went through the instructions anyway.

Madrone was doing a great job. Why did that bug Jeff so much?

Aboard Sharkishki
18 February, 1137

MACK CONTINUED TO CLIMB AT FORTY-FIVE DEGREES, his forward air speed pushing through 550 kilometers an hour, roughly three hundred knots. The dials were marked with both measurements and he could toggle the displays; the metrics had been retained to give the Aggressor pilot more of a "Russian head." Mack felt particularly Russian today—which translated into a foul mood. He acknowledged the range change and continued to climb, nudging the stick left as he reached fifteen thousand feet.

The MiG controls felt much different than an American jet like the F-15. Set subtly higher and further forward, the stick seemed to pull Mack toward the front of the plane, using a different twitch of his muscles. It handled well, though, even with its hydraulic controls—he did a roll for the hell of it, coming onto the new course for Test Range 4B.

Bastian still hadn't found him a command gig. No one else had stepped up either. Frickin' best damn pilot in the Air Force, and he was getting the leper treatment.

Knife was tempted to goose the burners, tuck the plane down, and run. He'd be in Mexico before anyone realized he was gone.

And what would he do there? Find a beach and some willing *señorita*. Hell, damn plane was worth serious bucks, even if the damn ex-Commies were flooding the globe with them. Spare parts alone would keep him in margaritas for the rest of his life.

He hated margaritas.

Could always fly to Brazil and look up that Defense Ministry honcho.

Have to refuel a few million times. Not even Raven could make it there on a full tank.

Knife held the MiG steady at fifteen thousand feet, watching the radar as it caught and painted the Flighthawks west of him. They altered course slightly to run by him. They'd turn, pretend to catch him from the rear—and all he could do was take it.

This was what he'd been reduced to—playing target sled for Monkey Brain.

Aboard Hawkmother
18 February, 1141

MADRONE PUSHED HAWKS ONE AND TWO AHEAD, CLOSing on the enemy fighter, precisely as planned. The MiG's radar spotted his two planes, but held course as they'd planned.

If it were a real encounter, he would have flown the U/MFs much differently. C^3 gave him several suggestions. The best had the two-ship split up right about now, with Hawk One vanishing into the ground clutter before beginning an end run toward the MiG's rear, where its radar coverage was poor. Then Hawk Two would disappear as well.

Smith would finally find Hawk One gunning for his tail. His only option would be to flood the afterburners and speed straight away, outrunning his adversary.

Which would take him into the second Flighthawk, waiting ahead. The small planes could outmaneuver the MiG; no matter what the bandit did, Madrone would get one pass with his cannon.

And one pass was all he needed.

But not today. Today he had to swing around the back, just as they'd mapped it out.

Make more sense to mount a front-quarter attack, rake the SOB. Not a high probability in a conventional fighter, but the Flighthawks and C^3 wouldn't miss.

The computer glowed at the top of his head.

Why not do it, just for giggles? Frost that asshole Smith and his jerk-face smirk.

Aboard Sharkishki
18 February, 1145

MACK RAN HIS EYES OVER HIS INSTRUMENTS. HIS RIGHT engine had the temp indicator pegged at the extreme edge of the acceptable range, a bit hotter than the left. Fuel burn seemed constant, and the two power plants seemed to be working in unison. Mack suspected the gauge was flaky—he was always suspecting gauges were flaky.

As he looked back at the windscreen, he realized the two Flighthawks had deviated from the planned course. Instead of flying in the planned arc, they were heading straight for him.

Oh, real funny, Zen.

"Yo, Gameboy, we sticking to the program or do I get to shoot these suckers down?" he asked.

"Gameboy to Hawk Leader," boomed Zen over the circuit. "Kevin, you're off course. Is there a problem?"

"Yeah, like I believe you and Monkey Brain didn't cook this up on your private line," said Mack.

He said it, but he didn't transmit. He rolled the MiG, accelerating at the same time as he swooped around to outfox Zen and his nugget sidekick controlling the U/MFs.

Aboard Hawkmother
18 February, 1153

MADRONE COULDN'T TELL AT FIRST WHAT THE MiG WAS doing, and C³ offered no clues. He started to cut power, then realized Sharkishki would try to slice behind his two planes. Kevin nudged Hawk One north, intending to send the two planes in opposite directions, ready for anything Mack might pull.

Pain crashed into his skull, pushing him back in his chair. He gave the computer full control of the two robots. The fight drifted to the edge of his consciousness as the heavy control helmet seemed to shear his skull in half. The crankshaft of an immense engine revolved around and around at the top of his head, its counterweights smashing against his cranium, pounding through the bone into the gray matter beneath. Madrone tried to relieve the pressure, but couldn't, felt himself weighted down, pushed back by the pain.

He heard a tapping noise somewhere in the com set.

Rain.

His Theta metaphor.

Relax.

He tried to conjure the jungle, the rain just beginning, the dark shadows around him.

"Knock it off! Knock it off!" screamed Zen.

The rain surged, but the pain backed away. Madrone realized he was hyperventilating. He controlled his breaths, let his shoulders droop, found Hawk One and Two under control, approaching from opposite ends toward the MiG; the computer had followed his directions without being distracted by his pain.

"Knock it off!" repeated Zen.

"Hawk Leader acknowledges," said Madrone, retaking control of the planes and sending them back toward their prearranged course.

"What the hell happened there?" said Zen.

He seemed to be talking to Kevin, but it was Mack Smith in the MiG who responded.

"Microchip Boy came at me for a front-quarter attack," said Smith. "I just waxed his tail."

"You were out of line," said Zen.

"I held the wrong course a little too long," said Madrone. The pain was gone; it had been an aberration, probably because he'd been breathing too fast. "Let's try it again."

"I think we ought to go home," said Stockard.

"Jeez Louise, I can't make a mistake?" Madrone snapped.

"Come on, Zen. Don't be a baby," said Mack. "Just because I spanked Junior."

"I think we could run through the scenario again," said Geraldo. Her voice sounded like a soothing whisper; Kevin caught a glimpse of her, standing at the side of him, long hair, much younger.

How did he see her beyond his visor array?

His mind projected her, just as it did with the Flighthawks.

No, not like that. But it felt the same.

His memory created the image. But it had distorted it as well. She didn't really look like that; he'd never seen her that young.

"You sure, Kevin?" asked Zen.

"Let's go for it," said Madrone.

"All right. Everybody back to their starting positions. This time, exactly as we planned."

Aboard Raven
18 February, 1213

"WHAT HAPPENED?" BREANNA ASKED JEFF AS SHE BE-
gan the bank at the end of the racetrack pattern they were
flying.

"Kindergarten bullshit."

Bree said nothing as she pulled the Megafortress through
the lazy turn. They were at thirty-five thousand feet, well
above the action. Jeff's annoyance was interesting; while it
was true that Madrone and Smith had disregarded the planned
scenario, Jeff himself had said during the briefing that they
could freelance as circumstances allowed. Granted, it was
early in the exercise, but the fact that Madrone had taken the
initiative there seemed to her a good thing.

Kevin had definitely changed since ANTARES began. He
was more confident, more self-assured. He seemed to be
working out; his chest and arms had bulked. She was annoyed
with him, though—he'd made, but then blown off, a date with
her friend Abby.

Very un-Madrone-like. But people did weird things when
they were in love.

"They're in position," said Chris Ferris, her copilot.

"Try it again," said Jeff over the shared circuit.

Aboard Hawkmother
18 February, 1227

KEVIN STEADIED THE TWO ROBOT PLANES ON THEIR
course. Actually, the flight computer did—he simply acqui-
esced to its suggested course.

Maybe Mack was right. Kevin was just a monkey here; the
computer could fly the planes without him.

True enough, but that didn't make him useless or unim-
portant. On the contrary. He could go anywhere. He had no
limits. He told the computer what to do, and it did it.

What had the red shock of pain been? He didn't have control over that. It was a storm that had struck without warning.

He could go anywhere. He hadn't completed an actual refueling yet—that was on tomorrow's agenda. But he had no doubt he could master it. And then, what were the limits?

Whatever his mind flowed into, ANTARES, the gateway, C^3—those were the limits.

He could get beyond them. He didn't want to be tethered to dotted lines laid out on maps. He wasn't a monkey boy or microchip brain or whatever Smith decided to call him—he was beyond that.

Madrone felt a twinge in his temple, the hint of the headache returning. He concentrated on his breathing, and the twinge receded into the pink space beyond the edge of his vision.

Where did it go? He slid out toward it, focusing his thoughts into a kind of greenish cone, his curiosity forming into a shape. But he couldn't penetrate the haze; his vision darkened and he began falling out of Theta.

He heard the rain of the forest, returned to full control. He moved the Flighthawks farther apart, closing on the MiG at ten miles.

C^3 gave him a warning: *"Connection degrading."* The Flighthawks had extended to nearly twenty miles ahead of Hawkmother. The 777 couldn't keep up.

He backed off his speed. He hadn't been paying enough attention. He had to learn to segregate his thoughts, to monitor the computer but to think beyond it as well.

The difficulty was the pain.

Maybe. He didn't have control of everything, not even his own mind, not yet anyway. It worked in a way he didn't completely understand or control.

The MiG sat at the apex of a V, dead meat between his two planes, his two hands.

If his curiosity were a snake, it would slither beyond the edge of his brain, over the round seam that marked the end of his universe.

The autopilot system of the Boeing. Thick metal levers and motors.

No vision, but the radar.

Safety protocols suspended. The autopilot was off. It was helpless, just watching.

Could he switch it on?

No. Yes?

No. It was off.

Could he be in all three planes at once? Guide them all? Hawkmother's seat felt foreign to him, deliciously unfamiliar, spiking his taste buds.

He slipped. His body began to sink.

He could hold it.

The tingle again. A harsh red circle around his head. A massive band of pressure, thick oily pressure erupting below his head, his neck on fire, the flames of pain consuming the center of his being.

Aboard Sharkishki
18 February, 1250

MACK'S ALTITUDE HELD STEADY AT 7,500 METERS, roughly 22,500 feet. The Flighthawks passed by and began banking for their attack. Monkey Brain was doing it by the book this time, and so did he, flying exactly on the prebriefed course.

Kick on the afterburner, tuck down, head for the open sea. Be over the Pacific in what? An hour?

Easy. Except with the afterburner he'd blow through his fuel and bail out over Baja.

Go west, young man—buzz L.A. Why the hell not? His career was toast anyway.

If the future really was bleak, maybe he should look up that Brazilian geezer. Or just hang it all and fly airliners for a living.

Yeah, right. That was fine for some guys. Hell, you couldn't argue with the bucks or the time off. But Mack needed more; he needed the edge.

The Flighthawks roared up behind him, closing to point-blank cannon range. They were directly behind his wings, vectored at a slight angle.

"Bang-bang you got me," he said over the radio.

Then he realized they weren't stopping.

Aboard Hawkmother
18 February, 1257

GERALDO'S VOICE BURST ALL AROUND HIM.

"You're off the chart," she told Kevin. "The peaks are overlapping. Your heartbeat is at one-fifty. Your brain waves are off the chart."

Did she mean he was out of control? Pain pressed against him from all different directions. His head was a block of glass being broken into a million jagged pieces.

Except that if it were glass, the pain would have stopped. Madrone tried to breathe, tried to relax—he forced himself back into the jungle, into his Theta metaphor, the pathway for his control.

Someone spoke to him, a woman with a deep voice. From behind the greens and browns and blacks. She spoke Geraldo's words, urging him to breathe slowly, but it wasn't the middle-aged psychiatrist speaking; it was a dark woman, a beautiful woman.

Karen, his wife.

No, not Karen. Someone infinitely more beautiful. He could see her through the dark trees. Rain streamed down her naked body, coursing over her breasts and hips.

Come to me, darling. Come.

The Flighthawks were above him. They had a target in sight, closing on a collision course.

C^3's safety protocols had been suspended.

Who did that? Had he?

The pain flashed in waves. Madrone tried to push himself back into the Flighthawks, back into control.

Aboard Sharkishki
18 February, 1301

MACK PUSHED HIS LEFT WING DOWN, DROPPING THE MiG into a violent, sliding dive. The Flighthawks had caught him flat-footed; they were closing so fast he couldn't even hit his afterburner and rely on his superior speed to get away. All he could do was duck.

He slammed the MiG through a series of hard rolls, taking close to ten g's as he jerked violently down, the MiG just barely controllable. Gravity pirouetted against the sides of his body, punching so hard that even the advanced flight suit he wore couldn't ward off all of the pressure. A black cowl closed around his head. His eyes stopped working together;

he saw the world as two circles of spinning blue and brown in a thick bowl of grayness. Knife lost sight of his instruments, of the cockpit; he flew by dizzy feel, the stick his only consciousness.

Somehow he pulled out as the spin threatened to overwhelm him. Somehow he managed to get the MiG moving in the direction opposite the one he'd started in, gaining speed.

Knife pushed his wings flat. The world expanded around him, the effects of oxygen deprivation receding. One of the Flighthawks shot ahead, well off his left wing, but where the hell was the other?

He started to move his head around the cockpit, and belatedly realized he was flying upside down. Still disoriented, he swooped right, losing three thousand feet in a roll that brought him nearly to the desert floor.

The second U/MF was on his tail, over him about five hundred feet, still trying to close.

Knife knew he should call time-out, push the mike button and yell knock it off. He might already have done that—his brain was so scrambled he couldn't remember whether he had or not.

But Goddamnit. If Zen and his shadow were going to play for keeps, so was he.

He forced his hand to the throttle, notching his speed back. He could feel the Flighthawk trying to close.

He'd pull his nose up at the last second, send the son of a bitch right into the dead lake bed. Easy as pie, as long as he kept his head clear and his speed up high enough to avoid stalling.

Madrone would smash the $500-million Flighthawk to bits. Let him explain that, the SOB.

Aboard Hawkmother
18 February, 1307

KEVIN'S THOUGHTS AND IDEAS STREAMED THROUGH THE blue sky, comets jittering and disintegrating. He thought of sending the Flighthawks crashing into the MiG.

The idea remained there, a contrail in the jungle sky.

He grabbed for it desperately, trying to wipe it away.

"Knock it off! Knock it off!" Zen yelled.

The red disappeared. The sky and rain forest disappeared. And then he felt Hawk Two, felt the wind coursing below his wings. He relaxed, put his nose up, and circled away from the MiG, breaking pursuit.

Kevin's head pounded; his heart thumped against his chest. He wanted to turn the two robot planes back over to their flight computer, but he dared not. He couldn't be sure what other ideas sat out there, ghosts ready to jump in and take control.

"What the hell's going on, Kevin?" asked Stockard.

"Hawks One and Two returning to base," he answered. "Requesting permission to land."

Aboard Raven
18 February, 1313

ZEN PUNCHED THE TRANSMISSION SWITCH ANGRILY. THIS time it had clearly been Kevin's fault; Mack had flown the pattern perfectly until the Flighthawks homed in on his tail. If anything, Mack had waited too long to take evasive maneuvers. It was a miracle there hadn't been a collision, and at least a minor miracle that he hadn't lost Sharkishki.

Jeff had screwed up too. He hadn't told them to knock it off soon enough, hadn't taken over the Flighthawks the instant his command wasn't obeyed.

Why? Because he thought he'd been a little too harsh on the first go-around?

"What are we doing, Gameboy?" asked Mack. He sounded winded, his voice hoarse.

"Calling it a day," said Jeff. "Return to base."

Dreamland Security Office
18 February, 1315

DANNY SLID INTO HIS DESK CHAIR AND OPENED THE folder of FBI foreign-contact alerts in his lap. Officially known as Monthly Referral of Foreign and Suspicious Contacts (Form 23-756FBI/DIA), the five pages of eight-point single-spaced type strained Danny's eyes as well as his patience. The report compiled rumors and rumors of rumors about base personnel and their alleged contacts with foreigners; he was required to acknowledge any that pertained to Dreamland personnel and indicate what he intended to do about it. If the report had added anything to base security, he might have at least felt more comfortable about it, but the real goal was clearly COA—cover our ass—on the FBI's part. Every conference a Dreamland scientist attended was listed, along with a roster of foreigners; any potential contact was noted by Bureau spies or sources. An engineer who found himself in the same cafeteria line with a British journalist would rate a paragraph. If he'd been served by a Mexican national, he'd get two paragraphs. And if he'd had the misfortune to be at the cashier when a Russian scientist entered the room, he'd get an entire page.

Danny skimmed through the report with as much attention as he could muster, looking for "his" people. Lee Ong had been to a lecture sponsored by the Department of Energy on utilizing computers for some sort of nuclear-test thing; someone from Taiwan had been there. Blah-blah-blah.

Freah yawned his way through the rest of the report until he came to a three-paragraph account detailing a "contact meeting" between Major Mack Smith and a high-ranking member of the Brazilian defense establishment. The details were trivial—the FBI agent fussed over the cigars they had smoked—Cuban Partagas, blatantly illegal, blah-blah-blah.

Brazil was said to be trying to buy MiGs from the Russians, the agent added, almost as an afterthought.

Danny hit a combination of keys on the computer, calling up a file that compiled data from foreign-contact forms—official paperwork that was supposed to be filed by certain key personnel when they were approached by a foreign national.

Smith hadn't reported the incident.

Not necessarily a big deal. Except that he was assigned to the top-secret Advanced MiG project.

Danny reached to the end of the desk, pulling over his thermos to pour a cup of coffee while the computer fetched Major Smith's personnel records.

Flighthawk Control Bunker
18 February, 1400

ZEN PUSHED THROUGH THE CONFERENCE ROOM DOUBLE doors so fast he nearly slammed into Chris Ferris, who was reaching for one of the doors.

"Knock if off means *knock it the fuck off*," he said loudly, wheeling toward the large table at the front of the room where the rest of the ANTARES/Flighthawk team had gathered. Everyone in the room froze.

Everyone except the two people the comment was directed at.

"No shit," said Mack.

"I did knock it off," said Madrone.

"You didn't knock it off fast enough," Jeff told him. He pushed on the right wheel of his chair, maneuvering as if he were a fighter lining up his enemy in his gunsight. "What the hell happened?"

"Nothing happened," said Madrone.

"You got that close on purpose?"

"I wasn't close."

Zen whipped his chair around, facing Mack. He'd expected Smith to be wearing his usual smirk, but instead found the pilot frowning.

Maybe the encounter had actually done some good, instilling a sense of humility in the conceited jerk.

Fat chance.

"What's your excuse?" said Zen to Mack.

"Aw, fuck you, Stockard. He's the one who screwed up."

"You didn't break off right away."

"I don't have to put up with this bullshit." Mack started for the door.

"Hey. Smith. Smith!"

Jeff wheeled after him, then stopped a few feet from the door, impotent as Mack stormed away.

He told himself to calm down—his job was to keep everything professional, not throw kerosene on the fire. Jeff wheeled back toward the front of the room, corralling his temper. The different tapes of the mission were stacked near the players; an airman assigned as one of the mission assistants waited at full attention near the machine, his bottom lip trembling. Jeff slid near him, trying to smile.

"At ease, Jimmy. Relax," he whispered. "Breathe."

"Yes, sir," said the young man, who neither relaxed nor stopped trembling.

"Okay," said Zen, willing his vocal chords to project their characteristically soothing, in-control tone. "Let's go through this, from the top, bit by bit."

BREE WATCHED HER HUSBAND AS HE STRUGGLED TO maintain control. Long before she'd met him, he'd earned his nickname "Zen" because he could be calm under the worst circumstances. That, of course, was before the accident; since then, Jeff had much less patience for minor annoyances, and tended to struggle to project his former calm.

It wasn't just the accident. Jeff seemed uneasy with being in charge—or rather, with standing back and letting other people take control. He wanted to jump in and do it himself.

Unlike her father. Bastian wouldn't have roared in cursing. He would have found a way to make Kevin and Mack feel like peas, if that's what he wanted them to feel like, yet stay in the room and actually learn something.

Bree still thought Jeff was overreacting, at least a little. The review of the C^3 control tapes showed that the safety parameters had somehow gotten turned off—a programming glitch that Little Miss Jennifer Gleason was responsible for, though no one seemed to want to say so out loud.

Breanna watched Gleason flick back her hair as she tried to account for the problem. She looked more like a '60's hippie than a scientist on a military base.

Most of the men panted after her.

Not Jeff. And if Gleason tried anything in that direction, she'd scratch the little banshee's eyes out.

Dreamland Administrative Offices ("Taj"), Level 1
18 February, 1545

DANNY CAUGHT COLONEL BASTIAN ON HIS WAY OUT OF his office for a lunch so late it could be considered dinner.

"Talk to me," said the colonel, waving off Sergeant Gibbs as he headed for the door.

Freah followed silently as Bastian made his getaway. Bastian grumbled about something, passing the elevator in favor of the stairs. He swiped his card in the reader and pushed through the door, practically leaping from the landing to the steps as he did his customary double time up to ground level, where the general cafeteria was.

"So?" he asked.

"I have to talk to you in private," said Freah. "Personnel matter."

Bastian stopped abruptly. "Why didn't you tell me?"

"Hard to get a word in these days."

Dog smiled. He folded his arms around each other in front of his chest and leaned against the metal pipe of the railing, as deliberate in his nonchalance as he had been in his rush. "This private enough?"

The entire building was swept for bugs daily; everyone entering the building passed through a sensor array that beeped if a paper clip or earring was out of place. In theory, it was as secure as anywhere on the base except the command bunker.

Still, it was a stairwell.

"Go ahead, Danny," prompted Bastian. "What's bothering you?"

Danny told him about Smith and the Brazilian official. No one knew what the two men had been talking about, but the Brazilians had been inquiring about MiG sales with the Russians. At the same time, there were rumblings in the Brazilian government about military takeovers and coups.

"None of what you've said implicates Mack in any way," said Bastian when he was finished.

"I know that," said Danny. "Except that he didn't report the contact."

"You sure somebody didn't start this as a rumor to nail him? Smith is not the most liked person in the world."

Freah shrugged. His team had pulled Mack out of the Mediterranean during the Somalian matter, rescuing him after disabling the plane his kidnappers were fleeing in. Otherwise, Freah had had very little contact with the man.

"I'm not accusing him of anything except not noting the

contact," said Freah. "In and of itself, that doesn't call for the death penalty. However—"

"However it's not good," agreed Bastian. "What do you suggest?"

"Full security check for starters. Tail him when he's off base. Do the phones, the whole shebang."

"Pretty big invasion of privacy for forgetting to fill out a form."

Danny didn't say anything. Bastian finally sighed.

"All right. Go for it," he said. "I have a temporary assignment for him as a liaison with the Department of Energy; it's due to start in a week or two."

"I don't know, Colonel. It's classified?"

"Yes, but it's one of those BS things—it involves reviewing sites that are about to be closed for possible test sites. It was mandated by the last Congress, but the Administration has pretty much already dictated what the report should be. It's a holding pattern for him until a prime spot comes up."

"Doing what?"

"F-22. Mack would go in as the operations director on the test squadron. Important job—assuming he takes it. He's turned down everything anyone's offered so far."

"I don't know if I'd sign off security-wise."

"Well, the liaison thing will give you time to form a definite opinion, no?"

Danny nodded.

"You really think he's a traitor?" said Dog, his voice more incredulous than before.

Freah shrugged. "I learned when I was a kid you can never read somebody else's mind."

"Well, my mind says I'm hungry. How about some lunch?"

"Colonel, it's almost dinnertime."

Bastian smiled as if he were apologizing for having so much to do he couldn't get out for lunch.

"I have to get this going," said Danny. He took a step down. "I'm going to need you to sign the finding," he added, referring to the paperwork that allowed the procedures to proceed.

"After lunch I'm going over to the Megafortress simulator," said the colonel, glancing at his watch. "Half hour there, maybe forty-five minutes, then back to the office. Catch me and I'll sign."

"Can't get enough of the Megafortress, huh?" asked Danny.

"Hey, the computer tells me I'm getting good," said Bastian, resuming his upward jog.

Dreamland Bunker B, Subbasement
18 February, 1545

KEVIN PUNCHED THE SIDE OF THE HALLWAY WALL AS HE walked to the elevator. He hated Jeff. Who the hell did he think he was, criticizing him? No one else in the freaking fucking world had mastered ANTARES, and the Flighthawks, and the interface, and all the other crap so quickly, so easily as he had.

Damn him. Damn him.

"Kevin, excuse me."

Madrone turned and saw Geraldo, hurrying toward him. He felt an impulse to jump into the elevator and shut the door, but resisted, waiting for her.

"Thank you," she said. As they got into the car, he saw how old she was, how old and small. He'd never noticed it before.

"What happened during the last exercise?" she asked.

He shrugged. "I told you. Nothing."

"I saw wave patterns I've never seen before. Explain to me what you felt."

"I felt, you know, like I was flying. I had control of the planes."

"Did you?"

"I may not be as good a pilot as Zen or Smith," he said, "but I'm getting there."

She looked at him oddly. He resisted the impulse to keep talking—that was how they got you.

Was she one of them?

"How have you been sleeping?" she asked.

"Fine."

She put her hand to his skull where the spider had been implanted. Her touch was gentle, but still he winced. "Headaches?"

"No."

"This doesn't hurt?"

"No."

"You're afraid when I touch?"

"No."

She pulled her hand down, smiling as if she had caught him in a fib. "We have a battery of tests we need to do." She glanced at her watch. "Eat first. I'll see you in an hour from now."

"Yup." He fixed his gaze on the floor. His head had been fine until she asked about headaches—now his temples felt like they would implode.

"Are you ready to fly without me?" she asked.

"You don't think I can handle ANTARES alone?"

The words came out so harshly they snapped her back. Madrone felt her stare stoking the pain in his head.

He couldn't afford to have her as an enemy.

"I'm sorry," he said. "I'm just a little tired. The, uh, the exercises wear me out."

"Of course. I understand," she said in a tone that suggested otherwise.

The elevator arrived at the main level. He smiled, ducking his head against the light, letting Geraldo go first. "I'm going to get some lunch," he told her.

She nodded and walked out of the hangar.

Madrone remained standing a few feet from the elevator on the long cement ramp. He put his hand on the metal rail, felt its coolness. He was tempted to put his head on it, let the cold metal soften the throb, but there were others around; they'd think it odd.

Aspirin, he told himself. He needed to get something for the headache.

He didn't have any back at his quarters.

Quarters—a stinking tiny little room the size of an old-fashioned phone booth.

He deserved better—he deserved a mansion with a pool and someone to fix dinner, someone to greet him at the door in a silk nightgown, fold him into her arms, lay back while he bonked her brains out.

Red railroad spikes smashed into his head.

He didn't want violent sex. He wanted to wrap himself in

the warm rain, he wanted to sleep, he wanted to breathe slowly, he wanted to escape, escape, escape.

Dreamland Bunker B, Computer Lab
18 February, 1600

JENNIFER GLEASON PULLED THE LAPTOP CLOSER TO her, punching the function buttons to redisplay the graphs. Sometimes it was easier to use the visual displays of the different control segments to catch anomalies in the programming, but the graphs were smooth.

The fact that C^3 had turned off the safety protocols bothered the hell out of her. The fact that she couldn't figure out why bothered her even more. But she believed she could isolate the problem; there was a flood of integer overflows in the code mandating approval of the pilot that either accounted for the error or would show where it started.

More worrisome was C^3's decision to ram the aggressor.

Assuming it had been C^3. Tracking Madrone's commands through the electroencephalogram graphs and the gateway registers could be tricky and time-consuming; ANTARES kicked up a lot of back-and-forth and superfluous code. But the major commands were all marked out clearly.

There was no indication C^3 had given the command either.

Jennifer slid over to another display, keying up a set of numbers that corresponded to command flags originating in the robots themselves. Even when flown directly by the remote pilot, the Flighthawks actually carried out many of the flight functions themselves. To lessen the communications burden between the main computer—C^3—and the planes, most of these were precoded in the robots' onboard brains. The Flighthawks, for example, could be told to land at such and such a place and would do so without further instruction, setting their own speed, trimming control surfaces, etc. Several two-and four-plane formations were hardwired in, as was the command to close on another plane's tail. Combining different commands would lead the planes to recognize an enemy, close to gun range, and fire.

Perhaps the error was in the fire command itself, or the

combination, she realized. It seemed far-fetched, since the presets had been thoroughly tested without incident for nearly two years.

The fire flag was not depressed.

But that didn't make sense—it *should* have been set by C³ at the top of the exercise.

The flags directing the planes to close weren't set either.

C³ could have sent a flow of commands to the planes for each movement. In other words, it had either not realized the command was in its library—unlikely—or decided not to bother with the preset—even more unlikely.

Jennifer wound a thick stalk of hair at the back of her neck around her forefinger and pulled at the roots. She was going to have to dump all of the com code from that sequence and go over it line by line. And she was going to have to do it on hard copy. It would take all night, at least.

Wearily, she punched in the commands and went to make sure the big laser printer was on. As the printing drum sucked up the first sheet of paper, Jennifer walked to the far side of the lab where Mr. Coffee sat alone on a long work bench. She took the carafe and started toward the door to fill it in the rest room down the hall. But then she realized she had the printer running; security regulations forbade her from leaving the room until it was finished, which wouldn't be for quite some time.

Fortunately, she had a jug of water for just such emergencies. She retrieved it from the bottom filing cabinet next to the old Cray and emptied it into Mr. Coffee, leaving it out on the bench so she'd remember to refill it later. Then she spooned some grinds into the paper filter and started the machine.

Only two more filters left. Have to remember to pick some up.

Waiting for the coffee to brew, she thought about her visit back home for Christmas. Her family lived in a large farmhouse in frigid northern Minnesota. As a girl, she'd stood before the front window with its sixteen small panes of glass, watching the sun rise over the glittering field across the road, the brown heads of weeds fluttering with the wind. The light flooded into the house from the window, turning everything bright and blurring the face of the grandfather clock near the fireplace.

She missed the sun, but not the cold.

Although Nevada could be damn cold too. She shivered a little, sliding her coffee cup across the black Formica top of the table as Mr. Coffee began doing his thing.

The door to the lab whooshed open behind her. Jennifer glanced back and saw Kevin Madrone standing awkwardly just inside the doorway.

"Kevin, come on in," she said, pulling out the carafe. A drip of coffee slipped past the drip guard on the hot plate. "Want some coffee?"

"How about aspirin?"

"Aspirin?" She filled her cup and slid the pot back into place. The coffeemaker spat a pent-up stream into the carafe, hissing loudly. "I think there's aspirin in the ladies room down the hall. Want me to get you some?"

As she turned back to face him, she realized he wasn't by the door anymore—he was next to her, so close he startled her. He started to say something, his hand reached for hers; confused, she jerked her hand up, forgetting she had the cup in it. The liquid flew wildly, splashing all over Madrone.

He stepped back, stunned for a moment. Then he plucked at the top of his flight suit and cursed.

"Shit! Shit! This is hot!"

"Oh, God, I'm sorry," she said, putting the cup down on the bench. "You just—you startled me."

"Why did you do that, you bitch?" said Madrone. His face turned red and his whole body seemed to rise up. Jennifer froze, overwhelmed and suddenly powerless to move. Madrone raised his right hand, and the space seemed to shrink to nothing, her world evaporating into a void of fear. Jennifer felt her throat click; she tried to raise her hands to fend off the oncoming storm, but could not.

"What's going on?"

The loud, sharp voice froze everything. Jennifer took a step back, glancing toward the door. Colonel Bastian was standing in the doorway.

"I uh, I spilled some coffee on me by accident," said Madrone.

Jennifer looked up at his face. Had she imagined his anger?

He looked small and meek, completely perplexed. The top of his flight suit was soaked with the hot liquid; a few drops plopped down onto the floor.

"Actually, I spilled it," Jennifer heard herself say. "I was working and I didn't quite hear Captain Madrone come in. When I turned around he was there and I'm afraid he startled me. I'm sorry, Kevin. Here, there are some paper towels right here."

But Madrone had already started away, head down, passing Bastian and continuing out into the hallway.

"Something wrong here?" the colonel asked her.

"Oh, no." She smiled weakly, then retrieved the paper towels to clean up the coffee from the floor.

God, he must think I'm a loony, she thought to herself.

"I was—I get wrapped up in my work sometimes," she said. She bent to the floor and began wiping up the mess. "I can be a real slob. I think I burned him."

"We can get someone to clean that up," suggested Bastian.

"By the time they clear security it'll evaporate," she said, trying to joke. Jennifer rubbed the sodden towel on the floor, scraping her fingertips. She pulled the roll close to her, worked her way slowly across the puddle. After watching for a while, Colonel Bastian bent, picked up the pile of wadded towels, and carried them dripping to the wastebasket.

She wanted to jump up and kiss him, feel his arms around her.

Wouldn't that be the topper—then he'd know she was crazy.

Bastian picked up her plastic coffee mug and refilled it as she finished cleaning the mess.

"Vikings, huh?" he asked, handing it to her.

It took a second for her to realize he was referring to the logo on the mug.

"Oh, yeah. Well, I'm from Minnesota." She looked into his steel-gray eyes for a moment, then glanced to the floor.

"I was wondering if you would kick on the Megafortress simulator for me," said Bastian. "Major Cheshire has gone home and I can't find Bree or anyone else."

"Oh," she said.

She would do anything for him. Anything.

The print dump. She couldn't leave it. Security.

He wanted her too, didn't he? His eyes said so.

No, not really. Jennifer took a sip of the coffee. "I would, but I have a job running through the printer and it's going to take forty-five minutes. I can't leave the room. Security." She shrugged. "It's a little silly, but—"

"No, no, that's okay," said Bastian.

He started for the door. Don't leave, she thought. Don't leave.

God, was she really in love?

The door whisked closed as she considered the question.

Dreamland Dorms, Pink Building
18 February, 2345

LYING ON HIS COT, KEVIN FELT A THOUSAND KNIVES JAB his head from every angle, tearing and twisting the gray matter of his brain. He'd taken four aspirin and two Tylenol besides, tried a hot shower and Geraldo's tea, yet felt as bad as ever.

What had happened this afternoon with Jennifer? The memory was lost behind the shards of colored glass prying open his brain. Karen was there, beautiful Karen, her eyes turning into snakes, her tongue fire.

And then Christina, his daughter, lying in the middle of the floor, crying softly but incessantly. Her sob reverberated in his head, his body trembling.

He couldn't save her.

Geraldo and her assistants had run him through a battery of tests. She said he passed them all—he knew he passed them all. But something was happening to him.

The headache. Geraldo said it was normal.

It wasn't as if he'd gone his entire life without headaches.

If he'd known Christina would die before she was two, he'd never have had her.

She rose from the floor. She walked toward him, sobbing, holding out her chubby fingers.

Kevin jerked upright. He felt as if he were still connected to ANTARES. His mind spread out before him.

He held his hand to his daughter. Her soft flesh brushed against his fingertips.

A team of doctors pulled him back as they touched. The doctors were laughing and sneering at him.

The pain flashed.

He was dreaming; he'd fallen asleep.

He could make it stop if he could breathe. He could make it stop if he could breathe.

He could breathe. Picture the air at the bottom of your lungs and push it up slowly. Very, very slowly.

"Push the air up slowly."

It was Geraldo's voice, but it wasn't her. The dark woman stood at the rim of his vision, hidden in the trees. He got control of his breath, pushed the air in and out slowly, very slowly. Rain began to fall. The harsh light that had hurt his eyes retreated. He was in the forest.

"Breathe slowly," she told him. "Gently."

Jennifer?

No, Jennifer was thin, almost a wisp, with light hair. This woman's shadow was thick and dark, more seductive, moving from beyond the trees. He reached for her. The pain crescendoed.

When he stopped screaming, Kevin found that he had fallen from the bed and was lying stark naked on the cold floor.

Allegro, Nevada
18 February, 2352

THE DREAM WAS FAMILIAR NOW, EVEN WITH ITS SLIGHT variations. Jeff sat on the beach as the sun rose midway in the sky, its brilliant red gradually fading to black. A cube appeared to grow from the center of this blackness, shining and yet still black somehow. The cube spun slowly, revealing itself as a three-dimensional computer chip coursed by veins and arteries. Sometimes he could see the blood pulsing in the veins; sometimes he saw millions of faces like reflections in the tiny solder points on the surface of the cube. But always what happened next was the same—as the cube expanded he realized it was growing inside his brain, obliterating him.

At that point he woke up. Always.

Jeff knew the dream was about ANTARES. He'd been

thinking about the project a lot, debating whether or not to volunteer as a subject.

Geraldo had suggested that he start the sessions again at some point, though she hadn't brought it up.

Getting back into Theta would be easy. He still had the chip with its connections to his nerve endings implanted in his skull.

He'd thought of having it removed when he returned to Dreamland. But while he'd been told the operation wasn't particularly difficult, he feared it could harm his vision and hearing. His legs were useless; he couldn't survive any other loss.

Bree said something in her sleep and rolled over, away from him.

Did he want to fly like that, though, using ANTARES? Letting the computer come into his head, suggest things—it wasn't flying. He might as well be at a desk, checking off to-do lists.

Was what he did now flying? Strapped into a special chair, pushing a pair of joysticks and watching the world through a high-tech video screen?

Zen shifted his head on the pillow. ANTARES didn't take over your brain. You did the thinking yourself, sending impulses the way you would move your legs and arms. Ultimately, you were responsible for everything—including your dreams and fears.

So why was he afraid of it? Why hadn't he insisted that he be the subject?

He knew that as he was currently the only Flighthawk pilot available, shifting to ANTARES full-time would have set the U/MF program behind schedule. But he could have insisted.

Was he scared? He'd done okay with ANTARES, but had never particularly liked the sensation. Now Geraldo had added powerful new drugs to the mix, actually changing body chemistry.

Kevin had changed in the short time since he'd been in the program. He'd become more—what was the word? Not just aggressive exactly, more just a jerk.

ANTARES? More likely a side of him Zen had never noticed before.

Tomorrow, he'd talk to Geraldo. Not about Madrone—

about becoming a subject again, or at least getting ready. He'd have to clear it with Bastian, of course, but in the end, he'd do it. There was no other choice.

Breanna rolled over again, this time toward him. She pushed her arm over his chest and back around his neck, nuzzling close. Zen turned his head to kiss her, slipping back toward the heavy blanket of sleep.

Dolphin Helicopter Transport
Approaching Dreamland
19 February, 0600

MACK SMITH FOLDED THE NEWSPAPER BACK IN DISGUST, just barely stopping himself from flinging it onto the floor of the helicopter.

"Team lose?" asked his fellow passenger, a jet-propulsion engineer named Brian Daily.

"Hardly," said Smith. He gave Daily a sideways glance. Ordinarily he wouldn't bother with him, but the story had pissed him off. "Fucking *L.A. Times*. You know what it says?"

Daily shrugged. The freckles on his face seemed to blanch a bit as Mack unfolded the paper and pointed to the article.

"Israeli Defenses Stand Down from Full Alert," said Daily, reading the headline. The article was a longish analysis of the state of the Israeli military, with three typos that Mack had seen without even paying much attention.

"No, it's this bullshit that pisses me off," said Smith. "Pound for pound, the best air force. Pound for pound, my fucking ass."

Daily tried peering at the article while at the same time leaning away from Mack in the seat. "I don't think they mean that as a slam."

"It's bullshit," said Mack.

"Jeez, relax back there, Major," said the copilot, twisting around from the front. "What's got you frosted?"

"Ah, nothing," said Smith. He twirled his arms around each other, pushing his head down toward his chest.

Why was he so frosted? Things like that were total crap, written by jerks who didn't have a clue what they were talking about. No disrespect toward the Israelis, who after all were kick-ass pilots, but *pound for pound the best*? Better than the American Air Force, which had whipped Saddam's butt a few years before? Hell, the stinking Marines were better, pound for pound. Even the Navy, for christsake.

No offense intended to the Israelis.

His rage was so great, Mack began racking his brain to see what he really was angry about. Not having a job—that was the problem.

And really, he'd been hard on Bastian the other day. He ought to apologize. And see if maybe Bastian had something for him yet.

Fresh off the helo, Mack headed to Bastian's office, jostling past the obnoxious Sergeant Gibbs and sailing into Dog's inner sanctum with a half knock and a hearty "Hey, Colonel." He slid over one of the visitors' chairs, leaning forward with his elbows on the armrests.

"I was a jerk the other day, cutting in front of the egghead," he told Bastian, waiting for the colonel to quickly persuade him that he was wrong.

"Why are you here?" Bastian replied.

"I was a jerk," Mack told him, still waiting.

Bastian glanced toward the door, where Sergeant Gibbs was standing.

"I will have a cup of coffee, Sergeant," said Smith, following the glance. "That'd be nice."

The barest hint of a frown appeared on Gibbs's face before he retreated into his own domain.

"They broke the mold," said Mack, gesturing toward Gibbs. "Fortunately."

"Yes," said Dog. Even ramrod straight in his chair, Bastian was not a tall man. Still, he dominated the space, his eyes hard in a face that seemed squared at the edges. He wasn't particularly handsome, Mack thought, but looking at him you could tell he was the kind of guy who made a decision and stuck to it.

The colonel slowly reached for his coffee. He took a sip, then spoke.

"As a matter of fact, Mack, I have made a few calls on your behalf, despite our recent interview."

"Oh?"

"There's nothing immediate that comes up to your level of expertise."

"Thanks, Colonel." Mack smiled, expecting Bastian to go on, but he didn't.

Sergeant Gibbs appeared with the coffee.

"Two lumps, huh, Major?"

"I like it sweet, yes," said Mack, taking the cup. He stirred the metal spoon around, tapped it a few times, then took a sip.

Have to give this to the sergeant—he made a mean cup of joe.

"You're on base early this morning," noted Bastian.

"Yes, sir. Running some last tests on the MiG."

"You still working with ANTARES?"

"Don't know that they're flying again today," said Mack. "But if they want me, I'm ready. We're about to shut down Sharkishki anyway. Couple more flights at most."

Someone must have told Bastian about his son-in-law's screwup yesterday, Mack realized. No wonder he was in a bad mood.

Time to change the subject.

"Obviously, I'd like to command a squadron, even if that's not possible right away," Knife told Bastian. "What I thought might work would be to go in as number two somewhere, you know, with a guy about to move out. Probably over in CentCom," he added, referring to Central Command, which had charge of a number of tactical squadrons and where, he believed, Dog had numerous connections. "Like to hit Italy. Couple of squadrons there, no?"

"Might work," said Bastian. "In the meantime, I have something for you. It's a political plum—temporary assignment with the Department of Energy, inspecting test facilities that are either slated to be closed or already are. They need a report on their suitability for Air Force bases. You can guess what the report's supposed to say," the colonel added.

"Sounds kind of like a—"

"It's definitely a holding pattern, definitely bullshit, but you'll interface with some Pentagon brass along the way," continued Bastian. "If that goes well, I may be able to swing something much better."

"Like?"

"Everything in due time," said Dog.

Mack fought down the impulse to try and wheedle more information.

Hell, he had been a jerk, getting down on the Air Force. Even playing ground FAC with some dusty Army unit in Korea would be a million times better than becoming a civilian. Quit the service and he'd end up flying 727's and learning to play golf.

No disrespect intended.

Mack jumped up, took a long swig of the coffee, and placed the half-full cup on the colonel's desk. "It better be a kick-ass one or I'll farm myself out as a free agent," he joked. "Maybe I'll go to Brazil—some old geezer tried to recruit me last month as a consultant."

Bastian said nothing.

Mack laughed. "Hell, maybe I'll go to work for the Russians. I can fly their planes too. Don't you think, Dog?"

Still nothing from the colonel. Some guys were just humor-impaired.

"Well, listen, Colonel, I won't keep you," said Knife, backing his way toward the door. "I appreciate your trying to help me. Anything you can do, I appreciate it."

Dreamland Flighthawk Hangar
19 February, 0630

"YEAH, RIGHT," SAID SCHNEIDER WITH A LAUGH AS ZEN wheeled into the Flighthawk hangar. "Like you could hit a barn from that distance."

"I did it," insisted Foster.

The two techies were responsible for the robot planes' engine systems. A few other members of the maintenance and prep team were hanging around, reviewing their punch lists and warming up to the day with coffee and some Danishes.

"Hey, Major," said Schneider, turning to Jeff. "Foster here claims he nailed a buck between the eyes from five hundred yards last November back in Pennsylvania with a pistol."

"Three hundred yards, with a Remington rifle," said Foster.

"I could believe that," said Zen, helping himself to some of the coffee but skipping the sweets.

Tough, though. A pineapple Danish practically winked at him.

"And I didn't shoot it in the eyes," added Foster. "You don't aim at a deer's head if you want to hit it."

"You mean you hit it by accident?" said Schneider.

Foster waved his clipboard at his friend. "Twenty-one points, and that's no lie," he told Zen. "You hunt, Major?"

Foster tried to swallow his words; Schneider shuffled his legs nervously. One or two of the other men glanced toward Jeff's wheelchair.

"I'm not much of a hunter," said Jeff, sipping his coffee as nonchalantly as possible. "Freezing my butt off in the woods isn't my idea of recreation. Chair's cold enough as it is."

"Yeah." Foster laughed nervously.

Jeff took a sip of his coffee. When he had first returned to active duty, the awkward silence would have annoyed him—he didn't need, and didn't want, pity. But he'd come pretty far in the last few months. He wasn't at peace with the loss of his legs; that was never, ever going to happen. But the awkwardness of others didn't offend him anymore.

If he'd been in a better mood—if he'd gotten more sleep—he might have made another joke, probably at Schneider's expense; doubtless the coffee fiend couldn't hit anything he was aiming at, starting with the urinal in the bathroom. But Zen just changed the subject, asking what kind of shape the planes were in. The crew dogs fell to with quick and very positive status reports. Four Flighthawks were now considered at full flight status; two more would join them late next month, with another pair ready for static tests and check-flights the month after. Components for additional U/MFs were said to be en route; by summer Dreamland would boast enough Flighthawks to mount a full squadron.

Satisfied, Zen pushed himself over to the elevator, riding down to the lab level and his office in "Bunker B." One of the project members had tacked a large poster of a Frankenthaler painting on the door; he'd thought it pretty weird when he first saw it, and his opinion hadn't changed all that much. It was called "The Human Edge," and he supposed it was meant to be a metaphor or something. All he saw were some colors splotched on a large sheet of paper; not too much human about that.

Zen opened the door and spun his wheelchair sideways to angle through the narrow passageway. He left the door open while he checked for e-mail. Jennifer Gleason had left a long note discussing yesterday's exercises; she had found an apparent glitch in C³'s interface with the ANTARES gateway, but needed some fresh tests to see if she was on the right track.

So it wasn't Kevin's fault at all. Or Mack's, for that matter.

Jeff checked the time on the note. Jennifer had sent it at 4:45 A.M.; she'd worked all night.

They could rerun the test tomorrow afternoon, assuming Madrone was up to it and Zen could find a free range. Between the Russian spy satellites and Dreamland's increasing activities, spur-of-the-moment test flights were getting harder and harder to arrange.

The weather module on Dreamland's automated flight-scheduling system gave him another caution—a serious storm had stalled over the mountains to the west. Except for a bit of turbulence, their test range should remain clear during their flight window, but the front was fierce and looked to hang around for a while. Ordinarily the U/MFs didn't operate in the flight areas that far west, but more routine test craft sometimes did, and the storm could complicate scheduling for some time.

Better to try and get it done ASAP. Jeff picked up the phone to start rounding up the troops.

But he found himself punching the extension for the ANTARES project offices instead.

Dr. Geraldo herself picked up.

"Doc, this is Jeff Stockard," he said. "I'd like to take you up on your offer to reinitiate the ANTARES sessions."

"Really?"

"Yes," he said. "Whatever we need to do."

"Well, you should begin with the drug protocol, and we'll have to talk to Colonel Bastian—"

"Let's do it."

Dreamland Dorms, Pink Building
19 February, 0806

SLEEP WAS A COUNTRY OF GRAY-SHROUDED HILLS, PALE yellow light, and a harsh sun, its purple-red globe directly overhead no matter how Kevin turned. Animals stalked the shadows, their low growls sifted by the rustle of the leaves into hints of human whispers. Snakes slinked just out of sight, ready for him, watching.

Madrone rolled over and over on his bed, got up in the dark and paced, threw himself back onto the mattress. Finally he realized it was after eight o'clock. He went quickly to the shower, standing in the stall stoically as the water first froze and then nearly scalded him. When he got out, he realized he had left his underpants on; he stripped them off quickly, embarrassed.

His daughter had insisted on wearing her underpants into the bath. Karen had screamed at him for letting her.

The phone rang. It was Geraldo. But rather than demanding why he was late, she asked if he could report to Hawkmother for another flight. They wanted to redo some tests, if he was up to it.

"Yes," he said. He hung up the phone and quickly dressed. Then Madrone hurried over to the Boeing's hangar, skipping breakfast, head pushed down on his chest. He felt as if it were raining around him.

"Kevin, hello," said Dr. Geraldo, greeting him as he walked across the tarmac toward Hawkmother. The crews were tending to the plane as it sat at the edge of the ramp.

"You look tired," Geraldo said. She touched him gently on the arm. Her fingers cleared the rain away; he felt as if he'd taken off a heavy hat. A smell like the smell of cookies baking filled the room, soothing him.

"I didn't sleep," he confessed.

Geraldo looked at him as if she were disappointed. She was counting on him, needed him, and he was hurting her. He could feel it—he didn't want to hurt her.

"It's okay," he said. He tried to laugh. "I just couldn't sleep. Too much coffee yesterday. Gave me that headache."

Her own eyes were heavy, with thick rings below them. He wanted to tell her about the nightmares, but he'd hurt her if he did. She was counting on him; she needed him.

As Christina had needed him. He couldn't fail again.

"Well, let's get going," he told her.

"Are you sure?" Geraldo asked him.

"Come on, Doc," he said, giving her a light tap on the back.

"You're staying on the ground today, right? I'm ready to solo."

"Well—"

"Don't worry, Mom, I'm okay," he said, starting to feel more sure of himself. "Cut the apron strings."

"Are you sure?"

"We're just rerunning the tests, right?"

"Jeff wants to rerun yesterday's encounter. There was some sort of computer glitch they need to take care of. If you have time, they want to start working on the refuels."

Kevin shrugged. "Cool."

Geraldo nodded. "After the flight is over, I'd like to run another full physical review. We need some fresh electroencephalograms and the standard EKGs. The whole physical suite," she told him, her voice still faintly tentative.

"Two days in a row?"

"I'm afraid so."

"My cholesterol too high?"

Geraldo smiled. "No, you're perfect. You've gained weight; we should probably do a body-fat analysis and another stress test. You're probably in better shape than when you started."

"I'm telling you, Doc, we're going to cure the common cold."

Madrone realized she was looking at his thumb. He spread his hands and held them up for her to see. "No more nail-biting either. No cigarettes. I'm a new me."

"Yes."

"Don't sweat it," said Kevin. He put his hand on the rail to climb up into Hawkmother. "See ya when school's over."

Hawkmother Cockpit
19 February, 0840

TRENT "TRUCK" DALTON CURSED SOFTLY AS THE CAP ON the Diet Coke slipped around the top of the bottle, stubbornly refusing to break open. Fortunately, there were ways of dealing with problems like this—he reached his hand into his survival vest and pulled out his long knife, gingerly setting the bottle on the top of the control yoke to saw the plastic retaining snaps in two.

"You're out of your mind," said the 777's copilot, Terry Kulpin. Kulpin had gotten up out of his seat and was pacing on the spacious flight deck behind him.

"What?" said Dalton. The plastic was so stubborn he had to use considerable force to finally get through the edge.

"You're going to cut off your hand. Then we'll have to scrap the mission totally and Stockard will kill us."

"Nah." Truck rolled the bottle and the knife did slip; fortunately, it missed his fingers. Kulpin whistled behind him. "Relax. See? I got it open. Hungry? There's some Twizzlers in my kit back there."

Dalton gestured with the knife toward the gym bag he'd stowed in the auxiliary station directly behind the copilot's seat. There were mounts for temporary jump seats there, but in the Boeing's present configuration the extended flight deck was just surplus real estate, adding to the ghost-town feel of the big plane.

"I don't like licorice."

"Suit yourself." Dalton stowed the knife and took a long slug of soda.

"Looks like hydraulic fluid," said Kulpin.

"Maybe that's what you saw yesterday—Coke."

"Very funny," said the copilot. Kulpin had noticed—or thought he'd noticed—a small trace of hydraulic fuel on the ground below the left engine during yesterday's preflight test. That had necessitated a massive hunt for a problem, delaying takeoff and almost scrubbing the mission. But no problem had been found, and the plane had flown perfectly.

"You keep drinking that stuff, you won't fit through the ejector hatch," said Kulpin.

"You planning on getting rid of me?"

"Depends on how I'm feeling."

Unlike conventional airliners and transports, the Dreamland Boeing was equipped with ejection seats for emergencies. The system included an emergency computer initiative or ECI that they had been testing before being drafted for the ANTARES test; once armed by verbal command from the pilot, the computer could pull the handle if it sensed the pilot had become unconscious. To the pilots, this was a bit like a James Bond device for getting rid of obnoxious backseat drivers. While there were several layers of safety procedures, they didn't particularly like the system. Preliminary tests showed that it, like the advanced autopilot it was part of, worked well.

"Man. You're finishing the whole bottle?" asked Kulpin.

"I'm thirsty."

"You don't think you're going to have to pee?"

Truck shrugged. "I never have to pee when I'm flying. I was a Hog driver, remember? You drive a Hog, you grow your bladder."

"Wing tanks."

"Exactly."

Not equipped with an autopilot until recently, the bare-bones A-10A Warthog was a very difficult plane to take a leak in; you had to work the piddle-pack into position while keeping the stick steady with a combination of body English and wishful thinking.

"You think I should go back to the ANTARES pod and check on Madrone?" he asked. "He's all alone back there."

"Probably jacking off." They both laughed—Madrone was a bit of a cipher. "Might as well work your way back and make sure he's okay. This is the first time he's flown without a baby-sitter back there," added Trent. He tossed the empty bottle to his copilot. "Just don't get lost."

"I may trip over something," said Kulpin. "That's what I'm afraid of. I fall behind one of those black boxes you'll never see me again."

Ten seconds after he disappeared through the bulkhead, Dream Tower gave the go to launch.

Sharkishki
19 February, 0950

MACK GLANCED AT THE SMALL FLIGHT BOARD ON HIS knee, where he'd mapped out a cheat-sheet with the parameters of his flight. He was supposed to duplicate yesterday's final run exactly, or as exactly as possible. It was trickier than it sounded, since he had to duplicate something he'd winged, and didn't have the high-tech-computer assistant pilots to guide him.

As usual, the computer geeks wanted the tests done a certain way, but hadn't bothered to explain exactly why. Undoubtedly, they thought the universe worked like one of their programs—plug in the values and go.

"Gameboy to Aggressor," said Zen in his helmet headset. "You're looking good."

"Aggressor," acknowledged Mack. He spun his eyes around the cockpit, checking his instruments. He needed to come up five hundred feet if he was going to do this right; he coaxed the throttle so he wouldn't lose any speed as he nudged his nose upward. The Flighthawks were ahead somewhere, still undetected by his radar.

"Let's rock," he said impatiently. "Madrone, get with it."

Hawkmother
19 February, 0954

MADRONE SAW THE MiG FAT IN THE MIDDLE OF HIS head, precisely midway between the two Flighthawks as they approached. The computer had yesterday's track duplicated exactly, making a minor adjustment to accommodate the MiG's slower airspeed.

It was going well. His headache hadn't reappeared, and the fatigue had slipped away once the metal band of the ANTARES helmet liner slipped over his skull. Even the stiff flight suit, with its spike running up and down his back, didn't bother him today.

If anything, he was bored. The computer flew with minimal input, tracing the course. He could, of course, think himself into either cockpit. He could roll quickly, shoot downward, climb, launch a front-quarter attack, obliterate Sharkishki.

Madrone leaned back in his seat. If he'd thought that yesterday, C^3 would have carried out the commands. Today it didn't. He'd learned to partition his thoughts, keep different strands going.

A new level. Even greater control. More possibilities.

The headache and the dreams were growth pains, his mind bouncing against the ceiling of the next level, breaking through it.

There were so many other things he could do. He could

reach out through ANTARES and go beyond it.

Kevin could feel the autopilot for the Boeing, hovering in the background. He saw it beyond the gateway.

He could use ANTARES to walk into the room and see the levers there. Once he saw them, he could work them.

Metaphors. Mastering ANTARES was a matter of finding the right metaphor—inventing the right language.

Madrone snaked into Hawkmother's cockpit. The radar inputs felt like small twitches on the base of his neck. He could almost see himself.

Ignore the returns painting the Flighthawks. It's too confusing. The controls are difficult enough. Difficult but exciting.

"Coming to Point Delta," said Zen somewhere far away.

Kevin jumped back to the Flighthawks and acknowledged. It was like passing between different rooms.

Or different parts of the forest. Lightning screeched in the distance. Madrone took a breath, suddenly anxious that the headache might return.

It might. He would deal with it.

The dark woman beyond the edge of his vision would help him.

Breathe, she said. *Breathe.*

The Flighthawks continued past the MiG as they had yesterday. C^3 threw up a dotted line, proposing that they turn and fly toward Sharkishki's tail. Madrone assented.

He could fly the Boeing if he wanted. The systems were complicated, but the plane itself was more inherently stable, easier to control than the Flighthawks. He could feel the control yoke in his hand.

A tremendous jolt of pain crashed into the back of his head, nearly taking away his breath.

Rain, she told him. *Stay in Theta.*

Rain.

Raven
19 February, 1005

ZEN GLANCED QUICKLY AT THE FEED FROM THE FLIGHT-hawk cockpits, then pushed the headset's mouthpiece closer to his face. "Repeat, Hawk Commander?" he asked.

"Nothing. No transmission. Sorry," said Madrone. He sounded like he was out of breath.

Jeff called up the optical feed from Hawk One as the two U/MFs approached the MiG. The overhead plot had everyone precisely in place. The planes passed each other and the Flighthawks began to bank behind the MiG.

How would an engagement like this go if there were thirty or forty planes in the air? Could Madrone really control it all?

Could he?

Zen studied the instrument feeds as the two Flighthawks spun around and began to close on Mack. The planes were in perfect mechanical condition, all systems in the green.

Damn hard just sitting here and watching, using the tubes instead of his visor. He ought to be in the cockpit.

That meant getting back into ANTARES. Two years from now, maybe even sooner, it would be the only way to control the Flighthawks. It was clearly the future.

Zen hit the toggle on the video feed, bringing the enhanced satellite view onto the main screen. He forced himself to focus on his work. The Flighthawks duplicated yesterday's near miss.

"Here we go," said Mack, tipping his wing.

"Breaking off," said Madrone. The two Flighthawks shot downward, rolling on opposite wings in a graceful arc back toward the other end of the range.

"Got it," said Lee Ong from the other station. Ong was watching the Flighthawks' computer systems. "I think that's what she wants."

"Close enough?"

"She didn't say to scrape paint," said the scientist. "All she really wants to see are what commands fired."

Zen checked his watch. They had exactly an hour and a half of time on the range left.

Might as well put it to use.

"Mack, what's your fuel?"

"You want kilos or you want pounds?"

"How's about time?"

"Forty-five minutes."

"What are we doing here, Jeff?" asked Madrone in his now-standard snot-ass tone.

"I'm thinking we can practice some tanker approaches. First we'll try a couple with the MiG."

"Why?" asked Mack. "Why not use the Hawkmother?"

"Because I want to work on theory first, then worry about dealing with the vortexes the Boeing kicks off," said Jeff. "Kevin, I want you to fly the plane, not C^3."

"Shit. He's going to have more trouble pulling up behind me than the 777," said Mack.

"Even if that were true, you've demonstrated twice now that you can get out of the way fast."

"Oh, thanks. Hear that, Junior? Dad doesn't think you'll be careful with his car."

"What's the course?" answered Madrone.

Jeff laid it out for them, setting Mack into a long racetrack orbit at eighteen thousand feet. Smith was almost surely right—the Fulcrum, with its closely spaced engines and knife-like wing surfaces and fuselage, threw wicked vortexes off its wings. It also didn't have a lighting system to help guide Madrone in.

But Zen stuck with it stubbornly. Mack gave another grouchy harumph before settling into his track, flying it flawlessly as the two Flighthawks closed behind him. Hawk One pulled to within twenty feet of the MiG's right wing, as briefed, held its position for ten seconds, then dropped back.

"He let C^3 handle that completely," said Ong. "Did you want that?"

"Hawk Leader, rely a little less on the computer assist with Hawk Two," said Zen.

"Hawk."

Zen glanced back at Ong as Madrone began his approach. Jennifer would have been hunched over one of the laptops, punching the keyboard furiously. Ong just sat back and watched, occasionally making notes on a yellow legal pad.

Hawk Two, now totally under Madrone's control, pulled to within twenty feet of the MiG, holding its position for ten seconds. Then it ducked down twenty feet, accelerated, and reemerged exactly under the fuselage of the plane. Madrone—flying without the direct aid of the flight computer's automatic pilot sections—held the pattern through Mack's banking turn.

"Okay, Kevin, impressive," said Zen.

"Hawk."

Hawk Two fell back.

"Getting some wild fluctuations in the command centers," said Ong. "I'm not sure what's going on there, Jeff."

Before he could answer, Bree broke in over the interphone. "Zen, Boeing is off track. Something's up with him."

Hawkmother
19 February, 1015

THE SHARDS CAME AT MADRONE LIKE BULLETS OF HAIL in a storm, bits and pieces of the Boeing pelting his head. He put his hand out to catch them—Kevin felt the metaphor in his mind, saw his palm extending and the hail landing, landing and building slowly and steadily. He stared at the hail, concentrating his thoughts—a snowball congealed from the mass, cold and wet but thick despite the heat of the rain forest around him.

He could feel the plane's wings. He saw himself in the air, gliding along at 10,322 feet, the back of his neck rumbling with the engines.

A great thirst.

I need fuel, he told himself. I can find fuel where?

A needle at the top of his head connected to a run of numbers—a computer link to the database, a CD listing of hex numbers recording possible emergency bases.

AH345098BC333.

Lightning spiked through his eyes. Metal began to boil at the sides of his temples.

Madrone's heart skipped erratically. His lungs, caught somehow out of synch, began to choke. He felt himself moving sideways, twisting though the air.

He had to analyze what had just happened. He'd crossed some sort of threshold, but he didn't have control of it.

It's all in the way you think about it, she coached him. *Find the right metaphor to organize your thoughts. They will extend themselves. You must be yourself, not the computer.*

His chest began to swell. His heart pounded out of control.

There were different levels to the brain. You didn't think about how your heart worked, but you could control the beat with the right sequence of thoughts.

Could he?

Yes, she said.

Last night's dream loomed, rising from the jungle floor. Madrone turned away from it, concentrated, found his breath. His heart—he felt the mass of it around his eyes, stopped it.

He gulped. Then slowly, he began pounding steadily, pumping blood through his body.

Control. You have control.

He didn't want to control his heart. He wanted to fly the Boeing.

Hail was everywhere, heavy baseballs of ice in a thick mix of rain. The storm thickened exponentially; he lost sight of C^3 and the Flighthawks, lost the Boeing, lost himself as the wind and rain swirled through his head. Parts of his body broke away, flesh ripping as bones flew in different directions. His head twisted out of its socket.

The jaws of the gateway clamped around his face.

Then he heard her voice.

Come to me, said the dark woman. *Come to me.*

DALTON JERKED AS THE BOEING FELL AWAY FROM HIM, the control column whipping forward. It was only a flicker, as if the plane had panicked for a moment, shutting down and then revving up.

The yoke was exactly where it had started, the HUD and multi-use displays exactly the same, all indicators in the green. The pilot blinked, scanned his gear again, tensed his fingers, and untensed them. The plane was off track and lower than planned, yet otherwise flew exactly level, all systems green.

"Did you feel that?" he asked Kulpin.

"What?" said the copilot, who was staring at the multi-use display at the extreme right of the control panel.

"It was like, the plane blinked," said Truck.

"Didn't feel a thing," said Kulpin. "But the computer seems to be concerned with our fuel reserves."

"What?"

"I just got a fuel report without asking for it," said Kulpin, turning to him.

"What the hell's going on?" he said. Then the controls jerked away again—only this time, they didn't come back.

Sharkishki
19 February, 1019

MACK CURSED AS HE CAME OUT OF THE BANK. STINKING Madrone was becoming as big a wise-ass as his buddy Zen. The damn Flighthawk was right under his fuselage, close enough to be a Goddamn bomb for friggin' sake. He couldn't see it, of course, but he knew the little robot turd was still stuck there like a cling-on.

Madrone was playing chicken with him, daring him to broadcast a "knock it off" and end the exercise. Then he'd snort to Zen over beers about how he'd wigged Knife out.

Fuck that. He'd hold the damn course now until he ran out of fuel.

Which might not be too long from now in the short-legged MiG.

Raven
19 February, 1021

ZEN SAW IT HAPPENING IN SLOW MOTION: MACK CONTIN-ued on his southern leg, hugged and shadowed by the Flight-hawks. Meanwhile, the Boeing lurched downward from its orbit, slashing toward him.

"Break! Break!" he yelled, desperately jerking the transmit button. "Gameboy to Sharkishki—break ninety. Everybody, knock it off! Hawkmother—what the hell are you doing?"

Hawkmother
19 February, 1021

HE WANTED HER.

Madrone felt her warm breath wrap around his body, her kisses dissolving his pain.

He would have her—his heart raced and his lungs filled

with air and he stood up, spreading his arms as he screamed—
He would have her!

He looked at the palm of his hand. The icy lump of hail was still there. He squeezed, and the mush of precipitation became the Boeing. The storm raged around him and he took the plane and tossed it like a toy glider, its wings unfurling as it caught the breeze.

He sat on top of it. The Flighthawks came and landed on his shoulders, flying.

They were trying to stop him. The idiots in the cockpit thought they were in control. They were working with the bastard doctors who had killed his daughter.

They could be dealt with easily—he covered them with ice, raining hail on them.

The MiG was more of a problem.

Sharkishki
19 February, 1025

MACK CURSED AS HE YANKED THE MiG AWAY FROM THE lurching 777, just barely managing to clear the tail section without scraping.

"What the fucking hell are you assholes doing?" he shouted. He was so angry his finger slipped off the transmit button for a moment. "Dalton, you shit. What the fuck? Knock it off, knock it off," he repeated, calling off the exercise.

"Knock it off," Zen said. "Flight emergency. Clear Range 4B. Radio silence. Hawkmother? Hawkmother?"

Mack pulled Sharkishki level, recovering from the quick evasive maneuvers. He craned his neck back to find out what had happened to the Boeing.

Damn thing had looked like it flew right at him.

He couldn't see it behind him. He took a breath, calming down as he leaned the MiG slightly, trying to get a fix on the stricken plane.

A black speck appeared over his left shoulder, just beyond the MiG's tailplane. It grew into a grayish ball.

One of the Flighthawks. It dropped below his wing.

Where the hell was it going?

Mack hit the throttle, goosing the tweaked engines. Even so, the U/MF missed hitting him by less than twenty feet.

Shit.

"Stockard, what the fuck is going on!" he yelled.

Hawkmother
19 February, 1028

MADRONE PUSHED THE BOEING DOWN TOWARD THE edge of the range, quickly descending through four thousand feet. One of the systems warned about stress to the control surfaces, but they were well within tolerance—he could feel the problem as a slight twinge near his temples.

He'd drop to fifty feet above ground. There, the effect of the ground clutter in radar returns would render him invisible. It was low, but not so low that he couldn't easily cut a course through the mountains.

He could let the Boeing's control computer fly the plane as soon as he figured out how to kill the safety restraints and reset the course. They were an electrified fence, sparking his body as he approached.

When he got beyond the fence, he could get rid of the pilot and copilot. He could see their seats, but not quite reach the release.

The damn MiG kept getting in his way, despite the efforts of the Flighthawks to run interference. They were unarmed, and he didn't want to crash into Smith, since that would cost him a plane.

Get rid of Hawkmother's pilot and copilot first. Smith was a blowhard; he'd never be able to stop him.

Zen called to him. Madrone turned away, closing the door on him.

He reached for the fence protecting the pilots. Sparks jumped and he jerked back, lost control of Boeing momentarily. The pilot pulled back on the controls, starting to take it out of its dive.

"You're not going to beat me, you bastards!" he shouted.

A latch sat on the side of the fence, held there by twisted wires.

He could get through it, if he was willing to ignore the pain.

As he touched the latch, the metaphor changed. He grabbed not metal but the arm of his young daughter, his baby.

She cried with pain.

He let go instantly, stunned.

"Christina," he said. "Baby."

She stopped sobbing and turned her eyes toward him, raising her head. The hair on the right side of her scalp fell away, just as it had during the radiation treatment at Livermore. Huge clumps dropped to the ground.

Her neck and the side of her skull boiled. The cancer burst through her skin, purple lumps like the thyroid they'd removed.

"Christina, Christina," he cried.

Lightning struck his eyes. His body convulsed with pain. He couldn't save his daughter; he was helpless, useless, worthless. His tongue trembled in his mouth and tears flowed. His cheeks melted as if the tears were acid. His chest convulsed as thunder shook the universe.

Come to me, said the dark woman, her voice muffled by the distance. *Come, Kevin.*

Who was she? A dream of Karen? Of Geraldo? Of some primeval lover stored deep in the recesses of his Jungian brain?

A metaphor, constructed by his mind, simply a metaphor for ANTARES.

Come to me, love.

Madrone felt his heart slowing. His lungs worked properly again. He pushed his hand, and it no longer held his daughter, but the wire around the fence latch. He pulled, and the metal gave way; he pulled, and the protective circuitry that had prevented him from gaining full control of the plane flew over his head backward.

He had it now. He had the course laid out. Get past the MiG, disappear into the mountains.

Then?

He would fly to the rain forest and the dark woman. He would find peace there.

Madrone pushed the Boeing back toward the ground, then

jerked her hard to the west, the mountain peaks looming ahead.

"MAYDAY! MAYDAY! FUCK!" YELLED KULPIN AS DALTON continued to struggle with the 777. They'd disengaged the flight computer and done everything else possible, but had only limited success regaining control. They were well beyond Dreamland's borders, accelerating as they flew southwest into commercial airspace. Dalton had managed to level off at three thousand feet, but now the Boeing slipped from his control once more, shuddering as she put her nose downward.

They were going to break the sound barrier again.

And on top of everything else, the environmental controls had freaked—it must be down to fifty degrees in the cockpit.

"We're going to have to bail," said Kulpin.

"Not at this speed," said Dalton.

"No choice," argued Kulpin.

"Pull, help me pull," he said, muscling the stick.

"I'm trying."

"We are going to have to bail," Dalton began.

He intended to tell Kulpin to radio their position and the fact that they were going out. He needed to tell Madrone what was going on, make sure the captain was strapped in and knew what to do. He wanted to start an orderly checklist, to keep things calm and precise and absolutely orderly, as if he were a cruise ship captain practicing a routine and boring lifeboat drill. But as he opened his mouth he felt his breath catch in the pit of his chest. His body slammed back on the seat and an anvil landed on his head. Somewhere in the back of his mind he realized he had been ejected from the plane, though he hadn't pulled the manual eject handles, let alone fooled with the automated sequence.

Sharkishki
19 February, 1038

THE AUDIBLE FUEL WARNING IN MACK'S EAR HIT A NEW octave as he pushed to follow the Boeing. Dalton and his copilot didn't answer his hails on any frequency, nor did Madrone.

At least the Flighthawks had stopped flashing in front of him, staying in a close trail behind Hawkmother. Mack recognized it as one of the preprogrammed flight positions.

As he closed the distance between himself and the big jet, the 777 took another lurch downward and the front end seemed to break apart.

"Shit, they're out," he said to Zen, yelling so loud it was possible he could be heard without the radio. "Fuck. They ejected. I think they ejected. Oh, Jesus."

He slid the MiG into a bank, searching for parachutes. The truth was he couldn't tell if they had ejected or if the front of the plane had blown apart—it was moving that damn fast.

Knife glanced at his fuel panel. Serious problems. Even if he turned back this instant, he might have to glide home.

He couldn't see the Boeing anymore. Sharkishki's radar had lost it in the ground clutter, but the IR scan showed the plane plummeting toward the mountains, a half mile ahead. He glanced over to mark the position with the GPS screen on the MUD. As he pushed the button, the Boeing disappeared from the screen.

"Plane's going in," he told Zen. He punched the IR gear, watching for the inevitable flare.

"Mack, what's your status?" demanded Stockard.

"I lost them. They bailed and the plane nose-dived. Can't find it on the infrared. I'm not sure why. Shit."

"What's your *fuel*, Sharkishki?" demanded Zen.

"Yeah. I have a fuel emergency. Returning to base," conceded Mack. "I'll upload the GPS telemetry. Aw, shit to fucking hell."

Raven
19 February, 1050

ZEN'S CHEST COMPRESSED AS THE BOEING DISAPpeared from the radar display. It felt like a snake had wrapped itself around him and squeezed.

He tried the override again in a desperate attempt to grab

control of the Flighthawks, but the screens remained blank, the connection severed.

"We'll be at Mack's mark in zero-two," said Breanna.

"Yeah," answered Zen. The snake squeezed tighter. He checked on the status of the SAR flight that had just scrambled out of Dreamland—a pair of helicopters, one a Pave Low with an extensive suite of search gear, were about fifteen minutes behind them. Edwards and Nellis both had other units on standby.

"Aggressor, how tight is your fuel?" he said, calling Mack.

"Under control," answered Mack.

Smith sounded more angry than concerned, though Zen thought he'd sound that way on fumes.

"There's a civilian strip in your direct flight path if you need it," Zen told him.

"No shit, Sherlock. Let me fly this one, all right?"

Normally, Zen would have told Mack to screw himself. But by now the snake had wrapped itself so tightly around his throat that he couldn't get a word out of his mouth.

He was so damn impotent without legs, tied into a stinking wheelchair, a gimp, a cripple, a helpless lump of nothing.

A flame flared in the middle of his head, surging and glowing, flowing into a perfect round circle, a sun that went from red to pink to chromium.

He was helpless. He was back in the F-15 where he'd had his accident, going out at low altitude, crashing into the ground, crushing his spinal cord and losing his legs.

"Nightingale One to Gameboy. Please state situation. Major Stockard?"

He wasn't helpless. He'd proven himself in Africa. Every day he got out of bed, he proved himself.

"Zen, the SAR flight is hailing you," said Bree over the interphone.

"Gameboy to Nightingale One," he said, muscling the snake away. "We have a plane down, two, hopefully three ejections. Rough terrain. Maybe the mountains. No fix, but we can make some guesses from the GPS where they were last seen."

"Copy that," said the Pave Low pilot, who had already been given the coordinates by Breanna. "Do you have anything fresh?"

"Negative," admitted Zen. "We're in the dark as much as you."

V
The rain forest

Aboard Hawkmother
Over Sierra Nevada Mountains
19 February, 1110

WHEN HE REALIZED THAT HE HAD SHAKEN THE MIG AND Raven, Madrone pumped his hands in the air, as elated as he had ever been in his life. But after he turned control of the Boeing over to the computer, his sense of triumph began to drain.

There were problems. The Flighthawks were in perfect shape, holding behind Hawkmother as it hugged its way through the mountain passes. But they were more than half-way through their fuel reserves; while their engines were thrifty in cruise mode, they would need to be refueled.

He could do that. They'd planned to. He'd gone through the simulations, and Hawkmother had been loaded with extra fuel.

But sooner or later he'd have to find fuel for the Boeing.

Where? It wasn't like he could put down at a gas station and pull out his credit card. Who the hell was going to give him jet fuel without asking a lot of questions? Or demanding a lot of money?

Why had he gone off without a plan? What madness possessed him? He tucked out of the mountains—L.A. was a vast glow to the left, the Pacific a dark haze beyond.

Madrone began to shake, his body suddenly cold. He felt

a light pop at the top of his head, and then he began to fall, or feel as if he were falling.

He'd dropped out of Theta.

The twinge of panic swirled into a full-blown typhoon. The entire Air Force would be after him, all of the military. He'd been screwed before—Army generals and personnel bastards and Pentagon phonies had screwed him out of his advanced-weapons project at Los Alamos, yanked his clearances. They'd claimed he needed a rest, but he'd known they were out to screw him because of what he'd done in Iraq. He'd shown them up, nailing those tanks with his men. Bastards.

Madrone forced himself to sit back in the seat. He was losing it, giving in to paranoia.

The headache started to return. He pushed air into the bottom of his lungs, loosened the muscles at the top of his shoulders.

He hadn't wanted to run away. But here he was. The pilot and copilot had ejected; he was in control of the ship.

They'd call it mutiny. Put him in jail for life, and he'd never see his daughter.

She was already dead.

Kevin ran his fingers across his forehead. He couldn't think straight. The universe was breaking apart.

He had to get back into Theta. Now.

Pej, Brazil
19 February, 1510 local

MINERVA LANZAS FOLDED HER ARMS ACROSS HER CHEST and leaned against the back of the bulldozer. The hazy sun cast a brown light over the dusty mountain airstrip, tinting the colors like a faded postcard. If she'd been in a better mood, she might have almost thought it romantic.

But if she'd been in a better mood she would not be here in Pej, caught between the Amazon and the mountains of Serra Curupira, in exile—Dante's third ring of hell.

Three months before, Colonel Lanzas had been one of the most important officers of the Força Aérea Brasileira, the Brazilian Air Force. She had obtained her position through the usual means—family connections, politics, sex, even skill as a pilot and commander. As commanding officer of an elite group of FAB interceptors attached to the Third Air Force south of Rio de Janeiro, she'd had power, prestige, and the potential for great wealth. She had managed to shed her third husband—a once-useful if pedestrian diplomat and military attaché—and begun to amass a personal following that extended to the Army as well as the Air Force. At thirty-one, she'd looked forward to a bright future not just in the military, but in Brazilian politics as well.

But then she had overplayed her hand, misjudging the ever-shifting currents of the country's politics. The result had been a disastrous showdown with the Navy—and then this.

Two decades before, the Brazilian Navy had attempted to expand its power by clandestinely adding aircraft to its fleet forces. Then, the Air Force generals had carefully parlayed news of this into a magnificent power play that assured them of dominance in the government for many years. So it seemed likely that when the admirals once again tried something by secretly purchasing Russian destroyers and sending out feelers for MiGs, the evidence would propel the Air Force to even greater heights. General Emil Herule hoped to become Defense Minister, a short step to President. Lanzas and the white-haired Air Force leader had done good business in the past, with an occasional foray into matters of pleasure; her decision to lead a flight to gather intelligence seemed a logical and profitable gesture.

Colonel Lanzas personally commanded a four-ship element of F-5E Tigers over the screening force around *Minas Gerias,* the Brazilian Navy's aircraft carrier. The film in her plane confirmed Air Force suspicions about the two new destroyers. Her camera also discovered that the carrier's catapults had been modified to launch Mirages—a fact confirmed by the takeoff of the planes.

The two Mirages attempted to intercept the Tigers. At some point, one of the Navy planes used its radar to lock on her group. There was only one possible response. Both Mirages were destroyed in the subsequent battle.

Minerva had splashed one of the planes herself. Like all of her engagements, it was short, quick, and deadly. But it did not bring the desired result.

Brazil in the 1990's was very different than the 1960's.

The President and his Cabinet backed the Navy in the inter-service imbroglio, even though the admirals had clearly violated the law. General Herule was reassigned to a minor desk job in Brasilia. Most of the generals and colonels who had backed him were jailed. Lanzas, after some negotiation, got off with mere banishment. Her family had helped finance the President's election, after all. Negotiations had been complicated by several factors, not the least of which was the destruction of the Mirages. A sizable payment from the colonel's personal fortune had finally settled the matter.

There had been rumors before the showdown that Lanzas possessed two atomic weapons. The admirals fortunately did not believe the rumors, or the negotiations might have been considerably more difficult. They considered that the woman colonel was like all women, a contemptible temptress ready to use her tongue in any way possible—something several of them could personally verify. Brazil did not have its own nuclear program, and even her wealth could not purchase a bomb from another country. Besides, who would be so unpatriotic as to bomb their own country?

But in actual fact Minerva Lanzas did possess two devices, though in some ways they were as impotent as the admirals' personal equipment.

Designed during a joint-service project with a renegade Canadian weapons engineer several years before, the warheads were to have been fired by a massive artillery device. The gun, had the design worked, would have propelled them roughly twenty miles. About as long as a desk, with the diameter of a bloated wastepaper basket, they had small payloads that were only a third as powerful as the primitive weapons dropped on Hiroshima and Nagasaki during World War II. The design was relatively primitive—a focused detonation of high explosives propelled a seed nugget of fission material into a small bowl shaped of plutonium at a speed and temperature just high enough to start a chain reaction.

The project itself was an utter failure. The artillery piece proved much more likely to shatter than launch even a dummy shell. The computer simulations of the warhead showed its yield would be very "dirty," with the long-lasting radiation likely to spread precariously close to the firing position. And finally, Brazil had never been able to obtain the plutonium the weapon's final design called for.

Lanzas had been assigned as a monitor for the project; her reports lambasted it. But when the government abandoned the initiative, she acquired several of the early shells with their high-tech explosives and trigger mechanisms through blackmail, bribery, and in one case, murder.

Her wealth was not so great that she could obtain weapons-grade plutonium. But she could find uranium, which not so coincidentally had been the subject of one of the earlier designs. Shaping the radioactive metal was expensive and dangerous, but in the end the only thing that shocked her was how small the radioactive pellets were.

The Navy adventure had interrupted her efforts to adapt the warheads for practical use as missiles. And while she had arranged for two top weapons engineers to follow her here within the next few days, she now faced an even greater problem—even if she managed to scrounge material for a missile chassis, she lacked a suitable plane to launch the missiles from.

Minerva tucked her hands into her leather jacket and surveyed the packed dirt strip. Ten bulldozers—"borrowed" from a rancher nearly fifty miles away—had carved an additional three hundred meters out of the rocky soil, making the strip just long enough to comfortably land her Hawker Siddeley HS 748, an ancient twin turboprop known to the Brazilian Air Force as a C-91. The sturdy but far from glamorous transport was now the centerpiece of her command. In fact, it was her only plane.

Despair curled around her like a snake, squeezing the breath from her lungs. Her money was nearly gone; she had no influence beyond this small strip. When she had arrived, she had hoped for revenge, but as the days dragged on it became increasingly clear that there would be no opportunity for it. When the strip was finished, she might—might—be lucky to host a visiting KC-130H and an occasional squadron of F-5's, or Tucanos, as they rotated north to patrol the Venezuelan-Colombia frontier every third or fourth month. Even that would only happen if catastrophe struck Boa Vista, several hundred miles away.

She told herself not to despair. Fate would deliver her an

opportunity, just as it had in the past. She would shape her bombs into something useful; she would find a way to use her charms and the last of her money. Fortune would send her a chance, and she would make the most of it.

At worst, she would have revenge.

Aboard Hawkmother
Over Pacific Ocean
19 February, 1302 local

MADRONE PUSHED HIS BACK GENTLY AGAINST THE SEAT, his head rising with the flow of air into his lungs. Slow, slow—he pushed everything into the breath, resisting the temptation to concentrate on the tickling sensation at the corner of his temples. He could hear the rain in the distance. Thick trunks of trees appeared before him, materializing from the fog. His lungs rose to the top of his chest, pushing him against the restraint straps. He had to hold his back perfectly erect, his boots flat on the floor.

In.

The storm drenched him with wet, sticky water. A torrent ran down the back of his hair to his neck to his shoulders, sizzling along the metal of his spine.

They were on the course he had plotted, running toward Mexico.

He needed to find a quiet airfield, a place big enough so he could land Hawkmother, but not quite so big that they would ask a lot of questions.

They would always ask questions. They were after him. They hated him.

Madrone forced himself back to the cockpit of the Boeing. He could land—he saw the procedure on his right, felt the way it would feel in his brain.

Find an airport now. The computer held a list.

They would use the identifier beacon to track him. He could turn it off by cutting its power.

Where was it, though? Beneath his left arm somewhere.

The 777 suddenly lurched to the left. Madrone realized he had done that with his inattention. He imagined himself in flight again, felt his brain floating with Hawkmother. The plane leveled out, pushing its wings level.

The rods of the interface that helped him work the controls spread around him, an infinite series of handles connected to clockwork. He stood inside a massive church tower. Bells sat above, worked by the rods. A large row of gears sat in a long rectangular box to his left. The mechanical gears of four massive clocks filled the walls. The tower smelled of stone dust and camphor. There were open windows beneath the clock faces. He could see through them to the outside. The tower sat in the middle of the rain forest. A storm raged all around.

He looked upward. He could see through the roof, though the rain did not fall here.

What was this metaphor? It had risen entirely unbidden.

The testing tower at Glass Mountain, where he'd been assigned when Christina was born. The place where they'd poisoned him.

Lightning crashed in the distance. Madrone turned his gaze slightly right, remembered his idea of the brain as separate rooms. He closed this one, put himself into the Flighthawks.

Less than an hour's worth of fuel.

He turned his gaze left, then stepped back into the Boeing's cockpit.

Two hours more fuel.

Refuel the Flighthawks. Then land, fuel the Boeing, take off, feed the robots.

Yes.

Pain shot from one side of his head to the other. His skull snapped upward, shoved up by a tremendous force at the base.

Breathe, he reminded himself.

He couldn't. A panel with his vital signs appeared before his eyes. The green line of an electrocardiogram waved in front of him, flashed into a snake.

Pain enveloped him. The Boeing lurched toward the waves. Warnings sounded—they were very close to the water.

A hundred feet. Fifty.

Kevin. Kevin, I'm here. I believe in you.

The dark woman emerged from the forest. Her eyes were dark brown, the same color as her hair, pulled back from her face and flowing over her shoulders. Her bronze breasts swayed slightly as she walked toward him, naked in the light, misty rain.

I am in control, he told himself. He visualized himself sitting in Hawkmother's cockpit. He pulled back on the yoke, pushing the plane away from the ocean. The plane responded easily, pushing her nose up in the rapid climb he set.

Climb to twenty thousand feet and refuel. Then find a civilian flight path. Have the computer keep the Flighthawks close to the 777, where they would be invisible.

Find a civilian flight to impersonate. Refuel.

The first thing he tried was tapping into the Mexican civilian control network. He thought there would be a database of flights, and that the Boeing's flight computer could somehow access it. But if that was possible, he couldn't find the right hook; his mind clogged and the best he could do was use the radio, talking directly to the tower at Hermosilla—a comical exchange of *¿Qué?* after *¿Qué?*

Then he got a better idea. He monitored transmissions from flights taking off from the airport, listening for call signs and then asking C^3 to identify the plane types. He wanted something similar to the 777 flying southward.

After several minutes, he found a 707 bound for Mexico City—AirTeknocali 713. It was a cargo plane, and its course took it over the Sierra Madres. Adjusting the Boeing's flight path to trail it was accomplished with a nudge.

Refueling the Flighthawks was equally easy. The Boeing extended the tail boom. The first buffet of turbulence off the big plane's airfoil pushed the nose of Hawk One down, but Madrone found that the eddy helped hold the small plane in place; if he backed the engine of the U/MF off quickly as he approached, the nose of the plane moved to the nozzle like iron shavings to a magnet.

The Mexican plane, meanwhile, lumbered ahead, rising to 28,000 feet but barely pushing three hundred knots.

Madrone couldn't make it to Mexico City, but that was just as well. There'd be too many questions there, and people expecting AirTeknocali. He found a smaller airfield nearer the coast, Tepic.

He looked to the right, examining the Boeing's controls. He pushed the throttle bar gently, then edged the control yoke to the left, getting onto the exact path of the Mexican plane, though he was about five thousand feet lower.

He looked left, climbing into the Flighthawks. He punched them out of the 777's shadow, felt the rush as their engines began to accelerate. The planes' relatively small power plants couldn't take them much beyond Mach 1.2, but they were considerably faster than AirTeknocali 713 and infinitely more maneuverable.

The Mexican plane grew in Hawk One's visual display. C³ began giving him readings on its bearing and speed, then realized what he was doing.

"Intercept in eighty-five seconds," the computer told him.

He pushed the two Flighthawks into a spread, their wings separated 131 feet, exactly an inch outside the Boeing's.

Until the last moment, Madrone intended only to scare the pilot of AirTeknocali 713 into changing course. He had a vague notion of forcing the pilot far inland, spooking him long enough so there was no possibility of him interfering. Concentrating on flying had calmed Kevin somehow, removed the pain to a faraway place, focused his thoughts. But rage seized him as he rode the Flighthawks toward the wings of the cargo jet. A claw grabbed for the back of his head; he heard a jaguar or another big cat growling behind him. The anger at losing his daughter, the anger at being betrayed by the Army, by the people at Dreamland, by everyone, boiled into its scream.

Madrone flashed inches from the windshield of the Mexican jet with Hawk One, then took Hawk Two so close the wing scraped the cockpit glass, breaking it. The Mexican plane bolted upward, then nosed hard toward the ground, its pilot jerking hard on the stick as his windshield exploded and the force of the escaping air sucked at his clothes. Madrone rolled the Flighthawks downward, his mind between the two cockpits, flying them as one plane, flying them as if they were his hands. He was a giant, a vengeful god seeking revenge against all who had tried to hurt him.

The 707—*their* 707—flailed helplessly, trying to escape his grasp. As the pilot or copilot radioed a Mayday, Madrone shot Hawk One back across their path. The visual input from the robot plane caught the cockpit. The pilot's seat was empty. The other man cried, eyes bulging as the jowls of his cheeks distorted with the violent gravity and atmospheric pressures.

The plane yawed into a spin.

Madrone pulled the Flighthawks back, rage spent. He told C³ to take the planes back to Hawkmother, then rushed away from them and their inputs, not wanting to know what happened to AirTeknocali 713, not daring to see the copilot's tears as the plane crashed into the mountain.

From Hawkmother's cockpit, he radioed Tepic and told him he had a fuel emergency.

He used English, but the response came in Spanish. He was cleared in to land.

As he approached, someone on the ground radioed him frantically. Was he AirTeknocali 713?

Yes, he said.

But the radar showed he was something else.

He'd turned the identifier off, at least.

He had no time to figure out if there was a way to spoof the radar or to puzzle out a proper response. Madrone was committed now. The fear and excitement of landing, the danger—it all calmed him, helping him concentrate. He didn't worry about red tinges reappearing at the edge of his brain, or fear the bizarre dreams and startling metaphors ANTARES imposed on his thoughts. He simply flew.

The flight computer walked him into the airport. The strip was short—they'd have to go right into reverse thrust.

Doable. A good wind had kicked up to hit him in the nose. No problem here.

He jumped back to the Flighthawks. Madrone put them in a very low and slow orbit over the waves. They would be just barely within control range when he landed, but there was no one nearby to spot them.

What would they do if there was trouble? They had no shells in their cannons.

He could crash them into his enemies, burn the bastards to hell.

No. He didn't want to hurt anyone. That wasn't him. He'd felt bad even for the Iraqis after they'd killed them in the tanks.

Madrone found himself in the tower again, the storm flashing above him. He took a long breath, but it didn't disappear.

Someone cried below. There was a growl—the guttural yap

of a jungle cat approaching its helpless prey. A jaguar about to strike.

Christina!

"I'm coming," he told her. "I'm coming."

He fell into Hawkmother's cockpit. The plane settled down perfectly toward the runway, guided by the autopilot. Dreamland's modifications to the airfoil allowed the plane to slow to seventy-seven knots without stalling; she could have stopped in half the distance.

The tower controller gave him a command. Madrone concentrated on steering, forcing everything else away. He spotted a plane being serviced near a hangar at the far end of the access ramp. He told the computer to take him there, felt a twinge of pain, but nonetheless realized his directions were being followed. His thoughts ransacked the computer, desperately searching for information on how to refuel the plane.

The onboard computer did not appear to hold the ground refueling procedures, but a schematic of the aircraft showed him where the main refueling panel was located on the fuselage.

He jumped to the Flighthawks—no one was nearby.

He jumped back to Hawkmother, saw from the video feed that a crew was refueling an old DC-9 in front of a warehouselike building at the right side of the ramp.

The tower tried again to contact him.

He had to get out of the plane and refuel it himself. He'd have to convince them somehow to help.

To do that, though, he had to leave Theta and ANTARES.

The big Boeing rolled slowly to a stop. He couldn't see the maintenance people working on the DC-9 anymore.

If he left Theta now, would he ever get back? If he got out of the plane, could he return?

Madrone took a deep breath, then closed his eyes and jumped.

He tumbled from a great height, passing through a thunderstorm. Time jerked sideways into a different dimension, as if each second split in half—one part fast, one part slow.

The thud when he landed shook every bone. When he opened his eyes, he was sitting in the ANTARES control seat, out of Theta, unconnected.

Carefully but quickly, Kevin removed the control helmet

and the skullcap. The cabin lights stung his eyes. He rose, pushing past the control panels to the door. He unlocked it and pushed it open, at the same time retrieving an emergency access ladder kept in a small panel at the side of the door. The ladder was no more than a roll of chain links and metal bars; it swung wildly as he descended, further distorting his sense of balance.

He tumbled as he reached the ground, arms and legs unfurling in the warm, moist air. He lay on his back a moment, his senses as limp as his body.

I've escaped, he thought. I'll never go back. I'm free of ANTARES; I'm free of the bastards trying to poison me, of Bastian and Geraldo, of Smith and Jeff. I'm free.

Why had they taken his daughter and sent his wife away? To turn him into a computer?

"Qué le pasa?" said a trembling voice above him. "What's wrong with you?"

He looked up and saw a mechanic. His mind seemed to snap back into Theta. He jumped up.

"Nada," said Madrone. "Nothing's wrong with me. I need to be refueled."

The man stared at him. He had come from fueling the nearby plane and smelled like kerosene.

"What is this?" asked the mechanic in Spanish. He swept his hands, referring to the plane.

"I will pay you well to refuel me," said Madrone. *"Petro, petróleo aviación démelo,"* he stuttered, struggling but failing to get the words into presentable Spanish. He tried again, his brain reaching for the right room—the right part of ANTARES and the control computer, as if they were still attached, as if they had to be there somewhere. But even as he tried to find the words, he knew he couldn't; he kept talking as he rushed toward the man, bowling him over.

Taken by surprise, the mechanic fell easily. They rolled on the ground, thrashing. Madrone felt everything as if it were being presented by the Flighthawk video feed. Then the Mexican managed to strike him on the side of the head where the ANTARES chip had been implanted.

The pain shocked him. The blood in his arms and legs drained away; his heart stopped.

Lightning flashed. He closed his eyes.

When he opened them, the mechanic lay limp on the ground, neck twisted.

The mechanic's assistant stood a few feet away, terror on his face. Madrone took a step and the man bolted.

Kevin ran to the fuel truck. The hose lay below the old McDonnell Douglas airliner, unattached. It rolled to an electrically operated spindle at the rear of the fuel truck, but Madrone didn't bother with that. Instead, he jumped into the cab. The motor kicked over slowly, then caught. He drove quickly to Hawkmother, hands shaking, thoughts careening as the hose clattered on the ground behind him.

Pain mixed with anger and grief. The bastards had made him into a monster, made him kill his own daughter, kill his friends. Everyone had turned him against him.

Hawkmother's fuel-access panel had been updated for the automated attendant system being tested at Dreamland; it whooshed open with a touch of the access button and a light blinked next to the receptacle access port, a guide for the robotic nozzle assembly. Madrone had no trouble inserting the fuel truck's old-style hose, but couldn't figure out how to get the fuel flowing. He punched the truck buttons madly, felt his head begin to ache.

He felt himself in Hawk One, circling above the ocean.

Madrone slammed the panel at the rear of the fuel truck, desperate. The hose jumped.

Sirens in the distance.

The jaguar raced for him, lightning flashing from its eyes. Run. Run!

He had to do this. For Christina.

For himself.

For the dark woman, calling to him.

The fuel flowed freely, monitored and helped by the Boeing's automated circuits, which could compensate for changes in the pump pressure and automatically controlled the flow.

The flashing lights of a police vehicle approached from the other end of the field. Kevin left the hose as it pumped, and ran to the Mexican he had killed on the tarmac. He searched the man's jumpsuit pockets for a weapon.

Nothing but a butane lighter and cigarettes.

Lighter in hand, he ran back to the truck and the hose. The

police were in a pickup truck, now a few hundred yards away.

He would pull the hose from the plane and set the truck on fire.

Wouldn't the Boeing burn as well?

Hawkmother wouldn't permit him to simply remove the nozzle. He pulled and twisted, but it wouldn't relent. He stared at the square buttons next to the receptacle assembly. Two were lit; pushing them had no effect.

He tried another, then a fourth. Nothing. He punched a large rocker switch, heard a *whoosh*. The hose fell into his arms.

The pickup slammed to a stop about thirty yards from fuel truck. The police jumped out, ducking behind the opposite side of the truck. A voice called over a loudspeaker in Spanish and then English for him to stop and step away from the plane.

The automated fueling system on the Boeing had stopped the fuel flow with a bubble of compressed air, then closed and safed its fuel system. Had Hawkmother been interfaced with the Dreamland system it was designed for, the automated control on the other end would have felt the puff, reversed flow momentarily, and then shut off the pump and retrieved the hose, assuring that there would be no spill.

Here, the pump momentarily hiccuped, confused by the backflow pressure. Rather than shutting down, it sucked and then spat harder against the vacuum—after a brief moment of pumping nothing, jet fuel poured out everywhere. The hose slapped up and down against the pavement.

One of the policemen fired at him. Kevin grabbed the hose. As he began to run out from under the plane, he slipped and fell headlong on the tarmac. Jet fuel washed over him as the lightning broke above; he rolled in the rain, splashing through the gas and fumbling for the lighter. He needed a wick—he tore at his sleeve for the cloth, but the ANTARES jumpsuit didn't give way.

He had a handkerchief in his pocket.

More shots. The dull, metallic click of an automatic weapon.

The pavement chipped near him. Time had split again; his brain fuzzed as if he were in the middle of an LSD-induced hallucination.

Madrone wadded the handkerchief, pushed it away, took the lighter, and clicked it. Flames burst everywhere.

Breathe, he told himself. Warmth enveloped him and he saw the dark woman a few feet away in the rain forest, beckoning as fire leapt up his shoulder.

Roll and breathe.

Agony.

The jaguar roared from the fire. Madrone took a long breath and pushed his hands down. The fuel truck turned into an outline of flickering red.

The chain ladder slapped against his hands. He pulled himself upward. The plane seemed unscathed, safe.

Kevin slammed the door shut, then jammed the helmet on his head. He was there, in the cockpit, surrounded by flames. He could see the dark woman and the jungle beyond.

The engines wound up.

More vehicles came, an entire armada. He began to back away, saw them all in the video.

Madrone looked to the right and he was in the Flighthawks. The U/MFs flashed upward from the ocean, streaking toward Hawkmother.

Back in the Boeing. Moving.

He would fly right through the trucks if he had to.

One was an armored car.

Hawk One streaked at the armored car, slashing in front of her. The vehicle slowed, but did not stop.

Crash into it.

No. Not yet. Only if necessary.

An access ramp paralleled the runway. It was wide and would be long enough for him to take off, but only if he started from the beginning.

He couldn't turn and keep the Boeing on the ramp. He'd have to back up.

Reverse thrust.

Hawkmother didn't like the sudden change of momentum. She rumbled as the engines tried to follow his commands. Slowly, she stopped moving forward. Then, trembling, she inched backward on the narrow pathway.

Hawk One and Two danced before the armored car and a sedan. The armored car finally stopped. A police car reached the runway and began driving parallel to him.

The armored car began moving again.

The runway. They thought he would use it and were trying to block it off, ignoring the ramp. Good.

He had it now. He jumped back into the Flighthawks, harassed a knot of men piling off a pickup truck, sending them to the ground.

He looked left. He was in Hawkmother.

Full throttle. Go. Go.

The fuel truck exploded. Though it was by now several hundred yards away, the shock wave nearly pushed Hawkmother off the narrow ramp. Her right wheels nudged the soft dirt.

He pulled back on the stick. The 777, not yet at eighty knots, far too slow to take off, hesitated. The safety protocols screamed.

He swept them away with his hand, demanded more thrust.

The armored car began to fire its cannon at him.

Now, he told the plane, and she lifted into the sky.

Dreamland
19 February, 1705 local

JEFF UNDID HIS RESTRAINTS AND LEANED BACK IN HIS seat as Raven rolled toward her hangar. The day had been impossibly long, and he'd had nothing to eat beyond the sludge from Ong's zero-gravity Mr. Coffee. But the way his stomach was roiling, Zen was glad it was empty.

They had found and retrieved the copilot with help of SAR assets from Nellis, working at long distance. But the storm over the mountains had whipped into a fury as they worked, hampering even Raven and its sophisticated sensors. The pilot and Madrone were still missing, and no one had found the wreckage of Hawkmother or the Flighthawks.

"Major, you need a hand?" asked Ong behind him.

Poor egghead looked like he was ready to fall down on the deck and sleep there.

"Nah," Jeff told him, swinging his chair out from its mounting. "I'm fine."

"Tight squeeze," said Ong.

"Yeah. You should see me trying to get into a phone

booth." He leaned forward, then levered his arms against the low-slung seat rests, maneuvering his fanny backward into the wheelchair. He supported his entire weight with his left hand, then walked it back a bit before sliding into the chair. He'd done it maybe a thousand times, but tonight fatigue made him slip a bit, and he nearly fell out as he plopped backward. He rolled to the hatch slowly, attaching the chair to the special clamps on the ventral ladder that allowed him to use the specially designed escalator.

Colonel Bastian was waiting on the tarmac. "So?"

"Dalton and Madrone are still missing. We think we have the area narrowed down," said Jeff.

"McMann told me they saw a chute," said Bastian. Colonel McMann was in charge of the search-and-rescue assets that had been scrambled from Edwards.

Zen nodded. "The infrareds didn't find anything there. They were going to wait until morning to send some PJs down unless there's a radio transmission. Bitchin' terrain."

Bastian nodded. "No use going out in this weather in the dark."

"Crew's beat," agreed Zen, even though he and the others had debated going back out.

"Dr. Geraldo tells me you want to rejoin ANTARES."

"Technically, I never left," said Jeff.

"It's a tight schedule until we get another Flighthawk pilot."

"I realize that," Jeff told him.

Bastian nodded, but the silence remained awkward.

"I thought I'd go downstairs and see if they made anything out from the mission data," said Jeff. "See if we can turn up anything. I had Ong transmit the data when we were inbound."

"Yeah, okay. Look, Zen . . ."

Bastian touched his shoulder, but didn't say anything. In the dim morning twilight he suddenly looked very old.

"I'm okay, Dad," he told his father-in-law.

Bastian nodded, then took his hand away. Zen gripped the top of his wheels.

"Dad?" said Dog, slightly bemused. Jeff had never called Bastian "Dad" before.

"Don't get used to it, Colonel."

"I don't know that I'd want to." Bastian gave him a tired smile, and waved him on.

Computer Lab
19 February, 1715

JENNIFER GLEASON SPREAD THE PRINTOUTS ACROSS the black lab tables, trying to see if there was a pattern to gibberish that had inserted itself into C^3's resource-allocation data.

Of course there was a pattern; there had to be a pattern. But what was it? Her diagnostic routines hadn't a clue. Baffled, she decided to get them all on a printout in one place, mark them, and see if anything occurred to her. Scrounging tape and a marker, she laid out the pages of the printout, then began the laborious process of highlighting the interesting sections.

Following their usual protocol, the entire test session had been recorded on the diagnostic computers. The flight computer's different functions were logged as they were monitored in real time, tracking flight commands and the U/MF's responses. She also had a hard record of C^3's processing and memory allocations, which corresponded with the various instructions and inputs on the log. Specific commands—takeoff, for example—always resulted in a certain pattern of resource allocations, in the same way human brain waves corresponded to certain actions.

The correspondences were all there, a perfect set of fingerprints showing that C^3 and the Flighthawks had worked flawlessly, at least until the point when Raven lost its link with Hawkmother over the Sierra Nevadas.

But the diagnostic program that she'd run to check for the correspondences had discovered a large number of anomalies in the allocations. Sparse at first, they'd increased dramatically by the time contact was lost.

They were short too, and didn't correspond to actual or virtual addresses in the memory or processing units. But they were definitely there—as her yellow marker attested. Jennifer climbed onto the table, bending low to mark them. She was about three quarters of the way through when the door to the lab slid open.

"Hey, Jen," said Zen, rolling in.

"Hi," she said, continuing to mark the sheets.

"What are you doing on the table?"

"Cramming for the test," she said.

"Huh?"

"Just a joke." She lifted her knees carefully and slid off the table.

"Some view," said Zen.

"If I'd have known you were coming I would have worn a miniskirt," she said.

"Seriously, what are you doing?"

"Something strange happened with the Flighthawk control computer," she said, explaining about the allocations.

"Maybe it's just a transmission problem."

"No way. We've done this a million times without anything like this showing up."

"Not with ANTARES."

"True."

"This related to the crash?"

"No."

"You sure?"

Jennifer tugged a strand of hair back behind her ear. "I don't see how. You have no idea what happened?"

"Kulpin thought the flight computer on the Boeing whacked out and somehow took over."

"Hmmmph."

"Possible?"

What if the gibberish were code from the Boeing's computer pilot?

"Well?" asked Jeff.

"I uh, well, probably not," she said. "We've never had that kind of problem with the autopilot before. It's basically a subset of the systems we've used in the Megafortress."

How could the Boeing's command computer leak across into C³?

Through the interrupts they used for the video, and to coordinate the flight information. But the gateway and thus ANTARES were in the way.

Impossible.

Impossible?

"Jen?"

"I just thought of an odd theory," she said, explaining it to him. Zen's eyes began to glaze after the first sentence, so she cut it short. "I'll have to review a few sessions to see if I'm on the right track. I'm not sure I'm right, but it might be a start."

"Do you have anything that can help us now? For the search?"

"Sorry."

Jeff started to roll away.

"Jeff, if you can get the hard drives back, we'd have a much better chance to figure out what happened."

"Figuring out what happened isn't my priority at the moment," he said. "I want to find Dalton and Madrone."

"So do I."

Aboard SAR Helicopter Charlie 7
Over Sierra Nevada Mountains
19 February, 1715

SERGEANT PERSE "POWDER" TALCOM LEANED AGAINST the door window of the Pave Low as the big helicopter struggled against the wind. The cloud hanging on the mountainside seemed like a massive bear, trying to protect her young.

"Fierce fuckin' rain," he groused to Sergeant Lee "Nurse" Liu, who was standing behind him. "I can't fuckin' see fuckin' shit."

"Sleet," corrected Liu. "Some of it's even snow."

"Whatever."

"Use Captain Freah's visor."

"Helmet's too damn heavy."

"Then I will."

Powder gave his companion a scowl, then braced himself to fit the smart helmet and its high-tech visor over his head. Freah's suggestion that they take the new device had seemed like a great idea—until Powder put it on in the transport out to Nellis. The helmet had been formed for the captain's head. It scraped the hell out of Powder's ears going on, but floated around freely like a bucket atop a water pump once on.

No wonder officers thought differently than normal human beings; their heads were shaped weird.

Normally, a Pave Low would ride with two officers—pilot and copilot—along with a pair of flight engineers and two crew members manning the guns. This craft, Charlie 7, had been flying nearly nonstop since before the crash, and was now on its third crew. Besides the pilots and the Dreamland volunteers as SAR personnel, it carried only one flight engineer, a staff sergeant named Brautman who had drunk at least four liter bottles of Coke since the Dreamland volunteers had come aboard forty-five minutes ago. He definitely had a caffeine buzz—his chin bobbed up and down constantly and his arms buzzed like a hummingbird's wings. Brautman kept getting up and down, pacing back and forth between the rear of the flight deck and the rest of the cabin, so jittery Powder felt like laying him out with a shot to the jaw.

"There, right there," said Liu, pointing to the ravine.

Powder flicked the visor into infrared mode. A brownish blob appeared at the lower left of the screen; the weather cut down greatly on the available detail, but there was definitely something warm down there.

"Get us the fuck down there," Powder yelled to Brautman, who relayed the request to the pilot without the expletive.

"Too windy," was the reply.

"Fuck that." Sergeant Talcom took off the helmet, and then nearly lost it as turbulence rocked the helo. Liu grabbed the helmet and Powder tottered forward, grabbing at the bulkhead like a drunken sailor.

"You gotta get us fuckin' down!" he yelled at the two men on the flight deck.

As a general rule, Air Force SAR helicopter pilots, and Pave Low jocks in particular, had boulder-sized balls. With the possible exception of their mamas, they weren't scared of anything. This particular pilot had flown deep into Iraq during the Gulf War, and had a scar on his leg to prove he had done so under fire. But he shook his head.

"The storm is too much, night's coming on, and that's not a man down there," he told Powder.

"How the fuck do you know?" demanded the sergeant.

"Because we've been looking at that spot for five minutes on the infrared," answered the copilot, pointing to the Pave

Low's screen. A strong gust of wind caught the helicopter, and he snapped his head back to the front as the pilot steadied the craft. "The scope is clear," he added. "No one's there."

"He's on ours!" answered Powder. He jerked his thumb back toward Liu. "Or something is! I'm fuckin' tellin' ya—our gear spotted something."

"Look, Sergeant, you do your job, we'll do ours," said the copilot. "And watch your language when you're talking to an officer."

"Hey, fuck that," grumbled Powder.

Liu squeezed next to him, the helmet on his head. The Whiplash crew members' discrete-burst com sets didn't interface with the Pave Low's interphone, so he hadn't heard the discussion.

"I see something," he shouted to the others over the whine of the engines.

"We know," said Powder.

"Not a person," answered the copilot.

"I know," said Liu. "But I have a theory."

"What?" said Brautman.

"If that object below is the ejection seat, which I believe it must be, then perhaps the pilot came out nearby."

No shit, thought Powder.

"In this storm, he would seek shelter," continued Liu. "There are caves on the south side of the ravine."

"We can look," said the copilot, all of a sudden Mr. Compromise. He said something into his mouthpiece and the pilot began nodding his head.

"You're a fuckin' diplomat, you know that, Nurse?" Powder told Liu.

The wash of the motors drowned out Liu's reply. The two Whiplash troopers resumed their posts at the windows, trying to scan through the heavy fog and drizzle.

The helicopter lurched sharply left, so quickly Talcom thought they were going in.

"Got something!" yelled the flight engineer.

Powder bent forward to look at the IR screen. A small greenish blob congealed at the bottom of the screen around other greenish blobs in a sea of fuzz.

"Our fuckin' guy?" he asked Liu, who was scanning with the CIV.

"Something," replied Nurse. "The rain and sleet hinder the sensors."

The pilots agreed the only way to find out was to go down there. But between the wind and the ravine, the closest the helicopter could come after three attempts was twenty-five feet.

"Tell the pilot to hold the fuckin' thing steady and we'll fuckin' rappel," Powder told Brautman.

"That's a hell of a fall," said the flight engineer.

"I ain't plannin' on fuckin' fallin'," said Powder. "Come on—it's gettin' fuckin' dark. We gotta kick ass here."

Brautman consulted with the pilots through his com gear. "He's up for it if you're up for it."

The helicopter stuttered against a wind shear.

"Fuckin' damn, let's kick ass."

"Hey," said Brautman, grabbing Talcom's shoulder. "You sure?"

"Fuck you."

Brautman laughed and shook his head.

"What?"

"You curse worse than anyone I've ever met."

"Fuck off."

"Ten bucks says you can't get through the rest of the mission without using the F word."

Powder snorted. "Sure. Now let's stop screwin' around and do it. Liu, give me the damn helmet back and put on your own. Mama always told me never go out in a storm without a hat."

The Pave Low reared sideways as the door slid open for Powder and Liu. The wash of wind, sleet, hail, and rain against Powder's body felt like a tsunami, sending him off balance into the bulkhead behind the cockpit. The sergeant smacked the back of his helmet against the metal and rebounded like a cue ball with bottom English.

"Bitchin' shit-ass weather," said Powder, grabbing for the side of the door. He was careful not to use "fuck." Ten bucks was ten bucks.

By the time he was three quarters of the way down the rope line, his thick weatherproof gloves were sopping wet. He managed to toe himself against a ledge six or seven feet over the cave Liu had spotted. The helo had descended a little further, but could hardly be called steady; one of the gyrations whipped him forward, and he just managed to avoid smashing his knee on the rocks. Leaning around the rope, Powder tried to see what the hell was below him—he didn't want to be climbing through this shit for a lost mountain lion.

He couldn't see much of anything except some very nasty-looking rocks. And sheets of rain, sleet, and snow.

Slowly, he worked himself down far enough to leave the rope. The helicopter began drifting backward as he went; he twisted and put one arm out to keep himself from smacking against the rock face opposite the cave. Finally, he found a ledge wide enough to stand on.

As soon as he let go of the rope, he slipped and tumbled halfway down a three-foot-wide crevice to his right. His curses became truly poetic, invoking the wrath not merely of God, but of the bastard recruiting sergeant who had steered him toward such a thank-shitting-less life. He continued to curse until he reached the cave, where he found Liu kneeling over a prostrate body.

"Alive. Barely. Hypothermia. Broken leg. Internal injuries," said Liu over the Whiplash com set. "It's the pilot, Dalton."

"Yeah. Think he'll survive a shittin' sling?" asked Powder.

"He better. An avalanche may cover the cave opening any minute."

"You're pulling my pud, right?"

"Too big to pull, Powder."

Talcom heard—or thought he heard—the rocks groan above. He popped out his walkie-talkie and told the crew to expedite the stretcher.

The wind died somewhat as they secured Dalton and brought him beneath the helicopter. The sleet compensated by kicking down harder.

Despite the fact that he was clad entirely in waterproof gear, water had seeped into every pore of Powder's body. Even his liver felt waterlogged. He sloshed against the rocks, trying to keep the stretcher from spinning too much as it cranked upward. It had reached nearly to the doorway when the Pave Low stuttered backward, pushed toward the jagged peaks by an immense gush of wind.

"Hey, you bastard," Powder shouted. "Crank him in before you go anywhere."

He and Liu stared at the aircraft struggling above them, no more powerful than a grasshopper caught in the fury of the storm. The front of the helicopter pushed upward, then steadied back, leveling off. Brautman appeared in the doorway, fumbling with the mechanism for the stretcher. Dalton disappeared inside the hull.

Then the rear of the MH-53 veered to the left, the front of the big bird tipping against the wind. Powder thought the idiot pilot had forgotten them and was taking off.

In the next moment, the helicopter's tail smashed against the rocks.

Dreamland Commander's Office
19 February, 1803

"EXCUSE ME, COLONEL," SAID SERGEANT GIBBS, OPENing the door to Dog's office. "Secretary Keesh is on the line."

Dog nodded, then turned back to Geraldo, who had only just come in. "I'm afraid you'll have to excuse me," he told her. "This isn't going to be pleasant anyway."

"I understand, Colonel." She stood. "I should be back at my lab in any event. You'll contact me when Kevin is picked up?"

Even though he was a big believer in remaining positive, Dog found it hard not to grimace. If Madrone had managed to parachute—and at the moment there was no reason to think that he had, based on what the copilot had said—he would have spent more than seven hours in mountainous terrain in freezing weather.

"It's okay, Colonel," said Geraldo. "I realize the odds. But it's best to sound positive."

"I'll keep you informed," he told her as she walked out of the room.

Ax held the door for her. The sergeant rarely, if ever, did that for anyone, Dog thought to himself before picking up the phone.

Ax soft on Geraldo?

No way.

"Stand by for Secretary Keesh," said an aide on the other line. The woman's voice sounded muffled, as if she were speaking from inside full body armor—undoubtedly standard issue for anyone on Keesh's staff.

"How the hell did you lose two airplanes?" demanded Keesh as the line clicked.

"Actually, sir, it was one 777 and two Flighthawks. We've recovered one of the pilots. Two others are missing, including the ANTARES subject."

Dog paused for effect, pushing around the papers on his desk. Among them was an old photograph Ax had found while going through some old papers the other day; it showed Dog at an air show standing in front of a P-51 Mustang.

Damn nice airplane. He hadn't had a chance to fly it, though.

"What is this going to do to the project?" Keesh demanded.

"At the moment, Mr. Secretary, we're in the process of recovering our people. We haven't even located the wreckage yet."

"You're taking your damn time."

There was no sense arguing with him. Bastian looked up as the door to his office opened again. Danny Freah stood there with one of his most serious expressions.

"With all due respect, sir, I'm advised by my security people that we're speaking on an open line," said Bastian.

"That's not going to get you off the hook, Bastian."

Dog was tempted—sorely tempted—to ask if Keesh thought he'd arranged the crash solely to make the Secretary look bad. But he merely told Keesh that he would keep him apprised through the proper channels, then hung up the phone.

"You're not here about that line being open, are you?" Dog said to Danny, who was still standing in the doorway.

"They've lost contact with the Pave Low that Powder and Liu were on," said Freah. "They think they went down. The storm's pretty bad."

"Excuse me, Colonel," said Major Stockard, rolling up behind Danny. "Can I get in on this?"

"I don't know that there's anything to get in on, Jeff," said Bastian.

"Nellis is asking for help in the search," explained Danny, who obviously had already told Zen what was up.

"Raven and the Flighthawks can help," said Stockard. "The IR sensors on the U/MFs are more sensitive than the units in the Pave Lows. We can get in through the storm while Raven stays up above."

"We just lost two Flighthawks," said Bastian.

"The Flighthawks had nothing to do with that," said Jeff. He gave his wheels a shove, then pulled his hands close to his body as the chair rolled across the threshold, narrowly clearing the doorjambs. "We can be off the ground inside of thirty minutes. Twenty, easy. Raven's ready to go. With the weather, the Flighthawks would extend our vision exponentially."

"I don't know Jeff. Those are our last two Flighthawks."

"Why do we have them if we can't use them?"

"You have to be tired as shit."

"Screw that."

Bastian folded his arms. If the Flighthawks ran into trouble in the heavy storm—and the weather report was anything but pleasant—Keesh would be unmerciful. Worse, the Flighthawk program might be set back six months or even longer.

But he had two missing men, plus two Whiplash team members and the crew of a Pave Low down. What was more important?

His men certainly. Unless you added in the lives of men who might be saved in the future by a squadron of Flighthawks.

As for Secretary Keesh . . .

"SAR assets are strapped. They're looking for help," added Danny. "That was the only Pave Low available within a two-hundred-mile radius."

"You sure you're not tired?" Dog asked Jeff.

"Of course I'm tired," said Zen. "But I'm not going to fall asleep now anyway."

"Go for it."

Sierra Nevada Mountains
19 February, 1934

POWDER SLOGGED HIS SODDEN BOOT UP AND OVER THE rock outcropping, forcing his foot into the small crevice. Then he boosted himself over the razor-sharp diagonal, finally onto solid and relatively flat ground. The CIV and its helmet were heavy, but they did at least give him a pretty clear picture, even in these conditions—the helicopter sat on its side about a hundred yards away, its nose pointed down the opposite slope. One of its blades pointed into the air like a giant middle finger raised against the storm. The rain and sleet had turned back into snow, which had already piled about an inch high against the fuselage.

"Shit," Powder told Liu, who was just clearing the ravine behind him. He pointed the flashlight attached to his wrist, showing Nurse the way.

"Light a flare," suggested Liu, pointing left. "We'll stage off those rocks if anything goes wrong."

The night turned crimson-gray, the flare burning fitfully in the wet snow. They walked gingerly, unsure of their footing. The crash had forced the front of the helicopter's fuselage together; Powder prepared himself for a gruesome sight.

He couldn't see much at first. Liu climbed onto the chin of the helicopter, draping himself over it and then smashing at the side glass with his heavy flashlight and elbow. Powder took out another flashlight from his kit and clambered up.

Someone groaned inside.

"We're here, buddy," shouted Talcom. Adrenaline shot through him; he reached his fingers into the door frame and somehow managed to pry it open, the metal twisting as he did so. He got to his knees and then his feet, pushing the bent panel away with all of his weight. The mangled hinges gave way and the door flew through the air and into the snow.

The pilot and copilot were still strapped into their seats. Liu leaned in, slinking over the men to check on them.

"Pulses strong," said Nurse. "Let's take this slow in case they injured their backs."

"Hey!" yelled a voice in the back. "Hey!"

Powder clicked the visor from starlight to infrared mode and scanned the dim interior. Fingers fluttered in front of a wall; the viewer made them look like worms in a lake, unattached to anything human.

The sergeant slipped the helmet back and yelled into the helicopter. "Yo!"

"Hello," yelled Brautman. "Leg's broke," he added, his

voice almost cheerful. "Otherwise, I'm cool except for whatever the hell is holding me down."

It looked like a good hunk of the helicopter wall.

"You say the F word yet?" asked the flight engineer as Powder tried to push his way toward him.

"No way," answered Powder. "You owe me ten."

"Mission's not done yet."

"Need a pneumatic jack to get him out," said Liu from somewhere outside the helicopter.

"Screw that." Powder straightened in a small spot between the forward area and what was left of the rear compartment. He had enough clearance to sit upright, but still couldn't see Brautman's head. "I said 'screw,' not the F word," he yelled back to the trapped crewman.

"I heard ya. You will."

Powder backed out, gingerly climbing atop the wrecked helicopter. Liu stood on the ground near the door—the chopper body had been squeezed so tight it barely came to his shoulders. Moving forward on his knees, Powder looked for something to use to help lever the rear door off its rail. When he couldn't see anything, he set himself at a forty-five-degree angle and managed to jerk the metal out in two loud rips, producing a two-foot-wide opening.

"I ate my Wheaties this morning," he told Liu as he leaned back to rest. His arm felt like he'd pulled it out of its socket.

The helicopter creaked as he spoke. He straightened, then realized they were moving—not far, not fast, but definitely moving.

"We may slide down the slope," said Liu.

"Shit," answered Powder.

"Get the pilots out one at a time, ASAP."

As Liu said that, he was already clambering back to the cockpit. He leaned in, trying to release the pilot from his restraints.

The helicopter slid some more, then stopped. Powder thought of trying to find something to prop it in place, but quickly dismissed the idea. He swung down and took the pilot's body from Liu.

The pilot was heavier than he thought, and Talcom's legs buckled as he carried the man toward the rocks they had pointed out before. The rocks didn't offer much shelter, but they were easy to find in the swirling snow and sat on the other side of a large crack, which might—might—mean they were safe from the slide. Powder laid the pilot as flat as possible, then lifted the crash shield on his helmet to make sure he was still breathing. When the man opened his eyes, Powder nudged his cheek with his thick thumb, then closed the shield. He took off the CIV and smart helmet, placing them next to the pilot, and ran back to the Pave Low. Liu was just lifting the copilot out.

"You're strong for a little guy, Liu."

"He's conscious," said Liu, holding the man in front of him as if he were displaying a piece of meat.

Powder clambered up onto the helicopter. The aircraft slid a lot this time. "Damn," he said, grabbing the copilot.

"I'm okay," grumbled the man. "I can walk myself."

"Yeah, okay," said Powder, ignoring him. He turned to get off the helicopter, then noticed something peculiar—though the Pave Low had moved several times, it hadn't pushed up any snow in front of it as it slid.

"That's because the whole sheet of ice is moving," explained Liu before ducking back inside the craft.

"Damn," said Powder. "Damn, damn, damn."

He helped the copilot back to the rock, then ran to Liu. The wind rattled the helicopter propeller back and forth. Powder heard a low rumble, as if a train were approaching from the distance.

"Liu! What the hell are you doing in there?"

"If we use this spar as a lever," Liu answered from inside the cockpit, "maybe we can move the wall away."

"The whole thing is moving," said Powder. "Feel it?"

"Quickly then."

"Shit." Talcom squeezed around Liu to push his legs into the small opening to the rear of the helo. There was a loud groan from outside as he did.

"Hope that was the Abominable Snowman," he said.

"Ice is giving way," said Brautman.

Powder wedged his foot against the metal side of the helicopter and tried levering the piece of spar in the opposite direction. As he did, Liu dropped the flashlight.

"Get the fuck out of here," Brautman told them. "Go."

"Now who's using bad words?" said Powder. The helicopter or the ice it was on slid downward, and he felt an empty impotence in his stomach.

"Screw this horseshit!" Talcom yelled, jamming his boots against the metal.

It snapped away, springing back as the door released from its latch. Snow and sleet and ice and rain fell through, twinkling artistically in the dim flare-light. None of them stopped to admire it—Brautman pulled himself upward through the hole, helped by Liu, who was outside. The flight engineer's leg trailed behind him at an odd angle, and Powder felt a twinge in his stomach, thinking of how the damn thing must feel.

The twinge was replaced by full-scale nausea as the helicopter jerked hard to his left, starting to ride down the incline. It had finally slipped on the ice—which also shifted in its own direction.

"Get the hell out of here! Go!" Powder shouted. He'd started to push himself upward when he saw something moving beneath the twisted metal where the snow was falling.

Dalton, still strapped to the stretcher.

Aboard Raven
19 February, 2010

HAWK THREE KNIFED THROUGH THE TURBULENCE, accelerating toward the jagged, snow-laden peaks where the Pave Low had disappeared. While the flight computer could cope with the strong vortices of wind easily enough, there was little it could do about the ice trying to freeze on the wings. The lower and slower Zen went—and to do the search properly, he had to go low and slow—the more precipitation clung to the control surfaces. While not enough to keep the plane from flying, it added considerably to the difficulty factor in the swirling winds near the crags.

"Sector Alpha-Baker-1 is clear," said Jennifer Gleason, who'd volunteered to come along and help monitor the scans. Major Cheshire had bumped Bree's copilot and was at the stick; Bree had slid over to the second officer's seat and was also studying the feeds.

"Alpha-Baker-2 is also clear," snapped Breanna. Both

women were examining the IR video from Hawk Four, which was being flown entirely by the computer through a ravine at the very northern edge of the search area. The weather there was not as severe and the terrain not as twisted as the area Zen was working himself further southwest.

Hawk Three hit a patch of clear air and shot forward as if her engine had ingested pure oxygen. Zen steadied his left joystick, glancing at the vital signs projected at the lower edge of the visor. Everything was in the green.

His attention back on the main screen, he saw a dull shadow at the edge of the approaching valley, below a triple-dagger peak. It wasn't warm enough to be a body, but since it was the first non-rock he'd seen, he switched from the IR to the optical feed.

"Computer, zoom in the dark object at the bottom of Hawk Three's visual feed," Zen directed.

The computer formed a box around the image, which seemed to burst into the middle of his view screen.

Ejection seat.

"Mark location," said Jeff.

"What do you have?" Jennifer asked over the interphone.

"Jeff?" said Bree.

"Excuse me. Are you manning your scans?" he snapped.

"Affirmative, Hawk Leader," answered Bree testily. Jennifer said nothing.

"Raven, I have a piece of the seat, I think, from the Boeing," Jeff said, technically speaking to Cheshire though they could all hear him. "I've marked it. I'll continue to sweep the sector. Hawk Four is going to stay in the pattern we planned."

"Raven Leader acknowledges," said the pilot. Although Jeff was actually sitting a few feet below Cheshire on Raven's lower deck, they had found it easier to communicate as if flying separate planes—which, of course, they were.

Zen pushed Hawk Three to the south, dropping her lower to scan close to a W-shaped ravine at the edge of a shallow mountain plateau. The severe storm shortened the IR's range considerably, though from a technical viewpoint the fact that he was even receiving an image was impressive. Even light rain played havoc with conventional FLIR systems.

As he neared the end of the ravine, a small shadow flickered into the upper right-hand corner of the view screen. He was by it before he could ask for a magnification; he pulled back on the Flighthawk's joystick, then felt the plane fluttering in the heavy wind.

"Disconnect in zero-three," warned the computer. The storm and jagged terrain degraded the link between the Hawk and its mother.

"Raven, I need you closer to Three," snapped Jeff. He started to pull up, but saw something in the IR screen at the right-hand corner. He pushed toward it, despite the disconnect warning that flashed in the screen.

"Disconnect in zero-three, two—"

Zen managed to nudge the U/MF upward at the last second, retaining the data flow. But the storm whipped hard against the small plane's wings. It pushed up and then down, yawing like a gum wrapper tossed from a car. Even with the assistance of the computer and the vectoring nozzles, Zen couldn't get it where he wanted.

"Raven, lower," he demanded.

"You want me to park on Mount Whitney?" snapped Cheshire.

"That's too high." He just missed a ravine wall as he tried to slide Hawk Three back toward the ridge where he'd seen the image. Hawk Three hugged the hillside, her altimeter nudging six thousand feet—half the altitude Raven needed to clear the surrounding peaks. This was too damn low for comfort, and even C^3 began doing a Bitchin' Betty routine, warning that he was going too low and too slow. Still, the only way to get a good view was to practically crawl across the terrain. Hawk Three's forward airspeed nudged below ninety knots.

Stall warning. But something hot, real hot, filled the screen.

Above—up. Jeff throttled and pushed the stick, climbing the side of the ridge.

"Disconnect in zero-three."

"Nancy! Closer!"

"We're trying, Zen!"

A red bar appeared at the bottom of his view screen as the computer continued counting down the disconnect.

But there was a man there. Definitely a man—two men, huddled.

As Zen went to push the GPS marker, the screen blanked into gray fuzz. The default sequence knocked the view screen back to the optical view from Hawk Four, which had just begun knifing east.

A magenta disc filled the screen; Jeff felt suddenly weightless, sliding backward. The right side of his head imploded, pain shooting everywhere—he closed his eyes as he spun back, caught by some trick of fatigue or exertion or merely disorientation. He couldn't see, couldn't think. Streaks of rain and lightning flashed by him, close enough to feel but not see. The world split beneath him, the fault line running through his spine.

Then he felt his toes. He could actually feel his toes.

The sun turned mercury red, then steamed off, evaporating in a hiss that filled his helmet.

An ANTARES flashback because he'd been thinking of Kevin?

Or because he'd taken the first dose of drugs as soon as Bastian gave the okay to rejoin the program?

That was less than two hours ago. The screen was back to normal—it had to have been a weird anomaly caused by the lightning.

And fatigue. He was getting damn tired.

"Sorry, shit, I'm sorry. The storm is too fierce here," said Cheshire somewhere outside of his helmet. She apologized for the wicked, disorienting turbulence shaking the plane.

Raven shuddered, trying desperately to fight off a wind shear that dropped her nearly two hundred feet in the blink of an eye. The plane pitched onto her side, just barely staying airborne.

"Zen, I can't get any lower than this."

"Hawk Leader acknowledges," he snapped. "C³, reestablish contact with Hawk Three."

"Attempting," answered the voice module.

"Try harder," he said, even though he realized the voice command would merely confuse the computer. He altered Hawk Four's course to close on the area Three had been surveying, and was within ten miles when the computer finally managed to restore full bandwidth with the U/MF.

Fail-safe mode during disconnect had caused the robot to fly upward out of the mountains. Because of that, Four was actually closer to the slope where he'd seen what he thought were men—or at least he thought it was closer, since he hadn't marked it. Zen let the computer put Three into a safe orbit at fifteen thousand feet over Raven, and brought Four into the treacherous peaks. He flew south, then circled back, pushing downward as he came.

A fire burned at the left-hand side of his screen. Above to the right loomed a large object.

The Pave Low. Men nearby.

Jeff quickly marked the location.

"I have them," he told Nancy. "Get me the SAR commander."

"Coast Guard asset Colgate is already en route to our position, Hawk Commander," answered Breanna from the copilot's station, where she was handling communications. "ETA is ten minutes. They're requesting you guide them in."

"I have a flare on the ground. Two figures near a rock, three figures. Something else in the helicopter," said Zen, nudging Hawk Four to get as close as possible in the storm. "Looks like the helicopter's moving, sliding or something."

"Opening Colgate channel. I think I'm getting something on Guard as well."

The helicopter seemed to hop in the screen.

"Colgate better get a move on," said Zen. "And Bree, if you can get the crew on Guard, tell them to get the hell off that ice. The whole side of that hill is heading for the ravine."

Sierra Nevada Mountains
19 February, 2018

POWDER SHOULDERED AGAINST THE HELICOPTER SPAR, then felt something shove down behind him. Metal crunched and crackled—he pushed around what had been a flight engineer's seat, kneeling and then crawling into the cabin opening. Dalton lay beneath some blankets just a few feet away, his legs exposed.

They were moving. The earth rumbled beneath them.

"Yo, Captain, I'm gonna cut you outta this," said Powder, feeling along the stretcher for the restraints. "I sure hope your back ain't messed up, 'cause we gotta go."

Dalton groaned, or at least Powder thought he groaned. Powder pulled his combat knife against the belts, slashing and hacking as the back end of the helo slid around. His hand flew free as he reached the last strap. He lost the knife but grabbed Dalton, pulling him backward as he pushed upward to get out of the fuselage. Dalton dragged behind, still attached somehow.

"Come on!" shouted Powder, pulling. Whatever held the pilot down snapped free. Powder got his elbow on the metal side below the open doorway and pushed upward like a swimmer trying to rise from the bottom of a swimming pool. He managed to get out of the fuselage, dragging the pilot with him as they tumbled into the snow and ice and rocks. Powder got to his feet, clawing in the direction of the others as the mountain rumbled beneath him. Something hard hit him in the chest, but he kept moving, churning his legs and struggling to keep Dalton in the grip of his icy fingers. After about five or six yards he fell sideways into a fissure of earth, then lost his balance backward.

Something grabbed his scalp, yanking at it but losing its grip; nonetheless, it helped him regain his momentum, and he threw himself and the injured pilot forward, scrambling as a pair of arms caught his side and hauled him upward.

"Shit fuck," he said, landing on the ground across the fissure near the rock, helped there by Liu and the copilot.

"You owe me ten bucks," growled Brautman on the ground.

"Fuck yourself," Powder said to him, easing Dalton to the ground.

"Want to try double or nothing?"

Despite the storm, they all started laughing.

Aboard Raven
19 February, 2024

RAVEN HAD BEEN OUTFITTED AS AN ELECTRONICS WARfare and electronics intelligence or Elint test bed, and her sleek underbody included several long aerodynamic bulges containing high-tech antennae. Though not trained to squeeze the last ounce of reception out of the equipment, Bree knew

enough to pinpoint the strongest areas of the PRC-90 transmission beacon as it bounced out of the rocks. The enhanced
gear in Raven gathered different parts of the broadcast, in
effect cobbling the full transmission from a series of broken
shadows. The problem was making the PRC-90 hear them;
the radios were strictly line-of-sight and the surrounding
ridges gave only a narrow reception cone.

"I think they're laughing," Breanna told the others on the
interphone.

"Laughing?" said Cheshire.

"Hang on." She clicked back into the Guard frequency.
"Charlie 7, this is Raven. Can you hear me?"

"Charlie 7. Got you Raven, honey."

The crewman was definitely giggling.

"Honey?"

"Kind of wet down here," responded whoever was handling
the radio. "Send some umbrellas if you're not picking us up."

Major Cheshire tapped Breanna's shoulder.

"What's up?"

"I think they're suffering from oxygen depletion or something," said Breanna, shrugging before giving the Coast Guard
rescue helicopter a vector to the crash.

"Colgate acknowledges. Bitchin' weather, but—we see
them, we see them!" said the Coast Guard pilot, his voice
suddenly jumping an octave. "We can get them as long as
they stay in the clear there. We can get them!"

"Raven acknowledges. We'll stand by."

ZEN TOOK OFF HIS CONTROL HELMET AND LEANED BACK
as Jennifer dialed the video feed from Hawk Four into a common channel, allowing the pilot and copilot to view the rescue
on one of the multi-configurable screens upstairs. It looked
almost—almost—easy from here, as the Dauphin helicopter
battled against the wind, rain, and sleet, hovering only a few
feet from the downed crew.

"Kick-ass," said Zen as Colgate took on the last man and
bolted upward. "Kick-ass."

"Yeah," said Jennifer.

C³ flew the two planes in an orbit at fifteen thousand feet,
now below Raven as she stayed well out of the way of the

rescue helicopter. Zen rolled his neck and stretched his shoulders, taking advantage of the break to relax a little. He took a long, slow pull on his Gatorade, getting ready to jump back into things.

He already had a grid marked out to resume the search for Madrone and the downed planes. Between this position and the spot where Kulpin had been recovered, they'd have a fairly decent idea where the wreckage ought to be.

Finding it in the storm, of course, wouldn't be easy. Even in perfect weather, the wreckage of an airplane could take days if not weeks to find.

And as for Kevin—given that they hadn't detected a beacon or a transmission from him, it seemed likely that he had gone down with the airplane.

"You've used more fuel than you planned," Jennifer told him. "With the storm."

"We're okay," said Zen. "You worried?"

"Not about you."

The way she said that made him think, for the first time, that maybe Jennifer was a little sweet on Madrone.

"We'll find him," he told her.

"You think?"

"I don't know," he admitted.

"Did he seem—has he been acting odd lately?" she asked.

"What do you mean?"

"He came on to me—just about attacked me—in the lab the other day. If Colonel Bastian hadn't come in, I think he would've . . ." Her voice stopped. "He might have done something."

"Kevin? Did you tell the colonel?"

"Well, no. I mean—I don't know. It was all so . . . just weird."

"Raven to Hawk Leader," said Cheshire over the interphone, her voice muffled because the helmet was on his lap. "Ready to resume search?"

"Give me a minute," he told her. He turned back to Jennifer. "Captain Madrone has been acting strange around you?"

"Just that time. He was like—I don't know. It was like a different person."

"I noticed something too," said Jeff.

"Side effects of ANTARES?" she asked.

"Maybe." Zen shrugged. He glanced down at his visor before putting his helmet back on.

Dreamland
19 February, 2043

THINGS AT DREAMLAND DIDN'T COME TO A STANDSTILL because of one crisis, however great it might be. And in fact, Dog believed that on the day Armageddon arrived he'd have a foot of paperwork to review and a dozen meetings to sit through before being cleared to see St. Peter.

It was only when the hunger pangs in his stomach echoed off the walls of his office that he realized it was nearly nine P.M. He made it as far as his doorway before being waylaid by Dr. Geraldo.

"I was just coming to see you," she said. "I checked over in your quarters but you weren't there."

"Going for dinner," said Dog. "Come on. You don't have to eat, just talk," said Dog.

"Actually, Colonel," said Geraldo, grabbing his arm, "this really should be discussed in your office."

Reluctantly, Dog led her back inside.

"I located Captain Madrone's ex-wife," said Geraldo.

"That was premature," said Dog.

"I understand that," said the scientist. "I thought, under the circumstances, it was appropriate." Geraldo rushed on. "In any event, she seemed to want to talk. Did you know that Kevin had a daughter?"

"I'm not sure I recall that," Bastian said. "I know he was divorced. How old is she?"

"She died a year before he was divorced." Geraldo shifted uncomfortably in her chair, her fingers smoothing her stiff gray skirt. "It was five years ago, while he was working on a project for the Army through Los Alamos. The project itself was in the Glass Mountains in southern Texas. He worked there for a while, before she was born, and then immediately afterwards before going back to Los Alamos. His wife actually didn't know what the project was. Kevin is very good at keeping secrets."

Bastian nodded, sensing that that was a severe understatement.

"I've checked myself," continued Geraldo. "It's still codeword-classified, and I haven't been privy to the details, but it dealt with nuclear weapons in some way. My guess, given his background, was that it had to do with tactical artillery, since I can't imagine that it would involve TOW missiles. It's probably irrelevant, except to Kevin."

Soon after his daughter was born, Geraldo continued, she had been diagnosed with a rare but always fatal disease, anaplastic cancer of the thyroid. Highly malignant, the cancer began in the thyroid gland but spread quickly throughout the body. In her case, it had metastasized in her brain, lungs, and liver before being discovered.

"She died within three months of the diagnosis. It was an ordeal, as you can imagine," said Geraldo. "Losing a child that young—losing any child, of course, it's traumatic."

"Sure."

"The etiology of the disease is not clear. There are many theories. But thyroid cancer in general has been linked to radiation."

"So he blamed his work," said Bastian.

"Oh, yes. He blamed himself and his work, and his superiors who had assigned him that work," said Geraldo. She explained that the safety precautions, let alone security procedures, prevented any young child from getting near radioactive resources or reactors. So Madrone had apparently concluded—at least for a short time—that he had somehow poisoned his daughter.

"Patently impossible," said Geraldo. "No way it could have happened. But in grief, we believe many things."

"So what killed her?"

"The disease is so rare that it's impossible to know. A random malfunction of genetics would be my guess, but it's the sort of thing I can't say. Only God knows." Geraldo shook her head. "What's important is that in his grief he became paranoid and suicidal. I use the terms advisedly; the ex-Mrs. Madrone says he saw a counselor."

"*That* is not in his file."

"Nor is the fact that his security clearance was removed for a time. It appears only that it lapsed as he was transferred. I'm still trying to reach his superior, a former Colonel Theo Glavin. I believe he's now a civilian with the Department of Energy." Geraldo spread her fingers for a moment, studying them before resuming. "Apparently this commanding officer was sympathetic, with his own child around the same age. He still sends Mrs. Madrone a Christmas card, though they were never really close. I only have this from the ex-wife, understand. Kevin was popular and had worked hard—you know how intelligent and likable he is—and everyone felt deeply sorry about his daughter's death. Beyond that, he was a decorated war hero. So apparently people thought they were doing good by protecting him."

Dog slid back in his chair. He too had felt sorry for people under his command; he too had often found a diplomatic way of getting things done without ruining a person's career.

"I don't like any of this," said Geraldo. "Kevin never told me had a daughter, just that he was divorced. And as for the rest . . ." She shook her head and refolded her arms in front of her chest. "Technically, none of this would have disqualified him for the program. He did tremendously well on the tests, and as far as I can see has gone further faster than any ANTARES subject, including Captain James. He has an incredibly supple mind. Perhaps that is how he was able to hide this from us, since I would have thought the tests would have revealed it."

"James was subjected to the same tests, wasn't he?" Dog felt all of his reservations toward ANTARES resurfacing. He cursed himself now for not standing up more forcefully, for not refusing to go ahead with it, even if it meant resigning.

He should have followed his instincts.

"We've improved the tests as well as the procedures," said Geraldo. "Or at least we thought we did. Knowing this— knowing how he reacted at a point of great stress in the past would have influenced me. I might have eliminated him from the program. But the fact that he was able to keep such a secret—that is extremely worrisome. I would not have chosen him for ANTARES."

"All right," said Dog. "Unfortunately, it may very well be irrelevant now."

Aboard Hawkmother
Over Central America
19 February, 2240 local

MADRONE'S THOUGHTS TWISTED AROUND THE COMputer's, tangles of wires that ran through everything he heard and saw. They pulsed red and black; at times he tried to follow them through the tangles, but got hopelessly lost.

The elation he'd felt at escaping the Mexican airport and refueling the Flighthawks had dissipated. Hungry and tired, he vacillated between wanting this all to end and not wanting to give up.

Bastian and the others would blame him for killing Dalton and Kulpin, not to mention whoever had died at the Mexican airport. They'd charge him with murder, treason, theft of government property—they'd invent charges to persecute him with.

They didn't need charges, the bastards. They wanted to kill him, the way they had killed his daughter.

Worse. They would keep him alive, hound him every day. They might even be manipulating this now—Geraldo and Bastian and Stockard had set him up, hadn't they? Made him join the program, then concocted a series of petty tests, waiting for him to snap. They knew about his daughter. They were probably working with the people who had made him kill her.

The bastards had planned it all. Why did they hate him? What had he done to them?

It couldn't just be Iraq. It had to be Los Alamos, something there. He'd killed one of the tactical artillery programs, made a few generals look bad by pointing out the obvious.

Madrone needed only a fraction of his attention, a small slice of his ability, to fly the planes. His mind hungered for more, ranging across the universe of possibilities in a feeding frenzy.

What would he do? He would crash the planes into the rain forest, be done with it all, end their plot against him.

He saw Christina lying on the hospital gurney, frowning at him. "Daddy," she said. "Daddy."

A cheap shitting gurney. The bastards didn't even have the decency to give her a real bed. She'd spent her final days in treatment, between sessions, dying, dying, dying in the mold-stinking hall as she waited.

By the time they reached the children's wing, her eyes were closed, and she would never reopen them. Even the doctor admitted it, the bastard doctor who wouldn't even give her morphine when she began to cry, the son of a bitch.

He wanted to kill them. He would kill them.

Lightning flashed and the plane lurched onto her right wing. Madrone had entered another storm, but it was the chaos of his mind that sent the aircraft reeling. There were so many conflicting emotions and impulses—suicide, revenge, hatred, love. They slammed against each other, physically pushing his head back in the seat, literally tearing at the neurons and other cells of his brain.

The ANTARES circuitry spat back wild arcs of energy into the system, befuddling the Boeing's control system; the plane began to yaw, threatening to slide into a spin. The Flighthawks, set by C^3 in a basic trail pattern, faithfully mimicked their mother plane, rocking behind her at 25,000 feet.

Madrone knew he had to end this somehow. The pain threatened to overwhelm him. He felt the faint pings at the corner of his temples that meant he was slipping out of Theta-alpha.

If he went out now, he'd never get back in time to prevent himself from crashing.

Part of him wanted exactly that. Part of him wanted to just crash into the jungle below—he was over Colombia now—end it all in a flash of flames.

But other parts of him wanted to live. And those parts won out. He saw the rain forest enveloping him, heard the music Geraldo had played. And he felt the dark woman approaching, the shadow who had come unbidden from the recesses of his desire.

Come to me, she told him. *I will show you the way.*

Madrone's rapid pulse eased. He felt his way into the cockpit of the big plane, stared for a moment at the holes the ejection seats had made, then took the controls firmly. The plane leveled off; he checked his systems, made a correction to deal with the fury of the storm.

He had less than an hour's worth of fuel left in Hawkmother.

Landing at a major airport or military base was out of the question. But where?

The database in the navigational unit covered only the U.S., Mexico, and Canada. He wanted something in Brazil, in the rain forest.

Have the Flighthawks scout for him.

He took a long breath, his head rising as he held it, and saw himself inside Hawk One. Madrone pushed down, gliding toward the earth like a falcon.

He tucked his wings back. The canopy exploded below. The jungle was everywhere, thick with green, howling with the screeches of animals.

A long strip.

No good. Military planes.

A bulldozed runway. Too short; probably a smuggler's haven.

The long river, winding past the marshes. Smoke curled in the distance, a fire fighting the drizzle.

Madrone shook violently as the skin on his face froze. He was back in the tower in the middle of the storm, pelted by hail. Lightning jagged all around him.

End it, growled the jaguar's voice.

He turned back.

End it.

The tower. He was on the range at Glass Mountain, siting the artillery, telling them where to fire.

No, it was the church where they'd held the service for Christina.

It was both of them together.

Kevin felt himself starting to fall. Concrete appeared to his right. Bulldozers. The runway was too short.

His temples stung. He held the stick of the 777 in his hand, smelled the incense from Christina's funeral, saw Jennifer Gleason tearing off her clothes.

"No!" he yelled. "Land! Land! Land!"

Pej, Brazil
20 February, 0340 local

THE PLANE MATERIALIZED FROM THE DARKNESS, BURSTing down from the mountains and steadying its wings over the mountains. Lights on, gear down, it was obviously going to land.

An hour before, Minerva had been unable to sleep and had decided to walk around the base in the fading moonlight—an unusual decision, at least so early in the morning. Had she had some sort of unconscious premonition?

If so, of what? Disaster? Other people's deaths?

She glanced toward the building where the security team she'd summoned on her radio was just now rushing into a jeep. When she turned back, the big jet, a Boeing 777 or something similar, lumbered onto the runway. Whoever was flying it was damn good, but still, he was trying to land in the dark on a concrete and packed-dirt runway. The plane's nose flared as the engines slammed into reverse thrust. Dirt and gravel shot everywhere as the aircraft funneled toward the jungle at the far end of the runway. It thumped from the concrete onto the dirt, blowing tires as it skidded. There was a shriek and then a boom and then a drawn-out hush. Minerva waited for the explosion and fire, the dust so thick in the air that she couldn't see.

Something whirled down at the top of the dust cloud. Two large birds fluttered above, buzzards expecting carrion.

As the dust settled in the moonlight, Minerva realized the Boeing had managed to stop at the end of the rampway. Even more incredibly, it hadn't caught fire and its landing gear was still upright.

She began to run toward it, coughing from the dirt in the air. The plane bore no markings, not even registration numbers.

What an incredible thing, she thought; if she had been more superstitious, she would have sworn it was a sign from heaven.

A stairway opened with a tart whoosh from the rear belly of the plane.

Minerva unholstered her pistol, waiting as two members of her security team joined her. Then she stepped onto the stairway, peering up at the dim red interior of the plane.

As she did, the vultures fluttered down nearby. They weren't birds at all; they were sleek black aircraft unlike any Minerva had ever seen. About the size of small automobiles, they seemed to her some odd offspring of a mating between

F/A-18's and UFOs. A small series of LEDs blinked along their noses, the lights flashing in a pattern that seemed to imply the planes were watching her.

There was a noise behind her. Minerva spun back to the airplane, holding up her pistol. A man in a black flight suit staggered down the steps.

"Help me," he said before collapsing in her arms.

VI
Goddess of war

Dreamland ANTARES Lab
27 February, 1000

IT WAS DIFFERENT THAN ZEN REMEMBERED—MUCH DIF-
ferent. Better. He strode across the plain, a light wind brushing his face. He walked—walked!—to the edge of the mesa
and looked out over the valley.

"You're in Theta," said Geraldo somewhere far behind him.

Jeff laughed. He spread his arms, then coiled his feet. His
knees felt so damn good.

He wriggled his toes for the first time in a year and a half.
He knew, or thought he knew, that he wasn't really moving
them—it was a hallucination, a dreamlike, vivid memory enhanced by ANTARES.

But what if the process somehow did make it possible for
him to feel his toes? ANTARES made unused portions of the
brain available—maybe it could do that with nerve cells and
the spinal cord as well. One of the doctors who had examined
him in the hospital thought the cord wasn't one-hundred-
percent severed; he thought it might be theoretically possible
for Zen to feel something, if not today, then in the future.

The day he'd heard that he'd felt so much hope. Then he'd
crashed back down as other experts disagreed and it became
more and more obvious he felt nothing at all.

"Jeff?"

He leapt into the air and began to fly. The light pressure

he'd felt from the wind increased exponentially. Pain shot through his head.

Stay in Theta, he told himself.

The bony plates of his skull tore apart. His head spun and he fell. When Jeff opened his eyes, he was back in the AN-TARES lab.

Geraldo stood in front of him.

"Good," she said. "You were in Theta for two hours."

"Two hours?"

The scientist smiled.

Jeff waited while the others recorded his vital signs and brain waves now that he was out of Theta. The changes in the system since he'd been involved in the program the first time were incredible. It wasn't just the circuitry or the drugs or even Geraldo's preference for using Eastern-inspired mental-relaxation techniques. Connecting to the ANTARES gear in the past had been painful—this was extremely pleasurable.

He could walk. He knew it.

ANTARES, or perhaps the drugs that helped enhance his connection with it, stimulated the crushed nerves in his spinal cord. The damn thing was going to make him walk again.

"Let's work with the Flighthawks," he suggested as Geraldo's assistants began removing the body monitor wires.

"No, Jeff, not today. It's not on the agenda. You said you wanted to start slow, and I agree."

"Well let's take another turn in Theta," he told Geraldo. "Let's go for it."

"Major. Jeffrey."

Geraldo's frown reminded Jeff of his grandmother's. She glanced at her two assistants; without saying anything they left the room.

"Jeff, you know we have to go slow," Geraldo told him after they had gone. "For one thing, Colonel Bastian hasn't given his approval for you to devote anything beyond minimal time. And I do have other subjects. Besides, the drugs are only starting to reach potent levels in your system. They're very new, and since you didn't use them before, I'd like to have a good, firm baseline to use as we proceed."

She had obviously conspired with her assistants against him, Jeff realized. Why? What was she up to?

"Is there something you want to say to me?" the scientist asked.

"In what sense?"

"In any sense." She folded her arms in front of her chest, studying him.

"Uh, no. You staring at me for any particular reason? I got boogers coming out of my nose or something?"

Geraldo finally laughed. "No, Jeffrey, not at all. Come on. Have some tea." She turned and walked across the large room, going through the open doorway and entering the small lounge area. Light jazz played in the background, music that Jeff had selected last week before his first attempt—failed—to get into Theta.

She's trying to seduce me somehow, he realized as he rolled his wheelchair toward the table area. Geraldo took a bag of cinnamon-apple herbal tea and placed it in a cup as she waited for the kettle to boil. She didn't disapprove of coffee or "real" tea, but she advised against it. As a physician, she said, she had some doubts about the long-term effects of caffeine.

"Jeff, do you remember the accident when you lost your legs?"

"I didn't lose them," he said. "I have legs just the same as you."

"They're not the same. Though I did misspeak," she said, correcting herself.

Geraldo was a viper. She came off like a grandma-type, but beneath it she was always plotting.

"I remember the accident," he said.

The electric teapot whistled. She poured out two cups. "Do you think about it often?" she asked, waiting as the tea steeped.

"No. At first, sure. But not now."

"Would you say you've accepted it?"

"Who the hell accepts something like that?" Zen struggled to keep his anger in control. Geraldo was trying to provoke him. "The thing is, see, you don't accept it. Not really. Never. But you, it's like you move to the next problem. A pilot, see—a pilot knows there's a checklist."

"Losing your ability to walk isn't the same as missing an

item on the checklist." She stopped stirring the tea for a mo
ment. "Do you think you'll ever walk again?"

The bitch must have some way of reading his mind while
he was hooked up into the machine.

They'd always said that was impossible. They'd claimed
they could only see waves.

But hell, if it meant walking again, he'd put up with it. He
could put up with anything.

"The doctors have been pretty much universal that I won't
walk. And, yes, it seems pretty evident, don't you think?" He
reached for his tea. He smelled it, could tell from the steam
rising that it would be too hot, held it in his lap. "Everyone
is in agreement that walking isn't in my future."

"But you don't agree."

Zen laughed. He really did like her; she really did remind
him of his grandmother. "The fact of the matter is, Doc, even
if I thought I could walk—hell, if I wished to right now—
wouldn't change a damn thing. I'd still fall flat on my face
and you'd laugh your ass off."

"I wouldn't laugh at you, Jeffrey," she said, so seriously
that he couldn't do anything but sniff once more at the tea.

Dreamland Hangar 1
27 February, 1000

LIKE EVERYTHING ELSE AT DREAMLAND, THE SURVIVAL
shop was on the cutting edge. While there were no masseuses
on duty, pilots suiting up for test flights had nearly every other
conceivable amenity. Their flight gear, of course, was custom
tailored; the men and women who prepared their suits could
embarrass a team of London tailors with their speed and ac-
curacy. The survival gear itself—parachutes, etc.—was
mostly standard issue, and received the same standard of care
administered at any U.S. Air Force facility: in other words,
the best possible. But the experts attending pilots before and
after their test runs included a nurse who helped make sure
the legs and arms and chests fitting into the suits were in top
condition. She had certificates in sports medicine and nutrition
as well as aviation medicine.

She was also as free with her advice as Ann Landers

Which meant that Dog got the full harangue as he dressed before taking the new EB-52 for a flight.

"You've put on two pounds since you've come here, Colonel," warned Nurse Yenglais. "Too much of the good life."

"Good life?" Dog slid his helmet liner on his head. "Are you implying I'm getting fat, Maria?"

"Six thousand calories," she said, undeterred. "At this rate, you will be outside of your ideal weight range in two years."

Which would still leave him about ten pounds lighter than nearly everyone in the Air Force at his rank. But Dog knew better than to voice that objection, and merely winked at the nearby staff sergeant who was performing what amounted to a quadruple check of his safety gear.

"See you all in exactly ninety minutes," said Dog, taking his helmet and striding for the plane.

The practice sessions that had started because he wanted to prove to his daughter that he could fly anything had become welcome escapes from the rigors of his desk job. In the space of two weeks, Bastian had made himself into an excellent Megafortress pilot, and in fact an important fill-in for test flights. The plane's flight computers even rated him the third-best EB-52 skipper on the base.

Which irked him no end. He didn't mind—*much*—that his computer scores were lower than Major Cheshire's. She'd been flying big jets forever, and had helped build the plane and spent more time at the helm every day than he spent at his desk.

But ranking behind Breanna was another matter. Never mind that Bree also had considerable experience in multi-engined jets, or that she too had worked with the designers and whiz kids on the Megafortress. Dog wanted to beat her.

Not too bad, of course. Just enough to show he was better.

"Colonel, you have five?" shouted Danny Freah just as Dog touched the ladder to board his plane.

"I can spare about three," he told the captain.

"Just, uh, can we talk over here?" asked Freah, gesturing with his thumb. Dog followed Freah a short distance away, out of earshot of the techies completing last-second checks of the new plane, which had been dubbed "Galatica."

"I've been talking to Jed Barclay over at the NSC. We have a weird theory about the 777."

Dog squinted into the sun. "More hiker reports, or has the Navy found something?"

"No. The Navy contacts turned out bogus, just as you predicted."

Despite several promising leads, the search teams had failed to turn up any wreckage in the Sierras, and the search had been extended to the Pacific, where the Boeing and Flighthawks could theoretically have flown after the pilots ejected. The fact that the big plane did not appear on any radars and had not been sighted, of course, argued against it continuing to the Pacific, but it had to have landed somewhere.

"You're going to think this is nuts," added Danny.

"If Jed Barclay came up with it, I will."

"It's more my idea," said Danny. "A few hours after Hawkmother and the Flighthawks disappeared, there was an incident at a small national airport in Mexico. A large plane set down there, using the registration and ID of a 707. A gang stole some fuel, killed a man, and blew up a tanker before taking off."

"A gang?"

"It's not a good fit, I know. But one of the reports states that other planes were involved, and that one swooped in low and tried to shoot up some of the security vehicles. It could have been a Flighthawk."

"I don't know, Danny. I'm still thinking it's in the mountains somewhere, buried under the snow."

"With no beacon?"

"Disabled in the crash."

"I checked some of the technical data out. Hawkmother could have reached Mexico. The airport is down the peninsula, in the western mountains not far from the sea."

"The Flighthawks would never have made it that far."

"They could have refueled," said Danny. "I checked that out too. There would have been just enough fuel for all three to have made it. It would explain why we can't find the planes, Colonel."

Bastian looked back at the sun. Sabotage had, of course, been considered from the start. But theft was a different angle, and most unlikely. Madrone was the only other person on the plane; it seemed almost inconceivable that anyone else had snuck aboard. The Army captain had no experience as a pilot.

beyond ANATRES, and even if he had been an ace, he would have had a difficult time in the cockpit once the ejection seats were gone.

"Maybe the computer was programmed to fly the plane away," suggested Danny. "Maybe ANTARES is the target. The Russians know about it. They obviously want it. I talked to Dr. Rubeo," added Freah. "He says it would have been impossible to preprogram the computer to take the plane without it showing up in the preflight dumps. Apparently, they download the memory before taking off for some sort of baseline check."

"Well, there's your answer," said Dog.

"Except that there were transmissions that the Flighthawk team can't account for. Rubeo told me to talk to Jennifer Gleason. I think there's something here, Colonel."

"If the plane were in Russia, you don't think we would have heard by now?"

"Maybe it's been cut up and shipped by boat."

"You realize the satellites have checked every airfield it could land on."

"Has to be somewhere. I don't believe in the Bermuda Triangle. Or space aliens."

"You're not angling to go down to Mexico, are you?" asked Dog.

"I have an FBI contact that can smooth the way. She speaks Spanish too. If you authorize it, we'll hop a plane this afternoon."

"She?"

"Debra Flanigan."

"Nothing I have to inform your wife about, right?"

"Colonel. Come on."

"It's far-fetched, Danny. More than likely the planes are lying in a million pieces and buried under a few feet of snow. There's been plenty of crashes like that."

"I think it's worth a shot, Colonel."

Bastian glanced at the waiting Megafortress, and thought of all the work that waited for him back at his office. Among the pink telephone message slips there were bound to be several from the Pentagon asking what was up with the search.

"Take a shot at it if you think it's worth it," he told Danny, lifting his flight helmet to his head.

Pej, Brazil
27 February, 1700 local

HE PLUNGED INSIDE HER AGAIN AND AGAIN, PUSHING himself against her body. Minerva's breasts curved against his chest and her lips pressed into his, warm electricity bathing his body. Madrone felt himself beginning to climax and tried to hold back, unwilling to let go of the moment, unwilling to lose the immersion in the beautiful dark breathlessness of her body. Her fingers reached across his back, the sharp nails teasing his muscles. Minerva's perfume eased into his lungs and he exploded, coming with a violent surge that shook her to orgasm as well. The warmth of the jungle settled around them; Madrone floated as the energy slowly dissipated. Finally, he rolled onto his back, lying on the bed as she nuzzled her face against his chest.

Lanzas had appeared at the bottom of the steps when he landed the Boeing. At first he'd thought she was an apparition, part of an ANTARES-induced dream. But she had proven very real, personally nursing him back to health, taking him to bed that first night. She had restored the plane, marveling at the Flighthawks. She had filled him with incredible energy and love and strength. She was not the dark woman of the Theta metaphor; she was better.

"Time now, my darling," she said. "Time to begin."

"Yes," said Madrone, though he made no effort to move. Neither did she.

"Our first step, today."

"Yes," said Madrone. He had told her how everyone was against him, how the scientists and militarists were seeking to destroy not just him but the planet, turning everyone to robots with their drugs and implanted chips. He'd been their first guinea pig. Minerva had agreed, and pointed out the obvious—he would never be safe until they were neutralized.

Neither would she. His enemies were already trying to get her. The Brazilian Air Force had sent a flight of Mirages over the base yesterday, obviously looking for him. Fortunately, Hawkmother and the U/MFs were well been hidden by netting.

The bastards. Puny Mirages. They would pay.

He saw it. He could feel the Flighthawks firing their guns.

Loading the planes with shells was child's play, a simple adjustment not worthy of his expertise. But the cannons were limited and Minerva had few other weapons—six early-version Sidewinders, a pair of runway-denial bombs, and a dozen antitank weapons "on loan" from an Army unit. Adapting them so they could be used with the Flighthawks taxed him considerably, even though ANTARES had greatly expanded his intellect.

Lanzas thought the antitank weapons were useless; they were wire-guided and meant to be fired from helicopters or ground vehicles. But Madrone was well schooled in Army weapons, and saw the TOW equivalents as the most versatile weapons imaginable—their rocket motors could be staged, the wire extended. Their slender shapes would fit well beneath the U/MF fuselages. With the proper modifications, they could carry warheads of several hundred pounds.

He saw the solutions before he did the computations. His brain unfolded in a million directions. Under Minerva's care, without the Dreamland bastards breathing down his neck, his powers increased exponentially. He ran to each corner of his mind, vibrating with ferocious energy. He felt connected to ANTARES at all times. Even though he was no longer taking Geraldo's drugs, he felt his hippocampus and other brain cells continuing to grow.

They couldn't control him now that he had gotten away. They couldn't use him anymore. He would turn the tables, destroy the bastards, all of them. And then he would be safe here, at the edge of the rain forest.

"What are you thinking?" Minerva asked, rubbing his chest.

"The cannons in the Flighthawks," said Madrone. "Boa Vista and Manaus will be destroyed."

"Think of something else for now."

Lanzas's hand slid toward his belly. Madrone drifted. He loved flying the Flighthawks, because it meant he was in Theta. But being with her was better, far better.

She rubbed his thigh with the palm of her hand. Then she pulled it away abruptly.

"You're right. You must go," Minerva said. "It will be late."

"A few more minutes won't matter," he said, rolling on top of her. "Our victims will wait."

Dreamland Computer Labs
27 February, 1700 local

JENNIFER GLEASON LOOKED UP FROM HER DESK TO SEE Colonel Bastian coming through the door to her lab. Instantly, her fingers felt wet and her heart fluttery; her tongue stumbled as she said hello.

"Dr. Rubeo said you might have some details about anomalies in the communications-and-control computer handling the Flighthawks during the Boeing flight," said Bastian. He smiled, then pointed to a chair. "Mind if I sit?"

"Go ahead, please."

She picked at her hair, trying desperately to stop acting like a teenager with a full-blown crush. She was, after all, a grown woman with a full-blown crush.

Jennifer reached to her desk drawer and pulled on it before remembering that she had locked it. As if that wasn't bad enough, she kept the key on a chain around her neck beneath her blouse. She could feel every millimeter of her skin turning beet red as she pulled the chain up discreetly and then bent to unlock the drawer. She retrieved the folders and got up, willing her legs to stop shaking.

"I think when you look at them side by side," she said, placing the folders down on a clear lab table in the corner of the room, "you'll see what I'm talking about."

"You haven't actually said what you're talking about," said Bastian.

For just a half second, she considered throwing herself in his arms. But the consequences of that—of his inevitable rejection—were too great. Carefully, slowly, she laid out the papers.

"These signals came across to our monitoring equipment from the Boeing. They're broadcast through C^3 via the 57Y circuit—"

"Jen." He touched her arm and she nearly exploded. "Skip some of the technical jargon, okay?"

She managed to nod, then pointed to some of the yellow markings.

"Early on I realized that they were part of the Boeing's computer-assist-pilot unit. It's obvious—you can see the coding once you know what to look for. What I didn't realize until a few days ago—well, yesterday actually—while we were doing some upgrades on ANTARES, was that the leak isn't accidental. It corresponds to specific wave patterns. It's a command."

"Something bothering you, Doc?"

"Didn't get much sleep last night," she said lamely, quickly launching into an explanation of her theory that minimized the technical aspects. In a nutshell, she thought that Madrone had somehow learned to use ANTARES to fly the 777, or that C³ had done so at his direction.

"It was most likely a combination of both," said Jennifer. "The system was hardwired to the Boeing for test purposes and ANTARES or Madrone may have exploited it. I don't think C³ could have decided to do it on its own, since I haven't been able to get it to do so in the simulations."

"Dr. Rubeo doesn't think it's possible for an ANTARES subject to do that," said Dog.

"That's not exactly what he said. He said, I believe," she added, "I believe he probably told you that it's technically difficult to maintain, and that we haven't any proof. This crossover may not be a deliberate crossover at all, just the code spooling crazily."

"Can you pin it down?"

"I'm trying to come up with some simulations that can duplicate the ANTARES code. Major Stockard may also be able to help once he's up to speed. Of course, if we had the hard-drive recorder from the computer in Hawkmother, or, uh, well, if Captain Madrone turned up, I mean if, when—"

"I have to say, Doc, the odds are pretty damn good he's dead."

Dog looked like he had the weight of the world on his shoulders. She longed to take some of it off—massage his back, kiss him. Jennifer felt an impulse, began to follow it, rising slowly from her chair.

But Bastian had already gotten up and was walking to the door. She froze as he turned.

"See if you can expedite the testing you need. If this is a problem with ANTARES, I need to know right away."

She managed to nod before he stepped out.

Pej, Brazil
27 February, 2100 local

MINERVA WATCHED AS THE FUEL-LADEN BOEING LUM-bered down the newly finished runway, struggling off the field though she had nearly tripled its size in just a few days. The left wing dipped down as the wheels were cranked upward, but it stayed in the air.

In contrast, the two small robot planes jetted off smartly in less than two thousand meters, even with massive bombs beneath their bellies. The JP 233 British runway-denial weapons had been obtained by Brazil through Italy several years before. Minerva had managed to obtain them from another unit for a price approaching ten times the commanding general's salary. And it was only that cheap because the man considered himself her ally and sometime lover. At least he'd had the grace not to ask questions.

Nearly as big as the U/MFs, the bombs cut down on the smaller planes' maneuverability and range. But Madrone had practiced with one yesterday; she was confident he would succeed. More importantly, so was he.

Madrone scared her. She was used to manipulating men, but with him it was beyond manipulation. He anticipated her darkest wishes and went beyond them. It was as if the devil himself had materialized before her.

Yet he could be such a gentle lover, so willing, so soft when she asked.

His suggestion that the antitank weapons could be altered and then fit to the U/MFs made sense to her, though her experts had deep reservations. Madrone's enhancements to the shaped-charge warheads, at least, could be easily implemented, and were even now being tested in a bunker on the other side of the hill.

The dimensions of the planned weapons gave her a better idea, though she didn't trust Kevin enough yet to broach it.

Perhaps it wasn't merely trust. Perhaps she knew that if she told him, he would dare her to use them. For that, she wasn't ready.

Colonel Lanzas had recruited two pilots to fly the Boeing. The exhausted state Madrone had arrived in made it obvious that he had to concentrate on guiding the two smaller jets and not worry about the 777. She did not completely understand the process—his description of ANTARES sounded like science fiction, as if he merely closed his eyes and wished the planes to fly. But there was no doubt that it worked.

Minerva folded her arms, gazing at the large plane disappearing into the distance. They had painted it dark green, making it more difficult to spot when it flew at night or over the jungle canopy. She watched it now disappear in the darkness above the trees, to a thought in the unrippled distance.

If the attack went well, the commanders of Number 18 Group and Number 16 Group would join her immediately. She would then approach Herule. Already in the capital, the general would be well positioned to apply pressure on the government.

That meant she would have to let him believe he was in charge.

Acceptable, for now.

Aboard Hawkmother
Over Northern Brazil
27 February, 2200

HITTING BOA VISTA TOOK NO MORE EFFORT THAN CLOSing his eyes and saying, "Be gone."

Madrone saw the runway as Hawk One approached. The threat screen remained clear even after he had dropped the parcel of Thompson-Brandt BAP.1000 antirunway weapons and their massive dispenser toward the center of the strip and swung to strafe the row of AT-27's. He demolished all but one of the half-dozen armed trainers, and set their hangars on fire before the ancient antiaircraft guns began spitting in the direction of the Flighthawk. The gunfire was optically aimed and easily ignored as he finished off the last trainer.

Manaus was a different story.

Two Roland antiaircraft missiles had been located at the base. Their radars were scanning the air as he approached. Additionally, four F-5Es were overhead, undoubtedly alerted by the attack on Boa Vista.

The American-built Tiger IIs were agile, capable interceptors carrying Mectron MAA-1 heat-seeking missiles as well as cannons. Patrolling in pairs at roughly twenty thousand feet, they were running two elongated ovals seven miles north and south of the base. Since the Boeing had to stay within ten miles of the two Flighthawks, it would be an easy target for the fighters when he attacked.

So he would nail them first, using Hawk One. Hawk Two, still carrying its ponderous bomb, would be held in reserve.

The Tigers' radars quickly picked up the Boeing, vectoring toward it and issuing challenges before Hawk One closed to five miles. Madrone's heart raced and the edges of his scalp tingled ever so slightly, as if a light rain had begun to fall on his head.

Her voice guided him:

Remain in Hawk One. Forget everything but the plane.

The U/MF's threat screen flashed red. The F-5's had picked him up somehow. But it was too late for them, very much too late—he edged right, wishing the targeting screen into place, the pipper stoking red as he cut a V in the sky, Hawk One diving and then bolting back behind the Brazilian interceptor. He lost ground, the pipper turning cold black, then starting to blink, changing to yellow, then red. Madrone squeezed, and it was like the first time with Minerva, all of his fears rushing out of him. His enemy burst into flames.

He edged left, his body the Flighthawk. His maneuvers drew him parallel to the second Tiger, the pilot so intent on attacking the Boeing that he didn't see the Flighthawk in the darkness beside him. Nor could his radar find it as it slid backward, slowing a moment to let its target get slightly ahead and below him.

Madrone climbed. He focused the Flighthawk's IR scan in the center of his head, tipping downward to accelerate into the attack. He saw the man fiddling with his gear.

The idiot was arming his Sidewinders.

The attack caught the F-5E midships. The cannon shells smashed the turbines cleanly in half. The front part of the plane plunged down immediately, tumbling over violently. The rear, containing the engines, tail, and wings, flew on by itself for nearly a mile, a headless horseman still seeking revenge in the night.

By then, Madrone had turned his attention to the Roland defense missiles. The two Marder chassis launchers were located at the western end of the base, on slightly elevated ground. He had to dive quickly to avoid their radar, which swept out to just under ten miles. One of the launchers fired as he dove, though it wasn't clear why exactly—the Boeing and the Flighthawks were still well outside the missiles' range, and the threat screens were both clear.

"Captain, we are under attack," reported Mayo, the copilot. The voice came at him from above, a terrible intrusion from the clouds.

"Stay with me," said Madrone, concentrating on Hawk One's threat screen.

"But—"

"You *will* stay with me!" he thundered.

There was no response. He checked Hawkmother's position on the God's-eye view—if the pilots pulled off, he would eject them.

He might just do that now.

The threat screen on Hawk One painted the coverage area of the Roland's radar as he closed in. The French-German unit was especially proficient at finding low-flying targets, but even it couldn't find something as small as a Flighthawk flying at only twenty feet off the ground. A second missile took off from the launcher at the right; Madrone guessed that in their excitement the crew had misidentified and fired at the wreckage of the F-5 as it fell to earth.

Or perhaps they could see him somehow. Perhaps the bastards who had tried to destroy Madrone had altered the radar on the Flighthawk, made it visible to the enemy.

It was as if an iron bar hit him in the forehead. Madrone slumped backward in the chair, losing everything.

We will destroy them, Minerva whispered. *We will destroy them for what they have done to you. And we will live together, safe in our home.*

Madrone felt his way back into the cockpit of Hawk One, saw the large radar dish of the Roland barely two miles away.

He waited until he was within a half mile to begin firing. At his speed and range, he got no more than five slugs into the hull of the SAM launcher. But they were more than enough to destroy her.

Flames shot everywhere. A fireball from the first launcher's missile struck the second, unarmed launcher, but Madrone decided to erase it as well.

From there it was a turkey shoot. He vectored Hawk Two in to drop the bomb while he searched for the remaining F-5Es with One. After he shot them down, he found and destroyed a flight of Mirage IIIs on the ground, and even wasted an old Starfighter that managed to scramble toward the runway to stop him.

By the time Madrone was done, the best combat squadrons of Força Aérea Brasileiria had been eliminated. More importantly, the only units in the western part of the country that answered directly to the Defense Minister—and thus would resist Minerva—no longer had planes to fly.

Dreamland
4 March, 1300

BREANNA PUSHED AWAY THE PLATE WITH HER HALF-eaten turkey sandwich and got up from the table in Lounge B. One of the fancier clubs on the base, Lounge B had been thrown open under Dog's all-ranks edicts, and now served a very passable lunch, as well as offering some convenient nooks and crannies for involved couples.

Which, in theory, Zen and Bree were. Though during the past few days they had been acting increasingly "married."

A terrible word in her book, which she equated with a range of disparaging adjectives, none of which included intimate. For the past week, Zen had consistently ignored her, claiming he was working. He'd spent all of his spare time either in the ANTARES bunker—or in that computer bitch's lair.

Jennifer Gleason. Bree would scratch her eyes out if they were doing anything.

She knew Zen, knew he wasn't like that. But he was human.

And he'd blown her off for lunch. She was due at a briefing

with Colonel Bastian in ten minutes, or she'd hunt him down.

Or maybe not. She was being silly. Most likely he was working—he was incredibly busy, after all. Besides heading the Flighthawk Program, he was currently the only person who'd been able to achieve Theta-alpha in the ANTARES program.

Not that she'd heard that from him.

Was she being silly? Jeff had been acting strange lately, distant, quiet, not talking to her. True, Zen did get moody at times—he'd always been that way, even before the accident.

But something was definitely different now. ANTARES made him edgy, darker.

Could be lack of sleep.

"Hey, Bree, how's it going?" asked Danny Freah, sauntering in. A very attractive woman appeared behind him.

"Hello, Danny," said Bree, her eyes following to the blonde. As tall as Freah, she looked like an aerobic instructor even though she wore a conservative pantsuit.

Freah was married, the SOB.

"This is Debbie," said the captain, gesturing to the woman.

Debbie smiled and offered her hand. Bree didn't take it. "I'm running a little late," Bree told Freah. "You see Jeff anywhere?"

"No. He supposed to be here?"

"He's supposed to be married," snapped Bree, storming from the room.

Dreamland ANTARES Lab
4 March, 1300

ZEN FELT THE RUSH OF ADRENALINE AS THE PLANE soared to fifty thousand feet. He pushed the rudder pedals— pushed the pedals, he could feel them, feel his feet! He hunted in the sky for his adversary, a MiG-29 somewhere below.

His feet! He could feel his feet!

He had to test this. Had to!

He stood.

Gravity slammed his head back. He fell into a void, every part of him on fire. He blanked out.

When he came to, Geraldo and her assistants were standing

over him. He was still in the ANTARES lab room, but they had removed his connections, all except the small wires that monitored his heart and the chemical composition of his blood.

"What happened?" he asked.

"We were going to ask you the same thing," said Geraldo.

"I guess, I guess the MiG nailed me when I wasn't looking," he said.

"Our tape of the simulation showed the aggressor still out of range when you blacked out," said Carrie.

She had her hands on her hips, her beautiful breasts thrust out. Zen hadn't realized how beautiful she was until now, for some reason. Shy and reserved, but the kind of woman who would turn into something in bed.

"Jeff, how do you feel?" asked Geraldo, pulling over a small metal chair on wheels. The assistants customarily used the chair while adjusting the connections; its steel gleamed even in the softly lit lab.

"Uh-oh, I'm a prisoner of the Inquisition," he joked, still looking at Carrie.

"Not an inquisition, Jeffrey," said Geraldo. "But I do have some questions for you."

Carrie glanced down at the floor. He thought her face had colored, but he couldn't be sure—she and Roger beat a hasty retreat, leaving their boss to talk to him alone.

It occurred to Jeff that he could wring Geraldo's thin white neck with one hand, though he had no desire to do so.

"Jeffrey, I'm frankly concerned about you," said Geraldo.

"Why? Because I got waxed by a MiG? It's flying Mack Smith's game plans. It's pretty good."

"It has nothing to do with the MiG," said the scientist.

He really could wring her neck. It wouldn't be difficult.

"When you're in Theta, do you have full use of your limbs?" she asked.

She knew. Somehow, the bitch knew.

She wanted to control him. She wanted him to remain crippled. A gimp couldn't take over like Madrone had.

But that was just a wild theory of Danny's. He'd taken Jennifer Gleason's ideas to the ridiculous, paranoid nth degree.

No. It had happened that way. Looking at Geraldo, seeing

her cloying, meddling way, Jeff knew it must have happened that way. It was the only explanation.

Of course he'd taken over. With ANTARES Kevin could do anything.

So could Jeff. He could walk. Not today, not tomorrow, but soon.

"Do you use your legs in ANTARES?" Geraldo asked.

"Of course," he told her. "So what?"

She nodded, then started to move away.

"Hey, Doc—hey! Where are you going?"

She stopped at the door. "Jeffrey, I'm thinking of talking to Colonel Bastian. I'm thinking."

She stopped.

Jeff realized he had gripped the tires of his wheelchair and started forward, jerking the wires that were still attached to his hand and chest from the machines.

Why am I so angry?

"I think we're going to put ANTARES on hold," she said. Her cheeks and lips were pale, but her voice was calm and smooth. "Not just you—the entire program."

"I'll fight that."

"You can go to Colonel Bastian with me. I'll set up the appointment myself."

"Don't do this."

"Something is happening to you that I don't understand. I care about you, Jeffrey."

"Then give me back my legs," Zen told her.

Her lower lip trembled, but she said nothing as the door behind her opened and she stepped out.

Pej, Brazil
4 March, 2350 local

MINERVA SHIVERED AS SHE SLIPPED FROM THE BED, chilled by a breeze from the balcony door. Naked, she walked to the draped French doors, checking to make sure they were closed and locked. Halfway across the room she felt a premonition of danger and sidestepped to the upholstered chair nearby. She lowered herself stealthily, eyes riveted on the doors as she reached her hand beneath the chair to the pistol holstered there.

Madrone murmured and turned over on the bed, lost in his dreams. He mumbled something, a string of curses, as she rose and walked, still nude, to the doors. She held the Glock against her body, where it couldn't easily be wrestled away; the small gun's plastic butt felt warm against the inside of her rib cage. She paused a foot from the doors, breathing as softly as she could, examining the shadows.

Nothing.

But she could not dispel the premonition. Lanzas moved to the side of the drape, pulled it back gently.

Nothing.

The feeling of danger persisted. There was nothing to do but confront it—she pushed the drape away with a flourish, her body tense.

Moonlight washed the narrow terrace with a golden yellow. Otherwise, it was empty.

She slid her fingers across the combination lock to the French doors. Minerva trusted the men stationed there implicitly—many were related to her, and the others had worked for her or her family for at least a decade. But she well knew men were fickle, susceptible to all kinds of temptations. The glass in the doors was bullet-proof, able to turn back concentrated fire from a .50-caliber machine gun. The lair itself nestled onto the side of a rocky slope, with no possible vantage for a gunman for over three miles.

The concrete felt ice cold, but she stood on the terrace anyway.

Nothing.

Quietly, she slid back inside. Madrone remained sleeping on the bed, hands curled in tight fists. She patted him gently, then took her robe from the floor. Wrapping it around herself, her gun still in her hand, she slipped into the narrow hallway from her bedroom. With every step she scanned carefully for any sign of an intruder.

Her caution and fear made her late, though only by a few seconds—the light on her secure phone began to blink as she entered her study.

She let her robe fall open as she picked up the phone, as if her breasts might once again seduce Herule.

Perhaps they did, for his tone was that of a compliant lover, not a fierce and at times tiresome mentor.

"You have done amazingly well," he told her in Portuguese. The words rolled from his tongue poetically—after having used so much English these past few days with Madrone, Minerva felt they sounded almost haunting.

"Are you ready?" she asked the general.

"The Defense Minister will resign tomorrow. Then, I will be appointed," said the general.

He had worked more quickly than she had dared hope, but she held her voice flat, as if she had expected even more.

"And?" she said.

"Of course you will be rewarded."

Minerva felt her body flush with anger. She was the one with the power. She deserved not just nebulous promises but tangible rewards—the head of FAB, a post in Brasilia, even her own portfolio as Defense Minister.

Why did she need him?

She should just destroy them all. She could tell Madrone about the nuclear weapons, have him adapt them to the antitank missiles.

Kevin would do it in an instant, no matter what technical difficulties there might be. He was a genius, and he was in love with her. Most important, he would want to destroy them all.

Herule sensed her anger. "The reward will be ample," said the general.

Was she being too greedy? Overreaching again? Or simply too ready to destroy?

The American made her that way, with his infectious rage.

The Boeing and its Flighthawks were more powerful than the entire Força Aérea combined. Yesterday, Madrone had demonstrated that the small planes could not be located by the P-95's attached to the Navy. Technically part of Força Aérea though under a Naval commander, the turboprop planes were equipped with surveillance radars that were the most powerful airborne radars in the Brazilian inventory. The Navy had come to look for her, though it had not dared to overfly her base. Madrone's Flighthawks had danced around the P-95 before it was turned back by a flight of T-27 Tucanos newly loyal to her cause.

There had been some tense moments. The pilots in the T-27's thought the Hawkos, as they called them, were going to shoot down the radar plane.

And themselves.

Madrone had toyed with them. Perhaps he had even contemplated eliminating them.

She would have to dispose of him eventually. It was more than a matter of control. He made her reckless, more vicious than she needed or wanted to be. He made her think of using the nuclear bombs against her own people.

He was her dark side. He asked about her lovers, and she thought of killing them all—a needless and empty gesture. Self-defeating. Her last husband had contacts with the Russians that could be used to obtain MiGs—what good would come from killing him?

Joy at the moment his face twisted white certainly. Great joy. But after that?

"Colonel Lanzas?"

"Yes, General," she said, her voice silky. "I will stay quiet the next few days and await your orders."

She hung up the phone before he could say anything else—before she could say anything else.

Carefully, she moved back to the bedroom. As she stepped across the threshold, something moved in the darkness. She dropped quickly, pushing down as she did to a firing position, the small Glock in both hands.

"It's only me, love," said Madrone, sitting. "Come to bed."

She placed the gun on the floor and slipped beside him.

"I thought I heard something. It was silly." She curled herself around his body. Her nipples rose against his warm skin.

"We will have to eliminate all of our enemies," he said.

"Things are progressing, love," she reassured him. She ran her fingers along his thighs and downward to the top of his calves, starting back slowly.

"Not just in Brazil," he said. "I have been thinking. Los Alamos. Glass Mountain. They are stalking us."

"Los Alamos?"

"Where they first found me. Glass Mountain is the worst. They poisoned me. Remember? Where the tower is."

"They would not dare to follow you here," she said, slipping her hand toward his groin.

"They would!" Madrone bolted upright. "They have to be stopped."

His heart pumped violently; she reached for him, but he pushed her hand back, sliding out of the bed and stomping to the balcony.

"They're after us," he snarled. "Don't you see? They want to destroy me. They'll destroy you too."

Madrone flung open the drapes, staring outside.

"Let's make love," she said softly.

"I have to crush them before they crush us," he said, his back still turned. "I have to destroy their tower. Completely."

"Yes," she whispered, holding her arms out and willing him back. "We will crush them all," she said as he came back to her. "You will have your revenge."

He crawled into bed like a jaguar, silently stalking its prey. She slid her hand down and found him already hard.

"Make love to me," she said. "And then we will plan how to deal with them."

"I leave in the morning," he said.

"In a few days."

"Now."

"Be inside me," she said, pulling him gently toward the bed.

Department of Energy South Texas District 2, Test Area 6
Joint Services Projects Test Facility (Glass Mountain)
5 March, 1730

ONE THING MACK HAD TO SAY FOR THESE CANDY-ASS Department of Energy test sites—they stocked them with delectable feminine talent.

He and Marine Colonel Robling were being ushered around the surplus base by a young woman who rated a ten on the Mack Smith scale of excellence. Her lips puckered ever so slightly, her neck a dainty, vulnerable white, as she drove the Jimmy with smooth, lithe twists of her head and arms. Her short blond hair jostled as she drove down the mountainside toward the artillery testing range, and her breasts—her breasts were so perfectly shaped that Mack had to rub his mouth with his hand to keep from drooling.

Fortunately, he'd given the front seat of the car to Robling, or he'd have melted into a puddle of water by now.

He'd make a play after dinner. He'd get her talking and then turn on the charm.

Assuming he could contain himself that long. He hadn't had sex now in three days, since the redhead at Chesterville.

Robling chattered away about how stupid the Army had been laying out the test site. It was his usual BS. Not that he didn't have a point in a way—there were no defenses here, aside from a few grunts in some Humvees near the perimeters. But the place had been used for artillery and short-range-missile testing, and who the hell would have attacked it?

They'd shut down all active testing here months ago, and according to Blondie the contractors had already completed site reclamation; Glass Mountain would be closed down in thirty days.

Blondie. Jesus, he'd forgotten her name.

"See now, your main building is very vulnerable from here," said Robling as they stopped atop a ridge. "Give me a Ma Duce and I could pin down a regiment there."

"Oh," said the guide. "Ma Duce?"

That's your cue, Mack realized.

"The colonel means a heavy-caliber machine gun," said Mack. "He does have a point. But this is a hell of a view." He released his seat belt—she'd turned around specially to ask him to put it on—and opened the door.

Geographically, the view consisted largely of wasteland, the all-but-shuttered administration building, and the roofs of the vacant bunker facilities dug into the opposite hillside. But Mack had other attractions in mind.

"This hillside presents a strategic possibility," said Robling as he got out of the truck. "If this facility were used as a base, a surveillance tower could be placed here."

Mack rolled his eyes. Robling took no notice of Cheryl—the name flashed back—as she got out of the truck and put her hands on two of the most perfect curves in creation. She turned her back, and her firm butt—it had to be very firm—made Mack realize he was having a religious experience.

"It is a beautiful view," said Cheryl, turning to Mack.

Maybe he wouldn't have to wait for dinner.

"As far as a tower goes," she continued, "we just took one down. You can see the concrete pads in the dirt." She walked toward Mack, nearly brushing him as she passed. "Of course, it was just a light structure used to observe operations on Range F, over there."

The range was in the valley. Robling jerked around.

"This place radioactive?" said Robling, alarm suddenly in his voice.

Mack tried hard not to roll his eyes. The colonel had asked the same question at some point at every base.

Cheryl smiled indulgently. "Of course not, Colonel. There were never live explosions here. Nuclear material was never even present except in minute amounts. Every precaution was taken."

"Can't be too careful," said the colonel.

Cheryl walked over to him and—to Mack's complete horror—patted him on the back, her fingers lingering.

Robling turned to her slowly. Mack felt violently ill.

As he reeled away, he heard a whine in the air above him. Instinctively, he threw himself to the ground.

Aboard Hawkmother
Over Glass Mountain
5 March, 1740

SHE WASN'T PHYSICALLY WITH HIM, YET MADRONE FELT Minerva's breath on his neck as he took Hawk One into the target. She nudged his shoulder gently, pointed him to the lab where the bastards had poisoned him.

They'd come so far in the past few weeks. With her inspiring him, he'd used his brain in ways he'd never imagined possible. He'd discovered how to mount two bombs beneath each Flighthawk without losing too much speed. He had examined the Boeing's ident gear and learned to spoof commercial identifying codes. He had even found out how to enter bogus flight information in the civilian networks as they tracked commercial flights, though that required help from Minerva.

Help she was only too glad to give—she loved him as deeply as any woman had ever loved a man. He could feel it in her touch.

Hawk One zeroed in on its target, the two AV-BP-250 550-pound rocket-powered penetrator bombs strapped to its belly ready. They had altered the fuses slightly to enhance their ability to penetrate these particular bunkers and explode on Level Three, where he had been betrayed.

So easy; he knew how to do it before he even looked at the weapons.

The bunker sat fat in the middle of his screen.

So beautiful, revenge. Unspeakable.

As Madrone pushed the trigger, he heard the bells from his daughter's funeral.

C^3 warned that it was losing the connection with Hawk One.

"You bastards," Madrone screamed over the plane's interphone circuit to its Brazilian pilots. "Keep me close to the Hawks."

"We are trying, Commander," replied the pilot. "You're flying too fast, much faster than your plan directed."

"Closer, damn you!" Madrone looked to the right, jumping into the Boeing's cockpit. He took control and slammed the thrusters himself.

Back in the Flighthawks.

The bunkers had already exploded. He made sure the control connections were strong, then threw himself into the cockpit of Hawk Two, which was zeroing in on the tower.

Something was wrong. The tower wasn't there.

Nausea ate his stomach; Madrone felt sweat starting to slide down his temples.

Did he have the wrong place?

Sitrep.

He was there. He'd hit the bunkers. There was smoke.

They had taken away the tower. There was a truck there, people.

The bastards, laughing at him. They'd tricked him again. *Laughing!*

The AV-BI napalm bombs in Hawk Two would put an end to that.

Glass Mountain
5 March, 1744

MACK SAW IT ONLY FOR A SECOND, AND ONLY FROM THE periphery of his vision. He was falling and confused, but he was certain, absolutely positive, about what he saw:

A Flighthawk, darting upward over the bunkers on the hillside.

He hit the ground face-first, too stunned to get his hands out to break his fall. Before Smith could roll onto his back, the small U/MF had disappeared in the twilight sky. In the next moment, there was a dull thud from the direction of the bunkers, then a series of progressively louder, though still muffled, concussions.

He jumped to his feet. Robling and Cheryl huddled against the truck.

"We're under attack!" Smith yelled.

The colonel grabbed for the Jimmy's door.

"No—that's the only target besides the administration building!" yelled Mack. "Down the ravine. Come on!"

He grabbed Cheryl and in the next moment found himself falling, the air on fire behind him.

Aboard Hawkmother
Over Glass Mountain
5 March, 1745

IN HIS EXCITEMENT, MADRONE FIRED BEFORE THE CURsor settled. The napalm bombs hit a few yards before the truck. But their beautiful red flames quickly covered the hillside.

The attacks on Minerva's Brazilian targets had been exhilarating. But this was something else entirely. When fighting the FAB, he felt jittery at times, worried about the planes or even slipping out of Theta. He was a young buck making love for the first time, worried about messing it up.

This—this was revenge, the long moment after orgasm, the deep comfort of success. This was beyond the petty victory of survival, the silly ego play of killing your opponent. This deepened his whole being.

Madrone sat in both Flighthawks and Hawkmother simultaneously, seeing the battlefield from every angle. He smiled as he pushed the planes down from opposite directions, slashing into cannon runs on the administration buildings. Bricks and mortar disintegrated in his path. Be gone, he thought—and they were.

The SUV's gas tank exploded with a fury, the gasoline erupting in a fireball high above the ground-hugging napalm. There were three people clawing down the ravine just below the hill, three easy targets for him as he pulled Hawk Two around for the kill.

He'd nail them left to right. The optical viewer magnified them, outlined their heads with the cannon's crosshairs.

As he started to push the trigger on the first target, the second turned toward him.

Mack Smith.

The shock threw him out of Theta.

Dreamland Commander's Office
5 March, 1800 local

JEFF STRUGGLED TO CONTROL HIS ANGER AS GERALDO laid out her arguments for Colonel Bastian. The program results weren't consistent, blah-blah-blah. The subjects were all proceeding much more quickly, blah-blah-blah. Wave activity unaccounted for. Perhaps feedback in the computer systems originating from the subject. Unpredictable lapses perhaps due to changes in the protocol. Given the inexplicable disappearance of Captain Kevin Madrone—

Zen finally lost it. "This isn't about Madrone, it's about me," he sputtered. "You think I'm hallucinating. I'm not. I don't think that I have my legs back. That's ridiculous."

"You personally have nothing to do with my recommendation," said Geraldo calmly.

"Bullshit. Those are my base hormone levels on your chart there."

"Major, you happen to be the only person who has gone through both the old and new protocols," said Geraldo. "It's not directed at you. But there's a clear difference between your present charts and the ones from the past incarnation of the program. The levels of dopamine, serotonin, and other neurotransmitters are clearly different, as are the brain patterns." She turned toward Jeff. "I don't know if we should terminate ANTARES completely. That may eventually be my recommendation. I need time to correlate it."

"There's no sense shutting down," argued Jeff, trying to keep his voice even.

"We're going to have to put ANTARES on hold," said Bastian. "Doc, draw up a plan—"

"That sucks shit," said Jeff, jerking his head toward him.

"Major," snapped Dog. He glared down at him, then turned his gaze back to Geraldo. "Draw up a plan to review the effects. Reinstate the Phase II psychological studies. Take Major Stockard off the drug protocol immediately."

Jeff grabbed his wheels angrily. Bastian glared at him.

Everyone is against me, thought Jeff. They want to keep me a cripple.

But that couldn't be true. Bastian had gone out of his way to help him.

"All right," Jeff said finally. "I think it's a mistake, but I'll go along with it. Remove the chip. I'll stop taking the drugs."

"You can't just stop taking them," said Geraldo. "We have to back you off gently. If you were to stop taking them, your body would try to keep up the level of neurotransmitters on its own. They'd actually increase for about a week, perhaps two. At some point, you would crash. As for the chip—I think it's safe to leave it in. You've had it for so long now, and removing it might cause complications."

"All right," said Zen, finally looking away from Bastian's gaze.

DOG FOLDED HIS ARMS IN FRONT OF HIS CHEST. IN less than three weeks, Zen had gone from a somewhat skeptical critic to the program's biggest booster.

Short of Secretary Keesh. Who was going to have a cow when Bastian told him the program was on hold.

So? It was the right thing to do, very clearly. Yet Dog had hesitated to say so just now, looking for the right words. The stress of running a high-powered command was turning him into Colonel Milquetoast.

"All right," he told Geraldo. "Give me a timetable for a report. Thanks," he added, dismissing them.

Geraldo started to say something, but Ax's sharp rap at the door interrupted her.

"Colonel, I'm sorry—you need to pick that phone up right now," said the sergeant. "Line three. It's an open line."

Dog punched the button and held the phone to his ear.

"Colonel, this is Mack Smith. I'm at Glass Mountain. It's just been attacked."

"Mack?"

"I'm calling from a pay phone, Colonel. A Department of Energy test range, dummy nuke testing—two hours ago, a little more, we came under attack by Flighthawks."

"What are you saying?"

"Flighthawks. They attacked a base in south Texas, Department of Energy District 2, Test Area 6."

"Hold on a second." Bastian stopped Zen and Geraldo, who were heading for the door. "Jeff, Doc, listen to this." He punched the button for the speakerphone. "Mack, do you have access to a scrambler?"

"Colonel, I'm on a fuckin' highway in God's country. I had the Ranger troop car stop so I could make this call."

"Can you get to a secure phone?"

"It'll be hours."

"All right. Jeff Stockard and Dr. Geraldo are here with me. Tell us everything you know."

Dreamland
5 March, 1814

DANNY FREAH LOOKED DOWN AT HIS BELT AS HIS ALphanumeric beeper began to vibrate. He was already en route to see Colonel Bastian, but the STAT notice took him by surprise.

So did the location—the secure video conference center in the Taj basement.

Danny quickened his pace toward Taj, the low-slung concrete building, its entrance glowing ever so faintly with the low-emission yellow lights. He strode past the security desk to the elevator.

"Subbasement Three," he told the automated system as he stepped in.

The elevator itself wasn't particularly fast, and the security scans that were required before it would move took forever. Danny waited impatiently, and not just because of Dog's message. He was supposed to call his wife in exactly twenty-five minutes.

Finally, the elevator lurched and began grinding its way downward. The doors hissed open, and Danny double-timed the short distance to the conference room, whose entrance was flanked by two of his Whiplash team members, Kevin Bison and "Egg" Reagan. Bison nodded, looking desperate for a smoke.

Inside, Jed Barclay's pimpled face filled the large screen at the front of the room.

"Mr. Freeman is still tied up in meetings on Brazil," Barclay said as Danny came in, referring to the National Security Advisor. "But the NSC has already scheduled a meeting on this for, uh, like, nine, uh twenty-three hundred hours our time, which is, uh, eight o'clock your time, I mean—"

"You don't have to convert it for us, Jed," said Colonel Bastian dryly.

"Thank you. Hi, Captain," Jed said to Danny, seeing him come in on his monitor.

"Jed." Danny nodded toward the glass slot below the screen, where a moving video camera focused on his face. Then he nodded to the colonel and Major Stockard, who was sitting grim-faced in his wheelchair. Dr. Geraldo and Lee Ong, the scientist responsible for the Flighthawk's physical systems, were sitting at consoles behind him.

"Just to review quickly for Captain Freah," said Bastian, "there's been an attack at a small Department of Energy base in southeastern Texas, formerly used to test short-range nuclear-delivery systems. We believe Flighthawks were involved."

"Well, that's not exactly, uh, with all due respect, Colonel," stuttered Barclay. "There has been an incident there, but officially we're not sure what the nature is. The state authorities believe it was terrorism."

"Mack Smith was there. He saw Flighthawks," said Dog.

"Mack?" Danny realized he'd practically shouted. It was

too late to bite his tongue, so he sidled into a seat without saying anything else.

"Bunker-penetration weapons and napalm," said Bastian. "And they strafed one of the buildings."

"The U/MFs are capable of carrying AGMs," said Ong. "However, that limits their performance. Additionally, they would require modification. Even if Hawks One and Two—"

"Which we lost," said Zen.

"Well, even in theory, if they were capable," said Ong, "their flight characteristics would be very degraded."

"But an attack could have been carried out by them," said Bastian. "Danny, can you lay out your Mexican theory?"

"There really is no theory," said Danny, hesitating. Ong and Geraldo had the highest clearances possible, and obviously Bastian had already made the decision that they could hear everything he knew about the possibility that Madrone had somehow escaped. But the fact that Smith had reported the attack had just set off an alarm bell in his brain.

"A large plane landed and stole fuel at a regional jetport on the Mexican coast the day Hawkmother disappeared," he told the others. "It was not necessarily our 777. In fact, some witnesses said it was a 707. We've had the entire area checked with U-2's without turning up anything."

"Satellites as well," noted Jed.

"The Flighthawks could never have gotten to southern Mexico," said Ong.

"They could have refueled off Hawkmother, right, Jeff?"

"It's possible," said Jeff, a little too defensively for Danny's taste.

"If that was him," said Ong, "where did he go next?"

"No idea," said Freah. "Like I said, there really is no theory."

"So he controlled the Boeing as well as the Flighthawks?" asked Ong. "Hard to believe."

"There have been some anomalies," said Geraldo. "And remember, the flight computers are actually the ones that guide the plane. The subject merely directs."

"Captain, maybe you should head out to Glass Mountain," said Barclay. "And maybe Major Stockard."

"How quick can you get out there, Danny?" asked Dog.

Texas was the last place he should be, but before Danny could think of a graceful objection, Dr. Geraldo looked up.

"Glass Mountain? I thought this was a Department of Energy site."

"Actually, the site is owned by an agency connected with the Department of Energy," said Barclay. "The Army conducted some tests there a few years ago."

"Colonel, Kevin Madrone was stationed at Glass Mountain. That's where he was when his daughter died."

JEFF WATCHED BARCLAY'S FACE AS GERALDO CONTINued. Jed was his cousin, and Jeff felt odd watching him on the screen, as if a home movie had suddenly become part of his work life. He could remember swinging him around by the legs only a few years ago, and adjusting his arms on a bat to hit right.

Jed probably still couldn't hit a good fastball. But he'd always been smart. And somehow he managed to land on his feet—against all odds, he'd not only managed to stay on in the Martindale Administration, but apparently had even more authority than before.

If Jed and Geraldo and Danny were right, Madrone was still alive.

But why would Kevin do this?

To screw Jeff up maybe. This would kill any chance of continuing with ANTARES.

Jeff saw the others glancing toward him every so often, as if he carried a disease.

Kevin wouldn't hurt people.

ANTARES enhanced your mental capabilities. It didn't change you. Geraldo had said that over and over. Hell, everybody knew that—Maraklov had been a traitor before he arrived at Dreamland; ANTARES didn't turn him into one.

Maybe losing his daughter had twisted Kevin somehow.

Had Jeff's losing his legs done the same to him?

IN DOG'S OPINION, THE VIDEO CONFERENCE WITH BARclay had accomplished little. Freeman and Defense Secretary Keesh were unavailable because of a crisis in Brazil, where a three-way conflict between the Navy, Air Force, and government was coming to a head. Apparently the conflict was going to be resolved by giving a number of Air Force generals an important role in the government—though why any military person in his right mind would want that was beyond Bastian.

Barclay would present Freeman and the other members of the National Security Council with the theory that the Flighthawks had survived and were involved in the attack. He'd also recommend that all of the places Madrone had worked in the past—starting with Los Alamos—be heavily guarded. In the meantime, Dog had to call his own boss, General Magnus, and update him.

Magnus wasn't going to like this at all. Or maybe he would. It would undoubtedly hurt Keesh and his sidekick McCormack.

It would also damage Dog, though at least he'd advised against proceeding with ANTARES in writing.

I'm thinking like a politician and a bureaucrat, Dog told himself. That's not who I am. I'm a pilot.

"Frowning a lot, Colonel," said Danny, waiting for him near the door to the conference room.

"Yeah."

"I have something I have to talk to you about," said Freah. He gave a short wave to Zen, who was just approaching. "It's trivial. Base stuff. But—"

"I'm a bit busy."

"Won't take that long. Minor discipline problem. But I need advice."

Freah never brought minor discipline problems to him. Bastian nodded at the others, then motioned Danny to the side of the empty room. Freah waited until the doors closed.

"Everything I said just now, during the session with Barclay, was absolutely true," Danny said. "Maybe it's just a coincidence, but I find it interesting that Major Smith was at Glass Mountain when it was attacked. He's the only witness that Flighthawks were involved."

"How many other people could ID them to begin with?" asked Bastian. "And there's no local radar coverage."

"My point exactly."

"What would his motive be?"

"I don't know. Maybe something to do with the Brazilian?"

"I doubt Mack's a traitor. And he couldn't have stolen the Flighthawks himself."

"Maybe working with Madrone. I'm overthinking this, I know, but Hawkmother's pilot was found pretty far north and a good deal west of the prime search areas."

"Happens. The search cone was based on the last course projection, but that's always iffy."

"Mack supplied the projection."

"You think he purposely threw off the search?"

"I'm not saying that," said Danny.

"No way."

"I know," said Freah. "But Major Smith has been at some very interesting places at very convenient times. It's my job to be paranoid about it."

"Jeff Stockard and Breanna were aboard Raven when Hawkmother went down."

"Or was stolen."

"Or was stolen," admitted Bastian. "All right. I'll get Smith back here right away. And I'll kill his transfer to the Raptor program."

"If he were on ice for a bit, that's all."

"They need someone right away." Bastian reached back behind his shoulder, stretching the tense muscles in his upper body. Personally, he hated Mack, but it wasn't fair to screw him out of this based on a vague suspicion and coincidence.

Not fair, but it had to be done.

"Thanks, Colonel," said Freah.

"You'll have to excuse me. I have to call the boss."

"Shit, me too."

Pej, Brazil
6 March, 0300 local

MINERVA LANZAS CURLED HER ARMS ACROSS HER chest, pacing in the dark night. She cursed herself for giving into him.

Did she have a choice?

A tower, enemies—he was out of his mind. She'd never see him again.

The idea clawed at her. Objectively speaking, it would be easier if the American completely vanished. Yet she didn't think she could live if that happened.

She couldn't really be in love; she would never allow herself to be so vulnerable. And yet, there seemed no other explanation.

The ground rattled gently. The large Boeing appeared over the mountain ridge, snapping its landing lights on as it turned abruptly to line up for the field.

Minerva trembled when the rear hatch opened and Madrone walked down the ramp and into her arms.

"I was so worried," she told him.

"Yes," said Madrone, pressing her so tightly to his body she thought her bones would break. "They are stronger than I imagined. I must go back. They'll never leave us alone."

Minerva tried to undo herself from his grasp, but couldn't. "Kevin," she said gently. "Let me go."

Instead of answering, he sobbed on her shoulder.

"Are you all right?" she asked.

"They are bastards," he wailed. "They're everywhere. Glavin is probably telling them what to do. I know where he is. He sent me a card, a Christmas card, the bastard. I know where he is. I have to go back. I must."

He said it so forcefully, with such finality, Minerva knew she would never convince him to stay.

Dreamland
7 March, 0800

MACK SMITH HOPPED OFF THE DOLPHIN HELICOPTER ferry feeling like a million dollars.

Or rather, *milioncino,* a *cool* million. *Lire.*

Italiano. Which he would soon be speaking. Because obviously Bastian had ordered him back here because a transfer had come through.

And the grapevine was already buzzing with the possibilities. Either the Raptor F-22 program, which found itself in need of a director of operations, or squadron commander with a wonderful bunch of *ragazzi* flying F-15Cs in sunny Italia.

Bene, bene.

He'd prefer the Raptors, but something told him he was bound for Italy, where wine was cheap and the babes didn't believe in wearing tops.

To the best of his knowledge, no squadron in the Air Force was currently commanded by a major, so a promotion would quickly follow. The pay bump would be nice. Maybe he'd buy a little speedboat. Nothing outlandish—just big enough to rock gently when he made love.

"Major Smith, sir, Colonel Bastian wanted to see you," said a sergeant near the ramp. "I was to expedite you there, sir."

Jesus, Bastian had turned into an A-one fella, Knife thought as he climbed in the black SUV the sergeant had brought to ferry him over to Taj. Mack was in such a great mood that he even took a seat when Bastian's muck-up-the-works Sergeant Gibbs greeted him at the door.

Actually, Gibbs seemed almost deferential, at least by chief master sergeant standards, not only offering coffee, but remembering how Mack liked it. When Bastian buzzed, the sergeant showed him right in.

"Hey, Colonel," said Mack, breezing past Gibbs and pulling up a chair. "So—what's so fantastically important that I had to peddle back ASAP, as if I didn't know."

Bastian frowned at Ax, who had brought a folder's worth of vouchers to be signed.

"So?" asked Mack as the sergeant left the room.

"I'm afraid I have bad news for you, Major."

It took every ounce of self-restraint that Smith possessed not to cover his ears as Bastian continued. He spoke quickly, concisely, and without bullshit—Mack was assigned to Dreamland for the immediate future.

"Uh, Colonel—there's a slot in Italy and, uh, F-15's and, uh, I was promised—"

"Your name was mentioned for that, yes. I'm afraid it's no longer viable."

"Viable? Viable?"

"Nor is the Raptor slot open. The Pentagon wants more flight testing with the MiG-29's. You're on that assignment indefinitely," said Bastian.

"Who screwed me? What the hell's going on here?"

"I don't know that anyone screwed you, Mack."

"Oh, bullshit, Colonel. This isn't about the attack at Glass Mountain, is it? I'm getting screwed by somebody here," said Mack. He just barely stopped himself from jumping to his feet, rising slowly instead. "Colonel, can't you do anything? I mean—my record, Somalia. I've been a team player."

"I told you before, I will do something. And while we're talking about your record, why don't you tell me about the Brazilian you met in Las Vegas?"

"I told you about that. He wanted to know about MiG-29's. I told him to fuck off."

Bastian said nothing.

"That's what this is about?" Mack was too incredulous to believe it. "Asshole buys me a drink and gives me a cigar? I don't even smoke cigars."

Bastian pushed a button on his phone, and Ax appeared at the door. "The sergeant will see to anything else you need."

Confused as well as furious, Knife got up and made his way out of the office, barely controlling his temper well enough to avoid punching anything until he got into the elevator.

Aboard EB-52 BX-5 Galatica
Dreamland Range 34
7 March, 1000

BREANNA GLANCED AT HER COPILOT AS THE EB-52 reached twenty thousand feet. Galatica was similar to Raven in general layout, though the Dreamland wizards had continued to tinker around the edges. The most critical upgrades were larger fuel stores and super-cruise engines, which were based on a Pratt & Whitney design for the F-22. In the fighter, the engines helped conserve fuel at Mach-plus speeds. Tuned somewhat differently and shortened considerably for the Megafortress, they nearly tripled the model's combat radius. With careful fuel management, Gal could take off from Dreamland, fly a mission to Russia, and return without refueling—while providing fuel to a pair of Flighthawks through an automated boom in the tail.

The refueling boom was one of a long list of items to be tested today. They were going to air-launch two Flighthawks, which hadn't been done from Gal yet, and run through an automated test suite on Galatica's tactical surveillance radar. That done, they'd burn off some fuel with a few crash dives and climbs to make sure the airframe and engines were up to the stress. Bree had in mind taking a shot at eighty thousand feet, which was currently the unofficial Megafortress altitude record.

"Handling like a fighter, even with all the extra fuel weight," said Chris Ferris, her copilot. "I thought the leading-edge flap was a little sluggish when we started to climb, but the computer recorded the specs at Dash-1."

"What about the gear?"

"Cleaned fine."

"I don't like the extra tires," said Breanna. "It all felt kind of storky."

"I guess. I kind of like the higher view."

The plane stood roughly four feet higher off the ground than the other models. Changes in the landing gear made heavy landings more manageable, an important consideration if the plane were carrying a full load of fuel and had to quickly return to a combat base. At the same time, the gear further protected the engines and any carriaged Flighthawks from debris at a less than perfectly groomed airfield during takeoff.

"All instruments in the green," Ferris reported, running through the indicator screens.

"Go for it."

"Dreamland EB-52 BX-5 Galatica to Dream Tower," he said immediately, clicking on the radio. "We're on station and preparing to dance. Cue the band."

Breanna rolled her eyes as her copilot and the tower controller exchanged a series of excruciatingly poor puns. When the controller reported that the weather was "sans polka bands, with trombones blowing from the west at two notes an hour," she decided she had had enough.

"Chris, we don't have all day."

"Just trying to keep everybody loose," said Ferris.

His poorly concealed smirk indicated that he had probably been waiting for her to reach her breaking point for some time. It was not out of the realm of possibility that he and the controller had some sort of bet riding on her reaction.

"Hawk Leader to Gal," snapped Jeff over the interphone. "Yo, are we dancing today or what?"

"Not you too," said Breanna.

"Hey, if the waltz fits, dance it." He'd laughed, saying the words so quickly it was obvious he'd rehearsed them.

"Oye."

"Let's rumba."

"I hope you're all enjoying yourself," said Rap, pushing the Megafortress into the long slope that would launch the U/MFs.

At least Jeff seemed in a good mood today.

"Flighthawk launch in zero-five," she told her husband. "Prepare for alpha maneuver."

"Rosin the bow, maestro."

THE AIR LAUNCH OF THE FLIGHTHAWKS WENT OFF without a hitch, as did the first refuel, despite the increased turbulence generated behind Gal by the new engine configuration. When Dreamland Control asked them to shift ranges to accommodate another flight, Jeff was happy for the break.

"Trail One," he told C^3 as Breanna brought the EB-52 southwestward. The computer informed him it was complying, and Jeff slid his flight-control helmet up over his head. He glanced at the console to make sure it duped the controls—it did—then eased back in the seat.

With both Jennifer and Ong tied up on other projects, they were flying without a techie aboard today. While Zen thought the minders had long ago become superfluous, he did miss having someone on the deck to joke with—or hand him a Gatorade during downtime.

He fumbled for his small thermos cooler stowed between the two stations, barely within reach from his seat in the widened Flighthawk control bay. The original B-52's had three different crew areas. The pilot and copilot sat on the flight deck at the top front of the plane. The electronics warfare officer and gunner had a cabin on the same level behind them, where their side-by-side seats faced the rear of the plane. Below and roughly between these two areas was a bay for the navigator and radar operator.

In the Megafortress, the pilot and copilot—along with the

extensive array of flight computers and advanced avionics—could handle all of the offensive and defensive duties as well as fly the plane. This allowed the other compartments to be modified and adapted according to the plane's specific mission. Raven, for example, had been intended as a test bed for advanced ECM warfare and Elint-gathering craft, and her upper rear bay included extensive gear for that mission.

Gal, intended from the start as a dedicated Flighthawk "mother" with AWACS-like tracking capabilities, had duplicate U/MF control consoles in the upper compartment as well as the lower, where Jeff sat now. Lengthening and reshaping of the plane's nose area during the remodel added two more seats on the flight deck, which would be used for the operators of the plane's long-range surveillance radars. The changes had also made the lower Flighthawk bay somewhat more spacious than the offensive weapons station of a B-52G, though most of the extra space was taken up by test equipment and recorders.

Gal's T/APY-9 surveillance radar had been installed, but its programming was not yet complete. For now, only the system's most rudimentary capabilities were available, though even these were impressive for a fighter jock used to the traditional limits of small-area pulse-Doppler units. Operating in F band like the AN/APY-2 in the AWACS/E-3, Gal's next-generation slotted, phased-array antenna was twelve feet wide, rotating in a slight bulge at the bottom of the fuselage roughly where the strike camera and ECM aerials would be located on a standard B-52. While only a third of the diameter of the APY-2, the radar had nearly the same range and capability as the earlier AWACS, with Pulse Repetition Frequency and environmental modes helping it pick up fighters "in the bushes" at fairly long range. At present there was no way to slave its inputs into C^3; Jeff had to manually send the feed to one of the multi-use display areas, read the plot, and take appropriate action. While most combat pilots would kill to have what amounted to their own personal AWACS unit, the procedure felt somewhat clunky in the Flighthawks' otherwise seamless overlay of information and control.

Jeff popped the top on his soda and sipped slowly, watching the control panel. The U/MFs sat in their trail positions as precisely as a pair of Blue Angels preparing for a flight show.

The T/APY-9 required a few minutes to "warm up"—the revolving radar unit slowly accelerated from idle (one turn every four minutes) to operational mode, which was four revolutions per minute. The spinning disk changed the plane's flight characteristics, and the pilots had to adjust their control surfaces and in some regimes their engine settings to compensate for it.

Jeff checked the unit's status on panel two of the starboard station, then told Bree that he was about to gear up.

"Hang tight a second, Zen. We need to run through a systems check up here," she replied.

"Roger that."

Zen listened in as the two pilots worked through a short checklist; the procedure mostly consisted of his wife saying something and her copilot replying "in the green" or simply "green," indicating that the item was at spec. But the snap in her voice fascinated Jeff, giving him a window into part of her that he hadn't seen before the Megafortress and Flighthawk projects were wed. He loved his wife for reasons that had nothing to do with the fact that she was an excellent pilot and a fine officer; in fact, while he'd known that those things were true when they dated and married, he hadn't paid much if any attention—they'd worked in what were then completely different areas. But over the past few months he had come to admire her on a professional level as well. There was a certain satisfaction listening to or watching her work, as if her efforts justified some judgment he had made: My wife is not only beautiful and a great lover and companion, but she can kick ass too. Zen knew it was probably just a selfish ego stroke, but he couldn't help smiling to himself as she and her copilot cleared him to start the radar.

"We'll be at the next mark in, oh, call it three minutes," Bree told him.

"Looking good," said Jeff, sliding on his Flighthawk control helmet.

"Sitting that close to the radar," joked Chris, "you won' need birth control tonight."

"Ha-ha," said Jeff.

"Fuel burn?" said Bree in her most businesslike voice.

Jeff jumped into the cockpit of Hawk Three and began descending, watching the radar plot on the left side of the screen supplied by T/APY-9. The feeds were being recorded and the diagnostics were all automated, but Zen didn't see the point of having the damn thing on and not using it. Smaller and stealthier than a normal fighter, the Flighthawk had a radar cross-section about the size of a sparrow's, but the T/APY-9 followed it easily as it slid downward. Jeff's rudimentary controls allowed him two views—full and close-in—as well as query and non-query mode, which attempted to identify targets through ticklers or ident gear. The finished product would be able to fall back on a profile library for planes that didn't respond, a feature C^3 already had.

Close-in mode painted the Flighthawk at two thousand feet AGL, five miles distant, which was the test spec.

"Gal, I'm going to push Hawk Three out to ten miles and then dial the radar down to ten percent, see if we can follow it. Give the radar a real run. What do you say?"

"Simulating a hundred-mile scan?"

"Two hundred radius, give or take."

"That's going to put you outside the test range, Hawk Leader."

"Roger that."

"Wilderness area," said Chris. "Sometimes they run tour helicopters up across the lake and around the mountain."

"I'll scan it first," Jeff said. He clicked the Flighthawk's radar into long-range search and scan while lowering his airspeed, making sure the air ahead was clear. Then he clicked the tactical AWACS radar's plot into long-range view as well.

Clear.

He tucked the Flighthawk on her right wing, nudging toward a vast orange-colored plateau. There were times when he flew that the universe seemed to open up; he forgot he was sitting in the belly of a lumbering bomber, totally absorbed in the experience projected on his visor. He forgot about everything and just flew.

There was a valley about a mile south. Ducking into its recesses would give the T/APY a real workout. Jeff nudged the fuel slider on the underside of the control stick, picking up speed before plunging with a glorious roll down into the canyon.

A rock outcropping jagged off the side ahead. He had to pull hard left. He tried hitting the rudder pedals, didn't get a response.

Of course not. His legs were useless. He had no rudder pedals.

Damn, he thought to himself, I haven't done that in months. ANTARES.

They were still weaning him from the drugs. Sometimes he thought of saving all the pills, taking them together, seeing if that might do it.

Zen pushed the idea away, concentrating on the flight, but he'd lost the magic. He began to climb mechanically, easing back toward Galatica as the bar showing the signal strength edged toward critical.

The Flighthawk was fat on the radar. But there was something else on the screen, at the far edge, something low and very small.

Not blue, as a civilian plane should have been coded by the gear.

Red with a black bar.

Another Flighthawk.

A spoof or bizarre echo.

Another contact swallowed it. A large civilian plane, flying very low, less than a hundred feet from the ground.

Jeff pressed the ident gear, but the contacts had disappeared.

"Bree, change course, go to 0145," he said, naming a vector to the southeast. "Go!"

"Jeff?"

"I need you to snap on that course," he said.

The Boeing complied, but the contact was lost. Jeff told C^3 to put Hawk Three back into Trail One, then slid his control helmet up and reached to the other panel. But he couldn't remember the right sequence to get the radar feed to replay off the test equipment.

"On course," said Breanna.

"Chris—a hundred, hundred and fifty miles ahead on this vector. There any military installations?"

"You've got us straight on for Mount Trumble and the Grand Canyon," said Chris.

"Beyond that."

"Have to look at the paper map."

"What's the story, Zen?" asked Bree.

"I think I picked up another Flighthawk."

"Jeff, no way. The radar probably just had a shadow or something."

"I think we have to check it out. We have the fuel, right?"

Breanna didn't answer.

"Nothing on the map," said Chris.

"No Army base?"

"Well, I mean, how far do you want me to look?" asked the copilot.

"Two hundred miles."

"Zen—"

"We have to check this out, Bree. The radar picked up a Flighthawk."

"At two hundred miles?"

"It was flying in front of a larger plane. I think it's Kevin."

"Geraldo said she thought he would try and hit Los Alamos. If he's still alive. And crazy."

"We have to check it out," he told her.

There was another long pause.

"Gal Leader concurs," she said finally. "Notifying Dreamland Tower. I'll see if there are any other government facilities along the route."

"In the general area. It could be north of our course," he added, picturing a pair of Flighthawks hugging the terrain en route to a target.

"Copy that."

Aboard Hawkmother
Over Hulapi Mountains, Western Arizona
7 March, 1120 (1020 Dreamland)

THE GRAY-STRIPED JAGUAR STALKED BACK AND FORTH as the wind gathered force, the trees stirring and then shaking. The cat stopped, looking upward as it scented danger.

But it was too late. Madrone opened his talons wide and caught his enemy behind the neck, twisting with a sharp jerk so hard that the sharp claws severed the head completely from the body.

The first Avibras FOG-MPN crashed through the roof and down into the floor of the reception area of the DOE building at Skull Valley; it cleared a large hole to the basement. Madrone managed a quick correction on the trail missile, getting it cleanly through the two holes and into the basement laboratory area where he believed Theo Glavin would be. Hawk One, which had launched the missiles, shot wildly to the right as a massive secondary explosion rocked the sky. Madrone pitched the plane upward, his sensors temporarily blinded by the massive explosion of a pressurized helium tank.

He'd blown it. Even with his modifications, using the short-range weapons had been a tremendous mistake. Minerva had been wrong—she'd tricked him somehow, keeping him from his revenge.

Madrone felt himself falling from the plane, tumbling toward the parched desert. He was out of Theta, about to die.

I just want to be left alone, he thought. I want to be at peace. I don't want to be a robot—I don't want revenge or to kill anyone. I just want peace.

I want to die.

Christina stood before him, crying.

But warm hands clamped around his shoulders, and Minerva whispered in his ear. *I want you. I want you.*

Even though he did nothing to initiate it, even though he didn't think of his Theta metaphor or try to control his breathing—Madrone snapped back into Theta, back in control of the Flighthawks.

Hawk One circled above the roaring flames of the Skull Valley DOE facility. Hawk Two, still carrying its missiles, hit its IP two miles from the target, approximately six miles from Hawkmother.

The security shack was the only part of the facility left intact. Madrone zeroed in on it from Hawk Two and fired one of the Avibras FOG-MPNs. As the missile sped toward its target, he saw a small culvert on the roadway about a half mile south. He targeted it and pickled, wiping out the only approach to the lab.

"Target destroyed," he told the Boeing's pilots. "Return."

He felt the pull of gravity as the pilots jerked the plane into a tight bank and hit the rocket-assist pods to accelerate. It felt good. He needed to get home, needed to wrap himself around his lover, sink deep inside her.

Aboard Galatica
Over Arizona
7 March, 1130

DREAMLAND TOWER HAD JUST REQUESTED ADDITIONAL information when the sky exploded fifty miles ahead of Breanna's left wing. The flare of the explosion seemed to tear the bluish haze in half.

"Holy shit," said Chris.

"Get a fix on the location. Tell them," Breanna said.

"I have Hawkmother on the T/APY," Zen told Breanna over the interphone. "That's definitely him. Seventy-five miles, correct five degrees south."

"Can you feed me the radar image?" asked Breanna as she worked onto the course.

"Negative," said Jeff. "Come on. They're pulling away."

"We're at the firewall."

"You're not going to let him get away, are you? Come on, Rap. Kick some butt."

Breanna touched the throttle slider, even though she knew it was useless—the engines were at the max. They were moving at nearly 565 nautical miles an hour, or Mach .95. That was a good deal faster than a standard B-52 could muster in level flight at 35,000 feet, and it was in fact fairly quick even for a Megafortress. They ought to be able to catch Hawkmother easily; the Boeing's top speed was "only" about 520 knots.

"We're falling back," said Zen.

"Are you sure you have live contacts?" Bree asked. "There's no way he could outaccelerate us."

"He is."

"You're positive it's Hawkmother?"

"Stay on this course."

"Gal Leader."

Dreamland Commander's Office
7 March, 1135

DOG HAD JUST STARTED TO THINK ABOUT GOING IN search of lunch when his phone buzzed.

"Bastian," he barked as he brought the receiver to his ear.

"Urgent transmission for you, Colonel," said Ax. "Tower on the line."

"Punch it through," said Bastian. He braced himself for the inevitable bad news. In the half second it took for Gibbs to punch the button and make the connection, he thought of Breanna and felt a twinge of fear.

"Colonel, Major Stockard thinks he's found Hawkmother. They're trailing them south of here," blurted the controller.

"What?"

"Hawkmother—there's been an attack."

"Okay. All right, I need this line—wait," he said quickly. "What other planes do we have in the air?"

"None at this time, sir. Satellite window reopens in ten minutes. Raven's due up at 1500."

"They don't have clearance to take off until I give it to you directly, do you understand?"

"Yes, sir," said the controller.

Bastian jumped to his feet and slammed down the phone. They'd outfit Raven and he'd go after them.

"Ax, tell Danny Freah to meet me over at the Megafortress hangar," he said, pushing into the outer office where his chief worked. "Call over there, find out who's on the duty roster. No, never mind—tell Major Cheshire to get there quickly. And have that plane fueled to the max. Go."

Madeira Hotel
Pôrto Velho, Brazil
7 March, 1435 local (1035 Dreamland)

WHEN GENERAL HERULE ENTERED THE ROOM TO BEGIN the meeting, Minerva felt astoundingly light-headed, barely able to believe she had lived to see this day. The general's personal bodyguard—wearing freshly adopted purple berets and matching epaulets as insignia—marched smartly into the hotel ballroom, flanking the doors. Their freshly polished boots reflected the sparkling chandeliers; the thick-paneled walls behind them showed off the sharp green of their khaki uniforms. Herule strode to the row of conference tables that had been set up in the exact center of the elaborate inlaid wood floor, standing at perfect attention. The sleepy town had been chosen as the site for the meeting because it was far from the capital; the hotel, finished only a few months before, because it could be easily secured. But in that moment it seemed to Minerva that there could not have been a more perfect and grand setting; the general filled the room with an air of majesty and power.

The incumbent President, mouth drawn and eyes baggy, entered from the side door not far from where Minerva stood. He'd made the long trip from Brasilia to this regional outpost just south of the Amazon by car; his body seemed to have absorbed every dirt and dust particle along the way. When he glanced toward her, she saw not the hate she expected, nor anger, but simply sadness and fatigue. His expression shook her, and as the leaders of Congress entered, she worried that she had been tricked somehow, trapped here while Madrone was far away. There were no admirals, no one, in fact, from the Navy.

Had they managed to obtain the upper hand again?

Her guards were with the plane. She was defenseless.

The general began dictating the terms of the President's "retirement," speaking with so little enthusiasm that Lanzas began to wonder if this was in fact a charade. Had she somehow been tricked again?

Madrone would meet his doom in America. What would she do then?

She steeled herself against them, stiffened her muscles. She would face them bravely.

"Colonel Lanzas," said General Herule. "Thank you for coming on such short notice."

She looked into his face. Herule flinched.

Betrayal. The bastard!

Minerva felt her heart fall into the pit of her stomach. Despairing, she cursed herself for being so foolish to rely on the two-faced bastard.

Then she managed a long breath, put her head back and her shoulders flat, determined to meet destiny with dignity.

"Colonel Lanzas shall be my Defense Minister," Herule told the others. "She is well suited, both through training and her family."

"Agreed," said Findaro, the head of the Army. A Congressman nodded near his side. "It is a wise choice."

"She will deal with the Americans," added Herule. Now his eyes held hers for a moment.

Lifted from the depths of despair, Minerva felt almost sexual elation. She had won after all.

Madrone was responsible. Madrone—her dark self. She regretted letting him go, even though she knew it was better to be rid of him.

The rest of the appointments, the rest of the meeting, passed quickly. Minerva gathered herself as the others started to get up.

"Well done, my dear," said General Herule, taking her hand and kissing it. "You almost seemed surprised."

"And you as solicitous as ever," she told him.

Herule laughed—then pulled her into a bear hug.

"We cannot afford to anger powerful forces to the north," he whispered in her ear. "There should be no trace of complications. If they or others could be blamed for complications, so much the better."

Minerva eased her hand down toward the general's groin and squeezed gently. The table and chairs made it impossible for the others to see—but if they did, so much the better.

"We won't have any trouble, my dear," she whispered.

Herule released her, his face a little flushed. "I will arrange a meeting with the admirals."

"I'll arrange it," she told him. "In a few days. They will come to me. In the meantime, I must get back quickly."

"Yes," said the general. "No complications."

"Of course."

Aboard Hawkmother
Over the Gulf of Mexico
7 March, 1540 local (1340 Dreamland)

MADRONE SENSED THEY WERE AFTER HIM EVEN THOUGH the threat scope was clear. He felt them trail him out of Arizona, down the eastern Sierra Madres. They might be too far for the radar and too smart to use the radio, but he knew they were there nonetheless.

Fear prickled along the back of his head, like an electrical current arcing from the spider.

He welcomed it; it made it easy to focus.

The bastards made their move as the Boeing crossed over the southwestern Caribbean. Two planes came for him at high speed, tickling the 777's identifier. As they came on, he told Gerrias and Mayo to hold their course.

He pulled Hawk One and Hawk Two closer to the 777, nearly touching the big plane's wing. They would be invisible to the interceptors' radar, but not their eyes.

If the enemy approached within visual distance, he would kill them.

"Brazilian Air 43, please identify your aircraft type and specify your cargo," said an American voice.

Gerrias answered as they had rehearsed—a benign cargo flight carrying medical supplies. The flight would appear on the international registries, synching with their IDs.

There were two planes, F-16's.

He would roll out from under Hawkmother as they approached. The only possible attack would be head-on.

Climb with the gates flooded, cannons blazing.

Madrone's body relaxed. He waited, absorbing the sky around him, feeling the vibration of the wind buffeting off the wings of the Boeing above him.

The interceptors acknowledged Gerrias's transmission. They continued toward them, closing to within eight miles, seven.

Then they turned northward, pretending to be satisfied with the explanation.

He avoided the temptation to go after them.

"They're gone," said Mayo finally.

"No," Madrone replied. "They trail behind still. Be alert."

"Yes, Commander," said the copilot.

They would never rest now that he had killed Glavin. Colonel Glavin had been the jaguar. Such a clever bastard—he'd pretended to be so concerned about Christina, apologizing after denying Kevin leave to go to the X-ray session that afternoon.

"If only I'd known what it was for," Glavin had lied. "Why didn't you say so? Kevin, all you have to do is ask."

The bastard. He had set everything up. That very day he'd suggested Livermore and the experimental treatment facility connected to the lab. He'd done it all so smoothly, so matter-of-factly, that Madrone had been bamboozled.

Maybe Christina hadn't even had the cancer until then. How clever these bastards were.

Eventually, they would get him. But not before he made them bleed.

Aboard Galatica
7 March, 1545

"TWO DEGREES DUE SOUTH. WE'RE STILL SEVENTY-FIVE miles behind," Jeff told Breanna.

"F-16's have broken off," said Chris.

"Copy."

"They didn't get close enough for a visual," added the co-pilot. "But the identification checked out."

"Yeah, I know, I heard the whole thing," said Zen. The F-16's had flown south out of Texas, and were at the edge of their range when Jeff finally managed to vector them toward the Boeing. Since there was no way to protect the radio transmission, Zen hadn't told them more than absolutely necessary—the plane flying south had to be identified.

If he'd ordered them to shoot it down, they wouldn't have. No Air Force pilot in his right mind would target what seemed to be a civilian plane—hell, even a military plane—without serious authorization. Even then, most would hesitate unless they had some clear indication that the plane was a threat and the order lawful.

Jeff didn't have the authority to give the order. Colonel Bastian had authorized them to trail Hawkmother and find its location; nothing more. The colonel had boarded Raven and sent a message that he would rally other forces to help. But they were so far away from Bastian that they couldn't directly communicate; unlike Raven, Gal lacked a SATCOM system.

"Where the hell do you think he's going?" Breanna asked

more than an hour later as they continued southward, heading for Panama.

"Damned if I know," said Jeff. "I thought Cuba, but he should have cut east by now."

"How's your fuel situation?" Breanna asked.

"You're reading my mind. Let's tank while he's flying a straight line."

They refueled as quickly as possible, but still fell gradually behind as Hawkmother continued onward, making landfall over Cartagena in Colombia. Flying at forty thousand feet, the stealthy Galatica and her Flighthawks passed undetected by the local air defense and civilian radars.

"We're not going to be able to follow him indefinitely," Breanna said as they approached Colombia, "especially not at this speed."

"We should be able to tank off someone in Panama."

"Negative," Bree told him. "There are no tankers available. Chris already checked. No tankers, no fighters. We're trying to get somebody out of Texas. I'd like to check back with the colonel as well. We haven't heard from him in a while."

"He said we might not." Jeff saw the 777's image start to blink—the plane was diving toward the ground.

"Maybe we can turn this over to one of the—"

"Bree—hold on." Jeff stared at the radar; Hawkmother had disappeared. "I've lost him."

He returned the Flighthawks to computer control, directing them into Trail One, then tried to work out the spot where Hawkmother had disappeared. Chris, working with the GPS and the CD map library, pinpointed the spot as a pass in the mountains just beyond the Orinco River in central Venezuela.

"No airport there," said Chris.

"I don't know that he landed; I think he just dropped closer to the mountains," said Jeff. "Hold this course, Bree."

With no way to refine the powerful radar in Gal's belly, Jeff decided he would use the Flighthawks as scouts, scouring the river valley and mountains. It was difficult, however, to fly both planes and still look at the T/APY; its plot took up too much space in the viewer and he could only toggle it in and out. He accelerated the U/MFs into a spread formation at Mach 1.2, gradually swinging them apart. Their optical viewers showed only a thick cloud deck until he dropped below five thousand feet at the very edge of his communication range.

Beautiful country. No airport, no Boeing.

He knew Kevin was out here. He'd get him back—then they'd get ANTARES back on track. And then he'd have his legs again.

"Hawk Four disconnect in zero-three—" warned C³.

"Zen, we're going to have to get approval from the colonel to land in Panama or someplace if we can't arrange a tanker," Breanna told him.

"We've come too far to lose him now," Jeff said, dropping his speed and nudging the U/MFs a little higher, strengthening the connection. "Give me more speed."

"We only have enough fuel for two more hours of flying time. And that's stretching it. We have to talk to Colonel Bastian."

"We can land without approval," he said.

"Jeff, that's not the point."

"Just do what you're told, Captain," he barked.

She didn't answer.

He toggled the radar screen back. Maybe something, seventy miles ahead, almost in Brazil. Very low.

"Stay on course," he told Rap.

"Gal."

She was trying to sabotage him, though. Chris was trying to raise Southern Command.

Why?

He was being paranoid. They were trying to find a tanker.

"Bree," he said, flipping on the interphone. "Listen. I didn't mean to snap at you."

"We're on course, Major," she said sharply. "Brazilian border in zero-six minutes."

The Boeing disappeared again. He jumped back in Hawk Three, skimming along the rugged terrain. The 777 needed a good-sized runway to land; it ought to be easy to spot.

Nothing.

Flight of F-5Es approaching from the east. FAB interceptors, Brazilian Air Force. Approximately fifty miles away, they were most likely patrolling the border, looking for smugglers. They weren't quite on an intercept, but would draw within five miles in three minutes. Their APQ-153 radars could detect a standard fighter at about twenty miles; the Megafortress and her brood would be invisible to the radar until well within visual distance.

The 777, on the other hand, ought to be on their screens already.

"Rap, there's a group of FAB F-5's flying near their border to the east of us. They're about fifty miles away. What do you think about hailing them to see if they've spotted Kevin?"

"Gal," she snapped, still plenty pissed.

Breanna was right about the fuel. Maybe they could use the base of the F-5's.

If Bastian approved. They'd have to get his okay. Breanna was right about that.

The Boeing flitted into the corner of the radar plot. He'd turned ten degrees north.

Where was he going?

BREANNA TOLD CHRIS TO GIVE THE FAB FLIGHT THE Boeing's course even though they did not immediately acknowledge.

"Maybe they don't speak English," said Chris when they still didn't respond.

"You speak Spanish?"

"Portuguese," he said. "No. Hold on." He leaned to one side, putting both hands over his helmet as if that might somehow make the transmission clearer. "Repeat?" he asked.

"What's up?" Breanna asked.

"F-5's are challenging us," Chris told her. He turned toward the multi-use display at the far right of his dash. "Shit. They're trying to tickle the ident gear."

"Activate it. Standard mode," said Breanna. The Megafortress's friend-or-foe identifier could be manipulated from the dash. Standard mode presented Gal as a B-52G.

"Still not acknowledging. Ten miles off, nine, eight," said Chris. "Should be within visual range, but I can't pick up any lights."

"Can they see us?" Breanna asked.

"I think it'd be kind of hard, even with this bright moon," said Chris. "But they know we're here. They're correcting, maybe coming on our radio signal. I'm going to try and hail them again."

Breanna started to answer, but Chris cut her off.

"Shit—they're charging their weapons. Shit—I think those idiots think we're Hawkmother. They want to shoot us down."

Aboard Hawkmother
Over Northwestern Brazil
7 March, 2220 local (1820 Dreamland)

"YOU WERE RIGHT, CAPTAIN," THE F-5E PILOT TOLD MAdrone. "We have the B-52 in range. He has two escorts."

A B-52? The plane must actually be a Megafortress, with two Flighthawks.

So Jeff had finally shown his true colors.

"Shoot him down," Madrone said. "Ignore the escorts—they are unarmed."

"Captain?"

"Ignore them. They'll flail at you but they won't strike."

"Understood."

Aboard Galatica
7 March, 2223

ZEN SLAMMED THE FLIGHTHAWKS AROUND, CURSING himself for concentrating so hard on finding the Boeing that he had left their flanks uncovered. There was no reason for the damn Brazilians to attack—but here they were, pedals to the metal, slashing in.

He tucked Hawk Four into a dive as she came out of her turn, building back her momentum. C^3 took Three in trail as he slammed forward, trying to get between the Tigers and Galatica. He had no shells in his cannon, but he activated the targeting radars anyway, figuring that even the limited avionics in the F-5Es would realize they were being cued for a shot.

Hopefully, that would make the pilots break off, or at least concentrate on the U/MFs.

Of course, it might only make them mad. The lead plane

didn't seem to be turning, even though Jeff was homing in on his nose.

THE NEED TO STAY CLOSE TO THE FLIGHTHAWKS CUT down on Breanna's options, and her fuel situation would make a rip-roaring climb to sixty thousand feet a Pyrrhic victory. Besides, they'd never outrun the Brazilians' missiles.

"Their weapons are charged!" warned Chris. "Still not acknowledging our hails."

"Trying to wave them off," said Zen.

"Hang with me, Hawk Leader," she said, punching the plane into a sharp roll as the first two-ship of Tiger IIs came on.

"They're going to send the second wave onto our tails as we turn," warned Chris.

If Gal had been armed, that would have been fatal for the Tiger IIs—the Megafortress's Stinger air mines would have turned them into flying spaghetti. But with no weapons and no diversionary flares, Breanna had only her wits and the EB-52's ability to zig in the air going for her.

She flailed left as one of the Tiger IIs closed to range for a heat-seeker. The Megafortress wallowed a little, held back by the trim flaps that compensated for T/APY's rotation momentum.

"Power down the T/APY," she told Chris.

"Powering down."

"Shit!"

Breanna looked up to see the nose of an F-5E looming in her windscreen. She plunged right, trying to swirl into a controlled roll, but briefly lost the plane as the wings inverted.

"Missiles in the air," said Chris.

His voice was so calm she knew they were going to get hit.

IF EITHER OF THE HAWKS HAD BEEN CARRYING AMMU-nition, Zen would have made short work of all four F-5's. But the pilots seemed to know that he was unarmed, and paid no attention to him even as he dove for them. Hawk Three closed on one of the F-5Es as it spun toward the rear of the

Megafortress. He saw its cannon begin to flash, and pushed Three close enough to break the cockpit glass in two, slamming his stick with a flare of body English to hold on to the Flighthawk. The Brazilian plane pirouetted away, breaking up; C^3 said Hawk Three had not suffered any damage.

As he swung toward the F-5E's wing mate, Zen was pitched sideways by gravity. Breanna swirled the EB-52 into a hard spin trying to escape a fresh attack.

"Tell them we're not Madrone," Zen said.

"I'm fucking trying," said Chris.

Aboard Hawkmother
7 March, 2230

HAWK ONE'S SYNTHETIC RADAR FEED FILLED THE CENter of his mind. Madrone watched a God's-eye view of the battle ten miles away from 65,000 feet.

He was a god, wasn't he? That's why they wanted to stop him.

Missiles flared toward the big black plane. It would be over soon.

Kevin felt a twinge in his stomach, then lost the vision, his body plummeting toward the mountains below. He'd slipped out of Theta.

Aboard Galatica
7 March, 2230

BREANNA PUSHED LEFT, THEN RIGHT, THEN LEFT, nearly warping the flaps and ailerons with her maneuvers. As she whipped back right she popped the leading-edge tabs, working them like air brakes to slam the big plane downward like a pregnant whale. Her wings flipped over, the stress on the spars so great the entire plane groaned. Rap cleaned the controls and grabbed the throttle, goosing it to the max a second before jerking the stick upward.

The acrobatics worked. The first missile sailed past, wide of its target. A second and third missile whipped past, the latter detonating on default about a hundred yards away.

A fourth was so thoroughly confused, it too exploded—unfortunately about twelve feet from the plane. Hot shards of metal ripped through Gal's fuselage, shorting some of the electronics and damaging the control surfaces on the right wing.

But it was the cannonfire of the F-5E Rap had lost track of that almost did them in. The first she knew of the close-quarter attack was a low thump behind her. Then she felt like someone was hitting the seat with a baseball bat.

The Boeing slid sideways. Bree fought it, saw the enemy's tracers blazing across the sky, felt Gal rolling on her wing.

"I have it," she told Chris.

"Yup," he said, broadcasting a general Mayday on the Guard frequency.

THE F-5Es SWARMED ON THE MEGAFORTRESS. ZEN pushed Three closer, nudging the throttle as the four planes dove. Another six were within two miles, homing in on the scent of blood.

With a cannon, they'd all be dead meat.

"Proximity alert," flashed on the screen, C^3 warning that he was within a hundred feet of the F-5E.

Jeff watched helplessly as the Brazilian lit his cannon. Tracers blazed across the EB-52's tail section, gouging a large hole in the fin. Zen could feel the shock behind him.

For a brief moment, the chromium sun that had been part of his ANTARES metaphor returned. He felt a flash of heat and anger. Then he put his finger on the throttle slider, accelerating Hawk Four into the midsection of the Brazilian fighter.

THE SHOCK WAVE OF THE EXPLOSION HAD AN ODD EF-fect on Galatica, actually helping Breanna stabilize her in level flight. Even so, there was no question that they were badly damaged. The emergency screens lit on the multi-use displays, and the computer flashed a warning on the HUD saying they had only forty-percent power capability in engines one and four.

"At least it's symmetrical," said Chris dryly.

The Megafortress's twin-tailplane, which extended like a V at the rear of the plane, had been severely damaged. Breanna nudged the plane into a very gentle bank, testing her control.

"F-5's have backed off. Zen got one," said Chris. "He rammed it."

"Hawk Leader?"

"I'm here, Bree. You guys okay?"

"For now," she told him. "Can you give me a visual on our damage? Start with the tail."

"Yeah."

The image snapped into the screen on her lower left panel, which was preset to accept the Hawk feed.

"Looks like a half-eaten waffle," said Chris. It was an apt description; much of the skin had been blown or burned off, leaving the honeycombed carbon-fiber guts exposed.

"We're stable. I can turn somewhat," Breanna told her husband. "We have to land ASAP, though. We've lost fuel, and we weren't exactly full to begin with."

"Your call," said Zen.

"Boa Vista's a hundred miles northwest," said Chris.

"I don't know." Breanna began banking in that direction anyway.

"Okay," said Chris, working the maps.

The plane bucked sharply.

"Fuel problem," said the copilot, punching his instruments. "Management panel won't come up for me."

"I have it. Find us a landing strip—even a highway at this point."

"Got an FAB strip five miles south of us. Primitive at best."

"Jeff, there's a strip at the edge of the jungle five miles south of here. Can you check it out?"

"Done."

It didn't much matter how long the strip was—they might not even make it that far. Two tanks had been shot out; the Boeing's automated fuel-management system had isolated the tanks, but apparently they were leaking somewhere in the feed lines as well. As Bree stabilized the engines, the monitor warned she was dry.

She thought of saying something to Jeff—maybe apologizing for not accepting his apology before. But the words didn't come and there was too much to do, keeping the plane steady.

"One of the fuel bags the system shut off sealed," reported Chris. "I'm trying to get it back on line manually."

"Give it a try."

"How long did you say that strip was?" Zen asked.

"Less than twelve hundred," said Chris.

"Try five thousand," said Jeff. "It's long, level, and concrete."

"Give me a vector," Bree said.

"You're nearly dead on. It's hidden by the ridges there. Sharp drop. Check the low-light feed."

The runway looked brand-new. Everything else—a few buildings, two hangars—looked ramshackle, even from Four's orbit at five thousand feet. An old propeller transport sat off the ramp.

"No tower that I can raise," said Chris. "Trying Guard. Trying everything."

"There are people there," said Zen.

"We're landing one way or the other. We're on final," she added as the moonlit runway suddenly came into view over the mountain.

She blew a tire as they landed, probably because it had been damaged during the attack. Chris struggled with the crosswind readings at the last minute, and Breanna lost engine one completely when she applied reverse thrust, but she still managed to hold the runway. A wide ramp sat at the far end; she felt her body starting to collapse as she headed for it.

"So, what happens now?" Chris asked.

"We call home," said Breanna.

"The question is, why did the F-5's attack?"

"The country's in the middle of a crisis," said Jeff on the interphone. He landed the Flighthawk and taxied behind them. "There's been a military coup."

"Just what we need," said Breanna.

"Shooting at us still doesn't make sense," said Chris. "Unless they thought we were on the other side."

"Which side is the other side, though?" said Bree.

A jeep waited ahead. A soldier stood in the rear, waving at them.

"Looks like he's smiling," said Chris. "What do you think? Pop out and have a chat?"

"Think he'll speak English?" asked Bree.

"Got me."

"Those fuckers tried to shoot us down," said Jeff.

"It wasn't exactly these guys," said Breanna. "Doesn't look to me like the F-5's came from this base. No support facilities."

"We're going to have to talk to them sooner or later," said Chris. "It's not like we're at war with Brazil."

"No?" said Jeff sarcastically.

The men in the jeep jumped out, waving and smiling. They weren't carrying weapons.

"One of us is going to have to try talking to them," said Breanna. "We have to at least get to a phone."

"I don't know, Bree," said Jeff.

"Sitting here doesn't make any sense," said Chris. "I mean, if they want to, they can just blow us up. But those guys down there don't look hostile."

"I think I'll go talk to them," said Breanna. "What do you think, Jeff?"

She could practically hear him debating it, tossing his head back and forth the way he always did. If the attack had been a case of mistaken identity, then going out was the obvious thing to do. Chris had broadcast their position, but there was no indication that any American units had received it; even if they had, it would take hours or even days for them to be found. In the meantime, their radio's range would be severely limited by the mountains.

On the other hand, the F-5 attack had hardly been a friendly gesture.

"I think our options are either to blow up the plane or talk to them," Breanna said when Jeff didn't answer. "And we don't have anything on board to blow up the plane."

"Blowing up the plane doesn't make sense," said Zen finally.

"I agree," said Chris.

Breanna hit the console switch to automatically crack the hatch, lowering the ramp to the ground. Then she got out of her seat. "You and Zen stay with the plane," she told her copilot. "I'll go see what sort of donkey train we're going to need to get help in."

Breanna made her way to the ventral hatch without stopping to talk to Jeff in the Flighthawk bay. After so much time in the air, her legs felt a little spongy; she wobbled a bit as she put her boot on the pavement. Gal's stilt landing gear disoriented her as well, and Breanna felt unbalanced as she turned toward the front of the plane, walking out from its shadow. A pair of two-and-a-half-ton trucks, canvas tops flapping, whipped out from behind the hangars and headed toward her.

Breanna paused to get her bearings. As she did, something large buzzed down from the air behind her, so close and sudden that she stumbled sideways and fell to the ground. The Megafortress and the ramp rumbled with the vibration.

A Flighthawk.

"I thought you landed, Jeff," she yelled, rolling to her feet.

As she rose, one of the men who had come to greet her pulled out an Uzi and pointed it in her face.

VII
Doom

Pej, Brazil
7 March, 2300 (1900 Dreamland)

AS SHE WALKED TOWARD THE AMERICAN PLANE, MI-
nerva's anger dissipated, replaced by a rush of awe and even
envy. The massive black plane loomed from the dark shadows
like a mythic beast, its sleek nose a sword thrusting from
massive shoulders. The plane towered above her on its gear,
with smooth skin like a dark shark in the night. It was so big
it seemed like another part of the mountain, pulled down in
an avalanche. Yet the F-5 pilots reported the big bomber
could turn as tightly as they could. Had the plane been armed,
the outcome of the battle would have been far different.

The two men guarding the hatchway snapped to attention
when they saw their commander approaching. She gave them
a salute, then took hold of the railing and walked upward into
the reddish glow of the interior.

The lower deck looked like a television studio control
room, with a wide array of monitors and a bank of computers
and other gear along the walls. She guessed this was the place
where the robot planes were controlled from—joystick con-
rols and extensive video banks sat in front of both seats,
somewhat similar to the arrangement in Hawkmother. The
seat on the right turned on a special rail; the crippled commander must sit there.

Minerva climbed to the flight deck slowly. Madrone said
he Megafortress had started as an old B-52, but this didn't

seem possible—the cockpit belonged in something from the twenty-first century, or maybe the twenty-second. A smooth glass panel covered the entire dashboard area; there were no mechanical switches or old-fashioned dials on its surface. Screen areas, instruments, and controls were all configurable, either by touch or voice command. The throttle bar between the pilot and copilot did not move, but responded to pressure input. Control sticks rather than wheels guided the plane once airborne; textured areas indicated sensor switches built directly into the stick surface. Dull yellow letters in the windscreen showed clearly that the heads-up display, rather than being mirrored from a projector, was actually part of the window surface.

The plane's potential as a scout, as a bomber, as the leader of a squadron of interceptors was limitless. With one Megafortress, she could dominate not merely Brazil, but all of South America.

But she had to give it back.

More than that. She had to find a way to get it back to the Americans without being implicated in its theft.

She would fly it first certainly.

And then?

Minerva slipped into the pilot's seat. She would never give it back if she took off. No pilot could. To fly this plane would be to relive the first moment, the first dream of flight. She could never give it back.

But she had to. The Americans would never let her be if she kept it. They would take the plane back by force and dispose of her like a cockroach who had wandered into their home.

She could fight off the Americans. She could destroy them.

Desire erupted inside her, the darkness of her soul spreading everywhere. She would keep the plane, she would keep Madrone, she would destroy anyone who dared oppose her.

With great difficulty, Minerva forced herself from the seat and out of the plane. She had to let go of Kevin before he destroyed her. Even if it meant cutting her chest open with her nails and tearing out her heart.

Aboard Raven
Over the Gulf of Mexico
7 March, 2100 local (1900 Dreamland)

"OUR TANKER IS SET," COLONEL BASTIAN TOLD NANCY
Cheshire, quickly reviewing their position on the Megafortress's navigation screen. "They'll run a track as far south as
possible. We have about an hour on our present course and
speed."

"Good enough," said Cheshire.

"I think being copilot may be more difficult than piloting
this plane," said Bastian. Even though they had two operators
aboard to handle the EB-52's radio-eavesdropping gear, Dog
was responsible for many functions that would have been handled by the navigator and weapons operators in a standard B-
52. Granted, the computer did much of the grunt work, but
just calling up the proper panels on the multi-use screens
seemed an art.

"You're doing fine," said Cheshire.

"I'm going to check back with the *Nimitz*," Dog told her.
"See if their planes picked up anything."

"Go for it."

Raven's gear made it possible for him to communicate with
literally anyone in the world, as long as they could directly
access satellite connections. Dog had preset the frequencies
they were using for the search, and found himself speaking
to a Navy flight commander in the southwestern Caribbean a
half second after punching the buttons.

Nothing to report.

Southern Command had tracked Galatica to Venezuela. F/
A-18's from the *Nimitz* had heard Chris Ferris, Gal's copilot,
as the plane approached Brazil, though he hadn't answered
their own hails. After that, the plane had disappeared without
a trace.

Brazil, Colombia, and Venezuela had all been enlisted in
the search, though they were told only that they were looking
for a B-52. Brazil had been fairly forthcoming, volunteering
two squadrons for the search and detailing the country's two
Grumman Trackers to help out, even though the radar planes

were optimized for naval operations and had only limited SAR capabilities.

The Venezuelans had fairly limited resources, but were also cooperating. Colombia, on the other hand, had balked, claiming to be very busy with an outbreak of guerrilla attacks in the south.

Not to jump to any conclusions, but it seemed the obvious place to concentrate their efforts. Unfortunately, it was currently out of range of the *Nimitz* and her planes. A second task force, which included a Marine MEU, was heading east from the southern Pacific, but they were still a good way off.

The com system flashed a line on Dog's screen, indicating that they had an incoming text message from Quickmover, the Dreamland C-17 dedicated as the transport for the Whiplash assault team. Bastian touched the glass surface next to the message, and the text appeared in its place.

"On station."

"Danny and his boys are orbiting off Mexico," Bastian told Cheshire.

"Transmissions, too far to get a fix, very weak. Could be a distress signal," said one of the operators.

"Give me a heading," said Cheshire.

"Lost it, ma'am," said the operator, Senior Airman Sean O'Brien.

"No way to pin it down?" Bastian asked.

"The problem is, Colonel, on those line-of-sight transmitters, you're dealing with very weak signals and at this point, really what you're trying to do is figure the bounces. This could have been fairly far away, possibly even in Brazil."

The computer flashed a message on the com line of the HUD:

"Incoming urgent coded Dog-Ears."

Dog had to give a voice command to allow Raven to unscramble the transmission. It was piped only into his headset.

"Colonel Bastian, this is Jed Barclay."

"Go ahead, Jed."

"Stand by for Assistant Secretary McCormack."

Raven's antennas provided a precise, clear pickup over the secure long-wave communications system, which had been originally developed for use by the President and the top brass in the event of a nuclear war. The transmission, conveyed at a slight delay because of the nature of the radio waves used and the distance they traveled, was nonetheless so clear that Dog felt his eardrums melt with McCormack's anger.

"What the hell are you doing, Colonel?" she demanded.

"We're conducting a search for Hawkmother and Galatica, an EB-52 that tracked her south after the raid on Skull Valley. I sent word of that quite some time ago," said Dog. "I've been in communication with Jed—"

"Colonel, the Secretary wants you to return to your base immediately. Immediately."

"Is that an order?"

"You know damn well I can't give you a direct order," she snapped. "General Magnus will contact you shortly."

The line went dead.

"What's up?" Cheshire asked.

"I'm in a whole heap of trouble," said Dog.

"Been there before," said Cheshire.

Not like this, thought Bastian. He couldn't leave his daughter and he couldn't disobey a direct order, which would undoubtedly soon be forthcoming.

His career would tank now anyway, with the loss of Galatica and its two Flighthawks on top of Hawkmother. Excuses wouldn't matter—look at what had happened to Brad Elliott.

Screwed every which way.

He needed to help Breanna.

More than likely it was too late. He had other responsibilities.

"We'll stay on course until we receive further orders," he told Nancy.

Pej, Brazil
7 March, 2330 (1930 Dreamland)

ZEN EYED THE BRAZILIAN SOLDIERS AT THE DOOR, WONdering whether their polite and even deferential air was a good sign or not. While they didn't appear to speak English, the soldiers who had taken him off the plane were well disciplined and well briefed, inspecting not just him but the ejection seat for weapons. They had even produced a receipt for his old Colt .45, which had been holstered in his gear. And

they had allowed him to wheel himself to his "guest room"—
a rather large storage room in one of the hangars.

Two soldiers stood silently next to the door, rifles in hand.
Others were apparently outside, since he could hear voices
and occasional laughs. They had offered food and water and
even some Brazilian beer, though Zen had declined it all.

An odd sound from outside startled him, and he looked
toward the doorway. Something big was being wheeled down
the hallway.

It sounded like one of the equipment carts in the hospital
where he'd spent so much time after his accident. His stomach
pinched and his side ached with the memory of his helpless-
ness and despair.

Two soldiers wheeled in a television set with a video player
on top of it. Zen expected a message of some sort; remembering Jed's reference to the Brazilian leadership scramble,
he thought he might even be treated to some sort of diatribe
about local politics. But the Brazilians had loaded in a tape
with old *Gunsmoke* reruns.

One of the guards handed his M-16 to his companion and
came over to watch.

If he had his legs, Jeff thought, he could overpower the
bastards.

And then what? Single-handedly take over the base? Might
just as well hope for Matt Dillon to walk out of the screen,
six-guns blazing.

The set of boots scraping in the hall were nearly muffled
by the volume of the television. Even so, Zen recognized the
scrape long before Madrone entered the room. He prepared
himself, gripping the chair rests tightly to check the anger
welling up. But rage deserted him when he saw the blanched
and hollow-eyed face of his friend.

"What's going on, Kevin?" said Zen.

Madrone laughed. "You know what's going on. You tried
to destroy me. You're still trying."

Madrone's body moved with jerks, his hands nearly flying
off his arms. He seemed about ready to fly apart.

"Kevin, it's Zen," he said. "Do you realize that?"

"What do you think, I'm stupid?"

"Are you all right?"

Madrone laughed.

"Why are you working with the Brazilians?" Jeff said. "What's going on? You look like you're a ghost."

"You know what's going on. I'm not working with the Brazilians. They're working for me."

"ANTARES has messed you up. I took the drugs too. I know what they can do. You have to come home with me."

Madrone snorted with contempt.

"Going off the drugs messes you up," Zen explained. "You become paranoid. Geraldo says—"

"I don't care what she says. I'll get her. I got Glavin. I'll get them all. I know you're going to get me. I understand that. But I'll take as many of you down with me as I can. I will."

"I'm sorry about your daughter."

"Bullshit! Bullshit! You were part of it. You *are* part of it."

Madrone's fingers slashed the air. His skin went from white to red in an instant. It stretched taut over the bones of his face, which seemed animated by a sirocco.

"You have to let us help you, Kevin," said Jeff softly.

Madrone blinked at him, then bent closer. For a moment, Jeff thought he had gotten through.

"I'll kill you all," said Madrone, his voice even softer than Jeff's. "All of you."

There was a burst of gunfire on the TV, so loud that Jeff jerked back apprehensively, turning toward the TV. When he looked up again, Kevin was gone.

MADRONE'S HEAD POUNDED AS HE WALKED FROM THE building. His mind had shorn itself into splinters, each wedge manipulated by the spider in his skull. New voices yapped at him, emerging from the maelstrom between the segments of his brain.

Zen is your friend. What was he trying to say?

Jeff was a victim just as Kevin was. They'd made him a robot.

Breanna too. And the copilot.

Kill them!

Zen seemed to think he could escape. Had he said that? Or had Kevin wanted him to say that?

The shadows closed around Madrone as he walked out into the night. The jungle—he was back in the jungle.

He was in Theta, connected to ANTARES. But he wasn't wearing the helmet, wasn't in the airplane or his special suit. There was no computer in sight.

Where was Minerva? He needed her.

MINERVA ALLOWED HERSELF A LONG MOMENT OF INdulgence, staring at the mountains from her balcony. The stars seemed to have a light purple glow tonight—destiny stars, an omen.

Good or bad?

Good. Only good.

The door opened in the room behind her. Minerva took one long breath, then slipped inside.

Kevin stood in the middle of the room. "Why did you bring them here?" he demanded.

"Kevin, I didn't bring them here."

"Zen and Breanna—you wanted them to come."

Minerva suppressed a shudder. "They followed you, love." She glided toward him, striving to keep calm. "You've forgotten? I know you're tired."

She wrapped her hands around his shoulders. His muscles were hard metal; his heart pounded crazily.

His madness had grown nearly uncontrollable in the past twenty-four hours; he was no longer simply dangerous, but crazy as well.

That ought to have made it easier for her to let him go. But it didn't.

"I always knew they were against me," Kevin said.

"Yes," she whispered.

"They're all bastards."

"You will carry out your attack in the morning using their plane. The repairs will be finished in time. I'm positive of it," she added, more to convince herself than him. "They will help." Minerva ran her hands across his shoulder, then slipped her fingers beneath the collar of his jumpsuit, sliding them to his flesh.

"They won't help me," he said fiercely.

Fear froze her hand. He might resist—he might even turn against her.

"The Lawrence Livermore Laboratories in San Francisco," she said. "Isn't that where they poisoned your daughter for the final time? Perhaps she was only sick until then—and that was where they killed her."

He'd told her several times about the treatment, performed near but not actually in the lab. Always he had spoken with anger, clearly wanting to destroy the place. It should have been his deepest desire now, the simplest way to hold him in her fingers.

But not today.

"I'm not going," he said calmly.

She slid her hand away, drifting back toward the chair in the corner of the room. The gun was beneath the cushion. If she killed him, what would she do?

Destroy the planes, get rid of the others. There would be no trace.

Better—take some of the remains and scatter them north near the border. Her people were already helping the American searchers and offering to do more. Of course, their every move had to be cleared with her.

It wouldn't be as convincing as her plan to send him back with the plane after pretending he had attacked her base. But luck seemed finally to have turned against her.

Still, the benefits were worth another risk. Her hand easing toward the pistol, she gathered herself to try again to persuade him.

"Whether you go or not, it is your decision," Minerva told him. "If you do, I will give you a weapon that will guarantee their destruction. I have two warheads," she added. Even as she said it—even though she knew it was merely part of her own plan to get rid of him—she felt a certain undeniable excitement, a lust for destruction that he provoked.

"The warheads have nuclear bombs. They are small and were designed for artillery shells. But you could adapt them. Take one. I need the other here, in case they attack."

Madrone drew back. She sensed she'd lost him, and fought

the impulse to go to him. She felt a tinge of fear, shame at her own desire.

And then she continued to speak.

"Do they still do those hideous experiments there?" she said. "They must have known what it would do to her. Perhaps they lied from the beginning."

"No!"

Kevin's whole body shook so violently that Lanzas reached for her gun. But Madrone only collapsed on the floor.

"They're my friends," he murmured as she folded herself over him.

He bawled like a baby on the floor. She loved him, she truly loved him.

"If they are your friends, they will help you," Minerva told him. "You'll take off before dawn. The plane will be repaired then. The skin on one of the rear stabilizers is being replaced with aluminum, which perhaps will alter the flight characteristics, but it should be manageable."

"What if they won't help me?"

"Then our men will fly the plane. Or you can," she said. "We'll do whatever we have to."

"Give me the bombs," said Madrone. He took a breath and raised his head.

"They are warheads only. I thought perhaps they could be placed on the tank missiles as you did with the explosives. They're about the same size. But there's no time."

"There's time. I can fix it." He'd changed back into the dervish, the determined avenger. His voice was resolute; the insanity had receded. "I'll destroy Livermore, and I'll destroy Dreamland, the base where they invaded my brain."

"We have to reserve one warhead for here, in case they attack," Minerva told him. "Could you rig it to explode from a timer or remote control?"

"Child's play. Quickly." He jumped up.

She realized she should let him go, but something deep inside her made her reach out and grab his arm. "Let's make love first."

Aboard Raven
Over the Gulf of Mexico
7 March, 2130 local (1930 Dreamland)

THE RADAR OPERATOR HAD JUST FINISHED TELLING DOG that the scans were clean when the yellow bar on the HUD flashed.

"Incoming urgent coded Dog-Ears."

Bastian snapped on the transmission.

"You've lost your mind," said Magnus.

"No, sir," said Bastian. "What I've lost is an EB-52."

"I'm not going to be able to bail you out of this one, Dog," said the three-star.

"I'm not asking you to bail me out, General."

"You are to set a course for Dreamland and return there without delay. The search will be handled properly, through official channels."

"I am official channels. As per—"

"Colonel!"

"Yes, sir," said Bastian. "We're heading to refuel anyway."

"Who's your copilot?"

"I'm the copilot."

"You know what I mean."

"Major Cheshire is acting under my orders," said Dog. "She filed a protest. It's in the log," he added, hoping they could add it retroactively.

"That may not save her either. Let me talk to her."

"You have to authorize it on your end," Bastian told him.

The line was silent for a moment, apparently while the general consulted with whatever technician was helping him complete the transmission.

"Is he going to yell at me?" Cheshire asked.

"I didn't realize you had such a sense of humor."

"The condemned always joke before the hanging."

"Major Cheshire?"

"Yes, General."

"You get home. Now."

"Yes, sir."

"Bastian, contact me when you're an hour from base. I'm in D.C. Find me. Out."

"Doesn't sound too pleased," said Cheshire.

"Probably had a long day," said Dog.

"What are we doing, Colonel?"

He couldn't leave Breanna; he just couldn't.

But it was senseless to stay here. Even without Magnus on his back, he ought to return. They had no transmission, no beacon, no sign of Galatica.

"Message, Colonel," prompted Nancy.

Dog looked up and saw the alert code, indicating the line was scrambled and from D.C. Sighing, he once more authorized the line. He was surprised to hear Jed Barclay's voice, not the general's.

"Uh, Colonel, I have e-mail here, came through the NSC public system. I believe you got a copy too at Dreamland. But I want to read it to you."

"What are you talking about?"

"Listen. 'Deposit sixty million U.S. dollars in the following account by 0600 Pacific Coast time, or Lawrence Livermore Labs will be destroyed, along with San Francisco.' There's some account numbers too, which seem to be linked to a bank in the Caymans, though I haven't been able to trace it yet. It's signed by Madrone."

"What?"

"I'd think it was just a loony, but there's a TIFF file attached."

"What's a TIFF file?"

"Tagged graphic. Very low resolution and primitive algorithms, no security at all. But basically, it's a photograph or a video frame. It's a picture of an EB-52 with damage to the rear. I'm guessing it's the one you're searching for, but there's no way to authenticate the picture or the e-mail definitively."

"Where did the message come from?" Dog asked.

"At the moment, I'm not sure. We've traced the e-mail back to Italy, but it probably didn't originate there."

"Okay," said Bastian. "Jed, have you been able to organize that surveillance via the satellites?"

"Yes, nothing there yet. I'll get to that in a second, Colonel," added Barclay. "There was another file attached to this e-mail. It had a line drawing. I'm not an expert, but it looks like a nuclear warhead. I'm trying to have it checked out now."

"What did your boss say?"

"He's en route to the White House to inform the President right now."

Aboard Dreamland Combat Transport C-17/D "Quickmover"
Over the Caribbean
2240 local (1940 Dreamland)

DANNY NEARLY SLIPPED OFF THE CREW LADDER AS HE descended into the belly of the C-17. Sergeant Talcom suppressed a laugh at the base of the ladder, but the rest of his Whiplash team members guffawed so loudly he could hear them over the whine of the transport's four powerful engines.

"All right, listen up," Freah said. "We're putting down for a while in Panama."

"We got a target?" asked Bison, practically jumping off the plastic bench.

"No. We're working on it. We have to refuel and the powers that be are gathering some intelligence."

"Translation: Some jerkoff in D.C. wants to go to bed," said Powder.

The others started to laugh again.

"You know, Sergeant, I hear the latrines here are a very interesting place to spend an evening. All sorts of yummy bugs to check out."

Danny had so much venom in his voice that not one of the others dared to as much as titter as he climbed back up to the flight deck.

Pej, Brazil
March 8, 0100 local (March 7, 2100 Dreamland)

BREANNA HAD SAT ON THE WOODEN CHAIR FOR WHAT seemed like several hours, exchanging glares with the male guards. They made no move to attack her, and had even been delicate searching her for a weapon; if she'd had anything besides her bulky Beretta, she would have been able to conceal it easily. Still, her vulnerability felt like a physical thing, pricking at her skin.

She worried about Jeff. He was due for another round of the diluted ANTARES drugs in two hours. Geraldo had told her that he had to take them within five minutes of her carefully worked out schedule, or else he'd begin to feel effects of withdrawal.

A burly airman appeared at the door carrying her flight and survival gear. He placed it on the floor next to the guard, but the soldiers waved her back into her seat when she rose to examine it. A few minutes later the same airman came in with a large bowl of food. This, at least, she was allowed to have. Despite the toughness of the beans, she ate it quickly, and slurped the thin broth at the bottom. She was done by the time Chris was led into the room a few minutes later. One of his guards carried his gear, placing it next to hers by the door.

"You're eating that shit?" he said.

"Better than starving."

"You don't think it's drugged?"

"If they were going to drug it, they would have made it taste better," she said.

"Think they'll release us soon?"

Breanna shrugged. She could hear Zen's wheelchair in the hallway.

Jeff rolled into the room, an ironic smile on his face. Before she could ask what was possibly so funny, a tall man entered behind him and began giving orders in Portuguese. The guards quickly grabbed the flight gear and thrust it at Breanna and Chris, though mixing up who belonged to what.

"We're being released," said Chris.

"I wouldn't count on it," said Zen, still wearing his bemused expression. It was a mask he sometimes used; maybe it meant he was planning something.

"Where's your gear?" Breanna asked.

"They made me leave it in the plane."

"What's so funny?" she said.

"I got a TV and you didn't," he said, then added, "They think I'm going to help fly the Flighthawks."

"What?"

"He speaks English," said Zen in a stage whisper. "He says we're going back north. They think we're going to help."

"That wasn't quite what he said."

Breanna looked up and saw Kevin Madrone standing in the doorway.

"He said you will assist me or be killed," said Madrone. "Hello, Breanna. Captain Ferris."

"I'm not helping you, Kevin. Your head's screwed up." Zen wheeled around to face him. "You're going through withdrawal from the drugs. ANTARES blew up your mind. Take it from me. You're screwy. Nuts."

Kevin glared at him, his eyes nearly popping from their sockets. And then he launched himself at Zen, flying across the room and swinging wildly. Jeff swung in his chair and managed to slip back so that Madrone fell to the floor. But this only enraged Kevin more. Breanna jumped to help her husband as Madrone's punches started to land, but found herself in the arms of one of the security guards. Another guard had a pistol in Chris's chest.

"Stop it! Stop!" she cried.

The soldiers tried to break up the fight. A rapid burst through the ceiling from an automatic rifle finally caught Madrone's attention, or perhaps his fury ran out; he allowed himself to be dragged off Zen.

"Kevin, what's happened to you?" Breanna demanded.

Madrone shrugged off the guards, then shook his head, catching his breath. "I didn't think you'd be in on this, Bree."

"Be in on what, Kevin? What's going on?"

"I'm not listening to you. I know you're going to get me, but I'll take you down too. I'll take enough of you down to hurt you."

"Are you involved in the revolt against the Brazilian government?" said Jeff. His voice was so calm he sounded as if he were a graduate student asking a question at a seminar.

Jeff had provoked the attack, perhaps thinking the surge of emotions would break through, Breanna realized. But it hadn't worked, at least not the way he'd hoped.

"There's no revolt," said Madrone.

"Sure there is. There's a new government already. You helped take over the country with Hawkmother and the U/MFs."

"People attacked us, and we neutralized them," said Madrone. "We're going to do that now."

"Christina died from a cancer that had nothing to do with you or your work, Kevin," said Zen. "It wasn't your fault. It wasn't a conspiracy. It was just—horrible luck. Look at me."

"Get them aboard the plane," Madrone told the guards. "Handcuff the ones who can walk."

"Who are you working for?" Chris asked.

"I'm not working for anyone."

"I wouldn't trust them," said Chris.

"I don't," said Madrone, leaving the room.

OUTSIDE, KEVIN STOPPED AND FELL AGAINST THE SIDE of the building, gasping for air. Had they been his enemies from the beginning? Or had they turned against him?

Betrayal was the worst crime. To go against your friend or your family or your lover—what could be worse?

To kill your own daughter.

He hadn't killed her. *They* had. The bastards.

When they closed in, he would kill himself. He would borrow a pistol from one of the men. He would get as much revenge as possible. Then cheat them.

They would come after Minerva to avenge their losses. She was still naive—she thought they would escape together when he returned, but he wouldn't return.

They would destroy her too. Worse, they would make her suffer as Christina had. He wouldn't let that happen again.

Kevin felt his body relax, the last vestiges of the headache sifting away. It was finished. He hurried to check on the men working on Minerva's weapon.

Dreamland
7 March, 2200 local

THEY LANDED PRECISELY AT TEN P.M., having pushed Raven to the max. Dog slipped out of the cockpit dead tired, and went straight to the waiting Hummer without bothering to stop to change out of his gear.

The inimitable Ax was waiting at the door to his office suite with a cup of very black coffee.

"Hey, Chief. Big shots want to bark at you," said the sergeant.

"What the hell are you doing up?"

"Never miss a hangin'," said Gibbs, who despite his bonhomie, wore traces of worry and fatigue in the cracks around his eyes. "You're supposed to plug into a conference call on the scrambled line. Mudroom's all set up downstairs."

"All right."

"I'll be down with the coffee soon as it finishes perkin'. Captain Freah landed in Panama," added Ax. "Standing by for your orders."

"Okay." Dog took a long swig from the coffee, then handed the cup back to Ax for a refill. "What, no paperwork?"

"At this hour SOP is to forge your initials."

Downstairs, Dog nodded at the pair of MPs covering the door and went inside the empty control room. Cleared into the secure video conference circuit, he found the others were already talking together.

"Colonel Bastian has joined us," said Jed Barclay in the White House basement.

"Colonel," said General Magnus gruffly.

"Good evening, Colonel." The screen flickered and a new face appeared on the screen at the front of the room. It was the President, Kevin Martindale.

"Sir."

"How real is this threat?" Martindale, dressed in a cardigan sweater, sat in a thick chair aboard Air Force One. Philip Freeman, John Keesh, and a grim-faced aide sat nearby.

"I'm afraid it's very real, sir," said Barclay.

"I want to hear Colonel Bastian," said Martindale. "Is ANTARES responsible?"

Bastian hesitated. "I'm afraid it appears likely ANTARES was involved. We're still trying to connect all the dots."

"ANTARES is nothing but grief. Promising poison. It's to end right now, on my order. This overrules *any* directive you may get from anyone else, no matter who it is."

"Yes, sir," said Bastian.

Keesh scowled in the background but said nothing.

"We've set up a net with ANG and regular Air Force units guarding San Francisco," said Magnus, apparently speaking from aboard another Air Force plane. "They won't get close."

"I think that's the idea," said Dog.

"What do you mean?" said the President.

"They've basically told us the target and when to expect them," Bastian said. "Either it's a decoy, or we're meant to shoot them down."

"We can't *not* shoot them down," said Magnus.

"We can't let them attack the laboratory or San Francisco," said Dog. "But there's something else going on. I had some of my people at the base examine the diagram. I've only spoken to them by radio, but they say it's very primitive, possibly attached to a very short-range-missile system. Even if it were fired from a Flighthawk—difficult but not impossible—the controlling ship would have to be within ten miles."

"If it's dropped by a bomber, it will be overhead," said Magnus dryly.

"Absolutely," said Dog. "As long as we know they're coming, we can cordon off an area twenty miles away, and be fairly confident of finding the plane, even a Megafortress."

"Maybe the attack will be carried out elsewhere," said Jed.

"That might be. But Livermore does fit," added Bastian.

"Jed has filled us in on the psychological implications," said Freeman, the NSC head. "Jed, run down the Brazilian scenario," he added.

Barclay's face came back on the screen. He had a bit of peach fuzz on his chin between the pimples, and looked as if he were going to cry. His voice shook a little as he began, but he spoke in coherent, long sentences.

"It's not a scenario exactly. I've been looking at the power struggle there, trying to coordinate some of the players against the intercepts we've had. The conflict between the Navy and the Air Force, that's legendary; they spy on each other back and forth. They have for years. A few months ago, there was a kind of mini-insurrection and the Navy people quashed the Air Force. The major players were cashiered or sent out to Amazon scratch bases, which is our equivalent of being detailed to guard latrines on the moon."

"We don't have posts on the moon," muttered Magnus, making his opinion of Barclay evident.

"Get to the point, Jed," prompted Freeman.

"As we know, this time fighting broke out, which resulted in a government crisis. The President resigned. Air Force people then pop up all over the place, starting with the Acting President, who was the Air Force Chief. Now it could just be the usual blackmail and skullduggery—"

"Jed," warned Freeman.

"Yes, well, the Defense Minister—this is all just the acting government, remember, but anyway—a Colonel Minerva Lanzas is due to be named Defense Minister when Herule takes over. He's the Prez. Lanzas was transferred from the biggest Air Force command to a mountain landing strip at the edge of the Amazon after the Navy brush-up, so that's a pretty dramatic turnaround."

"Is that site big enough to land a 777?" asked Dog.

"Not according to the Factbook," said Barclay, referring to the standard non-classified directory compiled by the CIA. "But our review of Satint shows it's been greatly expanded over the past month, maybe even more recently. You could land a standard B-52 there now, give or take. And," added Barclay, leaning toward the camera with just a hint of dramatic flair, "there was a two-engined jet on the ground there yesterday morning. It was obscured by clouds, but it seemed to be either a 777 or an Airbus, an Airbus, uh—" He faltered, trying to remember the designation of the large European-made plane.

"We need to hit that base," said Dog. "Now."

"Too far," said Freeman. "Too aggressive. Even if we had hard evidence—"

"The Whiplash Assault Team is in Panama," said Dog. "They were standing by to help a rescue. They can go there."

"Big risk, especially with the Brazilian government in transition," said Freeman. "We better talk to State."

The President, to his right, was looking at his watch. "General Herule won't be sworn in as Acting President until noon Brasilia time," he said.

"I'm not sure that's relevant," said Freeman.

"I can have my Whiplash Team on the ground at that base in two hours," said Dog.

"I say we take a shot at it, sir," said Magnus unexpectedly. "If young Mr. Barclay is right, it's a logical place. I trust Colonel Bastian's men to pull it off."

Keesh finally spoke up. "I have faith in Colonel Bastian as

well," he said. "But if we're wrong, it will be a grave situation."

"If our planes aren't on the runway, they don't land," said Dog. "Brazil has already offered to cooperate in the search. We can say this is just an extension."

Someone spoke off camera in the President's plane. He turned for a moment, listening as another aide whispered something in his ear.

"We'll deal with that in a few minutes," Martindale told the aide. Then he turned back to the camera. "Do it," he said. "And keep me informed. Jack," he added, apparently to the operator, because the circuit went gray.

Magnus reappeared on the screen. "This isn't very good, Colonel."

"No, sir. I understand that."

"General Olafson will coordinate the defenses out of the Fresno ANG base. Get with him."

"Yes, sir."

"And Tecumseh—no more road shows. You're to remain at the base. You're not a fighter pilot anymore. Your job is coordinating things from the ground."

The screen blanked. Dog sat in the chair, the tumult of the past few days catching up with him. He was still sitting there, legs stretched along the floor, when Sergeant Gibbs entered with the coffee a minute later.

"We still in business?"

"For now," said Dog, snapping back to himself. "Get me Captain Freah."

"Punch line five on your doohickey thinger and you got him," said Ax.

Pej, Brazil
8 March, 0401 local (0001 Dreamland)

MINERVA STOOD IN FRONT OF THE LARGE BOMBER AS her men worked feverishly to complete their work. They were used to fashioning spare parts for military jets, but the damaged Megafortress was an extraordinary challenge. Its wings and fuselage were made from an exotic compound that none of her experts recognized; they'd fashioned replacement panels from several sources, including Hawkmother. Madrone's EB-52 had also furnished the tail section, which proved remarkably easy to replace—a testament to the aircraft's design, meant to facilitate quick combat-area repairs. Her chief engineer assured her the plane would get off the ground, but would give no guarantees beyond that.

Minerva didn't need any. She had already constructed her own elaborate alibis and a cover story, pinning all of the blame on Madrone.

It wasn't the most airtight or even believable of stories, but it didn't have to be. As Defense Minister, she would be able to control any inquiries. And the main witnesses would all be dead:

Madrone and his friends, who would either be shot down by the Americans, or blown up when the bomb her people had added to the plane's tail exploded. It was set with both a timer and a radar altimeter, guaranteeing their destruction.

Her people at the base, who would be killed when her second nuclear warhead exploded at 6:50 A.M. She herself would only just escape the American madman's attempt to obliterate all Brazil. She would emerge victorious, having fought him off without the Americans' help. She would then launch an investigation to find out who had helped him, for surely even a madman could not have come this far without local assistance.

The conspirators would pay dearly. She would end up Brazil's heroine; the people would reward her with the Presidency and power beyond her dreams.

Even so, she longed to refuse to let Madrone go.

But Lanzas feared him greatly now; even more, she feared her own darkness. She had the strength to restrain only one.

No. She could restrain herself only if he was no longer with her.

Minerva climbed inside the plane to watch her men as they finished installing the six oversized steamer trunks containing the heart of the ANTARES equipment in the Megafortress's equipment bay. The devices plugged so simply into circuitry in the rear compartment, they seemed no more complicated than a stereo system. Two more went into the lower deck.

"We're ready, Colonel," reported Louis Andre, who headed the team.

"That's it? You're sure?"

"We followed Captain Madrone's directions to the letter. The computer panel says that its diagnostics have cleared."

He pointed toward the large screens at the two stations before them.

"Diagnostic complete. No errors. System ready," read the screens.

"The most difficult thing was arranging to keep the units in the fuselage cool," Andre told her. "We rerouted a duct in the plane. It may affect other equipment, but Captain Madrone did not seem overly concerned."

"Very well," she said. "Tell the captain we are ready for him."

Minerva allowed herself one last look at the flight deck before leaving the plane. An amazing warbird, a plane of immense potential.

She could learn much from the Americans. If she was willing to wait, rather than simply take their weapons, she would do much better.

It was a pity the 777 had to be destroyed as well. But there was no other way. Her course was set. To change anything now meant only doom.

Minerva considered not seeing Kevin off, but decided that that might upset him, and in some way tip her pilots off that they were about to die. So she waited by the plane for him to arrive.

A final kiss. A supreme indulgence. But after years of letting her body be used by others—wasn't she owed it?

Mayo walked toward her, saluting smartly.

"Madame Colonel," he said. Mayo was young, without a family; though he'd been with her a long time, she didn't feel his loss as much as she would that of Gerrias, who had three children. Still, she would make sure his parents had a double pension.

"You're confident you can fly this?" she asked, though Gerrias had assured her twice already it would be easy.

"Once Captain Madrone used his security codes to open the computer for us, we had no trouble with the controls. There is a computer that does all of the work. Of course, in flight there may be a few wrinkles."

"The small planes?"

"Picot declared them ready. Captain Madrone is inspecting them all. There are codes, apparently, that are entered directly into them. It is all voice-coded. Picot had no trouble."

"Picot is a genius."

"Madame Colonel, are we really attacking San Francisco?" asked Mayo.

"Not San Francisco," said Minerva. "A complex nearby."

"The Americans will try to stop us."

"If you are afraid, Lieutenant, Captain Gerrias can fly alone."

"I am not afraid. I don't know if it is right. Captain Madrone says all of San Francisco will be destroyed."

Minerva sighed. "Captain Madrone is brilliant, but unfortunately he exaggerates. You've been rewarded for the other flights?"

Mayo said nothing. She knew that he took the implication that he valued money above loyalty to her as an insult.

"Don't worry," she told him. "In a few hours, you will return here, and then—off to wherever you will. You are already a rich man, and you will be ten times richer."

"I fly because you saved me from death," said Mayo stiffly. "It is a debt I will never forget."

"A debt that will be discharged today. Start your engines. Quickly," she said, saluting to dismiss him.

Madrone approached from the runway.

"We are ready," he told her. "The Flighthawks are all fueled and loaded with bullets."

"Can you handle all three?"

"I can handle twenty."

The door to the hangar behind them creaked on its rusty wheel hinge. The three Americans and their guards emerged.

"Is that your robot master?" shouted the one in the wheelchair.

Even in the dim light, Minerva saw Madrone's face turn red.

"Calmly," she said, touching Kevin's chest. "He's trying to provoke you."

"What was it Mack called you? Monkey Boy? Microchip Brain? How's your thumbnail these days? Still biting it?"

"That's enough out of you," said Madrone.

"His hands are not bound?" Minerva asked the guards.

"To wheel his chair," said the guard. "If—"

Mayo, already aboard, spooled up the two outboard engines. They were surprisingly quiet for being so close, but even so drowned out the guard.

"He's harmless," yelled Madrone. "Just a cripple."

"You should have told us about your daughter, Kevin," said the woman pilot. "I'm so sorry—it must have been so horrible."

"You don't care. None of you care."

Minerva gripped Madrone's arm. In an instant, he had changed from a confident, cocky pilot to a trembling, fearful man. Tears rolled down his face.

She should have shot the Americans.

"They're trying to trick you, Kevin," she said. "Perhaps we should give them something to make them less disagreeable."

"Is she coming with us?" said the one in the wheelchair. "Your master?"

"There isn't room on the plane," answered Minerva.

"Actually, there is," said the man. "There are four stations in the cockpit, two downstairs, two upstairs, and that's not even counting the roll-out cot."

Madrone turned toward her. "Come with us," he told her. "You must."

"I have to attend to things here, lover," she said softly.

"You will come," he told her sternly.

She reached to pat his hand, then saw he had a pistol in it.

"Kevin." She stared, but before she said anything else she heard the loud whine of another jet popping up over the nearby mountain.

Aboard Quickmover
Over Western Brazil
18 March, 0445

IN A PERFECT WORLD, THE TARGET WOULD HAVE BEEN under real-time surveillance from an army of recon drones and maybe a satellite or two, with a highly trained team aboard a JSTARS command craft interpreting the images and giving advice.

But Whiplash operated in a decidedly imperfect world. So

the fact that Danny Freah was able to turn on his Combat Information Visor and get an image off the C-17's chin array of infrared and optical cameras as they popped up over the mountains two miles from the target seemed like a real luxury.

Which didn't make it any easier to read the blurs.

Danny pressed his hands against his helmet, trying to steady the image in the CIV. There were two large planes near hangars alongside the runway. The glowing bursts near the wings of the larger made it clear that its engines were just being started.

The EB-52? Too hard to tell.

Danny pressed the underside of the left lenses to adjust the contrast, reducing the image glare caused by the jet exhaust. He saw the image of a man in a wheelchair.

"Pop the ramp, we're going out!" he shouted to his men over the shared laser-com system. "Get the chutes! We have thirty seconds! Planes at the end of the ramp. Engines are hot."

The pilot, who was tied into the circuit, immediately cut in. "Captain, that's not the way we planned it."

"You go ahead and circle around to land. We'll try and pick off the guards holding the crew at Galatica. Just hold on your course," said Danny, who could see through the visor that the C-17 was aimed to pass right over the Megafortress.

"Captain, I can get back around and land in two minutes, maybe three."

"Too long!" said Danny. The people near the plane were moving. "Go! Go! Go!" he shouted to his men. He unhooked the feed from the back of his helmet, the wire whipping back as wind began gusting through the rear of the plane.

Danny's command was superfluous. Prepared for any contingency, the team members had been wearing their jump gear and night goggles on the approach. Team Jumpmaster Geraldo "Blow" Hernandez was already pushing guys out the open ramp. Danny went out with him, dragging his tethered rucksack clear.

He kicked his chute open on a two-count after sliding into the air. The cells flapped full and he swung backward slightly, his weight not quite balanced due to the rush. As he grabbed the toggle handles to steer, he realized he faced in the wrong direction; he leaned his body as he steered back, knowing that the ground would be coming up tremendously fast.

Low-altitude jumps into a combat situation were incredibly hazardous, as dangerous as jumping off a bridge with home-made equipment. A half second of disorientation could be fatal. That was especially true at night, even when you had help from advanced gear like the CIV. The images in the starlight view flared back and forth as Danny managed to steady his descent; the runway was dead ahead, fifty yards off, with the Megafortress beyond it. He pulled the right steering tog, hoping to coax his way across the runway and onto the parallel access ramp. He couldn't see any defensive positions, but as his feet accelerated toward the ground he saw the flare of tracers on his right.

Pej, Brazil
8 March, 0450

ZEN WATCHED MADRONE SWING HIS ARM AROUND, REvealing the gun.

"With us," Madrone shouted to Lanzas.

"Kevin, no," she said.

"They'll kill you here."

The Megafortress's engines roared. A soldier with a rifle came down the EB-52's ramp to see what was going on. Madrone fired his gun and the man's body flew backward. In practically the same motion Kevin grabbed Lanzas and threw her onto the ramp. One of the guards took out his pistol, but then slumped downward. Gunfire erupted beyond the runway—the plane passing overhead had dropped paratroopers.

It has to be Whiplash, thought Zen. He saw Chris lash out at one of the guards, then felt himself pitched to the ground. He swung his arms, but realized he was being dragged by his useless legs toward the plane.

"Up," Madrone told him. Automatic weapons barked around them. Madrone pointed a small, blocky pistol in his face. "I'll kill you, Zen."

"I can't get up."

As Kevin ducked down to him, something flew onto his back. It tumbled over his shoulder, a heavy weight that smashed against Zen's upper torso, pinning his right arm.

Breanna.

Madrone, somehow not surprised by her, nor fazed by the chips of cement and bullets dancing around them, grabbed her by her bound hands and pulled her to her feet.

"Help Jeff into the plane. Now, or you die here!"

"No!" she shouted.

"He dies first."

She reached for Jeff, starting to pull, going slow. Jeff tried to hold back, but Madrone pushed them both over onto the middle of the ramp. He swung his left arm wildly. Either he hit the lever to close the gangway, or someone in the cockpit issued the command; in any event, the ramp sprang upward moving quickly despite their weight.

As long as he was alive, Zen thought, there was a chance he could stop Madrone. He had to stay calm and work out a plan.

Then Madrone smashed Breanna on the head. Jeff propelled himself with an enraged shout, swinging both fists toward Kevin with all his might.

Had he connected, he surely would have knocked Madrone out. But he missed by at least half a foot. As his momentum carried him downward, he felt a hard smack against the side of his temple. He smelled the metal tint of blood tickle his nose. His lips tasted the smooth aluminum of the deck floor. Then everything went black.

DANNY HAD HIS M-16 IN HIS HANDS AS HE HIT THE ground, but the drop-off between the runway and the ramp kept him from getting a good view of the hangar area or the rest of his team.

It also made him lose his balance. He rolled forward, struggling to his feet. Snapping clear of his gear, he ran up the slope toward the ramp and hangar area, still without a target. He heard the distinct whap of a flash-bang grenade, thrown by one of his team members to paralyze the resistance.

The large planes near the hangars were definitely theirs. The EB-52 sat on the right. Someone fired from the ground near it; the shots were immediately answered with a spray of gunfire from the left.

Danny raised his rifle, clicking his thumb against the target switch that allowed him to use the CIV to aim.

Someone sat in the cockpit. He put the body in the cross-hairs and fired. The bullet hit the target square, but the figure remained unharmed behind the EB-52's thick glass. The 5.56mm bullets in the M-16 were no match for the reinforced windshield and hull of the Megafortress.

The Flighthawks should be more fragile. Danny clicked the visor into IR mode and began scanning for them.

MADRONE KICKED JEFF'S HEAD WITH HIS BOOT TO make sure he was truly unconscious, then leapt into the right control seat, quickly pulling the ANTARES head gear on. Breanna moaned behind him, but he didn't have time to worry about that now—he had to get into Theta and get the Flighthawks off the ground.

He felt his scalp tingle as soon as the liner band slid over the spider connection.

Already? The panel wire hadn't even been connected.

He stood in the forest, rain storming all around. Balls of hail pelted him.

Hawk One, start procedure.

Two, Three.

Systems green.

Go.

A NARROW FLARE ERUPTED AT THE EXTREME LEFT OF Danny's vision; by the time he turned toward it, two others had lit, small cigarette burns in the visor. He brought his rifle up and began to fire as the first object—undoubtedly a Flighthawk—moved behind a row of low bushes or some other obstruction. Danny burned the clip as it disappeared; he re-loaded quickly and hiked sideways to get a shot on the U/MFs as they rolled in the direction of the Megafortress. He figured he didn't have to stop them, just slow them down—the C-17 ought to be landing any second and would block the narrow runway. But as the first Flighthawk reappeared, some-thing hard slammed him down against the ground—a fifty-caliber machine gun had opened fire near the hangars.

His armor saved his life, but the heavy gun had cracked

the suit and possibly his shoulder blade. Worse, as far as Danny was concerned, the fire was so severe he couldn't raise his head or the gun. The Flighthawks whipped around the end of the runway, not bothering to wait for the Megafortress. They turned and thundered down the cement to take off—just as the C-17 appeared above.

Aboard Galatica
Lower Deck
8 March, 0453

BREANNA WRITHED ON THE FLOOR, HER HEAD STILL SPIN-ning from the bang she'd gotten as Madrone tossed her over his shoulders. She lay at the base of the Flighthawk tech station at the left side of the bay; the tubes were flashing above, and she could hear Kevin moaning and muttering to himself at Zen's control station. His arms flew in the air as if he were conducting some mad symphony only he could hear.

Struggling to rise, Rap pushed back against the side panel, and saw Jeff sprawled on the deck behind the seats near the hatchway. The sight of his helpless body gave her strength; she managed to push up against the panel, wedging her foot down, but then snagging her bound hands on part of the rail beneath the seat. She rebounded to the floor, then pushed back upright, still hooked on.

The main monitor at the station jumped through views. Breanna realized she was seeing the Flighthawk optics.

The technician's panel could access C^3. She tried rising, but remained snagged. She pushed down, felt metal scraping against her wrist. The pneumatic hoses that allowed the chair to be adjusted had been sawed or clipped apart; the entire base of the ejection seat looked as if it had been gnawed by a metal-eating squirrel.

The keyhole-shaped clasp at the left front of the rail covering one of connectors held her. No more than an inch and a half long and a quarter of that wide, the edge seemed sharp enough to cut the thick plastic binder on her wrists. Rap began razoring the strap back and forth, twisting at it. Slowly, ag-onizingly slowly, the handcuff began to give way.

She looked up. The screen had stopped shifting. The dark

runway ramp rushed by. The Flighthawk was taking off.

Red and yellow speckles appeared around the side of the runway—gunfire. A large store of fuel exploded beyond the hangar area, and the flames burst so bright that Madrone or C³ swapped out the IR for an optical view.

Zen groaned.

Rap looked over at him, then back as Madrone yelled something. A dark shadow loomed in the main display panel. A large bird descended, claws snatching at the air. Then everything turned red.

THE FIRST FLIGHTHAWK JUST CLEARED THE C-17. THE next one, however, crashed dead into the looming hull, which had thrust itself in front of him without any warning. Madrone fell backward in his seat, stunned into disorientation.

The storm raged. He was in Theta, but couldn't feel C³ or the robot planes anywhere.

ANTARES was an immense jungle, the vegetation cluttering, choking his mind. Minerva stood before him, naked. She reached for him, turned to fire.

He hated her. She was the enemy. She'd been sent by them to destroy him.

No.

He was in the cockpit of Hawk Three. He had the bomb strapped to the center hard-point. Takeoff had been aborted; he was dead on the runway.

Hawk One was in the air. Hawk Two had been destroyed. Galatica sat at the edge of the ramp, engines revving but motionless.

He'd die here, without revenge, without anything.

Good—Kevin wanted to die, wanted to end it. He'd be with Christina.

No—he had to kill the bastards. He wanted to see them cry as she had cried.

The attacking aircraft had crashed at the end of the strip. Even with its heavy load, Hawk Three had enough room to get in the air.

And the EB-52?

Probably not. But it would be better to die trying than to be killed on the ground.

Worst case, he'd target himself with the missile.

"Take off," he told the bridge. "Take off."

Pej, Brazil
8 March, 0501

THE EXPLOSION PRESSED DANNY AGAINST THE GROUND. He heard one of the other members of his team cursing in the com set, but as he turned to see if he could spot him, a massive fireball ignited behind him on the runway. Metal rained down; Danny curled himself into a ball as a series of thunderous explosions shook the air and ground.

He thought the Megafortress and the C-17 had collided, but as he twisted around he saw the plane was still back near the hangars. It must've been one of the Flighthawks.

"The wheels!" he yelled over the com set. "Try and hit the inside wheels of the Megafortress."

He flicked the sensors on the CIV, toggling from normal to IR and then starlight. He could see the top of the Megafortress, but to hit the tires he'd have to stand, exposing himself to the machine gun again.

The plane started to move. Danny jumped to his feet, raising his M-16 as a steam of bullets started whizzing by his head.

Aboard Galatica
8 March, 0501

MINERVA TASTED BLOOD IN HER MOUTH, HER LIP BLEEDING. The Americans were here; they were trapped.

Bullets splashed against the thick side glass of the cockpit as she pushed up onto the flight deck, half in shock. Mayo sat at the copilot's station, frozen.

"Go!" she yelled at him as a fresh spray of bullets panged against the glass and fuselage. The panels and skin were obviously thick enough to withstand the light-caliber weapons, but sooner or later the attackers would bring heavier guns to bear. "Move!" she told her pilot.

"Colonel, Captain Gerrias isn't aboard—"

"Just go!"

He put his hand on the slider between the pilot stations and the plane surged forward. A fireball erupted from the far end of the runway ahead.

"The other plane," screamed Mayo, backing down the engines quickly. "The wreckage. We won't clear the flames."

"We must," Lanzas told him.

"But—"

"Go! Just go!" Minerva reached over to the power console and punched the thruster so hard it nearly moved out of its retainer. The plane slammed forward, veering to the right. The flames loomed.

Better to go out in a fireball, she thought.

Gunfire rippled across the front of the outside of the cabin. The bullets made a lot of noise, but still didn't break through the hull. Minerva saw the flames ahead and began to close her eyes, then decided she would meet her fate bravely. She thought of Madrone, who had brought her to this.

The Megafortress shuddered and there was a roar behind and below her; she fell backward against the second set of seats. An alarm sounded and she heard the plane's computerized voice say something. For a second, she thought she could feel the flames burning her body.

In the next, they lifted off the runway.

It took her a moment to realize they were all right. She steadied her hands on the pilot's seat, watching as Mayo raised the gear and climbed rapidly.

"Do you have a gun?" she asked him finally.

"Yes." He reached into his vest and retrieved an old-fashioned revolver.

"Keep the plane below ten thousand feet no matter what," she told him. "Stay on the course north. I'll check on the others."

Pej, Brazil
8 March, 0504

DANNY'S FIRST TWO BULLETS TOOK OUT A TOTAL OF three tires, thanks to a lucky ricochet. But as the Megafortress lurched left on the runway, Danny felt himself pushed down again, hit by the massive machine gun on his left. This time, the gun's bullets managed to spin him around and somehow got a piece of the CIV, cracking it.

Which made him madder than hell.

Screaming, he rolled backward and began firing into the stream of red tracers. A huge ball of fire slammed into the top of his helmet, smacking him into the ground. Somehow, he kept firing.

When his clip clicked empty, he realized the machine gun had stopped.

He could feel a welt rising at the front of his head. Though a jagged line ran through the left quadrant, Annie's visor was still working—a body lay a few feet away from the machine gun fifty yards away.

Directly above it, four hot circles edged into ellipses over the mountain pass. The Megafortress had managed to clear the C-17 on the runway.

Aboard Galatica
8 March, 0510

BREANNA'S RESTRAINTS CAME APART WITH A SNAP, slamming her hands against the seat and panel so hard, she felt something snap in her left wrist. But she ignored the pain and jumped up, launching herself across the tech station toward Madrone.

The distance was farther than she thought. She fell across the technician's gear, grabbing Madrone's wires and loosening them. He didn't seem to notice, or at least made no effort to stop her. But as she squirmed to get more leverage, something grabbed her and threw her back against the rear bulkhead.

Lanzas.

"Strap the cripple into the seat and come with me," barked the Brazilian colonel.

"He's not a cripple. He's my husband."

"Do it now or you both die here." Lanzas had a revolver in her left hand. She edged away, watching Breanna carefully as she lifted Zen up and strapped him into the seat. He seemed thoroughly out of it.

Breanna leaned toward him, intending to kiss him. The Brazilian put the pistol on her neck to stop her.

"Nice try," said Lanzas. "Upstairs now. If you do anything, you will die. Kevin, we're okay."

Madrone took no notice of them. He seemed a zombie, completely oblivious.

Not sure what else to do, Breanna edged past and went up the ladder to the flight deck.

Dreamland
Secure Command Center
8 March, 0130 local (0530 Brazil)

"WE MISSED THE PLANE."

Colonel Bastian held the receiver away from his head for a moment, not because he was disappointed with Danny—he knew stopping them on the ground was a long shot—but because he was afraid of the answer to his next question. He glanced at Major Cheshire and Captain Arjun, the two Megafortress commanders alone with him in the Mudroom. Their consoles were locked out of the secure line and they watched grimly.

"Our people?" asked Bastian.

"C-17 crew is dead. One of the Flighthawks collided with it. Two more got away with Galatica. Captain Ferris managed to roll behind some barrels on the ground before they took off, and one of the Brazilian pilots surrendered," Danny said.

"What about Major Stockard and Captain Breanna?" he asked.

He meant to say *Captain Stockard,* but his emotions betrayed him.

"At the moment, we're not one hundred percent sure," said Danny. "We have Jeff's wheelchair, but not him. Ferris thinks they hauled Major Stockard aboard before takeoff. It's likely your daughter went too. We haven't secured the entire base," Danny added. "We will. Army Special Forces and airborne are inbound from Panama in Combat Talons and an AC-130. They should be here within twenty minutes. I'll have the hangars secure by then."

With only six men? But Danny wasn't known for exaggeration.

"All right, Captain, thanks. I want you to search the base carefully. See if you can find evidence that Galatica or the Flighthawks are carrying nukes."

"Nukes? In Brazil?"

"If there's anything else we can do from our end, let me know," Bastian told him.

The line snapped dead.

"There were no survivors from the C-17 crash. The Whiplash Team is intact and searching the base," he told the others, filling them in on the situation. Cheshire rubbed her tired eyes and turned back toward the situation map they'd been studying before Danny's call came through. The map showed the entire southern portion of the U.S., along with the defenses planned to stop Galatica.

Colonel Bastian picked up his stylus and traced it across the flat touch screen at his console, outlining in red the tracks General Olafson had given them to patrol. Raven and Iowa, a sister ship for Galatica named after the famous Naval battleship, would back up a quartet of AWACS planes that were forming a 360-degree radar picket around San Francisco. Besides their sensors—Raven's Elint gear, which could detect C^3's radio transmissions at roughly two hundred miles, and Iowa's admittedly unfinished T/APY radar—the planes would carry eight Scorpion AMRAAM-plus air-to-air missiles in their rotating belly launchers. They'd also have four standard AMRAAMs and four all-aspect Sidewinder AIM-9Ms on their wings.

The Megafortresses represented the last line of defense. A full squadron of F-15Cs, along with ANG F-16's and F-4's, Marine aircraft, and two Navy tracking planes manned the front lines. Meanwhile, a flight of F-15's, accompanied by a tanker, were working south, as were planes from two aircraft carriers in the Caribbean. Surface-to-air-missile batteries throughout the Southwest and ships all along the Gulf Coast had been alerted.

In theory, it was an impenetrable gauntlet no conventional aircraft could penetrate. But Madrone wasn't flying a conventional aircraft. He had a Megafortress, arguably the most capable bomber in the world. He also had two Flighthawks escorting him.

One Megafortress and two U/MFs against the entire U.S. military. Dog might take those odds. Surely a madman would.

Assuming it flew near top speed, the EB-52 would approach the mainland a little more than six hours from now. Nancy and Arjun, who would pilot Iowa, went over some fine points in strategy and timing their refuelings. Though he was essentially superfluous to the discussion, Dog followed it with as much interest as he could muster.

The alternative was to worry about his daughter.

"Let's do it," said Cheshire. She punched the kill codes on her terminal, deactivating the console, and stood.

Arjun rose as well.

"There's one thing I want to make clear," said Bastian, still in his seat. "If it comes down to it, if Galatica is there, you take your shot. Absolutely take your shot."

Arjun nodded.

Bastian looked at Cheshire, whose cheeks seemed to have hollowed out. "Major?"

"Yes, Colonel, I will."

The room's silence felt oppressive. "M-6 will back you up," he said. "Captain McAden is en route to fly it. We're still hunting down a copilot."

"Fenner should be here shortly," said Cheshire.

Dog nodded. M-6 was so new it hadn't completed its test flights. It hadn't even been given a name. Configured as an Elint-gatherer like Raven, she had two Flighthawk control decks like Iowa and Galatica, though only part of the U/MF equipment had been installed.

Bastian followed the others out into the hall and waited for the elevator to arrive. When the doors finally sprang open, Mack Smith nearly knocked them over.

"Colonel, a word," said Smith, marching preemptively down the corridor as if he were the one running the base.

"Why am I being shut out of this?" he demanded when Bastian joined him.

"What the hell are you talking about?"

"Madrone. The Flighthawks. Our Megafortresses are going to shoot him down. Why wasn't I informed?"

"Why the hell should you have been?"

"I'm the best fighter pilot on the base," Smith sputtered. "I'm head of the defense squadron. Shit, I'm one of less than a dozen active guys who has a shoot-down in the entire Air Force."

"Hold on, Mack," said Bastian. "First of all, I believe the defense squadron you're referring to was abolished before I even came to Dreamland. Years ago."

"That's irrelevant."

Dog turned toward the elevator. "Go to bed."

"This is because you think I sold out, huh?"

"Smith, there are times when you are just a pain in the butt, you know that?" Bastian pushed the button for the elevator to return. "And then there are other times when you are the biggest asshole in the world."

"Colonel, seriously."

"I am being serious."

"You have to let me help. There's nobody that knows what those Flighthawks will do like me. I've been flying against them for more than a year. Half of their damn programs are what I taught them. And Jeff," he added belatedly. "Come on—I can wax Madrone's fanny. Ask Jeff. I've done it already."

"Jeff isn't available to ask." Dog pushed the elevator button again.

"Where is he?"

"We're not sure."

Smith had a point, though Bastian couldn't help but remember the coincidences Danny had pointed out. Freah hadn't had time to follow through with any of his investigations.

"He's in on this, right?" said Mack.

"Jeff and Breanna are probably aboard Galatica, which Madrone seems to have taken control of. It will be shot down if it tries to attack."

"You can't shoot down Jeff and Bree."

The elevator finally arrived. Bastian entered; Mack followed. Both looked toward the ceiling, which in theory made it easier for the scanning devices to verify their identities. Still, the process took excruciatingly long.

"You have to let me do something," said Mack as the elevator finally began moving upward.

"What exactly do you want to do?" said Bastian.

"Help plan the defense at least. Be in the ball game. Come on. Use me. I know more about fighting the Flighthawks than anyone."

"I'm not in charge of the defenses," said Bastian. "They're already set."

"You think I'm a traitor, don't you?"

The elevator arrived at Sublevel One. Dog got out.

"Major?" asked Bastian.

"Put me in the game."

"It's too late, Mack," said Bastian as the doors closed.

Pej, Brazil
8 March, 0540 local

POWDER COVERED LIU WHILE HE RAN UP TO THE EDGE of the hangar building. One or two Brazilians had retreated here, though most of the Brazilians had fallen back to the far end of the base, far away from Hawkmother and the dilapidated hangars. Three low-slung buildings were visible there, defended by at least two small armored cars and some machine guns. For the moment, they seemed to be saving their ammunition.

Which was fine with Powder. Give the Army something to do when they finally got around to showing up.

Liu reached the edge of the building, then gave Powder a hand signal to come forward. Powder humped the ten yards so fast he nearly lost his helmet.

"Two guys, that way," said Liu.

"That it?"

"There was a light machine gun there, but Egg got him," said Liu, referring to another member of the team, Freddy Reagan.

"You see Captain Freah?" Powder asked.

"No," said Liu. "He hasn't been on the circuit since the planes took off."

"I heard him talking to Bison. They were setting up the Satcom."

"Maybe he's back by the C-17 wreckage, checking it out," said Liu.

"Doesn't look like they're too organized," said Powder.

"I hear something," said Liu.

"Uh-oh—duck!" shouted Talcom as an armored car rolled around the corner of the hangar and began firing at them. The ENGESA EE-11 was a very simple, no-frills truck equipped with a very basic machine gun.

And an equally basic but tremendously destructive grenade launcher, which fired a charge point-blank at the two Whiplashers.

Fortunately, it sailed past them, exploding nearly a hundred yards away.

"Next one ain't gonna miss," said Powder, already running toward the truck. He pulled a phosphorus grenade from his belt as he ran, thumbing away the tape that safed the pin and fuse. He set the grenade, tossing it at the last possible second as he threw himself to the ground.

The grenade wasn't powerful enough to penetrate the EE-11's armor, but Powder merely wanted to blind the gunners with the flash while he and his teammate attacked from behind. The machine-gun fire ceased as soon as the grenade went off. Powder, head down, jumped back to his feet and raced around to the rear of the truck.

Liu stood there already, staking it out. One of the vehicle's doors opened. Powder tensed, then realized that the hand that emerged held a white handkerchief.

"We ought to flatten the bastards," he said to Liu over the com unit.

"Just make sure they're surrendering," said a deep and commanding voice. He glanced back and saw that Captain Freah had joined them.

Aboard Galatica
8 March, 0545

MINERVA LASHED THE WOMAN PILOT'S HANDS BEHIND her with the string from her boot, wrapping the lace over Bree's wrists and then around a bolt at the side. It might not hold for long if she strained against it, but the American's struggles would at least warn her.

Where would they go? For now, they were running along

the course Madrone had plotted. But that was suicide.

Mayo nodded nervously as she slipped into the seat beside him. He began reading off bearings and instrument numbers—a status report. Everything was in perfect order.

"Why ten thousand feet?" he asked abruptly.

"Not now, Lieutenant. Just hold the course."

Mayo started to say something, but thought better of it. Minerva folded her arms, staring at the darkness before her.

Pej, Brazil
8 March, 0550

DANNY MADE SURE POWDER AND LIU HAD THE PRISONers under control, then approached the hangar building cautiously. He flipped Annie's CIV visor back into IR mode. There was one person in the hangar that he could see; he lay prone on the floor behind a desk or some boxes with a view of the doorway.

A flash-bang in his hand, Danny went to the entrance and crouched down. He couldn't see the man now—the boxes were too thick. He reached up with his grenade hand and flicked the visor into enhanced starlight mode. The aiming triangle appeared; he lowered his aim toward the boxes, then stepped forward, slowly turning his attention around the hangar.

Empty.

Something moved behind him.

He threw himself down, then saw it was only Powder.

"Shit, sorry," said his point man through the laser com.

"Down," hissed Danny, pointing toward the boxes.

Powder nodded, then began working his way sideways to the left. Danny slid toward the opposite wall.

"Get away from the gun, motherfucker!" shouted Powder, who'd come up behind the Brazilian.

Danny rose slowly. The Brazilian didn't move.

"He's dead, Captain," said Powder, moving in slowly.

"Hold on. Stop," said Danny. He clicked the CIV visor control, examining the object in front of the dead Brazilian. It looked like the guts of a small rocket, or maybe a large artillery shell.

"What's up?"

"There's a bomb or something sitting in the middle of the floor. It's got a timer. Go see if you can find some lights. No, wait a second." Freah lowered himself to his knees. There was a radiation symbol on the interior of the metal casing, heading about a paragraph's worth of closely printed letters. "You read Portuguese, Powder?"

"Negative, sir."

"Go get Bison," Danny said. "Tell him we have a bomb to disarm. Tell him it may be a tricky one, and to bring his full set."

"Sniffer too?"

"Especially the sniffer. And Powder, get the Satcom. Go very fast."

Dreamland
8 March, 0200 local (Brazil 0600)

MACK PACED OUTSIDE TAJ, TRYING TO CONTAIN HIS fury.

He knew exactly what Madrone would do, how he would fly. He'd get around the F-15's if they weren't careful.

Hell, even if they *were* careful. Because they'd be too damn full of themselves.

Been there, done that himself.

To be put on ice. Bullshit. Bullshit!

He could have the MiG fueled on his own authority.

Not armed, though. That would take an order from Bastian. Technically. Odds were no one would question him if he said it was approved.

God, they couldn't just leave him on the ground. At least let him talk to some of the pilots, give them advice.

They friggin' thought he was a traitor. Damn them all.

Pej, Brazil
8 March, 0613 local

"CAPTAIN, I'M ASSUMING THIS IS VERY IMPORTANT."

"Annie, I need your help," Danny said. The Army transports were just arriving outside, making it difficult to hear. "I'm looking at what I think is a nuclear warhead wired to a timer that's supposed to go off in thirty-seven minutes."

"Why do you think it's a warhead?"

"Our sniffer says it's full of uranium."

"Read me the scale level."

"Okay. Uh, hang on." He fumbled with the small Geiger counter, clicking it through its modes. About the size of a lunchbox, the field unit could detect the depleted uranium used for A-10 cannon shells at about fifty yards. Whiplash carried similar units for toxic chemicals and known gas agents. "497.83," said Danny, "on the, uh, hundredths, no, thousandths scale."

"That's fine," said Annie. "How large is the device?"

"About the size of an artillery shell."

"How far away are you?"

"About three feet, max."

"Tsk. I believe your unit may be doubling the reading."

"Is it a bomb?"

"Well, you're the one looking at it. The reading is certainly high enough. Interesting—you're in Brazil?"

"Interesting? What should I do?"

"Technically, Captain, I am not an expert on nuclear devices."

"The NSC is supposed to be getting me one," Danny told her. "But right now, you're the best I got, Annie."

"Well, thank you for the vote of confidence, Captain." Annie sighed. "What does Sergeant Bison think?"

Bison came on the line and described the setup of the wiring to her. Danny squatted down on his knees about a foot from the timer, which he had uncovered by pulling the top off the trunk that was inside the boxes. The timer had several folds of wires running off it, including one that led to a large brick of C-4. Bison thought that was a booby trap, and Klondike agreed.

"So what the hell do we do?" Freah finally asked his sergeant.

"She's thinking, Captain." Bison nodded a few times, then began describing the thick group of wires that fed into the front of the device.

Danny nearly had a heart attack as his munitions expert pulled at the winds of black tape.

"Wants to talk to you, Captain," Sergeant Bison said finally, giving the radio handset back to him.

"Creative," said Annie. "I'm not an expert on tactical nuclear devices, but in my experience, the device sounds rather primitive. Most likely it is primed by a focused explosive device, which would propel an atomic pellet into a cup of material toward the base. Rather like the Hiroshima bomb, in a way, except that there the mechanism—"

"As powerful as that?"

"Oh, no. Only half. Probably even less—maybe a tenth, assuming I'm right about your sniffer reading. I don't particularly like those devices; I saw two that malfunctioned in the Gulf, once when the consequences could have been very serious. Of course, the real key isn't so much the size of the warhead as the design of the explosive lens that initiates the reaction. An American bomb that size could wipe out a city the size of New York, whereas a Pakistani bomb would barely destroy twelve or thirteen blocks. They're quite hopeless as designers because they don't have the hang of focusing the explosion. On the other hand—"

"Annie, there's a timer on this thing."

"Yes, I understand that. Well, either you or Sergeant Bison has to take it apart. That's the first step. Undo the booby-trap component and then we'll tackle the timer. This way maybe we can see which of the wires are obviously fake."

"You don't think the booby trap might set it off?"

"Always a possibility."

Danny stood up.

"I can get the C-4 off no sweat, Captain," said Bison.

The weapons expert stooped over the bomb. Bison worked quickly—a little too quickly, it seemed to Danny.

"All right, get some screwdrivers," the sergeant said finally. Danny went over to the side of the hangar where there was a large tool case. He didn't realize until he was walking back that Bison had only sent him on the errand to make himself less nervous.

"Wasn't even connected," said the demo expert, pointing to the plastic explosive. "Just there to fake us out. I think."

"Maybe the whole thing is a fake."

"That I wouldn't count on."

Powder gingerly held up the small clock dial and touched one of the buttons on the side with the blade of the screwdriver. "Still giving me the local time, 0636. Still set to go at 0650. I think anyway. Could be a second sequence, like a countdown from there."

"Probably the detonation," said Annie when Danny told her over the Satcom.

"Can we stop it?"

"Long shot."

"Thanks."

"Just trying to be optimistic. Would you like to know what happened on *Jeopardy* tonight, or should we get to work?"

Aboard Galatica
Over Colombia
8 March, 0536 local (0636 Brazil)

ZEN DRIFTED IN AND OUT OF CONSCIOUSNESS FOR A while, strange visions twisting in his head.

He walked in midair toward the large crimson sun. His legs felt solid and strong.

A warning flashed. Bogeys. F/A-18's.

Zen's head cleared. He was at the U/MF observer station, the technician's bench next to the control seat. Two American F/A-18 Navy fighter-bombers were approaching. They might have caught something on their radar, though the threat screen indicated they hadn't picked up the lead Flighthawk, which was on an intercept vector from the southeast.

The Hughes APG-73 digital programmable radar of the F/A-18's rated among the best conventional radars in service; were the Flighthawk a conventional fighter, it could have been detected at no less than a hundred nautical miles, even in look-down mode, which tended to lower the range. But the Flighthawk was much smaller and considerably stealthier than a conventional plane. Its pilot also had the advantage of seeing exactly where the radar fingers were groping. By the time the Hornets finally detected the U/MF, it was less than eight nautical miles away.

It took nearly twenty seconds for the Navy pilots to realize the odd, unidentifiable returns on their radars were definitely a bogey. One of the pilots fired an AMRAAM, even though the Flighthawk screen showed he hadn't locked; Zen reflexively reached for the button to dispense chaff.

Madrone didn't bother, apparently realizing that he was so close and so fast that the missile, even if properly aimed, wouldn't be a threat. He was correct; C^3 flicked it off with a quick buzz of its ECMs, barely breaking a sweat as the missile sailed past, self-detonating about two miles away.

Madrone pressed a heads-on attack against the lead plane. The Hornet pilot handled it well, waiting until the Flighthawk began firing to make his move, a rolling dive to the right. Under ordinary circumstances against nearly any other plane, his tucking roll would have brought him behind the aggressor, leaving him with an easy Sidewinder shot. But against the U/MF, the Hornet pilot would have been better off pulling the yellow handle at the side of his seat.

Madrone tucked his nose and threw his tail out a bit, the vectored thrusters on the Flighthawk yanking it around so quickly that he closed on the Hornet's tail before the other plane completed its maneuver. He was within two hundred yards when he began firing the cannon again; two seconds later the back end of his target exploded.

As quickly as it happened, nailing the Hornet still took time. Had the pilot of the second plane been a coward or perhaps simply more prudent, the second F/A-18 could have escaped. But the Navy lieutenant in the trail plane was either brave or reckless, depending on the perspective; he pressed on toward the fresh contact his radar locked on eight miles away—the Megafortress.

Zen guessed that Gal's RWR had buzzed upstairs, for the plane suddenly lurched eastward. He reached to flip the screen into Gal's sensor array, which he could view but not control through the diagnostic station. Before he could complete the sequence and bring up the image, Madrone had begun to close on the Hornet's twin tailpipe.

The F/A-18's wing flared. He'd launched an AMRAAM. A second dropped off the rail. Then a long stream of red appeared, arcing from the nose of the Flighthawk. But Madrone had started to fire a few seconds too soon to score a fatal hit—the targeting control on C³ had always been slightly optimistic.

The Hornet veered upward, perhaps to try and outclimb its pursuer. All Madrone had to do was nudge his nose slightly to alter his aim and keep coming; the Flighthawk had built enough momentum to smash bullets through the right wing of the McDonnell-Douglas fighter, shearing it off between the outboard and inboard stores pylon.

Zen saw the Hornet's canopy fly away as the plane began to spin. The Flighthawk veered off.

Then he remembered the AMRAAMs.

"AIRCRAFT TARGETED. RADAR MATCHED FROM LIBRARY. ECMs prepared."

Minerva stared at the legend in the screen at the right side of the dash as the RWR continued to clang. The Megafortress had not only detected the missiles, but computed the proper response.

But it wanted her to authorize it. How?

"Activate ECMs," she said into her headset.

Nothing happened.

She twisted back to Breanna, then realized she wouldn't help.

"Use the word 'computer,' " said Mayo.

"Computer, activate ECMs," Minerva said.

"Acknowledged," responded a programmed voice.

The tone stopped. There was a flash in the sky two miles off their wing.

"Why are we not to go over ten thousand feet?" said Mayo.

Minerva turned toward her lieutenant. He stared at her. Before she could say anything, he pulled back on the stick.

With one hand, she reached for the controls. With the other, she drew the gun from her belt.

Mayo threw himself on her before she could retrieve the revolver. The plane lurched left as they struggled, the nose rising before abruptly pitching downward.

BREANNA HUNKERED DOWN AS BEST SHE COULD AS the two struggled. The plane rolled on its wing, pitching itself wildly toward the earth.

Gravity slammed her from two directions at once. The plane began to spin. She heard something pop a few feet away, and then a dark cowl tightened around her head, the violent g forces depriving her brain of blood.

"Let the computer fly it," she said, or maybe just thought— she didn't want to say anything, didn't want to help them. Negative g's tore at her body, twisting it like a bag of loose Jell-O; her head snapped back against the seat while her legs flew outward.

She remembered the night in the hospital with Jeff after his accident, the night that turned into a week that became a year, a dark hood around her head that had never completely cleared, a cowl she'd clawed and pushed and punched away.

The Megafortress stumbled through an invert and blood rushed to her head, and now Rap knew she was going to die, felt the grim weightlessness that precedes the final auger-in. The back of the plane lurched upward, a fish snapping its tail in the air as it arced over the water.

Breanna remembered the first day she'd seen Jeff, standing in the cockpit of a cranked-arrow F-16, a grin like nothing she'd ever seen before, and eyes—sparkling eyes that held the soft place inside her, that could ferret out her secrets. The afternoon they'd made love for the first time, she knew he would be her husband, knew she wanted to go nowhere else.

Her head snapped forward and then back twice, gravity pounding her face like a middleweight working a bag.

And then the storm was over. The engines' powerful thrust propelled them upward with a jerk. The computer had taken over and managed to wrestle the plane level.

Breanna twisted toward the front. Minerva sat in the co-pilot's seat, tensely guiding the plane.

Breanna let herself hang forward over the radar control console. All of the Megafortresses designed to work with the Flighthawks had locator beacons with an omnidirectional, "always-on" signal that could be read by standard IFF units about fifty miles away. The beacon could only be activated through the flight computer and required authentication to initiate, since it potentially could help an enemy find the otherwise stealthy plane. Staring at the inactive radar screens, Breanna made up her mind to find a way to issue the command. A headset lay at the base of the left tube; if it was active, her voice might just carry loud enough for the computer to respond.

She couldn't reach it, though. And there was no way to speak loud enough without the others hearing.

An auxiliary keyboard sat in the cubby below the tubes. She tried scrunching her body down—maybe she could get it with her teeth, somehow hit the right combination of keys.

Her arms suddenly sprang apart, freed. She fell forward, smacking her face on the tube. She pushed upward, determined to ignore the pain, make the most of this stroke of luck.

"No," said Minerva behind her. She put her hand on Breanna's shoulder and forced her back into the seat. Rap began to push back, but a knife slid along the back of her ear. The skin felt cold, and then as if it were pulling itself apart.

"I want you to fly the plane," Minerva told her.

"Me? You trust me to fly the plane?" Breanna began to laugh. "Are we giving up?"

"Hardly. Captain Madrone intends on bombing San Francisco."

"You're insane. I'll never help you."

"It's possible that I may be able to talk Captain Madrone out of it. In any event, you have a choice. Either you help me, and we possibly save San Francisco as well your husband and yourself. Or I kill you and let Captain Madrone do as he pleases."

"You're crazy."

"I am many things, but not crazy. I would prefer you to fly the plane," she added, pushing the point of the blade into Breanna's neck.

"What happened to your pilot?" said Breanna. But as she turned to face her captor she saw the answer—Mayo lay on the floor.

"He had only one bullet in his gun," said Lanzas. "It was unfortunate that it struck him in his head. Now—move him and fly the plane."

"Okay," said Breanna.

Dreamland
8 March, 0245 local (0645 Brazil)

THE BREEZE KICKED UP AS IOWA ROCKETED INTO THE sky, but it was an oddly warm breeze, as if the big plane's engines were warming the night. Colonel Bastian stared at the Megafortress as it rose, the tremble of its long wings reverberating in his chest. He belonged in the sky, not on the ground pushing paper. On any given day, the best use of his talents was in the air—and today was more than any given day.

More than likely, his flying days were over. Keesh would see to that. Not his flying days exactly—just his Air Force ones. The loss of the Boeing and Flighthawks was bad enough when it looked like an accident. But someone stealing a plane—that was a different story. And then losing a Megafortress and two more Flighthawks—Brad Elliott had been cashiered for less.

Not exactly. In Elliott's case, the thief was a Soviet spy, with the backing of a world superpower. Here he was simply a madman.

If Dog was going to be bagged anyway, why the hell not get his butt up in the air and do something?

Do what? Kill his own daughter?

What the hell kind of father would he be if it came to that?

The kind who had sworn an oath to protect his country.

What sort of oath had he taken when Breanna was born?

If he was there, he might be able to help her somehow. But then, hadn't that been the story of his life—he'd never been there when she was growing up.

The Megafortress began banking, heading south. Dog turned and climbed aboard the black Jimmy waiting to take him back to the Taj. The driver threw the SUV in gear.

They were almost at the building when Bastian put his hand on the young man's shoulder.

"Take me back around to the Megafortress hangar," he said. "Shed Two. Then knock off for the night."

"Sir?"

"You have forty-eight hours leave. I'd suggest you don't waste a minute of it."

Aboard Galatica
Over Colombia
8 March, 0545 local (0645 Brazil)

MINERVA HAD FIGURED OUT HOW TO PROGRAM THE course in on the flight computer, and was watching Breanna carefully. Rap flew the plane precisely as her captor directed, skimming across the ragged landscape just at the edge of a thunderstorm at 8,500 feet. Sooner or later an opportunity would present itself, even if it meant pushing the plane into a mountain.

"F-15's, twenty miles ahead at compass point three-two-zero," said Madrone over the interphone. He had one of the Flighthawks flying eight miles ahead as a scout, using its passive sensors to check for threats. "Two planes, one at twenty-five thousand feet. The second is at twenty-eight."

"Attack them," said Minerva.

"We can get by them," suggested Breanna. "It will be safer."

"Do it."

"Hold on. I'm going to take us out of this turbulence. Computer—"

"Don't change the course," Minerva hissed, leaning toward her.

"Do you want to get by them or not?"

"Don't change the course, or the altitude."

"I just have to get out of this storm."

Minerva grabbed her hand.

The Flighthawk screen showed the Eagles in a standard search sweep, running well off to the west. A standard B-52 would be clearly visible to them, but Gal had the profile of a barn swallow, and unless the plane made a sudden movement, the interceptors were likely to miss it.

"They're off my radar," said Kevin.

"If we switched our radar on, we'd see threats two to three hundred miles away," Breanna told Lanzas.

"Three hundred miles?"

"How do you think we were able to track you to Brazil? Gal is testing a—"

"The radar would also allow our enemies to see us coming," said Lanzas, her voice tired. "Please, Captain, do not test me further."

JEFF CURSED AS THE F-15s PASSED OUT TO SEA, AN-other chance lost.

"I know you're watching me, Jeff," said Madrone. His voice came from a small speaker in the console ordinarily used only by the Megafortress's systems. "Put the headset on."

Slowly, Jeff pushed upright and reached for the headset. His sore upper body moved like the works in an old rusted clock, creaking and cracking.

"Kevin, how did you manage to use that speaker?" he asked. "It's not part of ANTARES or C³."

"There are no boundaries I can't cross, Jeff."

"You flew Hawkmother too. How? Through the gateway?"

"I'm beyond ANTARES, Jeff. I don't need the computer."

"Show me. Take off the control helmet."

"Don't try and trick me. I'm not stupid."

"Withdrawal from the Theta drugs makes you paranoid," Jeff said. He turned and looked across the bay at the man who had been his friend. "It did it to me. It still affects me."

"It's not paranoia when people are really out to get you."

"I thought I could feel my legs," said Jeff. "It really tricked me."

"You're the only one playing tricks."

"I can't feel my legs, Kevin. It was a dream—a desire or something I can't control. It's not too late," he said. "Geraldo can help you. Take us back to Dreamland and surrender. I'll help you. I swear I will."

"Shut the fuck up!"

Stoking Madrone's anger was the only weapon Jeff had. Down here there'd be no one to stop him. Zen couldn't walk, but he would pit his upper body strength against anyone's. As soon as Madrone lunged, he'd grab his neck and strangle him. Whatever it took to subdue him, he'd do.

Whatever it took to help him, he'd try; he hadn't been lying about that.

"You going to hit me?" he told Kevin. "Come on, Monkey Brain. Hit me, Twig."

Madrone didn't move.

"What are you waiting for, Monkey Boy?"

"I'm not going to hit you, Jeff." Madrone's voice sounded sad, and far away. "You tried that before and it worked. But it won't work now. No."

"Come on, Monkey Brain. Microchip Head. Mack Smith nailed it for once. Come on. You're a wimp. Come on."

But Madrone no longer spoke to him.

Pej, Brazil
8 March, 0647 local

BISON'S HANDS SHOOK AS HE ANGLED THE SCREW-driver blade beneath the small metal band. He nodded. Danny closed his eyes.

Something snapped. But there wasn't an explosion.

"Okay, we're ready to work on the native timer and lock mechanism," said Bison. "It's hot."

As Danny relayed the information to Annie, he saw that his sergeant's hands were shaking violently.

"Undo the LED panel on the code-lock assembly right next to the explosive that launches the pellet," said Annie. "You see it?"

Danny told Bison. The munitions expert nodded, then pushed a Phillips-head screwdriver down toward the light green panel.

The blade slipped and clattered on the floor.

Danny grabbed Bison's arm as he reached for the screwdriver. "Kevin, let me try."

"I've d-done this a million times."

"I know. Let me take the responsibility, though. It's not just us who's blowing up."

"We evacuated the Army guys, Captain," said Bison, but then he slid back.

The panel wouldn't come off.

Bison held the Satcom to his head. "Now what, Annie?" said Freah.

"Try it again," she said.

"Shit."

"It's either that or reattach the timer and reset the detonation time."

"Jesus."

"You sound nervous, Captain. We will try sorting through the wires. Just don't cut them all. As I told you before, complete power loss will trigger—"

There was a click and the line went dead.

"Annie? Annie?"

"I think that storm's blocking the satellite," said Bison, working the radio. "Time's down to two minutes," he added.

Danny stared at the back of the LED panel. The large integrated circuit had several small solder points at the back, but nothing that gave any clue about how it worked.

"Let's short the thing out," offered Powder from behind him. "Dump it in water. I got a bucket right here."

"What the fuck are you doing here, Powder?" said Freah. "You were supposed to bug out."

"None of us are going to leave you, Captain," said Liu.

"Don't tell me you're all here. Are you?"

"No, sir. We're not here," said Reagan.

Danny turned his attention back to the Satcom. "Annie? Annie?"

Nothing.

He leaned over the bomb. He could cut the wire that connected the LED lock mechanism. Annie had said that doing that would probably kill power to the spytron, the highly sensitive and accurate trigger that activated an accelerating explosive lens around the "catcher's mitt" of uranium once the radioactive seed was launched toward it. But the explosive that sent the radioactive seed into the rest of the material would still ignite, as would the lens itself—a nanosecond or two too late to start a chain reaction maybe, but definitely in time to kill them.

"Everybody out of the hangar," Freah shouted, taking the thick combat knife in his hand and reaching it across the thick wires. "That's a fuckin' order. Get out of here."

"Captain!" shouted Powder.

"Go!"

"Nuke'll get us anyway, Captain," Bison said. "Rather be able to tell St. Peter I didn't run away."

"Just the explosive is going off," said Danny. "Go!"

"Klondike said that might not work."

"Go!"

"Thirty seconds," said Bison, studying at his own watch.

"Here, Captain," shouted Powder, running across the floor with a ceramic cup and a plastic gallon jug of water. He slipped on the smooth concrete, managing a leg-first slide near the bomb. He held the cup and jug out in front of him. "Douse it. We got nothing to lose."

"Twenty seconds. He might be right," said Bison.

Powder spilled water from the jug into the cup, his hands wobbly as he tried to slip it in place under Freah's hand.

Would that work?

If it didn't, he'd cut the wires.

Danny hesitated.

Do both at the same time.

"Fifteen."

One way or the other, everyone in the hangar would die.

Bison reached over, trying to steady Powder's hands. But he was shaking just as bad.

"Go!" Danny yelled.

"No time!" shouted Liu.

Danny closed his eyes and pulled back on the knife, sliding the blade through the collection of wires. He waited for the long millisecond before death, heard the fizzle of the explosion as it began.

But it wasn't the explosion at all.

"Jeez, Louise, that was close," said Powder. He pulled the LED into the water.

The fizzle had come from the clock circuit shorting.

"Captain, did you cut the wires?" asked Liu.

"They're cut," said Freah, looking at them.

"Shit," said Powder.

"Got Ms. Klondike!" yelled Liu.

Danny sat back on the floor. The fluorescent lights in the hangar seemed very yellow. Liu came over on his knees and held the handset to Danny's ears.

"Where have you been?" Annie asked.

"I cut the wires," he said. "Powder dumped the timer in water and shorted it. I think that saved us."

"No," said the weapons expert. "The mechanism is impervious to moisture. Water wouldn't have done anything."

"It fizzled."

"You cut the wires. It is odd, though—at least one end of the device should have exploded when all current was lost, unless the designer was completely inept. Are you sure you cut all the wires?"

Danny looked over at the harness. Fourteen of the sixteen wires had been cut clean; two remained.

"Shit," said Danny. Then he told her what he saw.

"Out of curiosity, Captain, what's your birthday?"

"Why?"

"I was thinking one of us ought to run down to Las Vegas and play those numbers on the roulette wheels."

Aboard EB-52 M-6
Dreamland
8 March, 0351 local

BOTH MCADEN AND FENNER INSISTED ON STAYING WITH M-6 even after Bastian ordered them to stay on the ground; he finally decided it didn't make much sense to argue with them. No one would blame them for flying, and besides, Magnus's order applied to him, not them.

McAden wasn't all that happy about taking the copilot's seat, but there Dog had an easier argument—Dog had very little experience using the EB-52's weapons systems, which were more easily handled from the copilot's station.

As they got ready to fly, a black SUV hurtled up the ramp toward them, blue light flashing.

Dog watched the Jimmy screech to a halt. Undoubtedly Magnus had gotten to the security people somehow; he was about to be placed under arrest.

He edged his hand toward the throttle bar. As soon as the men were out of the car, he'd hit the gas and lurch away. By the time they got back in the vehicle he'd be on the runway.

But instead of heavily armed security men, a thin figure jumped out of the Jimmy. Dog stared at the shadow, which seemed to have small wings.

Or just very long hair.

Jennifer Gleason. She waved frantically and ran toward the plane. Another person jumped from the SUV—Dr. Geraldo.

"What should I do, Colonel?" asked McAden.

"Let's find out what they want," said Bastian.

McAden dropped the ramp. Gleason appeared on the flight deck a few seconds later.

"Colonel, let me aboard," she said.

"We're just flying backup," he told her.

"I can override C³," she said. "I can send feedback through the command link. It'll break the connection with ANTARES and disable the Flighthawks."

"That'll work?"

"It's either that or you'll shoot them down, isn't it?"

"Colonel!" yelled Geraldo from below.

"And what exactly is your plan?" he asked the psychologist as she came up.

"I want to try talking to him," said Geraldo.

"It's not going to work."

"Better than shooting him down."

"We almost certainly will have to," said Dog.

Neither Gleason nor Geraldo said anything else.

"This won't be a joy ride," he said finally.

"I fly in Megafortresses every day," said Jennifer.

"Shut the hatch," Bastian told McAden. "Jen, show Dr. Geraldo how to strap herself in downstairs."

Aboard Galatica
Approaching U.S.
8 March, 0805 local (0705 Dreamland)

THE FINGERS OF THE AWACS GROPED THE AIR, REACH-ing for him, desperately trying to grab him. Two F-16's cruised not five miles to his left, at less than five thousand feet, determined to ferret him out.

The bastards would all miss. He was within sixty minutes of San Francisco, sixty minutes of having revenge.

And then?

Then they could kill him. He wouldn't even bother to run.

"Losing connection," warned C³.

"Closer," he screeched on the interphone.

"But—" Breanna began.

"Closer!"

The Megafortress lurched upward and to the left. C³'s warning flashed off.

"AWACS tracking," warned the computer.

"Impossible," Madrone muttered. The threat screen on the Flighthawk showed he was clear.

Breanna had tricked him—the F-16's had seen the Megafortress.

"F-16's being vectored for mother ship," said the computer. *"Attempting to activate ident."*

Madrone started to slip out of Theta. His view of the U/MF screen went blank.

Kevin took a deep breath, felt himself relaxing. The feeds returned. But he couldn't feel Galatica across the gateway. He was too drained, and his brain worked in slow motion—he had too much to hold in his mind.

"We're being targeted by a pair of interceptors," he told Minerva.

"What?"

"This!" He flashed the computer's threat screen into the cockpit HUDs.

He'd have to take over Galatica as well as the Flighthawks. He'd have to find the strength somehow.

ZEN SAW THE F-16s ON THE FLIGHTHAWK SCREEN AS they turned to target the Megafortress just under forty miles away. But the slippery black plane danced at the edge of their radar coverage; they would have to ride much closer to lock on. Most likely their rules of engagement demanded visual identification before firing anyway.

Or maybe not. The launcher indicators on the Flighthawk went red. Sparrow radar missiles were in the air.

BREANNA PUSHED DOWN ON THE STICK, AIMING TO USE the confusion to her advantage. But the plane moved in the opposite direction—Kevin had somehow taken control.

The rest was automatic. Tinsel shot from Gal's backside as its ECM computer zeroed in on the AIM-7Ms and knocked them senseless with a blast of Gangsta Rap fuzz. At the same time, Galatica accelerated toward the F-16's to keep its connection with the Flighthawks. The Air National Guard F-16 Vipers launched another salvo of missiles at approximately twenty miles; these two were easily confused.

Thirty seconds later, Hawk One began a front-quarter attack on the lead Viper. The fireball trailed across the left windscreen; as it flared out, a second appeared on the left.

"Why are you doing this, Kevin?" Breanna said.

"I'm destroying Livermore," he said. "They poisoned my daughter there with their radiation. They claimed they were treating her, but it was a lie."

"You'll destroy all San Francisco."

"So be it."

HE WANTED SAN FRANCISCO TO BE DESTROYED. HE saw it, saw Karen there, shriveling in the flash as the nuke went off. That would serve her right for giving up on him.

Maybe she'd been in on it.

He saw his wife crying at the graveyard, sobbing as she knelt on the fresh-packed dirt. Then he saw Christina, helpless on the gurney, head shaved, the tape for the lead shields still dangling on her skin.

She screamed like he'd never heard her. The two nurses came to wheel her away. He jumped for her, but some bastard grabbed him and held him back.

Kevin fell from the sky, tumbling backward into the jungle. He landed flat on his spine, staring up at the sun overhead. The red orb pulsated, then began to descend. He tried to get up, but couldn't.

IT TOOK JEFF A MOMENT TO REALIZE THAT NOT ONLY had the Flighthawks defaulted to Trail One, their favored preset mode, but that ANTARES was no longer hooked into C³. When he finally saw it, he grabbed for the controller with his right hand and threw his left on the two rockers that connected his microphone with the computer.

"Command authorization Zed Zed Zed," he said, telling the computer to recognize him. "Zero Stockard Zero."

"Zed Zed Zed."

"Erase ANTARES plug-ins."

"Command unrecognized."

"Computer: Delete the connection with ANTARES!"

"Command unrecognized."

"Manual control, Hawk One," he said, pulling back on the controller. The cockpit cam showed the rear of the Megafortress in the moonlight, flying above an array of jagged peaks.

Down, he thought, pushing the stick forward so hard it nearly snapped out of its socket.

HE NEEDED TO BE IN THETA NOW.

Christina's face floated in the dim blue void before him. Her mouth moved.

Daddy, she said. *Daddy.*

I'm here.

It's the computer. It took me away.

ANTARES?

Yes.

But how?

It sucked me out from inside you.

Christina?

It stole me. The computer stole me. It took me from your memory and destroyed you. That was their plan all along— to kill me by killing you.

Her eyes and mouth faded, leaving only the outline of her face. Lightning flashed behind him and he fell back in the tower. The last bits of his daughter disintegrated in front of him.

She was right. It wasn't Livermore he had to destroy. It was ANTARES.

BREANNA PULLED BACK ON THE STICK AS THE PLANE began plummeting toward the mountain peaks. She had the yoke pressed against its stop, but the plane didn't respond, its dive continuing.

Then, with a violent shudder, its nose began to jerk upward, and in the space of a few seconds it became a streaking roller coaster, whipping upward as the aerodynamic forces overpowered it.

Minerva was screaming next to her.

"Don't let the plane go through ten thousand feet. No!"

Breanna grabbed the stick back, not sure if Kevin had let go or not. They whipped up to 8,500 feet, going through 8,600 and accelerating.

"Help me," yelled Minerva. "We can't go above ten thousand feet."

"I have to override the flight computer," lied Breanna, who now had control.

"Do it!"

"Computer: override course settings, override command settings. Lock out autopilot section. Authorization Rap One-One-Two."

"Confirmed."

"Navigation screen." Breanna tapped the panel up and quickly hit the beacon code. In the meantime, she leveled off at 9,200 feet.

"What's so special about ten thousand feet?" she asked after checking the plane's systems.

Minerva didn't answer, but she didn't have to.

"We're booby-trapped, aren't we? Did you hear that, Kevin? Your lover wanted to blow you up."

"I heard," said Madrone.

And once more, even though locking out the autopilot should have isolated command at her console, Breanna felt the plane veer out of her control.

HE DIDN'T CARE ABOUT MINERVA ANYMORE. HE'D BEEN confused by ANTARES, the drugs, the computer, everything. Confused and tricked and used.

No more. Madrone eased back in the seat, in full control of the planes. Now that he knew what he had to do—now that his daughter had made it clear to him—he felt very calm and very strong.

He gave C³ and the Megafortress the new course, then pushed up his visor, looking across at Zen. His friend flailed at the control panel, trying to take command of the robot planes. He didn't seem to understand that Madrone and ANTARES could override any of his commands.

Or maybe he did. Maybe he struggled to keep from feeling helpless.

"That's enough, Jeff," Kevin said finally. He pulled his pistol out.

"Shoot me," said Zen.

"I don't want to."

"Thanks," said Zen sarcastically.

"You're right about ANTARES. I think you're definitely right," he said. "I'm going to fix it, once and for all."

Aboard M-6
Near Dreamland
8 March, 0715

DOG WAS A HUNDRED MILES SOUTH OF DREAMLAND when one of the AWACS in the net announced that it had found Galatica.

It had had a little help—the Megafortress had turned its locator beam on.

A quartet of F-15Cs scrambled to intercept. The controllers began jockeying other elements around, lining up the defenses.

Two of the Eagles had to turn back because of fuel. A pair of Navy jets moved up to take their place. Dog pushed M-6 to accelerate, but they were at least a hundred miles from the action.

"Swinging back—shit—Rock Two has contact!" blurted out one of the F-15 pilots. "Shit! Shit! Tally at five hundred feet, two o'clock. Jesus."

"Rock Two, clear to engage," answered the controller calmly, authorizing the pilot to shoot down the Megafortress.

"Rock Three to support," said the wingman, following his commander.

Dog closed his eyes.

"Break right! Break right!" shouted Rock Three. "Band— flare! God, oh, God!"

There was static.

Dog guessed that the F-15's had just been jumped by one or both of the Flighthawks. The AWACS vectored the Navy interceptors toward the Megafortress, then announced it had lost the locator beam.

"Plot an intercept for San Francisco," Dog told McAden softly. "Make sure it's good."

"Colonel, no. Stay on this course," said Jennifer. "I have the C^3 signal. They're eighty miles dead ahead. They're not going to San Francisco."

Aboard Gal
8 March, 0723

MADRONE HAD TO REFUEL THE FLIGHTHAWKS. WHILE the computer told him he could make it to Dreamland from here, another encounter would push the U/MFs into their reserves, depriving him of his margin of error.

Dreamland was barely two hundred miles from here. If he squinted just right, he'd probably see Las Vegas glowing at the edge of the desert.

He reduced throttle on the Megafortress, swinging Hawk Three up toward the tail even as the automated boomer lowered the straw.

It was sneaky of Breanna to turn the beacon on; he hadn't understood what it was until the AWACS latched on. He couldn't blame her, though. Under other circumstances, he might have done the same thing.

It didn't matter now, not in the least. Dreamland's point-defense MIM-23 I-Hawk SAMs wouldn't pick up the stealthy Megafortress until it was approximately ten miles from the base. Even with the long missile beneath it, Hawk Three ought to be able to get to within five miles before the batteries detected it. By the time they locked and launched, he would already have pickled, ending ANTARES forever.

He nuzzled the U/MF into the boom and began working through the refuel.

Aboard M-6
8 March, 0740

"THEY'RE STILL COMING," JENNIFER TOLD BASTIAN OVER the interphone. "Distance, approximately sixty miles."

"You ready, Devin?" the colonel asked McAden.

"I'll turn the radar on as soon as you give the signal," answered the copilot. "Won't take me ten seconds to target the Scorpion after that."

The Scorpion AMRAAM-plus air-to-air missile had a one-hundred-pound warhead and a radar that could track multiple targets, rejecting all but the tastiest. Like the stock model that had been in use for roughly five years, Dreamland's improved version moved at over four times the speed of sound and had a range of forty nautical miles—though in actual practice against a target as slippery as the Megafortress, the missile was best launched between ten and twenty miles away, or just beyond visual range. Assuming Gal stayed on course, and assuming McAden could get a lock, that would be three minutes from now.

Targeting the Flighthawks, which were considerably smaller than the Megafortress, was far more problematic. They'd be fairly close to M-6 by the time Gal was targeted. Jennifer would try to interfere with the C^3 link to keep them at bay.

It was possible, though just barely, that she might be able to succeed and they wouldn't have to splash Gal. Dog didn't dare hope that was the way it would play.

Flying without radar and maintaining radio silence allowed Dog to sneak closer to Gal without being detected; it was, he figured, the only way he was going to get close enough to nail them. But it was a calculated risk—the main defenses were still to the west, concentrating on protecting San Francisco. If they missed, the sky was wide open.

"Still on course," said Jennifer. "Two minutes."

Aboard Galatica
8 March, 0753

JEFF FLOPPED HIS HEAD BACK AGAINST THE SEAT, EX-asperated. Any good fighter pilot keeps a checklist in his head to cover any contingency—engine out, do this, do that, do this. Gear jammed, do that, do this, do that.

For the first time in his life, he didn't have a checklist.

No, it was the second time. The first time was after the accident that had left him paralyzed.

There had been a solution to that. Not exactly the solution he wanted, but a solution. He'd gotten out of the aircraft and lived.

And now?

If he'd had his legs, what would he do?

Leap out of the seat, throttle Madrone, disconnect AN-TARES.

He turned his head toward Kevin. Madrone sat ramrod straight, his hands moving as he flew the planes. He was conducting an orchestra, not working controls.

The sitrep played on the main U/MF monitor, overlaid over a GPS map. They were about eleven minutes from Las Vegas, with Dreamland a breath beyond that.

If he had his feet, he'd undo the restraints, leap out of the seat. He'd grab Kevin with his hand and pull.

He *did* have his feet. ANTARES wasn't lying. Yes, it screwed up his head—yes, it made him paranoid. But there had to be something there. There had to be. ANTARES was a computer—it didn't invent things, it worked with what was there.

So he could use his legs. All he had to do was trust them—trust ANTARES this one last time.

Otherwise they were all dead.

Carefully, stealthily, Jeff undid his restraints.

Aboard M-6
8 March, 0758

"SIXTY SECONDS BY MY WATCH," BASTIAN TOLD JENNI-fer and the others. McAden jerked in his seat, rubbing his hands together.

Bastian had just missed combat over Vietnam, but he had flown missions in the Gulf and Bosnia; he had two probable kills and had ducked three different enemy missiles, including an SA-2 "telephone pole" that came within a meter of taking off his tail. By all rights, he was a grizzled veteran, and shouldn't feel nervous.

He didn't. Which bothered the hell out him.

"They're tracking us!" yelled McAden.

M-6's RWR drowned out anything else he said.

"ECMs," ordered Dog calmly. "Jenny, go for it. Can you get them?"

"Attempting."

"Go to active radar. Target the Flighthawks too," Dog said.

"Nothing. Nothing. Nothing," said McAden, his voice getting progressively higher.

"Just get Galatica," Bastian ordered. "Open bay door."

"Opening! They have their ECMs. We're still being tracked! I can't lock them up. Attempting."

"Flighthawk approaching," said Jennifer. "Hold this course."

"We're spiked!" said McAden. One of the radars hunting for them had managed to slip around the electronic noise and locked onto them.

Ordinarily, Dog would goose some chaff and zig through the air, complicating the radar's job before it fired. But that would complicate Gleason's job.

So would getting shot down.

"Break it," said Dog.

"Trying."

"Frontal attack! It's a U/MF!" shouted McAden, but Dog had already seen the Flighthawk on his HUD. It grew from nothing to the size of a baseball, then flashed red, firing its cannon. Dog could see the tracer arching in the air toward his windscreen as he plunged M-6 toward the earth.

"Tracking! I have him," said McAden.

"No! No!" said Jennifer. "Feedback initiated."

"Fire the missile," said Bastian steadily.

The Scorpion dropped off the rotating launcher in the rear bay. Dog clicked into the command frequency, giving their position and the fact that they were engaging Galatica and had already launched a radar homer.

In the twenty or so seconds it took for him to do all that, the Flighthawk had flown over the Megafortress, curled back, and dived for their tail. The Scorpion's rocket motor ignited; the missile zipped ahead, then flipped back. But it was no match for the agile little plane with its vectored thrust and finely tuned airfoil. The Flighthawk flicked right and closed on M-6 as the AMRAAM-plus passed by.

"Air mines," Bastian told McAden. The copilot was half a step ahead of him, and had the Stinger tail defenses already on his screen. The air mines were a twenty-first-century version of the tail gunners who had cleared the skies behind Flying Fortresses fifty years before—they literally peppered the air with exploding mines.

There was only one problem—their range was three miles, the same as the U/MF's cannon.

"I have the Flighthawk circuit," Jennifer said, her voice level. "I'm applying feedback. Leave it alone. Hold our course."

"Acquiring target!" said the copilot.

"Fucking trust me on this, Dog. If I have one I can get the other. Fuck!"

Somehow, the word "Dog" didn't sound right coming from her mouth.

As for "fuck" . . .

"Colonel?" asked McAden.

"Stand by. Have you found the other Flighthawk?" he asked him.

"Negative. Gal is now locked, but the ECMs may make the missile miss from this distance. We can close."

Before Bastian said anything else, the U/MF behind them opened fire.

Aboard Galatica
8 March, 0809

SOMETHING FOUGHT HIM, SOMETHING HE'D NEVER FELT before. Images flashed before Kevin's eyes, strange sensations—the tower, the jungle, the jaguar, the dark woman, all being strangled.

A snake wrapped itself around his neck, squeezing.

Madrone began to fall from Theta. He conjured his metaphor, then heard Geraldo call to him.

A woman in a flowing dress with long, strawberry hair stood before him.

Jennifer Gleason.

She morphed into a massive cobra, its large mouth looming.

Then her fangs grabbed him from the side.

*   *   *

JEFF LAUNCHED HIMSELF BY SLAMMING HIS ARMS against the rests, screaming as he flung his body sideways out of the seat.

His legs *would* work. They had to.

He hung suspended in the air, balanced perfectly between thought and action, between will and reality. He thought he could do it and he would; he willed his legs whole and they were.

But Zen's legs were irretrievably paralyzed, and whatever he had felt while under ANTARES, whatever he wanted to feel now, he couldn't make them cooperate. The distance between the two stations was too great to jump across, even for his well-developed arms and shoulders.

Jeff Stockard crumbled in the aisle, the long scream twisting into an agonized plea to his legs, to God, to any power that could make him whole. In that instant he would have made any bargain, paid any price, for the thinnest, poorest connection between his mind and his legs.

But no bargain could be made. He crashed down against the floor, his hands flailing until they hit one of the connecting cables to Kevin's ANTARES gear.

He hadn't the strength or momentum to break the cable, but as he fell his weight and agony yanked it backward, pulling the ANTARES feed from its socket.

Aboard M-6
8 March, 0811

"GOT IT! GOT IT! *GOT IT!* " SCREAMED GLEASON. "NATIVE mode. Okay, okay, okay. Fuck, I have them. Fuck fuck fuck. Hawk One is in native mode. It'll circle Dreamland. Locking in. My password. She's secure. Shit! Shit! We got it!"

"Is it carrying a missile?" Dog asked quietly.

"Hold on. No. Shit, no. Fuck. Looking for the other. Damn—what do you mean, not on the circuit?"

"Jen?"

"The other Flighthawk! Where is it?"

"Something in Galatica's shadow," said McAden.

"It's in preset," said Gleason. "It's native because the connection broke. I can't get feedback until C³ is back on the
line because of the codes. What the hell is he doing?"

"Colonel?"

Bastian glanced at McAden.

"Shoot her down," said Bastian.

"Let me try contacting them!" said Geraldo.

"Shoot her down," repeated Bastian.

Aboard Galatica
8 March, 0811

BREANNA FELT SOMETHING CLUNK AND PULL BEHIND
her, as if the leading-edge flaps on the wings had suddenly
extended.

They had.

She grabbed hold of the stick, barely managing to take
control of the plane as it did what could only be called a belly
flop in the sky. Two of the engines surged, the starboard flap
deployed—Gal seemed to be having a nervous breakdown.

Breanna pulled back on the stick. The altimeter ladder shot
up wildly. Minerva lost hold of her knife—it clattered to the
deck, tossed there by the sudden rush of g forces.

She'd blow the plane. It was the only thing to do.

9,200—9,500—9,800—

They'd die in a second. But at least Dreamland would be
safe.

"No!" screamed Lanzas, lurching toward her.

Breanna shrugged her off and closed her eyes as the altimeter nudged ten thousand feet.

Dreamland
8 March, 0811

FOR THE PAST HOUR, MACK HAD SAT IN THE MIG ON
the runway, listening as the searchers continued to hunt for
Galatica. He had cursed when the F-15's closed in, realizing
that he wanted to be the one who nailed the plane.

And then, miracle of miracles, it had escaped.

Only to be found by Bastian, who was targeting it.

Figured. Damn bastard hogged all the glory.

Still, from the position Dog gave, Gal seemed to be relatively close and headed this way. Resolved to get into the fight, he requested clearance from Dream Tower.

Without bothering to wait for an answer, he depressed the throttle button and moved the bar to idle. Using an old Russian Istrebeitelnyi Aviatsionnaya Polk rapid-takeoff trick, he selected just the right engine on the start panel. Knife kicked on the battery and hit the start switch, sending a whoosh of compressed air into the starboard engine. The MiG rumbled to life; he waited barely a second as it spooled up. In that second he pulled his canopy down; by the time it snugged he had started forward, rushing into the air on just one engine. Only after he had cleaned the gear did he bleed air into the left power plant, jump-starting it. The MiG shot upward.

"Alert the Nellis patrols," he told Dream Tower. "I don't want those cowboys taking potshots at me because I look like a bad guy."

"Uh, Sharkishki, you're clear to take off," answered the tower belatedly.

Aboard Gal
8 March, 0811

THE STORM WAS SO THICK AND DEEP THAT IT TOOK MAdrone forever to realize that the connection to the planes had been lost.

The ANTARES helmet had been pulled half off his head. He had become another person, his physical self another robot to be controlled.

The Megafortress lurched upward. Madrone shook his head clear and lifted the visor. Zen floundered on the deck beside him, the control lead snagged around his arm. He was trying to pull it with him as he elbowed backward from the control panels like a swimmer.

More like an upside-down turtle.

Madrone quickly undid his restraints and leaned down to punch Jeff flat in the face twice as the son of a bitch struggled to roll away. But Stockard didn't give up, somehow continuing to push himself backward, dragging the cord with him. Anger propelled Madrone to his feet. He stopped Jeff with a sharp kick to his stomach, then stomped twice on his chest, slamming his heel into Jeff's jaw before Stockard finally stopped, his eyes rolling back in his head as he momentarily lost consciousness. Kevin braced himself for a truly awful kick—he would beat the pulp from the bastard's brain until the floor oozed with it. But as he started to swing forward, something held him back, a voice whispering to him from far away.

Jeffrey is your friend. He tried to warn you but you didn't listen.

"Give me the cord, Jeff."

Stockard, his head limp to the side, said nothing. Madrone reached down and put his fingers on Jeff's arm almost gently as he pried the cord away.

"I'm sorry, Jeff. It has to be this way now." He gathered the ANTARES wire into his hands, restored the plug, and wound the wire around the panel so it couldn't be easily removed again.

Aboard M-6
8 March, 0828

THE FIRST SCORPION MISSED, SAILING ABOUT A HUNdred yards wide of Galatica. For a second, though, it looked like the pilots had lost control of the EB-52, and Dog thought Gal would spin into the mountains.

Somehow, she didn't. Somehow, she began climbing again, and shook off the second and third Scorpions they had launched.

The fourth Scorpion lost its track and self-destructed.

They had two more left. The closer they got, the better their odds of nailing the plane. But McAden couldn't get a lock to fire.

"Hang in there," said Dog. "Jennifer, how's that second U/MF?"

"It's still in native mode," she said.

"They're zigging. Tinsel. Damn, jamming our radar again," said McAden. "Shit—we're blind. I just lost them. I'm guessing they'll dive down for the ground clutter, but I don't have a heading. Jesus, I can't find them. Scanning. Scanning."

"Jennifer, can you find Galatica for us? They've jammed our radar."

"ECMs are off," reported McAden.

"Working on it," said Jennifer.

"No contacts. Shit," said McAden.

"I'm sorry, Colonel," said Gleason from downstairs.

"Without a transmission from them we have nothing to pick up."

"Be ready," Dog said. "They're here somewhere."

Was Bree flying? She was this good certainly.

Bastian held his course for Gal's last position. He pulled up the com screen on his right MUD and hit the Dreamland reserve frequencies, punching in a combination to broadcast on all of the channels simultaneously.

"Rap, this is Colonel Bastian. You have to surrender, kid."

"Daddy?"

Hey, babe, he thought. Sorry. I am so sorry.

"Captain Stockard. Stand down," he said flatly.

"Shoot us down! There's a nuke on the Flighthawk! Shoot us down!" said Breanna. She started to say something else, but the transmission was abruptly killed.

"Yes! I have them!" said Jennifer. She fed the coordinates up to the bridge.

"I have a lock! Five miles!" announced McAden. "Colonel?"

Shoot us down.

"Colonel?"

"Fire missiles," said Dog. For maybe the first time in his life, for certainly the first time since joining the Air Force, a tear slid down his cheek.

Aboard Gal
8 March, 0832

As Madrone reentered Theta, he saw the launch warning. He felt the computer tracking the missiles as they approached, winced as one slipped out of the noise and headed clean for their hull.

Another ducked downward, confused, not a threat.

Tinsel, jammers, cut left, cut right, you're too high, easy pickings.

Accelerate, accelerate. Left, right, left, left again, fool the sticky bastard.

Dreamland lay just ahead. No one ever will go through this again. Never.

The Scorpion stuttered in the air, a half mile from the fuselage. It had him nailed, but staying on its target had exhausted its fuel. Kevin lurched to the right as it tried one last burst of speed and then exploded.

The shock wave nearly threw Hawk Three into a spin.

It was then that the other missile picked itself off the deck and nailed Gal's extreme starboard engine.

MINERVA FELT THE SHOCK AS THE AMERICAN MISSILE tore into the power plant on the right side of the wing. She spun around, nearly pirouetting out of the seat even though her restraints were snugged.

The plane stuttered in the air, but kept climbing. They passed through ten thousand feet, the Megafortress fighting off a yaw.

Gravity punched against her chest as the plane finally lurched into an invert and then began to fall from the sky. They would die now. She'd had the seats sabotaged and there was no escape.

She hadn't wanted to escape, not really. There had been hours to persuade Madrone, or even betray him, to simply call the Americans and surrender. But she hadn't.

Minerva felt a twinge of regret, a small wish that her fate had followed a different path. Then her body slammed back against the seat so abruptly that she nearly lost consciousness.

This is what death feels like, she thought to herself.

Then the Megafortress rolled level, and blood began returning to her brain.

Aboard M-6
8 March, 0838

"THEY'RE BEYOND US!" YELLED MCADEN. "EAST, AT two, no, call it one o'clock. Three miles."

"Radio the position to Nellis air defense and the rest of the net," said Dog, calmly throwing the Megafortress into the tightest bank he could manage to pursue Galatica. "Sidewinders up. Dr. Geraldo, if you want to take your shot, do it now."

Aboard Gal
8 March, 0840

MADRONE SAW THE MEGAFORTRESS'S EMERGENCY panel in part of his brain. The Scorpion had taken the power plant completely off, but had done only light damage to the wing itself. One of the fuel tanks had been hit by shrapnel, but the bladder material had quickly self-sealed. As potent as the Scorpion was, the EB-52's venerable airframe had survived considerably worse.

Madrone didn't care much for history. He dropped into Hawk Three and plunged out of Galatica's shadow. Dreamland lay thirty miles away.

Two F-15's approached on a direct intercept, along with four F-5's.

The Eagles were merely a nuisance. The F-5's weren't even that.

He accelerated toward his target.

"Kevin," said a familiar voice in his earphones. "You have to give up. You're sick. It's ANTARES."

Geraldo.

He killed the radio.

Aboard Sharkishki
8 March, 0848

MACK TRIED TO TELL THE NELLIS COWBOYS IN THEIR F-15's that they were getting the sucker play, but the idiots wouldn't listen. They charged at the Megafortress and the Flighthawk that suddenly leaped from its shadow like they were running down a piece-of-shit Chinese F-7/MiG-21 impostor.

A piece-of-shit F-7 wouldn't have jumped from 250 knots to Mach 1.2 in less time than it took for the lead Eagle pilot to curse.

Stinking Madrone. He flew straight out of Zen's book, no damn creativity at all. Though burdened by something that was increasing its radar signal for the F-15's, the U/MF blew past the Eagles, made a feint for the F-5's, which threw them in a tizzy, then ducked into the ground fuzz where no one could see him.

Mack waited for the U/MF to rise up behind the F-15's. When it didn't, he took a guess why—the larger return was being generated by a missile or bomb.

He had his passive sensors goosed to the max, but couldn't find the little bastard. He tucked Sharkishki lower, nudging back in the direction of Dreamland.

Guy comes this far, in this direction, has to be thinking of nailing Dreamland.

That or Vegas. Maybe they'd cleaned Monkey Boy out at the blackjack tables and he wanted revenge.

Mack might take a piece of that himself. He zipped over Interstate 15 at five hundred miles an hour. Trucks and cars veered every which way, the drivers obviously freaking.

Wimps. He had plenty of clearance, at least a good eighteen inches. Maybe even twenty.

Aboard Galatica
8 March, 0853

BREANNA PUSHED AT THE STICK, THE PLANE SWIMMING sideways in the air.

Why weren't they dead? Had Minerva been bluffing? What could be so magical about ten thousand feet if there wasn't a bomb in the plane.

Maybe hitting that altitude simply armed it.

Shit.

There was no time to curse herself. She'd lost an engine, maybe part of a control surface. She didn't trust the flight computer and had no copilot. Breanna would have to do everything herself.

Assuming she didn't blow up. And assuming Minerva didn't take out her knife and slit her throat.

Aboard Gal
8 March, 0855

JEFF LAY ON HIS BACK, HIS HEAD FLOATING SOMEWHERE in a black ball of fur that filled the Megafortress's lower deck. He heard Madrone grunting above him, working the Flight-hawk toward its target. He tried to push up, but pain shot through him. His chest and upper spine felt as if they had caught fire. He flopped back, overcome by the fear that not just his legs but every inch of him was paralyzed.

No, he told himself, I'm not giving up. Fight! Fight!

But no part of him moved.

THE TARGETING SCREEN TOOK OVER MADRONE'S MIND. Numbers drained off the right side, slipping into the hole where the rest of his life had already washed away.

He had to hit the second air shaft on the target, and he had to hit it just right. But that was the beauty of the Brazilian missile. It could be steered very precisely.

The bomb would only destroy the top portion of the lab. A second reinforced layer protected the computer itself. But they'd never get around the radiation. They'd wait a hundred years, maybe more.

The numbers drained away. The Flighthawk's pipper began to pulse, and the targeting bar went to yellow, ready.

He was now thirty seconds from his target. Time to unsafe the bomb, allowing the trigger to be activated as soon as the missile's engine ignited.

As he started to give the command, something told him to watch his back.

ZEN'S RIGHT BOOT LAY AGAINST THE CORD THAT CON-nected to the helmet. If he could kick it, he could knock it loose, knock if off Kevin's head.

His leg stayed motionless.

Of course. Useless damn legs. Useless damn body. He'd taken his best shot and now he was truly impotent.

"No!" he screamed, smashing his arm against the base of

the control seat so violently his whole body jerked away.

The cord caught on the tip of the lower flap hook on his pants. But it had been tied to the panel—putting pressure on it had no effect on the plug. Jeff cursed and tried to sit up, pushing away the pain, telling his body he'd ignored much worse. He had gotten his elbow below him and begun to lever around when Gal lurched hard to the right and downward. Jeff's efforts were vastly multiplied by the plane's sudden momentum; his body flew backward, tugging the wire and sending the ANTARES helmet flying across the cabin.

Aboard Sharkishki
8 March, 0855

MACK PUNCHED HIS THROTTLE AND JERKED THE STICK back, riding the massive thrust of the MiG's tweaked turbofans upward as he saw the Flighthawk cross above him.

Little bastard was fast and still off his screen. Mack had the Scorpion thumbed up, locked.

Go, baby, go.

The missile clunked off its rail. He lost a second in locking and firing the other missile.

They were going to miss.

Son of a bitch. Chaff. Zigging and breaking down.

That damn Madrone. Zen had taught him well.

Sidewinders up.

Too far.

Mack jammed the throttles all the way to max afterburner. As the MiG shot ahead on its fiery ride, the Sidewinder growled. He launched right away.

Aboard Gal
8 March, 0658

MADRONE'S MIND FLEW INTO A THOUSAND PIECES.

He tried to give the command anyway, tell the Flighthawk to launch.

Minerva. The dark woman of death.

Kevin opened his mouth, but the only word that came to his lips was "Christina."

As he said it a second time, he realized the connection with ANTARES had been lost.

Aboard M-6
8 March, 0900

"FLIGHTHAWK IS DOWN! FLIGHTHAWK IS DOWN!" SAID McAden. "Who got him? Shit! MiG bearing—it's got to be Smith!"

"The bomb," said Dog. "Was it on the U/MF or not?"

His eyes were pasted on the windscreen. Las Vegas sat peacefully in the distance.

"I'm tracking fragments," said the copilot. "Big hunk of something."

Dog waited. If the Flighthawk had had the weapon aboard, it might still detonate when it hit the ground.

If it didn't have it aboard, he had to take out Galatica.

He might still have to.

The city's neons seemed to flicker.

Crazy imagination.

No, a reflection from Galatica, passing ahead.

"Lost it. Bomb would have gone off by now," said McAden. "Galatica, two miles dead ahead. Low, erratic."

"See if they'll answer a hail."

Aboard Gal
8 March, 0906

LANZAS SEEMED DAZED NEXT TO HER. BREANNA DE-cided it was time to get her weapon. She slipped the restraints, then jerked the stick forward, sending the plane nose down.

Pushing away her com headset, Rap dove for Minerva, wrestling for the big knife Minerva had tucked in the other side of her belt. But the Brazilian she-wolf didn't try to fight her off. Breanna pulled the blade free, then pointed it at Lanzas.

"It's no use," said the Brazilian. "You can kill me if you want. The bomb will get us when we land."

"Kevin's bomb?"

"That's on the Flighthawk."

"We're booby-trapped," said Breanna. "Where is it? Where's the bomb. Is it on a timer? Or an altimeter? When does it go off?"

Lanzas said nothing more.

"Jeff, are you down there? Jeff, are you all right?"

He didn't answer. She tried the interphone circuit again, but got nothing.

"Kevin?" she said tentatively.

Madrone didn't answer.

The Megafortress accepted her commands without interference. Something had happened below—it might well be that both Jeff and Kevin were dead.

Breanna reauthorized the computer pilot, reasoning that Madrone had been able to take over the plane even when the computer pilot was off. The computer snapped in, almost eager; it blew through its self-diagnostics, reporting itself fit and trim. Rap glanced at Lanzas as she told the computer to hold the present course, then locked the controls with her voice command.

The Brazilian made no effort to stop her. She seemed to be in a trance.

Breanna stood, twisting her headphones off. But as she started to get up to go below, she heard a voice over the headset.

Still staring at Lanzas, Bree put the headset on.

"Bree."

"Jeff? Are you okay?"

"We landing?"

"I think we're rigged to explode. I'm not sure how, though—whether it's a timer or some sort of altimeter bomb."

"You sure?"

"I don't know if Lanzas is lying or not. But she was awfully worried about going over ten thousand feet."

"We did that already."

"No shit, Sherlock."

"I want you to eject."

"What about you?"

"Just do it."

"Don't be stupid, Jeff. Besides, she probably sabotaged the seats. The ones below were monkeyed with."

He didn't answer. She could hear him groaning and shoving his body around; he sounded like he did in the morning when he pulled himself from bed and went to the bathroom by crawling across the floor.

"How much fuel do we have?" he said finally.

"About twenty minutes worth. Maybe a little less. We're on three engines," she added. "A Scorpion took one off."

"That ought to stretch things a bit, no?" he asked.

His voice was so deadpan, she wasn't entirely sure he was trying to make a joke.

Aboard M-6
8 March, 0915

"GALATICA, THIS IS DREAMLAND M-6. DO YOU READ ME? Galatica, can you hear me? Please acknowledge."

Dog listened as both McAden and Geraldo took turns trying to hail the plane. They were about ten minutes out of Dreamland.

His fatigue was starting to set in. Fatigue and worry, mostly about his daughter.

"Dreamland M-6, this is Galatica," said Breanna. "I'm in control here. Repeat, I am in control."

"Bree," said Dog.

"Hey, Daddy. What the hell are you doing in a Megafortress?"

"I'm flying it," he said. "Bree—the nuke."

"On the Flighthawk."

"Mack Smith splashed it," said Bastian.

"Mack?"

"Insubordinate snot disobeyed orders, thank God," said Dog. "Now listen, little girl, you stayed out past your bedtime and I've come to bring you home. Set up for Runway One."

"I'm afraid we can't do that. We have a bit of a situation here."

Aboard Galatica
8 March, 0925

IN JEFF'S OPINION, MINERVA WAS BLUFFING.

On the other hand, nothing she'd done until now had been a bluff.

"Altimeter or timer?" Bree asked.

"Timer," said Jeff.

"Then we should land right now."

"Unless it's an altimeter. What's the lowest we've been?"

"Hold."

Jeff listened as Rap paged back through the logs.

"Three hundred feet. But if it wasn't armed until ten thousand, it could be anywhere below 4,500, I think. Minerva's still catatonic. What about Kevin?"

"I knocked him out. He wouldn't know anyway. She used him."

"So what's your call?" Bree asked, her voice as breezy as if she were asking about a basketball bet. "Altimeter or timer?"

"Have to be a radar altimeter."

"Why?"

"Because otherwise you could defeat it by landing someplace high. Lanzas would have thought about that, and suggested it as a way out. Do you know where it is?"

"If I knew where it was, don't you think I'd run back and find it?"

"I didn't realize you had a blowtorch handy," said Zen sarcastically. "Must be in the tail, where they repaired the plane. Maybe we can spoof the beacon."

"Jeff, even if you were right and you could find a way to do that, it wouldn't eliminate a timer."

"Well, let's take a shot at finding it. Check the course that Kevin programmed in. See how low he was going to go before making the attack."

"That was the three hundred feet."

"Probably below that triggers it."

"Well, great, that's an easy jump."

If it did have a radar altimeter, there probably would be a way to spoof it, Jeff decided. He could use a Flighthawk to detect it, or maybe examine the hull for a hot spot.

Except that he didn't have a Flighthawk. But Jennifer Gleason did.

"It's in native mode, orbiting above Dreamland," Jennifer told him. "I can unlock it. Can you fly it?"

"Not a problem."

As he waited, Jeff glanced over at Kevin, slumped in his seat. Zen had grabbed and punched him hard as he leaned over him; blood curled from his nose and ear. But for some reason Jeff thought it was more than the blow that had knocked his friend senseless. The fatigue of these past days, the drugs, fear, and maybe the realization of what he'd done— they must be at least as responsible for knocking him out as Jeff's fist.

Zen's wrist had swollen, either from the punch or the fall. He winced, but still managed a smooth handoff of the Flighthawk. He took the U/MF from its orbit and swung up toward the EB-52.

Odd to fly the plane from the panels without his flight helmet, almost as if he were working by remote control.

Which, of course, he was. All the time.

"Blew that engine clean off," said Zen.

"B-52's don't go down," said Bree. "I can tell you stories. Major Cheshire has a whole gallery of damaged BUFFs that landed in Vietnam with half the plane shot away."

Jeff tried infrared as he closed in, focusing on the tail section. Maybe there was a little part of the right stabilizer that wasn't as hot as the rest, maybe not. The repair threw everything off anyway.

"Going to put the fuzz detector on full," said Zen.

"Jeff, it's not going to make any difference."

"Knowledge is power. Just hold us level until the tanker gets here."

"I have an idea. Let's break off the stabilizer and land."

"What?"

"Let's assume the bomb is there, okay? What do we do? We can't eject, we can't land. We twiddle our thumbs for the next twenty years—or twenty seconds, until the timer nails us."

Jeff nudged the Flighthawk closer. There were intermittent signals.

"I think it is in the tail. Where they repaired the plane."

"Great. Snap it off and let's go home. I'm getting hungry."

"How do you want me to snap it off?"

"Shoot it off with the Flighthawk."

"You're out of your mind, girlie."

"Don't call me girlie while we're working."

Zen pulled up the armament panel. The U/MF was down to two slugs.

Not that he had intended on using them.

"Don't have enough bullets, Bree."

"Slice through it," she said. "Fly right into it. This way we'll be sure nothing else hits us."

"Rap, even if I managed to do that, how are you going to land without a tail?"

"You know how many times I've done that?"

"Zero."

"Hell, it was in pieces when I landed in Brazil. I've done it once a week on the simulator. Jeez, even my father can do it."

"I'm not worried about him."

"You have a better idea?"

HE DIDN'T.

Breanna decided that sooner was better than later—it wasn't like they were going to gain anything by waiting.

As they crossed into Dreamland's restricted airspace, she leveled at a thousand feet. The range was cleared; they had nothing but empty lake bed for miles.

Was snapping off the stabilizer better than letting the bomb explode?

Depended entirely on how big the bomb was. And where it was. And luck. And how clean a break Jeff got.

Three hundred feet was really too high to do this.

Small bomb wouldn't do much damage. Except for the debris and shrapnel and fire.

She could land without one stabilizer. Hell, she could land without the whole tail.

Of course, if Jeff missed and somehow took out the wing as well . . .

"We'll get ready to land," she told her husband. "You have

to hit me when we're at three hundred and fifty feet."

"Shit, Bree, we'll roll right into the ground."

"No way."

"Bullshit."

"We will if you miss and crash into the rest of the plane."

"Bree."

"On a ten count."

"Fuck you."

"With great pleasure," she said, watching the altimeter slip through nine hundred feet.

Aboard M-6
8 March, 0930

BASTIAN HEARD DREAM TOWER CLEAR BREANNA TO land.

"I thought you had a bomb aboard," he said, trying—and failing—to keep his voice calm.

"Probably."

"Well, what the hell are you doing?"

"Landing."

"Wait. We can figure something out," he said. "Maybe we can get some parachutes into your plane."

"No time. Relax. We'll be okay."

"Breanna Rapture Bastian Stockard—"

"Close your eyes, Daddy."

Aboard Galatica
8 March, 0935

HIS DAUGHTER WOKE HIM WITH HER WAIL. KEVIN JERKED back to consciousness.

He'd fallen asleep downstairs again. He had to get up and get her, before she woke Karen.

No.

He was in the Megafortress.

Zen had taken control of the Flighthawks.

They'd take him prisoner, make him go back into Theta, have ANTARES suck what was left of his mind away.

He couldn't let that happen. He pushed to get up out of the seat, got tangled in the restraints. He fell and rolled onto the deck.

JEFF'S HAND WAS SO WET WITH SWEAT THAT THE STICK slipped as he approached. He wrapped both hands around it, eyes and consciousness riveted on the screen.

He had Gal's speed nailed. The computer kept warning about proximity, which was good.

A quick plunge to the right, snap off half the tail on Bree's count.

"Okay. Ten, nine," said Breanna.

"Jeff."

Zen looked up. Madrone stood over him with his gun.

"Seven, six."

Jeff put his right hand up, his other on the stick. He felt Kevin pushing the gun down into the back of his neck.

"Five, four, three."

Madrone ripped the headset away. Zen took a breath, then bent the stick downward.

DREAMLAND'S EB-52 SIMULATOR WAS VERY, VERY RE-alistic. But it couldn't begin to approximate what it felt to lose your tail at 140 knots, 347 feet above the ground.

The Megafortress lurched upward, then flopped down like a flat stone, losing 150 feet of altitude in the blink of an eye. Breanna and the computer struggled to compensate for the ravaging forces of gravity and momentum.

She held the plane steady, but it slid sideways through the air. One of the flaps, damaged earlier by the Scorpion, flew off the plane. Something exploded behind them, kicking at the fuselage, pushing the nose upright at the last second.

They hit the ground rather slowly, at ninety-two knots. But they struck at an angle. The leading gear collapsed; the right-side gear twisted off, but remained under the plane. Gal spun wildly. Breanna felt something hot in her face, then lost consciousness.

Dreamland
8 March, 1008

CAPTAIN BREANNA "RAPTURE" BASTIAN STOCKARD
woke up in her father's arms. Her body felt as if it were
encased in cement. Her arms hurt. Her fingers fluttered.

Her toes were numb. She tried to bend her knee, felt nothing.

"Breanna. Bree." He spoke to her in his strong voice from
far away, beyond the mountains.

Whose voice was it? Jeff's?

Bree opened her eyes.

"I can't move my legs," she said.

"You've been immobilized," he said. "Bree. You're okay."

"I'm okay?"

"You're alive."

She remembered Zen in the hospital. She'd said the same
thing to him.

Breanna started to cry.

"The doctors say you're okay. We're going to put you in
the ambulance."

The tears flowed. God. To lose her legs.

"Yo. Good landing."

She turned her head. Jeff lay on a stretcher next to her.

"Jeff—"

"Kevin's dead," he said. "He got slammed in the landing.
Minerva bashed her head too. They don't think she'll make
it."

She didn't care about the others. She pushed her head up,
looking toward her feet.

You're okay, she'd told Jeff. You're fine.

What a Goddamn lie.

Oh, God, she thought. Oh, God.

Then she saw her right boot move, ever so slightly. She
pushed her left foot. It moved as well.

Thank you, God, oh, thank you, she thought as she slipped
back into unconsciousness.

*   *   *

DOG STEPPED BACK FROM THE STRETCHERS AS THE medics packed Breanna and Jeff into the ambulance.

"We made it," said a sweet, soft voice in his ear.

"Yes," he said. Then he turned and took Jennifer Gleason into his arms, his mouth finding hers in a long, glorious kiss.

VIII

"On review"

Dreamland
8 March, 1300

COLONEL BASTIAN SLID THE THIN YELLOW PAPER OVER
the center of his desk. His fingers brushed so gently along the
tissuelike surface, he might have been touching a baby's
cheek, afraid that if he pushed too hard he would somehow
damage it.

He had no memory of Breanna as a baby. He had pictures
of her mother pregnant, but no memory of her in a crib or in
his arms.

The report said she'd be fine—minor scrapes, a few bruises,
some smoke inhalation, nothing that would keep her off active
duty. She'd been lucky.

Lanzas had been killed. And Madrone, his unrestrained
body tossed and broken by the crash.

More than luck had saved his daughter. There was the
structural integrity of the plane, its ability to absorb massive
shock and trauma, the computer that had helped her manage
a semistable landing, the magnificent airfoil that had somehow
kept the Megafortress from becoming simply a rock.

The guts to try an outrageous solution. The skill to pull it
off.

Not luck at all.

His own decision not to shoot them down.

The right decision, because everything had worked out. But
if the nukes had been launched, and part of Dreamland had

been obliterated, if the nuclear fallout was now drifting over Las Vegas?

"Colonel?"

Dog looked over at the door. Sergeant Gibbs grinned wider than a jack-o'-lantern. "You're going to want to take this call right now, sir."

Bastian picked up the phone.

"Stand by for the President," said a woman's voice, so cold and quick it might have been an automated operator.

Before Dog could react, President Martindale came on the line.

"Colonel Bastian, damn good to be talking with you," said the President. The warmth in his loud voice stunned Bastian momentarily. "Damn good job out there. Damn good."

"Yes, sir," said Bastian.

"Tecumseh, I'm afraid I don't have much time to talk right now, but one of my aides will set up a visit."

"A visit here?"

The President laughed. "Unless you're thinking of going somewhere?"

"No, sir."

The President laughed again and hung up the phone. Bastian wasn't sure whether he was supposed to wait for someone else to come on. After two minutes with the dead phone next to his ear, he finally hung up.

The phone rang almost immediately. But instead of the White House, it was his boss—General Magnus.

"You disobeyed a direct order," said Magnus without any preliminaries.

"I did not," said Bastian.

"You were in the cockpit of that EB-52. Don't bullshit me, Dog. You had express orders not to be in a Megafortress."

"I was the most qualified pilot at the—"

"Just because you have your nose up the President's ass doesn't make you immune, Bastian," snapped Magnus. "And just because Keesh was man enough to say you opposed ANTARES when he resigned won't get you off the hook. That was still your man who almost fried San Francisco."

"I said from the get-go the project was ill-advised," said Dog, his anger stoking to match the general's. "I was under direct orders to proceed."

"That's the only reason you're still in the Air Force at all," said Magnus. "The only fucking reason."

Bastian had never heard Magnus curse or use an obscenity. It drained his anger away.

"Your status is under review," said the general.

"I'm being relieved?" Bastian said softly.

"Under review," repeated the general. "We'll see what the new Defense Secretary thinks," Magnus added. "Arthur Chastain is the likely replacement."

"I don't see how you can discipline a pilot for flying an airplane," said Bastian.

"That's not what we're talking about."

"You're taking away my wings? I can't fly?"

"Of course not. But you're not a pilot, Dog. That's not your job. You're the commander of the most important weapons-testing facility in the country, as well as Whiplash. When the shit hits the fan, your job is on the ground where you can control things, not in the air getting shot at."

"Yes, sir."

"You bet your ass there's going to be a full-scale investigation."

"I welcome it," Dog said.

"You don't have to lie." Magnus snorted. He too seemed to have spent most of his fury. "Get your p's and q's in line. The fallout on this one is going to be heavy."

The line snapped dead before Dog could say anything else.

Did the President's phone call mean he would survive this no matter what? Or did it simply mean the brass would stack the odds monumentally against him?

Dog got up from the desk. He felt depressed and tired. Under ordinary circumstances, he'd work off the cloud by hopping into a cockpit and getting some flying time. Throw himself into the sky, clear his head.

He glanced down at Ax's neat piles of paperwork and the reports waiting for his inspection.

He wavered. He was no good when feeling like this, out of sorts—how could he command anyone?

How could he expect others to follow orders if he disobeyed his?

Magnus hadn't said he couldn't fly. He'd said when the shit hit the fan, he belonged on the ground.

The general meant he belonged where he could control things. Truth was, with a fleet of Megafortresses, that might very well be in the air, not on the ground.

There was work to be done. Bastian sighed and pulled out his chair.

Then he pushed it back and went to find a plane in need of a check-flight.

DALE BROWN

WINGS OF FIRE

PUTNAM

PENGUIN PUTNAM INC.
Online

Your Internet gateway to a virtual environment with
hundreds of entertaining and enlightening books
from Penguin Putnam Inc.

*While you're there, get the latest buzz on
the best authors and books around—*

Tom Clancy, Patricia Cornwell, W.E.B. Griffin,
Nora Roberts, William Gibson, Robin Cook,
Brian Jacques, Catherine Coulter, Stephen King,
Ken Follett, Terry McMillan, and many more!

**Penguin Putnam Online is located at
http://www.penguinputnam.com**

PENGUIN PUTNAM NEWS

Every month you'll get an inside look at our upcom-
ing books and new features on our site. This is an
ongoing effort to provide you with the most
up-to-date information about
our books and authors.

**Subscribe to Penguin Putnam News at
http://www.penguinputnam.com/newsletters**